"Cat Sebastian is an author at the absolute top of her game."

—Erin Sterling, *New York Times* bestselling author of *The Ex Hex*

"[Kit and Percy's] sexual tension is a living, breathing thing on the page." —*BookPage* (starred review)

"Entertaining and delightful. . . . An irresistible story of love and adventure that will delight both newcomers and regular readers of queer romance." —*Kirkus Reviews* (starred review)

"Wielding a rapier-sharp wit and displaying an exceptional gift for insightful characterization, Sebastian fashions another fiercely romantic, fabulously sexy m/m love story that not only delivers a delicious surfeit of slow-burn sexual chemistry but also deftly illustrates the true complexity of all human relationships." —*Booklist*

Praise for Previous Books

"This book is a marvel and a gem."

—*New York Times Book Review* on *Unmasked by the Marquess*

"This book is a pleasure that cuts deep. It's a slow-motion stained-glass heartbreak, all sparkling color and velvet shadow and sharp edges slicing you without mercy."

—*Seattle Review of Books* on *Unmasked by the Marquess*

"Sebastian gives readers a beautiful, emotional romance between two people who are thoroughly perfect for each other; Alistair's response to Robin's revelations is as powerful and poignant as the couple's happily ever after is triumphant."

—Sarah MacLean, bestselling author, *Washington Post*, on *Unmasked by the Marquess*

"Sebastian sends out her Seducing the Sedgwicks series in style with this intimate Regency romance. . . . [A] delight."

—*Publishers Weekly* (starred review) on *Two Rogues Make a Right*

"Romance supernova Sebastian once again brings her A game. . . . The author's exquisite writing and vividly detailed love scenes between two realistically flawed protagonists make this a must-read for fans and first-timers."

—*Booklist* on *A Gentleman Never Keeps Score*

"Sebastian's latest elegantly and eloquently written Regency historical . . . slowly unfolds into an unforgettable love story that manages to be both sweetly romantic and sizzlingly sensual at the same time, demonstrating once again why Sebastian is one of the brightest new stars in the romance genre."

—*Booklist* (starred review) on *It Takes Two to Tumble*

"Sebastian crafts another enormously fun, sexy romp that is also touching. . . . Highly recommended."

—*Library Journal* (starred review) on *A Little Light Mischief*

"Sebastian shatters taboos and genre expectations, crafting searing, meaningful, unique romances—and she makes it all look easy."

—*RT Book Reviews* (top pick) on *The Ruin of a Rake*

"Another exquisitely written, deeply romantic novel from Sebastian."

—*Kirkus Reviews* (starred review) on *The Lawrence Browne Affair*

"Cat Sebastian's debut is an utterly swoon-worthy cross-class romance. Don't miss it!"

—Courtney Milan, *New York Times* bestselling author, on *The Soldier's Scoundrel*

Also by Cat Sebastian

WE COULD BE SO GOOD

A Novel

CAT SEBASTIAN

AVON

An Imprint of HarperCollinsPublishers

WE COULD BE SO GOOD. Copyright © 2023 by Cat Sebastian. All rights reserved. Printed in the United States of America. No part of this book may be used or reproduced in any manner whatsoever without written permission except in the case of brief quotations embodied in critical articles and reviews. For information, address HarperCollins Publishers, 195 Broadway, New York, NY 10007.

HarperCollins books may be purchased for educational, business, or sales promotional use. For information, please email the Special Markets Department at SPsales@harpercollins.com.

FIRST EDITION

Designed by Diahann Sturge

Library of Congress Cataloging-in-Publication Data has been applied for.

ISBN 978-0-06-327276-7

24 25 26 27 28 LBC 9 8 7 6 5

For S, a well in the desert

Part I
NICK

March 1958

Nick Russo could fill the Sunday paper with reasons why he shouldn't be able to stand Andy Fleming. Not only is he the boss's son, but rumor has it he's only slumming it at the New York *Chronicle* city desk—a job Nick has been hungry for ever since he first held a newspaper in his hands—because his father threatened to cut off his allowance. He can't type. He roots for the Red Sox. He has no idea how to buy subway tokens. He has this stupid habit of biting his nails and then, realizing what he's doing, abruptly stopping and looking around furtively to check if anyone saw him. He blushes approximately five hundred times a day. He has a cluster of tiny freckles at the corner of his mouth shaped like a copy editor's caret and, since Nick can't stop looking at them, those freckles are going to ruin his career.

With covert glances across the newsroom, Nick catalogs all the things he doesn't like about Andy and stores them up like a misanthropic squirrel. He's Nick's age, twenty-five or so, but has definitely never done an honest day's work in his life, probably not even a dishonest day's. He's gangly, not short, but maybe a buck thirty soaking wet. His hair is that in-between color that on women gets called dishwater blond and on men isn't called anything at all because it usually looks brown after being slicked back or combed smooth. But Andy doesn't slick his hair back. He parts it on the side like a six-year-old. Nick doesn't bother with any of that garbage, either, but that's only because his hair is curly and has ideas of its own. Nick's hair laughs in the face of pomade.

It's offensive, is what it is, that the boss's son thinks he's going to play at being a cub reporter. It's possibly even more offensive than the story behind how Nick got the job, which owes more to the old city desk editor going senile than anything else, but Nick isn't going to think about that right now.

The point is, Nick knows how to hate people. He's no stranger to a grudge. He ought to spend the rest of his career resenting the ever-living daylights out of Andy.

Instead he lasts less than a week. Less than a day, even. About forty-five minutes, to be exact, and that's Andy's fault, too.

Nick meets his doom in the *Chronicle* morgue, a godforsaken maze of filing cabinets on the third floor where seventy years of clippings are stored in some loose approximation of alphabetical order. When he sees Andy there, he supposes he has to give the kid some credit for knowing that the morgue exists in the first place, let alone where to find it. He's just congratulating himself on being gracious when he realizes that Andy doesn't have any of the file drawers open. Instead he's standing there, tugging at a drawer handle and swearing.

Well, he's saying things like *rats* and *jeez* and Nick thinks there might even have been a *gosh* in there.

"Can I help you?" Nick asks.

"Oh crud," Andy says, turning the bright pink of Coney Island sunburns. And then he collects himself, or at least he tries to. Nick watches it happen, watches the embarrassment subside and get replaced with a mask of affability. "Nick, right?" Andy asks. "This is embarrassing, but I seem to have gotten myself into a predicament." He gestures at the filing cabinet, where the end of his tie is stuck inside a closed drawer.

The first thing Nick notices is that Andy's tie is pale yellow with tiny white flowers scattered across it. Nick's own ties run the gamut from gray to blue to gray-blue to one that even has gray and blue stripes, not because he's particularly attached to those colors but because that's what normal people wear. Nick has spent years making sure that when people look at him, they don't see anything that sticks out like a sore thumb—they don't see anything at all, they hardly even see a person, just a man in a suit.

Maybe when you're the heir to a publishing fortune, you don't need to worry about that sort of thing. Instead you can spend your time dropping out of law school and dropping out of business school and then flitting between the capitals of Europe for a couple years, not that Nick has made it a point to learn all about Andy's history or anything.

The second thing Nick notices is that the drawer is jammed. Of course it is. Nothing in the *Chronicle* building works as it's supposed to, from door handles that require special jiggling to stacks of carbon paper that come tumbling down if you aren't careful to a cafeteria worker who prays loudly for you in Hungarian if you don't eat your potatoes. Figuring this out is a sort of organic hazing process that junior reporters and copyboys have to endure. It goes hand in hand with learning how the newsroom works; by the time you've mastered the hot-water tap in the eighth-floor men's room, you probably have a byline.

But nobody can haze the owner's son, even if he is here unwillingly. Nick isn't sure, though, what the alternative is; it's not like there's an operator's guide to how to survive in this place, and even if there were, it would be as thick as a phone book.

"There's a trick to opening it." Nick has to step close to Andy to execute the trick—close enough that he can smell aftershave, close enough that he can hear how fast Andy's breaths are coming. Jesus, the kid must have been in a panic when he thought he was trapped down here, tied by the neck to a couple hundred pounds of metal and old newspapers.

Nick shoves the cabinet with his shoulder and then pounds the lower left corner of the stuck drawer with his fist. It pops open, rolling out smoothly, as if judging anyone who ever doubted it.

"Oh gosh, thanks," Andy says. "And here I was, trying so hard to make a good impression. I offered to come down here and get the clippings myself instead of sending a copyboy."

Nick, fool that he is, recognizes this as both a confession and a dare. Andy Fleming—Andrew Fleming the fucking Third—is daring Nick to do the most clichéd thing someone in his position can possibly do and make friends with the boss's son.

Nick has never known how to turn down a dare.

"Next time," Nick says, "send a copyboy."

"Right," Andy says, sounding abashed. He makes a useless effort to smooth his tie, which is now hopelessly creased and probably ruined, and turns toward the elevators. "Thanks, Nick."

"Wait. Stay still." Nick can't send the kid back to the newsroom looking like he's been mugged. He reaches out and smooths Andy's tie as best as he can, then straightens his lapels, which had gone all askew when he battled the filing cabinet. "If you button your jacket, it'll hide the worst of the damage," he suggests.

Andy flashes Nick a smile, a thousand watts of professionally straightened teeth, and it's like a two-by-four to the head. It takes Nick a minute to arrange his face.

April 1958

From there, it's only natural for Nick to invite Andy out for drinks with the handful of reporters who're waiting to see whether they need to rewrite anything before deadline. And then after that, what can Nick do but keep an eye out for Andy? He can't let the kid wander around unsupervised, can he? It wouldn't do to let one of the copyboys find his desiccated skeleton shackled to a filing cabinet or trapped in the fire stairs. Workplace morale would plummet.

And it's not like anybody said, "Russo, babysit the boss's son," but when Nick gets sent out to cover a story, Andy tags along as often as not. There's a set of arcane and unspoken rules governing who sits where in the rows and rows of desks in the *Chronicle's* newsroom, but Nick clears off the desk facing his own, all but shoves Andy into the chair, then glares around the room, silently daring anyone who thinks they're going to argue with him.

"Why do you keep calling me 'kid'?" Andy asks one day as they're walking back from City Hall. "I checked your file and we're both twenty-five."

"I have a file?" Nick asks, not sure whether to be annoyed or weirdly flattered that Andy has been prying into whatever files the *Chronicle* keeps on its employees.

"Everyone has a file."

"I didn't realize we were the same age," Nick lies.

"Did you know the copyboys have a betting pool about how many times you'll smile in a week? The over-under's two. *Two*."

"There's too much goddamn gambling in the newsroom," Nick says, because it's true—a newspaper shouldn't have its own numbers runner, that's just wrong—and also because he doesn't want to let on that he's kind of impressed that Andy's in good enough with the copyboys to know about their secret bets.

"Is this part of your grizzled old reporter routine?" Andy asks, narrowly avoiding a puddle only because Nick grabs him by the sleeve and hauls him out of the way. "The one where you act like an ink-stained wretch, made of nothing but newsprint and subway tokens and paper cups of coffee?"

That's . . . alarmingly close to the image that Nick tries to cultivate. "It's because if I start thinking of you as an actual adult, I'll start wondering why you never have a pen. Or your keys. Or why you get east and west confused."

Something like hurt flickers across Andy's face and Nick wants to take back whatever it was he said, but Andy's good-natured mask is back in place. "I never confuse east and west. I just never know which direction I'm facing, so I can't possibly guess where all the rest of the directions are. And that reminds me." He gives a self-deprecating laugh that doesn't sound in the least cheerful. "I lost my keys again."

"No, you didn't." Nick digs into his pocket and pulls out a key ring. "Sorry. Forgot to mention it. One of the girls on the fourth floor found it and gave it to me to give to you."

Andy blushes hard, and Nick wonders which of the reporters on the fourth floor he has his eye on. That's where the women in fashion, food, and furnishings have their desks. Hmm.

"That's three times this week." Andy sighs, taking the keys and sticking them in his pocket.

Actually, it was five times, and six the previous week, but Nick doesn't mention it.

"Don't you have a doorman you can leave your keys with?" Nick asks.

"It's too mortifying. He's known me since I was a baby. And he knew my mother. I can't admit to him that I can't even keep track of a key ring."

Nick guesses that Pulitzer-winning war correspondents don't lose their keys much. But this is the first time Andy's mentioned his mother. She died last fall, and Nick only knows this because everybody knows it—the *Chronicle* even ran a two-column obituary, despite her being the publisher's ex-wife.

The next day, Nick comes to work with a length of string. "Give me your keys," he tells Andy.

Andy raises his eyebrows but complies. "This worked for my nephew," Nick says, prying the single key off the ring and threading it onto the string. "He kept losing his keys because he always had his hands in his pockets. Whenever he took his hands out, he'd send his keys flying." He ties a double knot, then holds out the resulting circle of string, the key dangling like a locket at the bottom. "Come here." He loops the string around Andy's neck, pulling his collar just loose enough to drop the key under his shirt. "Safe and sound." He pats Andy's chest, then pulls his hand away like he's touched a hot stove. What the fuck. Nick knows to keep his hands to himself.

Andy's hand goes up to his throat, but he stops himself and jams his hands in his pockets. He looks embarrassed, and Nick realizes that he might have got this all wrong—he never meant to make Andy feel like he couldn't take care of himself.

"I mean, you don't need to keep it like that," Nick says. "Do whatever works for you. It's just—it was bothering you, and I thought—"

"Thank you," Andy says. "It was thoughtful of you."

Nick wonders when the last time was that someone looked after Andy Fleming, before reminding himself that it's none of his business.

May 1958

Nick stretches his legs out, propping one foot on the seat in front of him. They're up in the nosebleeds—Nick'll be damned if he pays more than a dollar to see the fucking Yankees—which means half the nearby seats at this midweek day game are empty.

"This is quite the cultural experience," Andy remarks calmly as a man a few seats over whips out his dick and begins to piss in the aisle.

"What's the matter with you?" Nick shouts to the man. "Put that thing away. There are children here."

Andy's face is bright red and his shoulders are shaking. "'Put that thing away'?" he repeats.

"I'm not going to shout *dick* in public," Nick says reasonably.

"No, of course not. Look at me, forgetting my manners." Andy takes a swig from his beer, his lips curling in a smile around the mouth of the bottle.

It's a sunny day and they're in the part of the stands that isn't cast into shade by the bulk of the stadium. Nick has already taken off his coat, and now he begins rolling up his sleeves. Andy, of course, looks as cool as a cucumber. He always does.

Out of the corner of his eye, he sees Andy looking at him, watching as the fabric folds back to reveal Nick's forearms—too thick, too hairy, and marred by a couple scars. He fights the urge to push his sleeves back down. So what if Andy thinks he's rough or coarse—plenty of people do. He thinks Andy is spoiled and out of touch. They're both free to think all kinds of insulting things about one another. Nick doesn't care. Besides, Nick has a mirror and knows that anyone who looks at him and doesn't like what they see just has bad taste. What does it matter if Andy has bad taste? He's wearing boat shoes and linen pants at Yankee Stadium—taste doesn't get much worse than that.

"You know," Andy says conversationally, "I don't even care for the ballet."

Nick spins around to face him, and sees Andy with that fifty percent sheepish, fifty percent smug expression he's never seen on any face other than Andy Fleming's. "Bullshit."

The entire reason they're at this godawful stadium watching this godawful team is that Nick won a bet. Andy bet that some reporting Nick did on a fire at the Museum of Modern Art would wind up above the fold on the front page; Nick—trying not to be pleased by this vote of confidence, however delusional, laughed in his face and bet that it wouldn't. The deal was that if Andy won, then Nick had to go with Andy to the ballet. Otherwise, Andy would go with Nick to a baseball game. The only problem on Nick's end is that baseball in New York now means only the Yankees.

"I picked something I thought you'd hate," Andy says.

Nick feels a slow, reluctant smile spread across his face. "I probably wouldn't have minded the ballet." He knows what those male dancers wear. That would have kept his mind occupied for a couple hours, make no mistake, not that Andy needs to know about it. "I'd have probably liked the ballet a hell of a lot more than I'm enjoying this."

"Not a fan?"

"Christ, no. I only picked this because I knew you'd hate it.

Why do you root for the Red Sox, anyway? I thought you were from New York," Nick says, as if he hadn't spent half his life scanning the *Herald Tribune* for Andy's mother's byline right before reading the *Chronicle* from front to back.

"I went to boarding school in New England." The way Andy says it gently closes a door on that topic, and Nick is the last person in the world to push on a closed door.

"I hate everything about them," Nick says, gesturing toward the field with his beer. "I hate the stadium, I hate the fans, I hate the— Well, I'd probably like the players if they played on any other team."

"I wouldn't," Andy says mildly. "I can't stand any of them."

Nick can't imagine Andy hating anyone, can't imagine him holding a grudge or being petty. "I wouldn't have thought you had it in you."

There's the crack of wood against leather, then a whoosh of noise from the stands as the Yankees score a run. "Fuck that guy," says Andy. Another runner crosses home. "And him, too."

Nick laughs, half from the shock of hearing Andy swear, and half from the unfamiliar note of vehemence in his tone.

"Fuck him specifically," Andy mutters when Mantle steps up to the plate.

The beer man comes along and Nick flags him down.

"Mostly, I hate that they aren't the Dodgers," Nick grumbles, passing one of the bottles to Andy. This is his third beer and he's feeling honest, even though he knows he's dangerously close to being a walking cliché—the Brooklyn boy who misses his team.

Andy wordlessly holds up his bottle and knocks it into Nick's, almost solemnly.

"The only thing I don't hate here is the beer. Well, the beer and the company," Andy says a moment later, as if that's the sort of thing you can just come out and *say*, Jesus Christ. "But even the beer is better at Fenway Park."

"Fuck the Red Sox!" shouts someone in the row behind them.

Nick spins around. "Shut up, you," he growls with as much menace as he can muster. The man sits down, and fast.

"You do that really well," Andy murmurs.

"Do what?"

"Intimidate people, I suppose?"

"Gee, thanks."

"Stop. I mean, I know it's an act." He puts his hand on Nick's forearm, a glancing brush of soft fingertips across bare skin. "I know you aren't going to hurt anybody at Yankee Stadium."

"I'm not, am I? Let's see about that." He throws a glare over his shoulder just on principle.

"I might enjoy being thrown out of Yankee Stadium and sent to the drunk tank more than I'm enjoying the Yankees trouncing the Orioles," Andy says. "Let's keep that as a possibility for next time."

And there will be a next time, Nick knows. They'll come back to watch a team they both hate, to drink warm beer and marinate in the sun. He stretches his arm over the empty seat beside him and looks up, watching pigeons roosting in the rafters. Other birds swoop and dive, and Nick lets the warmth of the sunlight soak into his skin.

June 1958

want you to meet her," Andy says.

"I've met her. I've known her for three years, which is two years and ten months longer than you," Nick points out. Emily Warburton is, in fact, one of the handful of people at the *Chronicle*—in the world—that Nick would call a friend.

"I want you to meet her as my . . . girlfriend."

Nick mumbles something about third wheels and having to take a phone call, not sure why he's resisting this idea but resisting it anyway.

Andy gives him this flat, disappointed look that Nick recognizes because Nick invented it and now he's going to have to sue Andy for copyright infringement.

"Ugh, I can't believe you're going to make me say this," Andy says.

"Say what?"

"You're my friend. Right?"

Nick stares. What the fuck? Who asks that kind of question? "Yes?" he says cautiously, waiting for the catch.

"Right. So I enjoy spending time with you and Emily. Emily enjoys spending time with me and claims to enjoy spending time with you. You enjoy spending time with Emily, which I know because you voluntarily talk to her about non-work-related topics, and that's more than I can say for just about anyone else. I know you enjoy spending time with me for the same reason. So, it stands to reason that all three of us would enjoy spending time together. I want my friend to like my girlfriend. It's lunch, Nick, not six months in a submarine. And it's my treat."

Nick stammers out some kind of agreement, and then they work in mortified silence for the next hour.

Nick has never seen anyone fall in love before. But when he watches Andy put his hand on the small of Emily's back as they walk to the table, and when Emily smiles at Andy over her shoulder, he's pretty sure that's what he's witnessing.

For a minute, he's annoyed that he's about to lose his two closest work friends—or friend-friends, whatever—in one fell swoop. They're going to pair up and leave him alone. Or, Christ, they're going to try to pair him up with one of Emily's friends and eventually figure out that he's queer and then—well. It all ends with Nick losing his friends, doesn't it?

But then Nick recalls how Andy had proposed this lunch. *We'd all enjoy spending time together*, he had said. Andy was trying to tell Nick that he wouldn't lose anything by Andy and Emily pairing up.

Andy might be the most scatterbrained person Nick's ever met. He might be incapable of having a conversation without letting it spiral in a dozen directions. He might live his life in total ignorance of where he put his pen, hat, coffee cup, and press pass. He might subsist almost entirely on coffee and whatever food Nick reminds him to eat.

But he's really, really good at people—at guessing what a person might be feeling and knowing what it will take to make them feel better. It sounds so simple, so unremarkable, but when it comes down to it, Nick thinks it might be pretty rare.

And so he puts on his best smile, his most charming manners, and sets about trying to prove that Andy and Emily won't regret letting him hang around.

They make sense as a couple. She's sharp and a bit cynical, with dark hair and the air of always being on the verge of laughing. Her father is some kind of banker and her mother is a Rockefeller, so she's one of the few people at the paper who wouldn't be dating Andy to get ahead in the world. She's a general assignment reporter for the women's pages, but as far as Nick can tell, she mainly writes about sofas.

"There was a shipping error and the entire fourth floor is

covered in samples of upholstery fabric," Emily says, "all of which
deserve to be burned as an example." She pauses, watching as
Nick and Andy perform their usual exchange of pickles (which
Andy regards as an abomination) and tomatoes (which Nick main-
tains threaten the stability of his sandwich).

"You know," she says, "you can order sandwiches without tomatoes and pickles. They have people in the kitchen whose whole
job is to make sandwiches."

"But then Andy wouldn't get an extra tomato."

"I need my extra tomato, Emily."

"God forbid you not get your tomato, darling." And then Andy
and Emily beam at one another. Nick has to look away, because
what passes between them seems so fond as to be almost private.

That night, he can't settle down. He paces the length of his
apartment, from the empty spare room to the front door and back
again, until the old woman downstairs bangs on the ceiling with
her cane and shouts at him in Polish. He shouts back an apology
and makes a note to get her something nice the next time he goes
to the bakery down the street.

He's jealous. Not of either Emily or Andy, not exactly. It's envy
more than jealousy, he decides. It isn't even that he wants someone to adore him the way they obviously adore one another. It isn't
even that he wishes he had a chance to fall in love. He remembers
Andy's hand on the small of Emily's back as they walked out of
the restaurant. That's what he wants, and he doesn't even know
what to call it.

He changes out of his suit and puts on a pair of jeans and a
leather jacket, then heads out, up to Greenwich Avenue, where at
least he can find someone to take the edge off.

July 1958

Nick is pretty sure that if he hadn't first known his nephew—a fourteen-year-old who goes through life with untied shoes and perpetually skinned knees, surrounded by a chaotic cloud of comic books and pencils and baseball cards—he wouldn't know what to think about Andy.

In May, Andy gets stuck in the elevator at the criminal courts building for three hours, then turns up at the *Chronicle* looking mildly traumatized but bearing a box of doughnuts to apologize for cutting it so close to the filing deadline. In June, he's nearly run down by a cab on Canal Street, only stopped by Nick's hand darting out to grab his coat. In a single week in July, Andy bangs his head into the ladder of a fire truck while he and Nick are covering a warehouse fire, gets food poisoning from a chicken salad sandwich that Nick *tells* him looks bad, and is almost bitten by a guard dog at the scene of a robbery in the Bronx.

When, one Monday morning, Andy emerges from the elevator leaning on a cane, Nick takes one look at him and shakes his head. "Christ. You need someone to follow you around. An ambulance or at least a medic. Maybe a Saint Bernard."

"Nice," Andy says, looking like he's trying not to smile. "This is how you treat the wounded?"

"What was it this time? You already have elevators, fire trucks, and taxicabs. A helicopter? A hot-air balloon?"

Andy looks like he'd rather do anything than answer. "A boat, actually."

Nick bursts out laughing.

"This is a place of business, gentlemen," shouts Jorgensen, the deputy city desk editor.

"A boat," Nick says, when he gets himself under control.

"The decks are quite slippery, I'll have you know," Andy sniffs. "Even slipperier when you accidentally step on a fish."

Nick falls off his chair, which sets Andy off laughing, and Nick is so unprepared for the baritone rumble of laughter that he doesn't even notice when he hits his head on the corner of a desk.

"You're bleeding," Andy says, stricken. Nick brings his fingers to his temple and they come away red.

Jorgensen rolls across the room on his chair, tosses the first aid kit onto the floor where it lands beside Nick with a metallic clank, and rolls back, muttering something about how it's a dark day when reporters start acting like giddy schoolgirls. Nick is dimly aware of a grumble coming from the direction of the copyboys' bench, and he realizes he's probably smiled enough in the past two minutes to make a mess of their betting pool for the entire month of July.

Andy hobbles over and with some difficulty lowers himself to the floor. "May I?" he asks, his hand an inch from Nick's forehead.

"I'll be fine," Nick says, from reflex as much as from anything else. He's been patching himself up for a long time now.

Andy rolls his eyes. "We both know that if you bleed on that shirt, you're going to gripe about it for the rest of the day. Let me stick a Band-Aid on your forehead so we can move on with our lives."

Nick sighs. "Fine. Have it your way."

Andy brushes the hair away from Nick's temple and peers at the cut. Nick finds himself looking up into a pair of caramel-brown eyes. "It's not deep. You won't need stitches and it won't ruin your pretty face."

Nick can hardly breathe. "What are you, a nurse?"

"As you've noticed, I've had a lot of experience on the receiving end of first aid. Now sit still while I put iodine on it."

Nick does as he's told, only wincing a little as the iodine stings his cut, distracted by the way Andy bites his lip as he focuses. A few wisps of hair fall onto his forehead as he works, and Nick resists the urge to put them back where they belong.

It's no good, looking at a colleague that way. There are plenty of places where he can look his fill and plenty of people who won't mind looking back. The *Chronicle* isn't one of those places, and the owner's son isn't one of those people.

"There now," Andy says, smoothing a Band-Aid across Nick's temple, the pads of his fingers gentle. "Good as new."

"Thanks," Nick says, his voice a little rough. "Jorgensen would have let me bleed out."

"Who gave you the first aid kit, you pair of ingrates?" the editor shouts.

"Back in his day they didn't have Band-Aids," Nick continues. "They just slapped mud on their wounds and went back to drawing the news on the walls of their caves."

"I can still hear you," Jorgensen says.

"It's nice when the elderly keep their hearing," Andy observes.

"I'll have you both writing obituaries if you don't get your acts together," Jorgensen says.

And for a minute, Nick thinks that obituaries wouldn't be so bad if he got to write them with Andy.

August 1958

He is such a liar," Nick murmurs into Emily's ear before twirling her around. They're at some nightclub in Midtown. Everyone's rich and white and the music is embarrassing. Nick can't believe the things he does for friendship.

"Ooh, I'm pleased to hear it," she says as he reels her back in. "But what did he lie about?"

"He told me he couldn't dance." Nick looks over Emily's shoulder to where Andy is dancing with Emily's sister. He looks elegant, like he always does, only more so because his suit is a bit sharper than what he wears to work. Nobody will ever accuse him of being an inspired dancer, but he looks effortless as he glides Jeanne across the floor. How a man who can't cross a room without tripping over a shoelace and also losing his wallet can look like that while dancing is a mystery to Nick.

"Well, you can hardly expect Andy to actually admit to being good at anything, can you? Hell would freeze over."

Nick snorts. "Excellent point."

"I dare you to compliment him and see how red he goes. He probably had years of dancing lessons. They wouldn't have let him out of Groton if he hadn't at least been able to manage a serviceable foxtrot and maybe even a waltz. You, however, are doing something more than serviceable. Why don't you have a girlfriend?"

Nick's ready for that question; he always is. "I have a lot of girlfriends."

She pulls back and looks him in the eye. "You've taken Ruth Fisher out for dinner a couple of times and she says you're a perfect gentleman. And Lilian Corcoran said pretty much the same thing."

Ruth is one of the paper's food and recipe writers. A couple times a year, she and Nick try new restaurants and then attempt to duplicate recipes. If their standing dates make people think that Nick is interested in women or that Ruth is interested in anything other than where to buy the best imported olive oil, so be it. As for Lilian, she's a staff photographer who lives with another woman in a one-bedroom apartment on Prospect Park West. They invite

Nick over for supper every month or so and never ask whether he has a girlfriend.

"Are you suggesting I *shouldn't* be a perfect gentleman?" Nick asks, raising an eyebrow.

She hums skeptically. "We've known one another awhile, haven't we?"

Nick misses a beat and nearly steps on Emily's foot.

"Oh, for heaven's sake," Emily says, pinching his shoulder. "Stop looking at me like I'm about to peel off my false mustache and reveal that I'm three KGB agents in a trench coat." Then, before Nick can make sense of this, she changes the topic and they spend the rest of the song laughing and talking—Emily doing most of the talking and Nick doing most of the laughing. Honestly, he can't even pretend to mind getting dragged out to make a fourth with whatever friend of Emily's needs a date.

At the end of the song, Nick feels a hand on his shoulder, and turns to see Andy.

"Afraid I have to steal my girl back," he says, keeping his hand on Nick's shoulder but not looking away from Emily.

Then Nick takes a turn around the dance floor with Jeanne, listening as she talks about the movie they all saw last week while he keeps his eyes on Andy and Emily. Emily has on a dark blue cocktail dress, one of those two-layer affairs—a strapless bodice with sheer, foamy fabric that drapes over it. Andy's gaze keeps straying to Emily's shoulder and collarbone, as if mesmerized by the hint of skin he can glimpse through the sheer overlay. The look of—Christ, that was longing—in his eyes makes Nick feel like he shouldn't be watching.

He wonders what they're like when they're alone. He assumes they're sleeping together, because it's obvious that they're crazy about one another, and why shouldn't they be? Probably Andy is attentive and careful. And based on how decently he dances, he can probably go the whole time without spraining anything or concussing himself.

When Andy glances up and catches Nick's eye, Nick's first impulse is to look away, embarrassed. He is, after all, being a giant pervert, imagining his friends in bed. But he holds Andy's gaze, not really sure what Andy can see in his own expression and for the moment not caring.

September 1958

"Emily wants you to come for dinner," Andy says, then clears his throat. "I want you to come for dinner."

Emily and her sister live a few blocks away from the Metropolitan Museum of Art, in a brownstone that apparently belongs to an aunt who spends most of her time traveling. Nice work if you can get it, Nick supposes.

Nick expects sandwiches or maybe scrambled eggs. Maybe some Chinese delivery eaten in front of the television. After all, the Warburtons don't seem like the kind of family where girls learn how to cook at their mother's knee.

Instead the door to the brownstone is opened by an aproned waiter. Jeanne appears a moment later, wearing a black dress and dangerous-looking heels, and for a moment Nick goes a bit faint over the idea that he's being set up with this woman who he actually likes very much. How the hell is he supposed to weasel his way out of this one? "Emily and Andy are upstairs with everybody else," she says. "You'll need a drink in each hand if you want to catch up."

Everybody else means six strangers whose names Nick immediately forgets. He feels like he's been ambushed into spending time with rich people. He resists the urge to straighten his tie. He's rumpled and covered in ink, because he always is, and if anybody has a problem with that, they can very much go fuck themselves.

Nobody, it turns out, has a problem with that. Or, if they do, they pretend not to. Or, just as likely, they're too tipsy to notice.

One of the women is an artist. She wears trousers and has her hair down and Nick is massively intimidated. The other two women work at the museum with Jeanne, but Nick hardly gets a chance to say a word to either of them because they sit very close on the couch, their heads bent together, their voices inaudible to anyone else.

Of the three men, one is a friend of Andy's from prep school who is currently going to law school at Columbia and hating every minute of it; he is, therefore, sauced. Another of the men is a banker who spends the evening doting on Jeanne.

And the third man. Well.

"Nick, right? Emily told me I'd *particularly* enjoy meeting you." His voice goes all singsongy on *particularly*. His name is Ted and he's a few years older than the rest of them, a bit over thirty, and apparently he works at an art gallery where Emily's boss did a photo shoot.

"Did she?" Nick raises an eyebrow.

"She said we might have some friends in common."

Nick would put the odds at zero that they know a single soul in common. Which means only one thing. "I suppose we go to a lot of the same places," he suggests blandly.

"I bet we do," Ted says, a grin spreading across his handsome face.

Nick is going to kill Emily. Or thank her, possibly. This guy doesn't look like an undercover cop, at least. There's no way Emily Warburton knows anyone so lowly as a cop, so that's some comfort. How, though, did Emily figure it out? Andy doesn't even know.

When Ted talks to Nick, he's flirty and camp and not making any secret of who or what he is. But when they sit down at the enormous linen-draped table and eat honest-to-God pheasant, he reins in his whole demeanor and becomes only a little bit camp.

Nick has always counted himself lucky for being able to blend in with everyone else. He can pretend to be like any other man, and he's fortunate that it's even an option for him. But he's twenty-five and he's already tired. He's so careful, all the time, about everything, from not letting himself look too long at other men to being almost paranoid about who he picks up.

But the stakes are too high for anything else. He'll lose his job if he gets arrested or if the *Chronicle* finds out he's queer. He'll never get another job at another newspaper. The situation with his family will be unbearable. He'll wind up waiting tables on Mott Street or knocking heads together outside a bar.

He knows things are different for artists and maybe they're different for people who work in art galleries, too. He tries not to think too hard about it, because otherwise he starts to feel penned in.

After dinner, everybody goes back out to the living room and drinks disgusting things out of little glasses.

"You're scowling," Andy says, coming over to sit on the arm of the sofa nearest to Nick.

"It's the crème de menthe," Nick says, eying the green liquid distastefully. "It's like drinking toothpaste, if toothpaste got ideas above its station."

Andy takes his glass, empties it into a potted plant, and hands it back to him.

"You're very drunk," Nick observes.

"Absolutely pickled," Andy agrees, enunciating every syllable. "But what's the matter with you, for honest this time, Nicky."

Nick gives it slim-to-none odds that Andy will remember any of this tomorrow, so he can give him something like the truth. "Sometimes it's a tightrope walk, you know? And it's not fair that I have to be on the tightrope when other people just go for a stroll down the fucking sidewalk. And some people have decided that sharks aren't so bad. Or maybe they decide to say fuck the sharks, you know?"

"There are sharks on the tightrope?" Andy asks seriously.

"No, there are sharks in the water underneath the tightrope. Keep up. But me, if I fall off, I get eaten."

Andy nods. "It's not fair," he agrees. "I don't want you to get eaten by sharks."

A minute later, Ted comes over, a little too casual, a little too close. "I'm afraid I have to make it an early night. I'm heading in the same direction as you, Nick, if you want to split a cab." He holds Nick's gaze as he speaks.

"Thanks," Nick says, and gets to his feet. But before he can follow the other man out of the room, Andy is hugging him.

"What's this for?" Nick asks, letting his hands rest on his friend's back and trying not to think too much about it, keeping his body rigid so he doesn't sink into the touch.

"It's the wine," Andy mumbles into Nick's shirt.

"It sure is," says Emily, coming up beside them. "Let the nice man go, darling." Then she turns to Nick and winks, mouthing *go*.

Nick goes. He catches up with Ted at the door and they take a cab to Ted's apartment on University Place. He pushes the man onto the bed and gives him what he wants, but keeps his own clothes on, smelling Andy's aftershave on his collar.

October 1958

Nick wakes to the sound of his phone ringing. Not many people have his number. The *Chronicle*, of course, but it's early Sunday morning. It's probably his mother, which means bad news. Nick stumbles down the hall in the darkness and snatches the receiver from the cradle.

"Hello," he says, his voice sleep-rough.

"Nick, is that you?"

"Andy?" Nick's pulse speeds up.

"I have a leak in my sink."

"You have a leak in your sink," Nick repeats, waiting for his brain to catch up with his ears. It's still dark out.

"Well, it's under the sink, to be exact. You know the pipe that's shaped like . . ." His voice trails off, and Nick can picture him making an S in the air with his finger.

"Don't you have a super or something?"

"The superintendent's wife is in the hospital having a baby. I called all the plumbers in the phone book and nobody's answering. Which, considering that it's six in the morning on a Sunday, isn't much of a surprise. So I called you. I woke you up, didn't I. I'm so sorry."

"And you called me because I'm the only person you've ever met who knows how to use a wrench."

"Pretty much."

Nick remains silent for a moment, not knowing how to take this. On the one hand, of course he can do something about Andy's sink. On the other, he isn't sure he likes the idea of being the handyman.

"How bad a leak are we talking about? A trickle? A gush? Only when you turn on the faucet or all the time?"

"All the time, and in between."

"Okay. Do you have a bucket you can put under there while you're waiting for me? The trains will run slow at this hour, so I don't know how long it'll take me to get up there."

"Nick, will you really come? Thank you, thank you—"

"Bucket, Andy."

"No, I don't have a bucket, but I put a soup tureen under the sink to catch the water."

"Okay. Let me get dressed and I'll come over. What's your address?"

He doesn't bother shaving or showering, just throws on a pair of jeans and a sweater and walks out the door. A minute later he's back for his own bucket and his toolbox, because there's no chance Andy has so much as a wrench.

"I've had to empty the tureen ten times," Andy says by way of greeting when he opens the door.

"Yeah, we're talking about the tureen later. Who doesn't have a pot? Where's your kitchen?"

"On the left. Nick, what would I do with pots or pans?"

"I'm not answering that." Nick crouches in front of the sink and shoves the bucket underneath before removing a half-full piece of crockery. So, this is a soup tureen. It's made of white china, but the rim and handles look like they've been dipped in gold. "You are a disgrace," he says, handing it to Andy.

"That's a horrible way to talk to fine china," says Andy.

The leak looks like it's coming from the water-supply line, which he had already guessed. He gets out from under the sink and takes his sweater off, not wanting to spend the rest of the morning in soggy clothes.

"Hand me the basin wrench, will you?" he asks when he's back under the sink.

"You're going to have to give me more than that to go on."

Nick ducks out from under the sink and rolls his eyes. "You're lucky you can get by on your looks." He retrieves the basin wrench and then the regular plumber's wrench, just in case.

At first, he thinks the connection might be too corroded to be tightened, in which case he'll have to turn off the water supply. And then he'll have to get ahold of a plumber who's willing to come over on a Sunday morning. His brother will know someone. Nick tries not to think about the fact that he spends most of his life doing his best to avoid talking to his brother but would get him on the phone in a heartbeat for Andy Fleming's fucking sink. But it's a moot point, because finally he gets the nut to budge, and the leak slows to a trickle before finally stopping.

"You'll still need to call a plumber," Nick says when he gets to his feet. "But that'll hold at least for a day or two." He puts the wrenches back in the toolbox, then brushes off the front of his jeans. When he looks up, Andy has an odd expression on his face.

"Do you want some coffee?" Andy asks, his voice strained.

"Uh, sure," Nick says. "If it's not too much trouble." A mood of intense awkwardness has settled over the kitchen and Nick has no idea why.

Andy doesn't move, and instead keeps looking at a spot near Nick's shoulder. "Here's your sweater," he says, thrusting the garment at Nick and turning toward the icebox.

Right. Things got awkward because Nick is standing half naked in Andy's kitchen. Well, maybe not half naked, because he has on jeans and an undershirt, but the undershirt is sleeveless and Nick is suddenly very conscious of every inch of his exposed skin.

Andy doesn't want the reminder that his friend isn't like him—that Nick has more in common with plumbers than with people who went to Ivy League colleges and live in—he looks around—extremely fancy apartments that really ought to have better pipes, what the *hell*.

There's nothing wrong with plumbers. Obviously. Nick would prefer to spend time with almost any plumber, even the ones his brother knows, than any of Andy's Ivy League friends. He just doesn't like the reminder of the gulf between them.

He pulls the sweater over his head, and when he finishes straightening the sleeves, Andy is holding out a cup of coffee, his face back to normal. In his other hand is an enormous percolator.

"I put in milk but no sugar," Andy says. "Why are you laughing?"

"You realize that percolator could have held three times as much water as your fancy soup holder."

Andy shoots him a scandalized look. "Like hell I'm getting my coffee maker dirty."

"But you don't care what happens to your soup thing, which probably cost fifty— You know what, I can tell from your face you're about to tell me that it cost more than I pay in rent and I really don't want to know what your soup heirlooms cost."

"Nick, my life and my health depend on this percolator. We both know that. But I will literally never use that soup tureen. Well, maybe after I'm married. Maybe Emily really likes soup and French porcelain. Stranger things have happened."

Nick takes a sip of coffee to hide his expression. He's unaccountably glad that he has his sweater on. "When you and Emily get married, huh? Have you asked her?"

"Not yet." Andy scuffs his toe on the floor like some kind of kid. "Soon, though."

"I'm happy for you." And Nick is. He really is. If he's jealous, it's probably only a faint pang, and he's been through worse.

November 1958

Ohne of the cops took it," Nick says.

"Could have been a bookkeeping error," Andy points out.

"A bookkeeping error that makes fifteen manila envelopes disappear from the police evidence safe, along with twenty thousand dollars cash and a couple of handguns?"

"Could have been one of the civilian clerks."

"Could have been little green men." Nick throws his hands up, exasperated.

"Look, we both know it was probably a police officer, but Jorgensen will have a stroke if you even suggest printing the names of the cops, even without any insinuation that they were at fault."

"I know." Nick throws his pen onto the desk. That evening, they filed a depressingly basic article stating the bare facts and repeating the police commissioner's promises to get to the bottom of the missing evidence. "What kind of bullshit is it that they put this statement out at five on a Friday afternoon?"

He gets to his feet and begins pacing. The newsroom is relatively quiet, only a handful of reporters on the night desk. Without the usual steady thrum of voices shouting into telephones and the clatter of typewriter keys, it seems deserted, eerily silent. Someone has turned off a few of the overhead fluorescent lights. He can hear the hum of a vacuum cleaner somewhere else on the floor.

Nick knows that getting the NYPD's hackles up is playing with fire. He already worries that any man he talks to is a plainclothes officer waiting for the right moment to arrest him—something that happens to queer men every goddamn day in this city. Nick would be done—fired from the *Chronicle*, exposed to his family, thirty days in jail. He doesn't need to paint a target on his back by pissing off the force as a whole.

The thing is that Nick hates the cops and he'll happily play with fire if that's what it takes to chase down a good lead. If Nick gets burned, it's not like it'll matter to anyone but himself.

"Twenty cops were working in the office that day," Nick says.

"Twenty cops were working when the items were discovered to be missing," Andy corrects, because he's doggedly accurate about news for someone who, at any given moment, has about a fifty percent chance of being able to accurately tell you the date. Nick supposes it's because he was basically raised in newsrooms, but maybe it's in his blood. Now when they go out to cover a story together, Nick isn't babysitting Andy. Andy's pulling his weight and then some.

Other reporters have started to refer to them as a single unit—NickandAndy or RussoandFleming—and Nick has to fight not to smile whenever he hears it. He has to remind himself that this is temporary, that soon Andy is either going upstairs to do whatever publishers do, or he's going to leave to work somewhere else. He's not spending the rest of his life covering minor police corruption stories with Nick, and the fact that Nick has any feelings about that whatsoever is a problem.

"Right," Nick agrees. "So we need to know the last time anyone noticed envelopes and guns in the safe, and also who was assigned to the office since then. Who gets assigned to the Property Clerk's Office, anyway? What did they say?"

Andy flips through their notes. "'Officers assigned to light duty,'" he reads.

"Okay. The first thing I want to know is whether that's a fairy tale. Are these cops really too sick or injured for regular duty, or are they the problem cops that no captain wants to deal with? Usually light-duty officers do desk work in the precinct."

"Really?"

"According to—" Nick nearly says *according to my brother*, but stops himself just in time. He doesn't want to talk about Michael. He doesn't want Michael's presence to intrude on this space that he's made for himself. "According to a source. But possibly not an accurate source."

"A cop?"

"Yeah."

"Can you call him and get a statement?"

Nick almost laughs. "Not that kind of source."

Andy raises his eyebrows but doesn't pursue it.

"We should go home," Nick says. "Tomorrow we'll find someone at the Property Clerk's Office who wants to talk. One of the civilians."

"Tomorrow's Saturday."

"They'll be working." Nick stops pacing and looks at Andy. "Sorry, you probably have plans."

"Yeah, to go to the Property Clerk's Office with you."

Nick bristles. "You don't need to. I can handle it on my own."

"Nick, stop being stupid. It's been eight months. Do you really think it's a hardship for me to spend time with you?"

His phrasing makes Nick look hard at him. *Spend time with you*, not *chase possible leads*, not *cover an interesting story*. Not even *do my job*. Of course they enjoy spending time together, but that doesn't mean anybody has to say so out loud.

Except—why the fuck not? Is Nick so mired in gay paranoia that he can't even admit to being friends with another man without thinking vice cops are about to crawl out from under the desks and arrest him? Is he so used to being lonely that even companionship feels dangerous?

Or maybe it's just that he knows that his friendship with Andy isn't the sort of thing you can talk about in public. At least not on his side.

It's late, and he's tired in every possible way. His guard is down, and maybe he's feeling things that in the light of day won't amount to much.

Or maybe he'll wake up and be stuck with the knowledge that he's in far, far over his head.

Andy sighs and looks away. "Sometimes you look at me and I wonder what I did wrong," he says.

"What?" Nick asks, appalled and a little hurt, but it comes out angry, as it so often does. "You don't do anything wrong. Ever."

"Sometimes I say something that puts your teeth on edge, but I don't know what. I wish I did so I could stop doing it."

"If I'm thinking something stupid, that's my problem."

"It really isn't." Andy actually sounds frustrated now, and a little cross, which he never does.

Nick gets ready to fight that point, but then he replays the last few minutes in his head. He looks out the newsroom windows, over the tops of the trees in City Hall Park and the empty courthouses. "You're my best friend," he says, hoping it doesn't sound too babyish, hoping it isn't a nail in his coffin.

He turns around in time to see Andy's face light up. It's the brightest thing in the shadowy newsroom, the brightest thing in the city, and all Nick can do is stare.

December 1958

Nick arrives at the last possible moment. Which, on New Year's Eve, means half past eleven. He can't believe he let himself get talked into going to Andy's father's ritzy party.

Although, looking back, Andy hadn't so much talked him into it as calmly said that he'd personally like it if Nick made an appearance.

And so Nick put on the dinner jacket and black tie that he had, like a fool, bought for the occasion, and because of which he'll be eating beans and spaghetti for a month. But, for reasons he doesn't want to think about, he hates the idea of looking scruffy in Andy's father's Upper East Side apartment.

When he enters, he's hit with a wall of expensive perfume and music from a live band. Who the fuck has space for an entire live band in their apartment? Andy's dad—Nick's boss—that's who. Andy's own apartment, only a few blocks away, seems modest in comparison.

He snags a shrimp and makes his way across a marble-floored hall as if he has somewhere to be, but that's the number one rule for not looking like a fool: act like you know where you're going. The place is clogged with men twice his age and women wearing enough jewelry to give them a backache and Nick suddenly feels very young and very out of place.

Emily, sharp as ever, sees him first and calls his name. She has on a floor-length gown made of pale blue chiffon dotted with tiny sparkling crystals, which Nick recognizes because she described it to him at great length last week when they went to see *Cat on a Hot Tin Roof* for the second time. (Nick is realizing that there are distinct advantages to having a friend who knows he's queer, and one of them is discussing Paul Newman.) She looks even more beautiful than usual and he feels his mouth tug up into a smile just at the sight of her.

Beside her is Andy, and—well. He's staring. Nick adjusts his stupid bow tie before he can think better of it. Andy probably just isn't used to seeing Nick as anything other than rumpled and in need of a shave. Or, worse, maybe Nick looks ridiculous in his suit, like some kind of dockworker who's been scrubbed up and crammed into a tux.

"You *do* clean up nice," says Emily, kissing him on both cheeks.

"Wish I could say the same for you," says Nick. "Too bad you're such an eyesore." Emily pinches his arm and then drifts off.

As for Andy, he always looks sharp. Nick doesn't know where he buys his clothes and suspects he doesn't want to know, and that he especially doesn't want to know what they cost. Andy looks like he's made for black tie. Nick begins to suspect that Andy has something done to the rest of his suits, because if he went around looking like this all day, nobody would get anything done. The *Chronicle* would grind to a halt and there wouldn't be a single progressive paper left in New York.

Someone taps a spoon against the side of a glass and shouts something. It's apparently one minute to midnight.

"I'd better see where Emily's got to," Andy says. For a minute he looks like he's about to bring Nick along, but instead squeezes Nick's arm and takes off.

Nick remembers staying up late as a kid, back when they still lived in the old apartment in Flatbush. At the stroke of midnight, people would throw their windows open and make a racket with whatever they had on hand—pots, pans, wooden spoons. It was a far cry from champagne and a live band and a suit he can almost afford. He feels the usual mess of relief that he isn't there anymore mixed with an utterly misplaced nostalgia.

Somebody starts counting down, and then everybody else joins in, but Nick lights a cigarette and looks out the window, at the checkerboard of light and dark windows across the street, at the barely visible stars in the sky, at the streetlights below and the reflection of the red ember at the end of his cigarette. Anywhere but at Andy and Emily kissing as 1958 gives way to 1959.

When he turns around, they're still together, foreheads almost touching, Andy murmuring something and digging in his pocket, and—that's a ring. Of course it's a ring. Then Emily is laughing and planting little kisses all over Andy's face, and Andy is wrangling the ring onto her finger, and Nick feels like he should be anywhere else.

He pushes down whatever he's feeling before he can give it a name. He's always known how this story ends. They're crazy about one another. They're lucky, and he's happy for them.

And, selfishly, Nick knows that Emily is the best possible person Andy could marry, because Emily likes Nick.

Nick will always have a place in Andy and Emily's life. They'll invite him for dinner, let him play with their kids. They won't care that he doesn't golf or have a yacht or speak with the right accent. Even when Andy moves on from the newsroom to greener pastures, there will be a place for Nick in his life.

He makes his way to where the couple stands.

Part II
ANDY

CHAPTER ONE

March 1959

Nick's on the phone when Andy gets back from lunch. From the way Nick is drumming his fingers and the depth of the crease between his eyebrows, Andy guesses it isn't going well.

Nick looks up, and whatever he sees in Andy's face must not be good. "Can't hear you," he says into the phone. "Line's gone bad." He drops the receiver into the cradle and gets to his feet.

Andy sinks into his chair at the desk across from Nick's. "Who have we alienated now?" he asks, trying to sound normal.

"You look like shit. What happened? How's Emily?"

"She's fine," Andy lies. His entire goal in life is to delay this conversation until after they leave the office, preferably until they're somewhere dark and with a liquor license and where nobody can watch Andy fall apart. Well, nobody other than Nick.

"Yeah, well, you sure aren't. What's the matter?" Nick is still standing, his hands braced on the desk as he leans forward, almost looming over Andy. "You know you're going to tell me eventually, so just spit it out."

Andy lowers his voice even though this will be common knowledge in a matter of hours. "She called off the wedding."

"She did what?" Nick sits heavily in his chair and stares at him. "Are you sure?"

Andy lets out a humorless laugh and scrubs his hand along his jaw. "I'm sure. She met someone else in London. Her mother's cardiologist."

"Her mother's— Do I look like I give a fuck who? Jesus Christ. I thought she was smart."

Andy glares at him. "She is. These things happen. You can't always control who you fall for."

Something complicated happens to Nick's face. He holds up his hands. "Sorry."

"You're supposed to be friends with her. Don't be a jerk out of loyalty to me. She's having a rough—" He swallows and, *shit*, he's going to cry in the middle of the newsroom, which is the only thing that could make today any worse.

"All right." Nick takes a clean handkerchief out of his desk drawer and slides it over to Andy. "Let's get out of here," he says, checking his watch.

"It's too early to leave." It's barely three. Andy can't remember the last time either of them went home before seven.

"I was figuring on spending the rest of the afternoon getting the runaround from the mayor's office and then heading over to the first precinct to see if I could get a quote from the captain about the fires in the warehouse district."

"*Another* fire?" Andy asks, momentarily distracted. There's been a string of highly suspicious warehouse fires in the area just below Houston.

"No, but the building that burned down on Tuesday is owned

by the deputy mayor's brother-in-law." He waves a sheaf of papers that Andy recognizes as copies of deeds from the city register's office. "But that can wait until Monday—"

"Like hell it can—"

"Honestly, with you in this state we aren't going to get much of anything done anyway."

Andy frowns. It's pitiful to drop a lead because Andy is *sad*. His mother filed a story half an hour before Andy was *born*, for God's sake. But Andy already knows he isn't cut from the same cloth as either of his parents. The story wasn't going in tomorrow's paper anyway, though, so Nick has a point.

Andy twists the handkerchief in his hands. "I don't want to go back there."

"Where?"

"My apartment." He doesn't want to explain, doesn't want to think about how empty the place is despite it being cluttered with all the stuff of his mother's that he still hasn't thrown out. He definitely doesn't want to think about all the different varieties of loneliness he's experienced in the twenty-five years, on and off, that he's lived in that apartment, all the times he's woken up there alone, and how little he cares to repeat the experience. He ought to have gotten a cat, but he'd probably forget to feed it. He'd forget he had a cat in the first place. One day he'd absentmindedly arrive at work with the cat on his shoulder.

He drags his mind away from the imaginary world in which he could take care of a cat or himself or a fiancée, and looks instead at the handkerchief, white cotton, crisp and smooth. He wonders if Nick irons them himself.

"You'll stay with me," Nick says.

Andy looks up abruptly. "I can't—"

"Because if you don't, then I'm just going to have to spend the night wherever you do wind up staying, which means the food in my icebox will go to waste."

"I don't have any clothes."

"I'll get your things." Nick has a key—he has multiple keys, because Andy's occasionally still go missing, disappearing into the same abyss as his handkerchiefs.

"Nick."

"Yeah?"

"Thanks."

Nick scowls. When he gets to his feet, he claps a hand on Andy's shoulder.

Andy teeters on the brink between misery and unhinged laughter as he lets Nick all but shove him into a chair in an empty office one floor down from the newsroom. This floor is a hangover from the *Chronicle*'s glory days, when every square foot of the building was crammed full of reporters and clerks and copy editors, not to mention the rest of the staff that makes a newspaper run. Now it, like approximately a third of the building, collects dust. If Andy had his way— Well, no use thinking of that, especially not today.

It's a relief to be out of the newsroom, with its typewriters and ringing telephones and raised voices, its harsh overhead lighting and the cloud of smoke that lingers even after everyone has gone home. He usually doesn't mind it—likes it, even, because it's fundamentally impossible to feel alone in a newsroom. But right now he doesn't want to be looked at, a fact that Nick somehow picked up on without Andy having to say anything.

Sometimes it's a bit mortifying, the way Nick sees right through Andy's attempts to seem normal. He can't remember exactly when Nick started looking after him like a lost dog, but he isn't complaining. He sort of does need looking after, at least if he wants to keep up the facade of being a functioning member of society. Nick seems to have accepted that Andy's a mess and not inquired too closely into it. (Emily had done the same, but Andy refuses to think about that right now.)

He's never been. . . . competent, he supposes. There's scatterbrained and then there's whatever Andy is. He wouldn't have gotten through school without classmates reminding him about assignments, janitors returning lost notebooks, and a fair amount of money to smooth the way.

The fact that his father thinks he's going to run the *Chronicle* as soon as next year is, frankly, insane.

"Did you manage to eat anything at lunch?" Nick asks.

Andy tries to remember. There had been a piece of bread, he thinks, and maybe some butter, but after that he was distracted by his world crumbling around him and all that.

"That's a no," Nick says. "I'll have something sent up."

"You sure you don't want to tuck me into bed?" Andy grumbles.

Nick mutters something unintelligible before stomping off in the direction of the elevator.

A few minutes later a copyboy arrives with a cup of coffee and one of those black-and-white cookies from the deli downstairs, which is fine, but then he sticks around, lurking between the office door and the elevator bank, trying to look inconspicuous and failing by a mile. "Seriously?" Andy asks when he's half done with the cookie. "Did Nick tell you to babysit me?"

"No," says the copyboy. Walter, Andy thinks. "Mr. Russo said I had to stick around until you finished the cookie."

Andy sighs, shoves the rest of the cookie into his mouth, and shoos the kid away.

He's fine. Or, he will be. Weddings get called off all the time, don't they? But whenever people talk about it, they speak about embarrassment or inconvenience or even scandal, but all Andy feels is . . . heartbreak, he supposes, with a side order of loneliness. He loved Emily. He still loves her, although knowing she doesn't love him back anymore makes him feel awkward and conspicuous about it, like he's clinging to some embarrassingly passé fashion and hasn't noticed everybody else moving on.

Abruptly, he realizes that even though he isn't thinking in terms of inconvenience or scandal, his father will. He gets to his feet, downs the rest of his coffee, tosses the paper cup in the garbage, and hits the elevator call button.

"Mr. Fleming is on a call," his father's secretary says when Andy approaches the publisher's office.

"Could you tell him it's urgent?" His father has to find out from Andy before he finds out from anyone else.

The secretary's left eyebrow doesn't quite rise—she's paid too well for that—but it flickers. "Of course, Mr. Fleming." She repeats Andy's message into the telephone and then gestures him into his father's office.

"What's the matter?" his father asks before the door is even shut.

"We've called off the wedding." Andy sits in one of the guest chairs and braces himself.

His father stares. "By that, I assume you mean that Miss Warburton called off the wedding, and you're being too gentlemanly to say so. Because when we spoke a few days ago, you were asking whether to take two weeks off for your honeymoon."

When Andy doesn't answer, his father sighs and takes off his glasses. "She went to London to look after her mother when Mrs. Warburton had a heart attack, didn't she?" his father asks. "That was six weeks ago. I believe you mentioned she was due to return last night." Andy can almost see the pieces falling into place in his father's mind.

Andy isn't going to give away Emily's private business. Frankly, there's no succinct way to tell the story that makes either of them look particularly good. Emily fell for another man, and even after being rejected by that man and returning home heartbroken, she still doesn't want to be with Andy. Nobody comes out the winner in this story.

His father wordlessly opens a desk drawer and takes out two glasses and a bottle of what Andy knows is top-shelf scotch. He fills both glasses and pushes one across the desk to Andy. "Are you all right?"

Andy tries not to look surprised, but it still comes as a bit of a shock when his father acts like he cares. It's probably cynical, but Andy doesn't know what else to think when his father, who was little more than a passing presence in his life until Andy's mother's death, suddenly decides to play the part.

He downs about half his glass, buying time to come up with an answer. "About as well as can be expected."

"Thank God she isn't working at the *Chronicle* anymore," his father says.

Andy suppresses a shudder. What would he say if he ran into her in the elevator or the cafeteria? What would *she* say? But she gave notice when they got engaged, so at least that's one thing he doesn't have to worry about.

"Did something happen?" his father asks.

Andy catches himself biting his nails and quickly returns his hand to the arm of his chair. He knows that his father isn't asking if Andy did something to screw this up, but the truth is that he wishes he had an answer. There must have been something, even though Emily said it wasn't his fault. But as far as he can remember, things were perfectly normal between them before she went to London. The first couple of letters he got from her seemed normal, too. After that, not so much, but he chalked that up to her anxiety over her mother's health. It hadn't occurred to him that spending over a month in a strange city looking after a sick parent was anything out of the ordinary; he would have done the same for his own mother if he had gotten the chance.

Maybe if he had done something as soon as Emily had first seemed distant, maybe if he'd gotten on the first flight to London, maybe if he'd sent more flowers or written more often or done *something*, he could have prevented things from going wrong.

Instead he's left believing that it's just him. That he's in some way insufficient—which is, of course, true. He's forgetful, absent-minded, perpetually late, easily flustered, and lazy. Emily never once acted bothered by any of that, but probably after spending time with a man who doesn't have any of those deficiencies, she realized how bad she had it.

He can hardly blame her for leaving.

CHAPTER TWO

Andy isn't surprised when Nick decides that the situation calls for a liberal quantity of cheap alcohol, applied like some kind of emotional first aid. He steers Andy past O'Connell's, the usual reporters' haunt, and to a hole-in-the-wall bar on South Street that smells like cigars and has dusty photographs of boxers on the wall.

By the time they get to Nick's apartment, Andy is several drinks to the better and a little unsteady on his feet.

"One more flight," Nick says, tugging Andy by the elbow. "Up you go. Christ, you're a lightweight."

Andy braces a shoulder against the wall as Nick jiggles the key in the lock. "It sticks," Nick grumbles. "There we go."

Andy hasn't ever been to Nick's apartment and doesn't know what to expect. He has the vague idea that Nick ought to live in the sort of apartment that looks like a miniature spaceship, with one of those sofas that's about as comfortable as a stack of corrugated cardboard. Everything should be uncompromisingly shiny and utilitarian and probably metal.

But there is no way any modern space-age apartments exist in this part of town. Based on the neighborhood, he'd imagine something shabby and tenement-like. Not that he's entirely clear on what a tenement looks like, at least not this side of Jacob Riis, so his information might be a good seventy years out of date. But he can't imagine anything *nice* in this part of the city.

The neighborhood is, to put it charitably, a bit rough, on the southwest fringe of Greenwich Village. Bands of children roam the streets at hours when they surely should be in bed. People shout at one another in languages Andy can't identify. A few blocks to the east, long-haired bohemians play the guitar and smoke grass; a few blocks to the west, actual longshoremen drink in dingy bars.

It's not a neighborhood where Andy would feel especially safe, at least not on his own, but nobody's going to bother him with Nick around. That's probably true for war zones and East Berlin as well as the seedier edges of the Village—Nick just doesn't look like the kind of person it would be smart to mess with. Part of it's his size, sure, but most of it's just that he projects the air of being someone you wouldn't want to go up against in a fight. He looks like he's ready to handle whatever's thrown at him, whether it's a punch or a breaking story, and after a year Andy knows this impression is correct. Nick is frighteningly competent.

Look, Andy knows that he's a walking disaster. He knows that he's clinging to a veneer of professionalism by the grace of God and his last name and every trick his mother ever taught him. Sue him if, on his first day at the *Chronicle*, when he already felt like a fish out of water and was pretty sure the day wouldn't end without him being exposed as a complete incompetent, he attached himself to the most intimidating person in the newsroom, the one person who looked like he might have clawed his way in. And it's worked out, hasn't it?

Andy didn't expect that they'd actually become friends. He

certainly didn't expect that any friendship between them would be easy. But it is. Sure, Andy has to be careful not to look too appalled when Nick casually alludes to things like working what amounted to a full-time job while still in high school. And Nick has to patiently explain things like how to pay the electric bill and change the typewriter ribbon and not get mugged on the subway. But these are details. Andy's never been too bothered by details.

In any event, Andy is prepared to look unbothered by whatever Nick's apartment turns out to be. He knows that he's sheltered, but he also knows that life exists outside the Upper East Side. He just never quite knows what that life is going to look like or how he's supposed to react.

Now, as Andy basically falls through the door, he lets Nick steer him to a squashed-looking floral sofa that's about ten times more comfortable than it has any right to be. He sinks into its cushions and takes stock of his surroundings. Most of the apartment's walls are painted a warm yellow, but some are brick. One wall is covered floor to ceiling in bookshelves. The floor is chaotically uneven wood planking, with an array of mismatched carpets scattered around and an odd patch of linoleum over by the kitchen. Everything is worn and faded; nothing is what Andy, to his mortification, still thinks of as "good." He wouldn't know how to go about acquiring anything in this apartment. The only obviously new items are a television and a record player.

"I'm putting your bags in the spare room," Nick says.

"You have a spare room?"

Nick snorts. "You thought I was inviting you to sleep on my couch? I mean, the room isn't much, but—"

Andy flings a sofa cushion across the room, missing Nick by a yard.

A moment later, he hears sounds coming from the kitchen—the water running, doors opening and shutting.

"Another drink?" Nick calls.

"Sure, why not."

Nick brings over two glasses of what looks like whiskey. "Budge over."

Andy manages to haul himself upright and takes the offered glass. Nick, meanwhile, lights a cigarette and passes it over. Andy doesn't really smoke, but he always wants a cigarette when someone else is smoking, so Nick just preempts the whole song and dance by giving him one straight off the bat.

"I ran into Emily at your apartment," Nick says. "She was picking up some things so you wouldn't be bothered by seeing them there."

Andy doesn't know what to say to that, and it doesn't matter, because Nick keeps talking. "She looked awful. She obviously felt awful, too. She cried all over me."

There are probably a dozen things he ought to be feeling, but primarily he's glad Nick didn't try to shun Emily. "I feel bad for her."

"Me too. She fucked up—"

"She really didn't. She met someone else and didn't want to dump me over the telephone."

"She fucked up," Nick repeats, more firmly now. "But who hasn't? Well, you haven't. But you're the exception."

Andy's given up trying to correct Nick on this bit of lunacy. "Go to hell."

"Come on." Nick takes a drag from his cigarette. "You lead a blameless life."

Andy doesn't know how to answer that, so instead he watches Nick's hand idly opening and closing his lighter. "I feel guilty for having slept with her. Is that strange? It was only after we were engaged, but now we're not getting married and I feel like I did something wrong."

Nick looks away and shakes his head. "Only you, Andy."

"What's that supposed to mean?"

"Only you would manage to make this whole thing into your own fault. Did you make it good for her?"

"Did I *what?*" Andy sputters.

"I'm trying to figure out what you have to feel guilty about. Did you make it a pleasant experience for her?" Nick articulates these last words deliberately, as if otherwise Andy might not know what he means.

"Uh. Yes." Andy and Nick *never* talk about sex, at least not any sex that either of them has. It's a sort of conversational third rail that they're very careful around. Andy thinks it's probably best to steer clear of any topic that might make Nick feel like he has to either lie or sidestep the question of who exactly he sleeps with. Andy has seen Nick look at men, and he'd noticed that Nick never talked about women, but he didn't put two and two together until Emily did it for him. Until Nick went home with that friend of Emily's last fall.

In any event, Andy knows that Nick sleeps with men, and Andy's pretty sure that Nick knows that Andy knows, but they sure as hell aren't going to talk about it.

"And she wanted it?"

"Yes, Jesus, what do you take me for?" Andy sputters, coughing on the smoke.

"And you used protection?"

"Oh my God, yes." Andy collapses to the side and buries his face in the couch cushions.

"Then I think you're fine. Say ten Hail Marys, et cetera."

Andy starts to laugh, the sounds muffled by the cushion. He knows it isn't that funny, and that the combination of stress and alcohol has gone to his head, but the idea that Nick thinks sex is fine as long as you wear a rubber and everyone has a good time strikes Andy as the funniest thing he's ever heard.

He feels a hand rest between his shoulder blades. "Hey. Hey now, Andy. You okay?"

Andy twists around so he can see Nick's concerned face. "Yes?"

"You asshole, I thought you were crying." Nick takes his hand off Andy's back and flicks him on the ear.

Andy rolls over and puts his feet in Nick's lap, watching a curl of smoke drift toward the ceiling. Nick begins to unlace Andy's shoes, muttering something about animals who wear shoes indoors. Andy can't imagine why animals would wear shoes anywhere.

He thinks about the handful of times he slept with Emily, furtive episodes when her sister wouldn't expect her home, careful and maybe a little fumbling on his part. It was . . . good. Fun, even, after that first time. Actually, even that first time was fun, with both of them giggling over his total failure to get the rubber on, and then the giggles giving way to something else entirely. Emily was beautiful and a little bold and he felt so lucky that he got to be with her in that way, in any way. He always felt lucky around her, lucky that he was going to get to spend the rest of his life with someone he loved and who loved him back, because even if everything else was up in the air, at least he had that settled.

He wants to talk about it—wants Nick to reassure him that this will somehow end well, but there isn't anything Nick can say, and he doesn't want to bore Nick with his worries anyway, not when Nick is being so good to him. And honestly, he'd rather talk about Nick. He's always been curious, and alcohol has made him reckless enough to get awfully close to that third rail. "Did you ever sleep with a woman?" he asks, reasoning that he's not asking directly about anything queer.

Nick lets out a choked-sounding laugh and pauses in unlacing Andy's shoe. "Christ, Andy."

"Sorry, you don't have to answer that."

"No, it's fine. Yes, I did. Any chance I had, for a few years there. I kept thinking that it was something I'd get used to with enough exposure, like gin. It didn't work," he adds after a minute.

There's a lot unsaid in between those words—how Nick must have felt about it in order to keep having sex that he didn't particularly want to have. "Not everyone's a gin drinker," Andy says inanely.

"Made my peace with being a whiskey man," Nick says, bringing his glass to his mouth and taking a swallow. "She was your first serious girlfriend?" Nick asks, not meeting Andy's eyes. For a moment, Andy is confused, because he's mentioned some of the women he's dated. Nick knows that he came close to being engaged a couple of times. Then he realizes Nick is still talking about sex.

"Not in the way you mean," Andy says.

"You're good-looking and rich. You'll find someone else in no time."

Of course he'll find someone else. Finding someone isn't the problem. Keeping them is. "I'm not rich," he says, because this is an old argument between them.

"Course not. You're poor, with those fifty-dollar shoes."

"I didn't say I was poor—"

"Right, you're middle class. Like plumbers and accountants."

"Like . . . a very fortunate accountant, maybe."

Nick snorts.

"*Emily* is rich," Andy clarifies. "Her father owns a bank and her mother's family doesn't work at all, as far as I can tell. *My* father owns a newspaper that hasn't turned a profit since 1946. I have my mother's apartment, a closet full of clothes, and a salary that would barely pay for Emily's hats."

He thinks, maybe, that this is one of the reasons he felt safe with Emily—she would never have needed to depend on him.

It's going to be fine, though. He already feels the edges of the wound closing up. On a squashy couch, as his best friend goes on a rant that would probably get him put on the FBI's radar, if he isn't there already by sheer virtue of working for the *Chronicle*, as he balances a whiskey in one hand and a half-smoked cigarette in the other, he knows he'll be fine.

"Come on," Nick says, gently slapping the side of Andy's thigh. "Time for bed."

"S'early." Andy has sunk deep inside Nick's sofa. He's a part of the sofa now. He's never getting up.

"Your eyes are already shut."

This is true. He still isn't getting up. A hand wraps around his wrist and tugs. "Up you go. Your room's at the end of the hall. Dresser's empty, if you want to unpack."

"Bossy," Andy mumbles, but he gets to his feet and stumbles toward the spare room.

When he opens the door, he has to blink to make sure he's seeing clearly. It's tiny, hardly bigger than the bed, but it's freshly painted and the narrow bed has cheerful yellow sheets and a couple of blankets folded at the bottom. His suitcase leans against a small chest of drawers, beside which is a battered bookcase that's empty except for a stack of dog-eared comic books.

Andy has a spare room, too. It's a repository for out-of-season clothes, luggage, magazines he might read one day, about seventeen boxes that belonged to his mother and that he has no intention of dealing with, a record player that needs to be fixed, and various other items that don't belong anywhere else. This room has none of that attic quality.

It is, in other words, a guest room. But for who? Nick's family lives in Brooklyn and would hardly need a place to stay just across the bridge. And Nick never mentions any out-of-town friends. The fact that there are things about Nick that Andy doesn't know makes him feel oddly jealous.

He opens the suitcase and finds two stacks of neatly folded clothing, his toothbrush and razor, and the book that had been on his nightstand. His glasses are even in there, and Nick must have gone digging through the nightstand in order to find them—Andy's been looking for them for weeks and had almost given up hope. He dumps it all into one of the dresser drawers and goes to find Nick.

"Thank you for getting all my things. I don't think I thanked you yet."

Nick looks up from the copy of *Sports Illustrated* he's reading. Nick's the kind of person who reads an entire magazine, cover to cover, then throws it away. It's amazing what some people are capable of. "You thanked me half a dozen times."

"There aren't any pajamas, though."

"Shit. You can borrow some of mine."

Andy glances up and down Nick's body. If Nick believes Andy can fit into anything of Nick's, he has another think coming. "I mean, I can try."

Nick looks at him oddly but disappears into his bedroom. He emerges a moment later with a pair of striped pajamas. "There's a clean towel in the bathroom and the shaving cream's in the medicine cabinet. And if you need anything else, just ask. Oh, and drink this before you go to bed." Nick goes into the kitchen and Andy follows, watching Nick fill a glass of water at the sink. "Aspirin's in the medicine cabinet."

"You realize I'm a grown man, yes?" Andy rolls his eyes, but he drinks the water. A draft of cold air makes him turn to find the source, and he sees that the kitchen window is propped open. "Do you want me to close that?"

"It has to stay open," Nick says.

"To make it enticing for burglars?"

"This is the fifth floor. Nobody's coming in the window. No, it's for . . . ventilation."

There's a distinct pause there before *ventilation*. "For ventilation," Andy repeats, raising his eyebrows. But Nick doesn't elaborate, so Andy lets it drop and gets changed into his pajamas.

Andy climbs into bed and drifts off before he even knows he's shut his eyes. When he wakes, the door to Nick's room is already shut with no light coming from beneath it.

The sunlight is coming from a strange direction and the sheets are all wrong, so Andy's already braced for disaster before he's even fully awake. When he opens his eyes, the reality of the previous day comes crashing back to him, but the blow is softened by the realization that he's in Nick's apartment. He can hear the sounds of someone moving around, which must mean that Nick is already awake.

He makes a halfhearted effort to arrange the bedcovers neatly and stumbles out to the kitchen, where he finds Nick making breakfast.

More specifically, he finds Nick in his underwear making breakfast. He's wearing boxer shorts and a sleeveless undershirt, a cigarette between his lips, the beginnings of a beard already showing on his jaw, and in general looking every inch the ruffian.

"Good morning, sleeping beauty," Nick calls out without turning around. "There's some coffee on the stove. Two eggs or three?"

"Two." A patch of dark hair is visible at the neckline of Nick's undershirt, and Andy finds this . . . arresting, somehow. He already knew it was there—Nick loosens his tie and undoes the top button of his shirt at the slightest provocation, so Andy's had glimpses. But Andy must be a bit hungover or maybe he's dealing with some emotional fallout from yesterday, because the fact of Nick in his underwear seems like a riddle that Andy can't quite solve. "Did I take your only pair of pajamas?" he blurts out.

"Nah, I never wear them. Those were a gift." Nick turns and looks at Andy, his gaze skimming up from where the pajama bottoms trail on the floor to where they barely cling to Andy's hips. Nick is an inch or two taller than Andy and probably forty pounds heavier, if not more. Andy has always been whip thin, and Nick is—well. All you have to do is look at him to see where that extra weight goes. His arms and shoulders are—

"Milk's in the icebox," Nick says, flipping an egg. "Sugar's on the table."

Andy pours himself some coffee and sits at the kitchen table. His head's still a little foggy from last night's drinking and he realizes that his eyes are sort of glazing over as he watches Nick cook. It's just eggs. He's watched people make eggs before, hasn't he? There's nothing so mesmerizing about it. Andy's just tired and emotionally overwrought.

Nick comes over to the table with two plates of eggs and some toast. "Want to play tennis later?"

Andy looks up in alarm. "Jesus, Nick, I got jilted; I'm not dying." Nick hates tennis. He's decent at it, which somehow only makes him hate it more. Last summer, Andy convinced him that he had to learn to play golf or tennis in case he ever needed to cultivate country club types of sources. This was horseshit. Andy wanted someone to play tennis with, and knew that with golf as an alternative, Nick would agree to tennis. Nick drew the line at buying tennis whites, saying that they could play at public courts like normal people, and Andy conceded.

Andy thought that Nick would make a grouchy, recalcitrant student, but was pleasantly surprised to be wrong. Nick watched, he listened, and then he did as he was told. Later, as they were cooling down on the side of the court, sitting with their backs against the fence, Andy said as much.

"If I only did what came naturally, I'd be knocking heads together outside a bar on Flatbush Avenue," Nick said.

"What does that mean?"

"Just that I knew that if I wanted to get away from my family, if I wanted to be able to take care of myself, I'd need to work at it. There's no use fighting the person who's trying to teach you, whether it's your boss at Woolworth telling you how to put things on shelves or some skinny WASP telling you how to serve a tennis ball."

That was one of a handful of times Nick mentioned his family.

Andy, no stranger to mixed feelings about family, recognized it as an area closed off by police tape.

Now Andy looks across the table at Nick, at his rumpled hair, at what he realizes is a vastly superfluous quantity of food. "You can't possibly want to play tennis."

"What I want to do is keep you busy. It's a beautiful day." This is only true if you're grading on a steep curve—the weather's decent for New York in March, meaning it's not raining and there isn't any slush on the ground. "Linda probably has a tennis racket you can borrow."

"Linda?"

"Linda Ackerman. Remember her from—" Nick sighs. "From Emily and Jeanne's dinner party. She was the artist with the long black hair and the trousers. She was looking for a place, and I mentioned that there was a room for rent in my building. She's right next door."

It's odd to think of one of Emily's circle living in Nick's world, and something of Andy's confusion must show on his face because Nick nudges him under the table with his bare foot. "Want me to go ask her if she has a racket?"

"You ought to get dressed first," Andy points out.

Nick rolls his eyes. "Great idea. I'd never have thought of that myself. Good thing you came to stay with me." He ruffles Andy's hair on the way to his bedroom and Andy doesn't even protest.

CHAPTER THREE

"Let me get this straight," Andy says as they walk approximately half a mile through a dark and damp tunnel, "the only way to get to Brooklyn on the subway is to switch trains and then pick our way through a maze of murderer-infested tunnels?" Something scurries across his foot, which is a shame because Andy is going to have to burn his shoes at Nick's mother's house. Not the best way to make a first impression.

"No," Nick says. "There are lots of ways to get to Brooklyn. But this is the fastest way to get to Bay Ridge on a single fare from my place."

When they finally get to the right platform, Nick lets three trains pass by, each bearing destination signs for places Andy has never heard of—Culver, Brighton, Sea Beach—before a train arrives with the correct sign: a brief *4th AVE*. It's been forty-five minutes since they got on the subway and he thinks they're still in Manhattan. Granted, it's Sunday morning and trains are running slow, but it seems to Andy that if Nick deliberately chose his apartment for how inaccessible it is to and from his mother's house, he couldn't have done any better.

"We should have packed a lunch," Andy says.

"I told you to eat that bagel."

"I wasn't hungry then," Andy says, definitely not pouting.

That morning, Nick had grimly set a cup of coffee before Andy. "I have to visit my mother," he said, in the same tone that people in movies use to break the news that they have to go off to war. "You should come with me. It'll be fun."

"Yeah, you're really selling it," Andy had said. But of course he's tagging along. He wants to meet the family that Nick has spent a year mentioning as infrequently as possible. It's getting increasingly difficult to pretend not to be dying of curiosity when Nick drops a casual reference to some or another member of his family, like when he mentioned that one of his brothers is a priest. A priest! Imagine burying a lede like that.

Andy knows that the only reason Nick's bringing him along is because he doesn't want to leave Andy alone with his broken heart. And Andy probably ought to have insisted that he's a grown man who can be left up to his own devices for a few hours and all that, but he's only human, and he wants to meet the Russos.

"Why do you have to visit your mother today, anyway?" Andy asks. Over half the seats in the car are occupied, so they're sitting immediately next to one another, and every time the train takes a bend, they slide together. Nick reaches out and braces an arm on one of the poles.

"It's her birthday."

"Her birthday!" Andy definitely does not shriek. "And we're arriving empty-handed?"

Nick lifts the brown paper sack he took from the refrigerator that morning. "I brought meat."

"You brought meat."

"She always says there's no good Italian butcher in the neighborhood, but really she just doesn't like the butcher because he's from Florence. So whenever I visit, I bring her some sausage and veal shanks."

"But I don't have anything for her."

"We can say the veal shanks are from you. Or the sausage, if you want."

"I'll tell you what you can do with your sausage," Andy grumbles, and then winces, because he didn't mean to make a dirty joke but managed to do it anyway. When he looks over, Nick is shaking his head, but not unfondly, Andy hopes.

Many, many stops later, Nick nudges Andy and gets to his feet, and they emerge onto a platform that's simply marked 77 in the usual tile mosaic. They climb the stairs and all of a sudden they're on a street that's lined with blocky brown apartment buildings and typical-looking storefronts, but along the side streets are these little houses that look like bungalows and make Andy feel like he's far outside the city.

"So this is where you grew up?" Andy asks, very casual, as if he isn't dying to know.

"No." No explanation, no elaboration. Nick is clearly in a mood, his expression shuttered, his posture wary and tight, as if he's expecting an attack. He's prone to sullen moods and usually Andy just jollies him into a more cheerful—or at least less sulky—frame of mind. But something about his demeanor today seems serious, and Andy worries that if he tries his usual tactics, Nick will think Andy's dismissing whatever's upsetting him. He plainly doesn't want to visit his mother—the mother he's hardly ever mentioned—or isn't delighted to have Andy tagging along with him, and both of these topics seem potentially dangerous, so he needs to step carefully.

"Do you want to tell me why all the plants are withering as we walk past?" Andy asks mildly as they turn onto a side street. "And why all the animals are running away from you? I mean, you don't have to, but it's an option."

Nick snorts. "Just grouchy."

"Yeah, yeah. Likely story." He nudges Nick with his shoulder and Nick nudges him back.

"Here we are." Nick stops in front of a small white house. "You hold this." He passes Andy the parcel of meat as they climb the steps. He holds up his fist as if to knock, then apparently thinks better of it and opens the door. "Mama!" he calls.

"Nicky!" comes a shout from inside the house, and then Nick is being hugged by a tiny round woman with salt-and-pepper hair. "Too skinny," she says, looking him up and down. She turns her attention to Andy.

"Mama, this is Andy. I told you about him. We work together."

Not sure what else to do, Andy holds out the meat. "Pleased to meet you, Mrs. Russo. Happy birthday!"

Nick's mother shouts something in Italian over her shoulder and two small children come racing through the house, although how they're managing to pick up that kind of speed in such a small space, Andy can't fathom. In a sitting room, a couple of men sit in front of the television.

"Christ, Nicky," says one of them, a dark-haired man who looks startlingly like Nick but maybe ten years older. "Nice of you to show your face around here. Who's your friend?"

Beside Andy, Nick goes rigid. "Andy, this is my brother Michael." Then he turns to his brother. "I just saw Chrissy and Danielle. Is Sal here? Where's Bev?"

Michael ignores Andy and looks Nick over, radiating disapproval, although Andy can't imagine at what—Nick's wearing the navy crewneck sweater that Andy got him for Christmas and a pair of wool trousers. "Bev's in the kitchen," Nick's brother finally says. "And Sal's with her."

There's something about the man's tone that makes Andy think that Sal, whoever that is, shouldn't be in the kitchen. It also makes Andy think that if this is how Nick's brother usually acts, it's no wonder Nick doesn't enjoy coming home. But what does Andy know? He doesn't have siblings. He really doesn't have any experience with family whatsoever.

Nick introduces Andy to two old women and one very old woman, all dressed in black. They're apparently aunts, or something like aunts, and before Andy can figure out how there could be any doubt on that score, Nick is gone, and Andy's left behind, attempting to have a conversation with three women who apparently don't speak English. One of them hands him a glass of something sweet and alcoholic.

"Nick's looking after me because my fiancée left me for her mother's heart doctor," Andy says when conversation flags. And by "conversation," he means smiling broadly and then taking a long sip of his mystery drink, as if he's on a television commercial for whatever this stuff is. It tastes a little like ginger ale but is a confusing orange color.

"Heart doctor?" repeats one of the women.

"Cardiologist," Andy agrees, as if this explains everything.

One of the merely old women says something in rapid-fire Italian to the very old woman, who then turns to Andy, frowns, and says something that makes the other two laugh. For lack of any better idea, Andy smiles, drinks some more, and looks around the room.

One wall is covered in photographs. Most of the recent photos are of Michael and what Andy assumes are Michael's wife and children. But the older photographs catch Andy's eye, especially three separate portraits of boys on what has to be their First Communion. Andy guesses he's looking at Nick and his brothers. There's also one wedding photograph of a tiny woman and a large man, presumably Nick's parents. He knows Nick's father died when Nick was still pretty young.

"Jesus, Andy, there you are," says Nick. He says something in Italian to the women, which results in the oldest getting to her feet and pinching his cheek and murmuring something in his ear that makes Nick blush.

"You shouldn't drink what they give you," Nick says, looking at Andy's mouth. "They've been in training for decades." He reaches his hand out, as if to wipe away whatever he sees there, but then shoves his hand in his pocket. Andy wipes his own mouth and the back of his hand comes away stained orange.

"What did she say to you?" Andy asks as they leave the room. "You blushed. I've never seen you blush."

"She wants to know when I'm bringing a girlfriend home."

Andy doesn't know what to say to that, but it doesn't matter anyway because now they're in a hot, crowded kitchen and he's being introduced to another half a dozen women. Some of them are chopping or stirring or peering into the oven, but the others are just chatting and occasionally sneaking a taste of whatever's on the stove.

The conversation in this room is entirely in English, which would be a relief except that now Andy knows for certain that everyone is talking about him.

"Don't they have food where he comes from?"

"The first time you ever bring anyone around and it's not even a girl, Nicky?"

"He works at that paper? Don't let Michael sit next to him."

"Sal," Nick says to a teenage boy Andy hadn't noticed, probably on account of the kid lurking in the corner between the refrigerator and the back door and also on account of him being built like a broomstick. "We're going out back. Want to come?"

Nick leads the way out the back door to a fenced-in yard. A handful of old men are lawn bowling and pay no attention to the three newcomers.

Nick sits on the brick steps. Andy sits beside him on one side, Sal on the other. Nick gets out a pack of cigarettes and lights two, handing one to Andy.

"Can I have one, Uncle Nick?"

"No," Nick laughs.

"I'm fourteen!"

Nick doesn't dignify this with a response, just shakes his head. "How's school, kid?"

"Not bad."

"Straight As?"

"B-plus in Biology."

"How's home?"

"Oh, you know."

Nick grumbles something unintelligible, then lowers his voice so Andy can barely hear him. "He's not smacking you around?"

"Shh!" Sal looks around furtively, checking that the door is still closed. "No."

Nick's jaw is clenched so hard that Andy can almost hear his molars grinding together. "You know where to find me if you need me."

"Yeah. Dad doesn't like those articles you've been writing. The ones about the cops."

Nick takes a puff from his cigarette and taps the ash onto the ground. "Yeah, well, that sounds like it's his problem."

"Just thought you should know, if he seems like more of a—if he's more difficult than usual."

"Thanks, kid."

Sal gets up and joins the old men on the lawn, and Andy is left not knowing what to say about any of that.

When they sit down to dinner, fifteen people crowded around the table, Nick and Andy wind up wedged together in a corner.

"Whatever you do, do *not* stop eating," Nick warns.

This, as it turns out, is not a hardship. There are noodles with tomato sauce, which is ordinary enough, but this sauce is spicy and filled with green things and tastes different from any other tomato sauce Andy has ever eaten. There's also meat, rolled up and filled with cheese, and several vegetable dishes that Andy can't identify but that he eats anyway. A few loaves of crusty bread get passed around the table, too. And there's wine—so much wine.

No fewer than six people ask Nick when he's getting married. And Nick, for some reason, seems unable to deflect. Andy's seen Nick brush that question off a dozen times and his inability to do so now makes Andy wince. Nick's discomfort is obvious and Andy doesn't understand why his family keeps pressing the point. Well, that isn't true—they probably do it because they want Nick to be happy, and marriage seems like a good indicator of happiness. Andy understands that; God knows he does. But feeling Nick go tense beside him makes Andy want to yell at all these nice old Italian people.

He's so wrapped up in Nick that he almost forgets his own troubles, until one of Nick's aunts points a fork at him and turns to the man sitting beside her. "His girlfriend left him for a heart doctor." So *now* she speaks English?

The man looks appraisingly at Andy and shrugs. "A heart doctor, though," he says in a tone that suggests that getting jilted in favor of cardiologists is all anyone can expect. That maybe Andy should have considered medical school if he didn't want to get jilted. That Emily did what she had to do, because who could turn down a heart doctor?

He starts to laugh. He had known that eventually he'd find the whole affair with Emily—well, not acutely painful, at least. He just wasn't expecting it to happen a mere forty-eight hours afterward.

"The liquor's finally gone to your head," Nick says as Andy hides his face in his napkin and tries to stop his shoulders from shaking with laughter. Under the table, Nick pinches his leg.

By the time they get back on the subway, Andy isn't steady on his feet. Not even close. "Come on, lightweight," Nick says, steering him toward a seat at the end of a mostly empty car.

Andy sits but Nick stays standing, his hands in his pockets, facing the subway map. "I grew up here," he says, pointing to a spot east of what Andy thinks is Prospect Park. He doesn't have his glasses on, so it's anybody's guess. "Flatbush. They only moved out here a couple years ago when my brother got promoted to detective. It's his house."

If Nick is in a mood to talk about his family, Andy is going to take advantage of it, but figures he has one, maybe two questions before Nick clams up again. He has to choose his questions wisely.

"Your family kept asking why you don't have a girlfriend," Andy says. "They don't know?"

Nick gives him a sharp look.

"Sorry," Andy says, holding his hands up. "I'm never sure whether I'm supposed to pretend that I don't know."

Nick sighs and sits beside Andy. "No, don't pretend. I'm not used to talking about it, that's all. I feel like cops are going to jump out from under the seats or something. Anyway, no, my family doesn't know. And they won't. They aren't— It isn't an option."

"I'm sorry," Andy says, for lack of any better ideas.

"They're never going to let it rest. They're never going to get a clue and stop asking. And if they do get a clue, that would be worse."

Just lie to them the way you lie to everyone else, Andy wants to shout. But maybe lying to your family is a bad idea; Andy wouldn't know. "I'm glad you don't go too often, then," Andy says, and it must sound more fervent than he intended, because Nick's expression goes all baffled and dopey the way it does whenever he has to deal with the fact that anyone gives a shit about him.

Andy yawns. It's the middle of the afternoon, but he's fading fast. The wine made him sleepy, and now the rocking of the subway car is threatening to knock him out.

"Go to sleep." Nick's voice is little more than a whisper.

For a crazy moment, Andy's tempted to put his head on Nick's shoulder—something he's never done to anyone in his life. Nick's had a bad day and Andy wants to make it better, but obviously snuggling on a train—or anywhere—isn't going to fix anything. This is what too much day drinking will do to you, he supposes. He tips his head back against the window and closes his eyes.

CHAPTER FOUR

It occurs to Andy late on Monday afternoon that he probably ought to spend the night at his own apartment. He isn't feeling fragile—honestly, he hasn't since Saturday—and there's no reason for Nick to keep putting him up.

"I should have taken my suitcase this morning," Andy says as he watches Nick clean up his desk, going through his usual end-of-the-day ritual of separating pens by color and tucking books and files into drawers, aligning the typewriter so it's parallel to the edge of the desk. Andy just leaves everything piled exactly where it is—he'll only mess it up again the next day.

"Huh?" Nick jams carbon paper into the wastebasket.

"Do you want to bring me my suitcase tomorrow? Or should I pick it up now?"

"I was going to make minestrone soup," Nick says. "You like soup."

"I do like soup," Andy agrees. "I take it that's an invitation, not you taunting me with soup I don't get to eat."

Nick takes a ball of paper out of the wastebasket and throws it at Andy's head.

At nine o'clock, Nick is still stirring the pot of soup and Andy is sitting at the kitchen table, his legs stretched out and a bottle of wine mostly empty.

"You can stay, you know," Nick says, his back to Andy. "I have the space. I could use a roommate."

Andy's monumentally grateful that Nick's back is turned and that he can't see whatever Andy's face is doing right now. At the idea that he could stay here—here with Nick in this tiny apartment with its wall of books and record albums, the noisy radiator and the sofa that barely fits them both, the cabinet full of mismatched dishes and spices Andy doesn't recognize—Andy's heart gives an extra thud. "Are you sure? I promise I'm not going to cry myself to sleep if I have to go home."

Nick turns around, his arms folded across his chest, like he's furious that Andy's making him say this. "It's nice having you here. I hate cooking for myself. I wind up eating scrambled eggs or Chinese food every night."

It's nice having you here is practically florid language from Nick Russo. Andy has to try not to look shocked. "Well, we can't have that."

"Exactly. You'd be doing me a favor."

Andy manages not to roll his eyes. "Okay. You'll have to let me pay half your rent."

"Really?"

Andy laughs and tips his chair back on two legs. "Why do you look surprised? You asked me!"

"My apartment's a dump! Also, stop tipping back in your chair like that. I don't want to have to clean your brains off my linoleum."

Andy settles the chair firmly on the floor. "Was I supposed to say no? Oh my God, you're making this so complicated. And your apartment isn't a dump."

"You'll really stay?" Nick looks . . . relieved, maybe. Like he was worried about Andy saying no, and not like he only made the offer because he feels bad for Andy.

"Yes. Jeez. Give me some soup, already, will you."

They eat the soup and finish the wine and linger at the table long after both are gone. And Andy doesn't admit to himself until he's in the narrow bed in Nick's spare room—his room, now?—how relieved he is. He hates being alone—it's pathetic, he knows it's pathetic, he'll never admit it aloud, and it would probably take a dog's age on an analyst's couch to deal with—but that's the truth of it. It comes from too many mornings waking up to a note on the kitchen table, too many letters with foreign postmarks. He knows why he's this way and that doesn't make it any less embarrassing.

He doesn't feel great about Nick having figured all this out. Sure, it counts for something that Nick has seen the worst of him and likes him anyway, but it smacks of pity and Andy does have a little pride, or at least enough that he doesn't want his best friend to treat him like some kind of emotional charity case.

Still, though, Nick did say that it was nice having Andy there. Nick, who only admits to having emotions when he's under actual duress, wouldn't have said that unless he meant it. As Andy burrows under the pile of blankets, this thought pleases him more than he knows what to do with.

Every morning, Andy meets with his father at nine o'clock, right before the editorial meeting, and they both act like they aren't losing sleep over the future of the *Chronicle*. Andy sits on his hands so he doesn't bite his nails, Andy's dad nervously polishes his glasses like he's going to face a firing squad if a single smudge is left on a lens, and they both engage in the fiction that Andy is ever going to run the *Chronicle*.

Actually, Andy's becoming increasingly concerned that for his father it isn't even a fiction. People usually realize Andy's incompetent pretty quickly and he can't imagine what's taking his father so long.

"Where were you last night?" his father asks on Tuesday morning. "I couldn't get ahold of you."

"I'm staying with Nick Russo for a while." Andy isn't sure why he includes Nick's last name. His father knows the two of them are friendly. He could hardly mean any other Nick.

"There's going to be a write-up in the *Daily Mirror*'s gossip column about the broken engagement. I should have expected it. I'm afraid you might be newsworthy just by virtue of being your mother's son." Andy's a little impressed that his dad managed a full sentence about his mother without soaking the whole thing in disapproval and resentment, so impressed that he doesn't argue that it's probably Emily's family that makes their broken engagement newsworthy.

"Thank you for letting me know," Andy says.

"Would you mind getting me my wheelchair?" his father asks. "I don't want to bother Evelyn."

For the past year, there's been a wheelchair discreetly tucked into the coat closet in his father's office. So far, his father is usually able to walk, albeit a bit unsteadily and with the help of a cane, but his bad days are coming more often.

Andy pushes the wheelchair so it's parallel with the desk chair and then braces it in place as his father makes the transition.

"I can't run this paper from a wheelchair," his father says. "I'm retiring in September."

That's six months. Six *months*. Andy wants to say that his father could run the newspaper from a wheelchair or a hospital bed or a hot-air balloon and do a sight better than Andy could on his own two feet. Andy can't run his own life; there's no way he can be trusted with the livelihood of the *Chronicle*'s hundreds of employees, not to mention the responsibility of not fucking up the *news*.

He can't just come right out and say that in no way is he ever running the *Chronicle* or anything else. It's too embarrassing. He's never actually had to explain to anyone that he's a disaster—that's how obvious it is.

"I'm not ready," Andy finally says.

"You'd have help," his father says, sounding far too reasonable for a man who's obviously suffering under some kind of delusion. "Lou Epstein will still be managing editor. He's been in this business nearly as long as I have."

"Then make him the publisher!"

"That's not how it works," his father says, not without sympathy. "You'll *own* the *Chronicle*."

"*You'll* own the *Chronicle*. You're not dying."

"Not yet."

Andy pinches the bridge of his nose. They've already had this conversation half a dozen times. His father, at sixty-five, believes his days of usefulness are coming to an end; Andy doesn't see why the publisher of the *Chronicle* needs to be able to walk or hold a pen or do any of the things that Andy's father is finding increasingly difficult.

"Nobody will respect a twenty-six-year-old publisher," Andy says, and he already knows what his father's answering argument will be.

"They respected me when I was twenty-six, and your grandfather when he wasn't much older than that."

Andy wants to argue that this was because his father had been twenty-six in the twenties, when rules were different, and his grandfather had been that age in the late 1800s, when rules were nonexistent. But that isn't the problem—the real problem is that his father and grandfather had the kind of personalities that commanded the attention of an entire room and the will to execute any plan they thought of. Andy apologized six times that morning to the man at the bagel shop for not being able to make up his mind about whether he wanted cream cheese and still would have forgotten his bagel on the counter if Nick hadn't reminded him.

Andy doesn't know if his father simply never bothered to get to know him and therefore can't see how bad an idea this is, or if he's so desperate to pass his life's work on to his only son that he's refusing to see reason. Either way it's a depressing thought.

"One other thing," his father says, his face carefully neutral. "Consider how it will look if it comes out that you've abandoned your apartment to live with a bachelor friend in a seedy neighborhood."

Andy's first thought is that he's never mentioned Nick's neighborhood, but he shouldn't be surprised that his father made it his business to check the file of anyone Andy was spending time with. The first part of the decade left its marks on Andrew Fleming Jr.: once he realized that the FBI had a file on him the size of a phone book, he started keeping tabs on everyone around him, because there's nothing like being accused of being a Soviet spy to make a man a little paranoid that the people around him might be reporting to Uncle Sam. Or Uncle Khrushchev, for that matter.

Andy's second thought isn't a thought at all, but a bone-deep sense of mortification. "Sir, what are you saying?"

His father sighs and takes off his glasses to clean them with his handkerchief. "I'm suggesting that whatever you do, you do it with your eyes open."

"I'm not— *Dad.*" He squeezes his eyes shut, hoping that when he opens them, he won't be in a room where his father is accusing him of having a queer affair with his best friend. Or, not accusing so much as being blandly indifferent, which is even more rattling.

His father is right that staying with Nick poses a risk: people love jumping to conclusions, especially scandalous conclusions, and that's exactly what they'll do even if nobody knows about Nick's private life. While it's normal enough for young men to have roommates, it isn't normal for a man in Andy's situation—a man who owns his own apartment and whose father has multiple spare rooms.

But Andy isn't going to leave. He hates living alone; he likes living with Nick and Nick likes it, too. Andy's mother never went in much for motherly advice, but one thing she was fond of saying was that if you want something, you have to grit your teeth and jump in with both feet—that it matters less how you land than that you get there in the first place. Andy had always grimly thought to himself that this was exactly what you'd expect from the life philosophy of a person who went to war zones for a living. Andy was happy shrugging his way through life.

Right now, though, there isn't anything his father could possibly say to dissuade Andy from staying in Nick's spare room. He remembers his parents hollering at one another, his father shouting that Andy's mother was going to get herself killed, his mother shouting back that at least she stood for something, and Andy thinking, disloyally, that his father was right. And he had been right, in the end.

He and his father have never really fought—even their disagreements about Andy's future at the *Chronicle* are just conversations. Conversations they both hate, but still just conversations.

He grips the arms of his chair, braced for the full force of his father's wrath.

Instead he gets a half smile and a sigh, neither of which he can begin to decipher but which leave him with the distinct impression that his father doesn't particularly care what kind of mess Andy makes of his life.

The story, as Andy and everybody else know it, goes like this.

Andy's grandfather, Andrew Fleming I, arrived at Ellis Island round about 1890 with a nickel in his pocket or whatever they call nickels in Scotland. He spent the next few years doing honest upstanding American capitalist things that definitely had nothing to do with any of the waterfront gangs that ran half the city in those days.

Somewhere around the turn of the century he met an enterprising young reporter named Cecilia Marks, who was making a name for herself by getting thrown into prisons in order to interview murderers, stowing away on steamships, chaining herself to various legislative buildings, and in general making herself irresistible to the likes of Andrew Fleming I, who had never met a danger he didn't want to embrace with both arms.

When the paper that employed Miss Marks threatened to fold, Andrew did the only sensible thing a man could do in that situation and bought the paper. Suitably wooed, Miss Marks became Mrs. Fleming, even though in the newspaper she retained her old byline. The paper succeeded; more papers were acquired; a son was produced, staid and responsible in a way that shocked the sensibilities of both of his parents. Young Andrew went off to fight a war, survived it, returned home to find that his father hadn't, and took over the *Chronicle*.

In the twenties, the *Chronicle*'s circulation exceeded half a million, which was none too shabby in a city that already had a couple dozen daily papers, not counting the weeklies, not counting the Black papers or those in other languages. The *Chronicle*'s success carried on through the thirties and right on through the war, not stumbling in the least when Fleming, again following in his father's footsteps, married his star reporter. He divorced her almost immediately—but not before fathering a child.

The circumstances that precipitated Andrew Fleming and Margaret Kelly's divorce were well documented, having occurred in the newsroom of a major newspaper, surrounded by journalists with steel-trap memories and a penchant for gossip. Andy's mother wanted to go to Germany to see what in hell was the matter over there. The *Chronicle* had always been progressive, and had only become more so under the stewardship of Andrew Fleming II, and while the staff might take their quarrels with one another about Stalin to the pages of the paper with unfortunate frequency, everyone agreed that Hitler was just a dirty fascist.

But Andrew Fleming insisted that sloping off to fascist countries was not something that the mother of a newborn did; his wife accused him of being a fascist sympathizer. She went to Reno for a quickie divorce and then directly to the *Herald Tribune*, a betrayal that smarted much more than when she subsequently took up with her photographer in Berlin.

This left Andrew Fleming with an infant and a paper to run. Only one of those required his personal attention and it wasn't the baby. When Margaret Kelly returned to the States, she scooped the child up and deposited him in an apartment on the Upper East Side with a succession of housekeepers.

She then went back to Berlin, and then to Prague and London and Paris. She was there for the liberation of Dachau. As a woman, she didn't have official press credentials, so she made her own access, and in doing so made herself something of a legend.

The first words Andy remembers reading were his mother's reporting on the fall of Paris. Every few months she returned to New York with stories and presents and new scars and more gray hair, and he almost felt guilty for wondering why she wasn't around more, because he was so proud of her. She went to Nuremberg. She went to Moscow and East Berlin, and then to Korea. She came back to the States long enough to shout at Senator McCarthy, then went to Budapest and won a Pulitzer. She likely would have kept on in precisely the same manner, darting from conflict to conflict, if she hadn't been caught in a bombing in Algiers. At her funeral, several of her colleagues told Andy that it was how she would have wanted to go, as if this was supposed to bring him some comfort, as if she hadn't told him so herself enough times that whenever he saw her off at an airport, he never quite expected to see her again.

Andy's father, meanwhile, built the *Chronicle* from something of a communist-inflected scandal rag to a respectable, if unapologetically progressive, newspaper. The taint of communism lingers, though, and is largely to blame for the way circulation plummeted after the war.

And so when Andy thinks of the *Chronicle*, when he thinks about journalism, he thinks of both of his parents and two of his grandparents. If anything is in his blood, it's this.

And the fact that it's all going to go to hell on his watch keeps him up at night.

The subway lurches to the side and suddenly Andy gets a clear look inside the newspapers of two fellow passengers.

"Look," Andy whispers, jabbing Nick in the ribs.

"Ow! What is wrong with you?"

"The paper!"

Nick follows Andy's gaze. "Yes, Andrew. People read the *Chronicle*. This can't be the first time you've seen someone—"

"Not the front page, dummy. The article. They're reading your article."

"Huh."

Ever since the news of the money missing from the police evidence locker, Nick's been on that story like a dog with a bone. It's not that the amount of money stolen was so huge; it's not like this is the biggest police corruption scandal they're likely to cover this spring, let alone this year. It's under Nick's skin, and whenever he writes about it, the paper gets a flood of letters. New Yorkers love stories about dirty cops, even if Nick—at Jorgensen's insistence—has been very careful not to come right out and say what everyone already assumes, which is that the money was stolen by the police, and that access to the evidence locker is considered something of a perk.

Last week Nick went up to Rikers Island to interview a recently convicted safecracker about what you'd have to do to break into the specific model of safe the police used. Then he interviewed the security company who made the safe. The resulting article should have been anticlimactic—just two different kinds of experts agreeing that this safe couldn't be broken into without leaving marks. But instead Nick's story is . . . Well, it's entertaining. There's a colorful old jailbird and a buttoned-up security executive and both of them are all but holding up signs that say "It Was an Inside Job."

No wonder people are reading it on the train, their eyes darting quickly from one line to the next, smiles tugging at their lips even though it isn't even nine in the morning and nobody should be smiling. Especially not about dirty cops.

"I have a lunch date with a secretary from the Property Clerk's Office," Nick says when they're in the elevator heading up to the newsroom.

"Tell her I say hi," Andy says.

Nick's been buying this girl lunch once a week and she tells Nick the names of cops who've been assigned there. He's trying to figure out why cops get assigned to the Property Clerk's Office. Theoretically, it's supposed to be staffed by officers with injuries minor enough that they can work desk jobs. But in practice, dozens if not hundreds of cops with similar injuries *aren't* reassigned. Instead they do desk work in their regular precincts.

There's no love lost between the police commissioner and the *Chronicle*. But now Nick is waving a red flag in front of a bull, and the readers love it and Jorgensen and Epstein love it and so Nick isn't stopping.

And now Andy knows Nick's brother Michael is a cop in addition to being a nasty piece of work. It's not that he thinks Nick's interest is purely personal—but it's always seemed at least a little bit personal and now Andy has a clue as to why.

He can't help but think that if he were Nick, he'd want to be a bit more careful. A lot more careful, really. He wouldn't want to provoke the police. Aren't plainclothes cops forever going into queer bars and arresting men as soon as they show interest? It would be easy for them to ruin Nick's life, if they knew.

He wants to ask Nick to back down, to leave this story to

someone else, even though this is absolutely none of Andy's business. In fact, the *Chronicle* is very literally Andy's business, and it's served by Nick continuing to dig. The fact that Andy would still prefer for Nick to leave it alone is just another reason why he isn't fit to run the paper.

On Wednesday morning, Andy waits until Nick is arguing with Jorgensen about changes the editor wants to make to one of Nick's stories, then he dials a familiar number, holding his breath as he waits to see who will pick up the phone.

"Warburton residence," says Jeanne. Andy breathes a sigh of relief—Emily rarely answers the phone unless she's expecting a call, but he doesn't know what he'd have done on the off chance she answered. Probably hang the phone up, to be honest.

"Hi, Jeanne. It's Andy."

"Oh, Andy, how *are* you?" Jeanne sounds like she actually cares. One of the strangest complications of this whole mess is that this person he was ready to regard as a sister for the rest of their lives is now demoted to being a near stranger, and they're both supposed to act like it isn't a loss.

"I'm fine. I called to see how Emily was. She didn't seem— Well, honestly, Jeanne, she seemed awful on Friday. I'm worried, but I can't call her myself, and I'm not sure that I even want to. I'm not even sure it's my business how she's doing."

Jeanne sighs, and through the line he hears the flick of her lighter. "She's better than she was last week. She really got her heart trampled on by that fellow."

"I'd ask if there was anything I could do, but I think we both know the answer to that is just to keep away."

"I'm so sorry, Andy."

After hanging up, Andy looks up and sees Nick leaning against his own desk, his eyebrows raised.

"I had to know how she was doing," Andy protests. "I can't pretend I don't care."

"You don't have to explain to me," Nick says, holding his hands up. "I called yesterday while you were in a meeting and made Jeanne put her on the line. Is that okay?"

"You don't have to stop being friends with her just because . . ."

"Just because she broke your heart?"

"Well, yes." The fact is that Nick and Emily *were* friends. Andy had liked it so much—he liked the idea that they all fit together. Usually bringing a date to meet his friends felt like brokering peace at a NATO summit, but if NATO were made up entirely of twelve-year-olds at their first mixer. It wasn't at all like that with Nick and Emily.

"Just so you know," Nick says, "if I'm ever in your place, I expect you to hold a grudge for the rest of your life. Give them the evil eye when you pass on the street. Spit after you say their name."

Any man who breaks Nick's heart will be lucky if all Andy does is give them the evil eye and hold a grudge, but he doesn't say so.

At eight thirty in the morning the newsroom is always like a coiled spring, still lacking the movement and energy of later in the day, but with plenty of latent force if you know where to look. Most reporters, except those on the night desk or manning the wires, don't wander into work until ten or eleven, but Andy gets in before nine in order to match the schedules of marketing and circulation, then usually stays until the paper goes to print—about nine at night. It's a long day, but he's never minded because it beats the hell out of his empty apartment.

Now, though, Nick is mirroring his schedule.

"It's not like I can go back to sleep after you crash around the kitchen," Nick grumbles, which is a lie, because Nick wakes up first every day and starts a pot of coffee. "So I might as well go in."

Whenever Andy attempts to protest, Nick shuts him up with a glare, making Andy suspect that Nick secretly likes waking up early. This is the most disturbing thing he's learned about Nick or possibly anyone.

That morning, there's a manila interoffice mail envelope sitting on Nick's desk when they get in. Andy brings a paper cup of coffee to his mouth and absently watches Nick unwind the string from around the button and empty the contents onto the desk.

What falls out is a book. Usually interoffice mail envelopes bring nothing but rejected expense reports and a stapled packet of receipts. He tries to remember if Nick mentioned ordering a book for one of the stories he's working on, but even if he had, it wouldn't likely be about Roman chariots or whatever this is. *The Charioteer* by Mary Renault.

Nick opens the book and almost immediately slams it closed.

"Something wrong?" Andy asks, even though it's pretty obvious that there is.

"No," Nick growls.

"Who sent it?"

"Doesn't matter."

"Is someone bothering you?" A list of people who could blackmail, extort, or otherwise harm Nick spools out in Andy's mind.

The police. Whatever mob connections dirty cops inevitably have. The mobsters who run half the queer bars in town. An ex-lover.

"No, Jesus. Leave it be." Nick drops the book and the envelope in a desk drawer, then slams it closed.

Nick puts a sheet of paper into his typewriter even though they both know he doesn't have anything to write at the moment. Andy watches him expectantly.

"Fine. Christ," Nick says after a few minutes, leaning back in his chair and looking at Andy in a long-suffering way, as if Andy's been interrogating him this whole time. He opens the drawer and takes the book out like he's handling a live grenade, shoving it across the surface of both of their desks. Thank God the newsroom is mostly empty, because the whole operation looks deeply suspicious.

Andy picks it up. It's a perfectly ordinary book—not photographs of Nick doing something incriminating, not a threat, not a demand that Nick drop that evidence story.

Andy flips the book over and reads the description. It seems perfectly innocuous and then—ah. He has to read between the lines, but there it is. Whatever's going on in this book, it's queer. Furthermore, it's not a proper book at all, but a bound galley— the sort of thing sent out to book reviewers in advance of the book's publication. He knows perfectly well that Nick doesn't write book reviews. "Who sent this?"

"One of the reviewers who— Christ, Andy," Nick says, as if Andy's been prying instead of just sitting there, wondering why his friend is acting like he's under attack. "He has reason to believe I might be interested in the subject matter. He thought I might like it."

Andy raises his eyebrows. He definitely wouldn't have guessed that Nick had ever been involved with anyone on staff.

Nick shakes his head. "Not because—not like that. We ran into one another at the sort of place nobody goes to unless they're—" He doesn't finish the sentence, and honestly Andy's shocked he got that far, but even at this hour there's enough noise in the newsroom to make their conversation unintelligible to anyone who might be trying to overhear. "He's sent me other books and I've just about had it."

"With books? With this book reviewer?" It doesn't take Andy long to figure out who this reviewer is—the *Chronicle* only has so many critics, and only one keeps an office in the building. Nick surely is aware that Andy knows all this.

"With his books," Nick says. "Jesus. They're enough to give anyone nightmares."

Andy furrows his brow. He's still trying to figure out whether he's going to need to fire a book reviewer today. He was hoping he'd manage to live out the rest of his life without firing anyone, but he'll cheerfully fire anybody who harasses Nick. "I don't follow."

Nick lights a cigarette. "So, he sends me any queer book that comes his way. He means well, but these books all end with someone dead or in a lunatic asylum."

"I suppose that's because—" Andy begins, thinking aloud. Probably any kind of happy ending would be seen as condoning homosexuality.

"I know why," Nick snaps. "I just— It makes him happy that these books exist. And sure, they're Literature, I guess." Andy can hear the capital *L* and any other time he'd laugh. "But they keep me up at night. I'm done with all that bullshit."

When they get home, Andy watches Nick retrieve the book from his bag and shelve it under *R*, for Renault, but he pretends he isn't paying any attention.

CHAPTER FIVE

L ate Friday afternoon, as they wait for the elevator to take them down to the lobby, Nick announces that he isn't going directly home. He takes his key ring out of his pocket and tosses it to Andy. "Let yourself in and I'll be back by nine."

"How mysterious."

Nick only shrugs.

"I can't believe you won't tell me what you're doing," Andy says, and he isn't pouting but he isn't *not* pouting, either. He lowers his voice even though there isn't anyone nearby. "Either you're meeting with a source that I'm not supposed to know about, or you're"—here, he drops his voice to a whisper—"cruising."

"Where did you learn that word?" Nick looks so aghast that Andy starts laughing.

"I'm a man of the world." In truth, Andy has been working up to saying something to Nick for days—as much as Andy would prefer to throw himself down an elevator shaft rather than discuss sex, he has to figure out a way to let Nick know that Andy's presence in his apartment doesn't need to hamper his . . . well. His private life. And Nick has inadvertently provided him with a perfect opening.

The elevator doors open and they step inside.

"I can't believe you think I'd"—Nick makes a vague gesture with his hand behind the elevator operator's back—"and then come back and make dinner."

"I had no idea— Wait. What are you making for dinner?"

"Omelets."

"I had no idea omelets were incompatible with . . ." He copies the same vague gesture Nick made.

Nick shoots him a glare.

"You know you're allowed to, um, have a social life even though I'm staying with you," Andy says when they're out on the street, valiantly trying to keep his voice casual.

"A social life," Nick repeats, flat. "Right. I'm going to bring people home and introduce them to you."

"Would that be so bizarre? I introduced you to Emily."

Nick lets out a crack of laughter. "The people I meet aren't Emily."

"But what does that mean? I'm too snobbish to rub shoulders with whoever you date?"

"Date!" Nick leans in and hisses, "It means that whoever I get with in the back room of a bar or the subway toilet isn't exactly a date."

"The—" Andy stops himself, realizing that shouting *the subway toilet!* in the middle of a rush hour crowd isn't exactly discreet. "People do that?"

"And here I thought you were a man of the world."

"Anyway, my point holds."

"I really appreciate your permission to get my—" Nick clears his throat and Andy's pretty sure that's a flush he sees high on Nick's cheeks. "But it's only a source."

If he's meeting with a source, then Andy doesn't need to ask what story this is for: it'll be the dirty cops and the missing money. Andy dangles the keys from his fingers. "I don't need these. I'll wait in that café on the other end of Barrow Street and you can come find me when you're done." The idea of being alone in Nick's empty apartment feels all wrong, like Nick's absence will be a tangible thing, like it might sink into his bones and never leave.

Andy hails a cab because he doesn't feel like crowding into a subway car with everyone else hurrying home to start their weekend, and Nick isn't around to give him Looks about it. He has the cabbie drop him off at Sheridan Square, in front of a bookstore where he can buy something to keep himself busy for the next few hours. Then, armed with a pulp detective story, he turns down Barrow Street in search of that café.

One thing he likes about the Village is that there are more people on the sidewalks than there ever are on the Upper East Side. There are little old ladies dragging groceries in handcarts, and there are men in suits awfully like his own. At this time of day, there are always people out walking their dogs after getting home from work. There are parents with children in strollers and old men sitting on stoops. But there are also young women with cropped hair and wearing trousers and young men with slightly longer hair and . . . well, they're also wearing trousers, obviously, but a bit on the tight side. A lot on the tight side.

Maybe it's because of that conversation he just had with Nick, but he's aware of an atmosphere in the neighborhood that he's always known is there but hasn't ever properly noticed. It's different, *knowing* men are looking at one another, compared with *noticing* that men are looking at one another.

And maybe he's noticing a little too obviously, maybe he's letting his gaze linger just a little too long on one man who walks past him—leather jacket, jeans, an honest-to-God *beard* on his *face*—because that man looks back over his shoulder and throws him a glance that Andy couldn't misinterpret if he tried.

He does try. A little. He doesn't want to think of the possibilities that exist in a world where he returns that glance. Everything is simpler and safer if he doesn't think about that, and Andy has long since made peace with being the kind of person who doesn't swim against the current. He has enough trouble without borrowing any.

When he gets to the café, he snags a table near the window and orders a cream cheese sandwich on date bread, which seems to be on the menus of half the coffee shops and cafés in the city. They're never particularly good, but they're never bad, either. He also orders a cappuccino, which will probably keep him up too late, but when in Rome.

The book, however, is dull, and Andy ought to have known better than to try a new author when he has nothing else to do with himself. Someone left a copy of the *Village Voice* on the table next to him, so he flips through it idly. He reads half a dozen papers a day, but he's never done more than skim through the *Voice*. It isn't the *Chronicle*'s competition and it isn't the *Chronicle*'s audience. It has the tiniest fraction of the *Chronicle*'s circulation. There isn't any comparison. The style is looser and less serious, but somehow more insistent. The writing feels conversational, but like an important conversation, like a conversation he's a little pleased with himself to be a part of.

He gets lost in the *Voice*'s world of blistering reviews of movies he'll never see and meandering paeans to music he's never heard of. And then he turns the page and sees a headline that seems like it might be visible from space: "Revolt of the Homosexual."

He feels his face heat and reminds himself that he isn't doing anything wrong. He's reading a newspaper. Hundreds of other people have read this same article. The article is styled as a dialog between two men: one a homosexual and one a self-described "straight guy." His focus skitters wildly across the page, picking up a phrase here, a jarring slur there, and he forces himself back to the beginning.

Why have so many fairies come out in the open recently? Wherever I go I run into them—the Village, East Side, Harlem, even the Bronx, Andy reads. And then the answer: *We no longer have the energy to hide. You can't know the strain on a person in always pretending.*

He realizes he's biting his nails and forces his hand around his now-cold cup of coffee. That's Nick the man is writing about. That's Nick, and it's the people in tight trousers walking around this neighborhood, and he's pretty sure his freshman year calculus professor, and at least one of the boys from his dorm, and—

He thinks about that man looking back over his shoulder at him, and he thinks about what some other, braver version of himself might have done, and he has to admit to himself, even if never to anyone else, that the article is talking about him, at least a little. At least theoretically.

Not really, though, because Andy likes women. Dating women isn't a burden to him. He isn't hiding, like that man in the article.

Sure, he's looked at men and felt the same thing as when he looks at women, but he's always known he wasn't going to do anything about it.

When he learned the words for men who liked men, he knew they didn't apply to him, couldn't possibly apply to him, and thank God for it because Andy had enough problems without being queer. Those words weren't for men who could have happily, cheerfully settled down with a woman. Nothing about that life he could have had—the life he'll wind up having with someone he hasn't even met yet, the kind of life he *wants*—feels like hiding.

Andy reads the rest of the article as carefully as he's ever read any piece of newsprint. He reads the demand for acceptance and basic rights, the rejection of shame and fear. He reads the calm rebuttal of all the usual arguments against homosexuality, and the statement that it makes no sense to argue against a thing that simply is.

Andy ought to have guessed that there were people campaigning for homosexual rights in the same way that people campaign for the rights of any subjugated group, but seeing it in print makes it real. That's what newspapers do, isn't it? They make things concrete, they make it hard to look away.

He imagines what would happen if the *Chronicle* printed something like this—a call to arms. And the fact is that he can't. He can't imagine any paper doing it, but here one is, right in front of him.

He goes back to the beginning and reads the article another time, and by the end his sweaty fingers have picked up some of the newsprint. He feels like the text of the article has gotten under his skin, inside of him, because he can't stop thinking about it.

The café gets louder, and a man helps himself to the empty seat at Andy's table. When he finally looks at his watch, it's past nine thirty.

It isn't like Nick to be late. In fact, Nick's more likely to phone the café to leave a message letting Andy know there's been a change in plans than he is to forget they have plans in the first place. But Andy didn't give Nick the name of this place, did he? He only said the coffee shop on Barrow. Even sitting in it, he can't remember its name—it's one of dozens of similar places with similar round tables and similar rickety chairs. Nick may even have gone to some other coffee shop on Barrow and not found him.

Another half hour passes and Andy decides to leave. He doesn't have a key to Nick's apartment, but he heads there anyway. If Nick isn't there, Andy can always go to his own apartment; his keys are still at Nick's, but the doorman will let him in.

But he already knows he won't do that. If Nick isn't at his apartment, Andy will sit on the stoop and wait for him. There isn't any question.

When he arrives at the building, he looks up, counts to the fifth floor, and sees that the light is on in Nick's apartment. Did Andy forget to turn it off that morning? Usually Nick checks before leaving, with some pro forma grumbling about not having stock in the electric company.

The building door is wedged open, which the woman on the third floor insists on doing when her kids are out playing and she doesn't want them to bother her to come open the door. But it's long past ten now, and even in this neighborhood there aren't any children out in the streets anymore.

He climbs the stairs—four flights are as grueling as they were a week earlier—and sees that Nick's door is ajar. He immediately pushes it open, ignoring the flicker of worry that he might be interrupting burglars. "Nick?" he calls. No answer. "Nick!"

Nick emerges from the bathroom, half his body lit from the too-bright bathroom light and the other half in shadow. He's holding something to his face. His white shirt has a dark stain running from the collar to the waist.

And Andy must be tired or something, because the first thing he thinks of is meeting his mother at the airport and seeing a fresh scar on her temple, a scant inch from her eye, and being immediately, irrationally furious that she thought it was all right to be anywhere near shrapnel or bullets or whatever the hell had hurt her this time. Couldn't she just be safe? Couldn't the only person he loved try to take care of herself, for Andy's sake if not for her own?

It was a useless thought then, and it's a useless thought now, so he grits his teeth and hopes Nick has a first aid kit.

"Hey," Nick says, his voice a little slurred.

Andy drops the newspaper and crosses the room in two strides. "What happened to you?" This close, he can see that Nick's lip is split. He pushes Nick's hand away and sees a nasty gash and the beginnings of a bruise running from his temple to his jaw.

"Kids," Nick says.

"Street gang?" There are bands of teenagers all over Lower Manhattan who like to fight one another, but what kind of lunatic kids would go after someone like Nick?

"Something like that."

Well, that's a deeply unsatisfactory and unconvincing answer, and Andy will get to the bottom of it, but not while Nick is bleeding all over himself.

"Sit," he says, as firmly as he knows how, pointing to the kitchen table.

To his surprise, Nick sits. Andy takes off his coat, then washes his hands, wets a dish towel, and pulls the chain to turn on the kitchen light. Up close, he can see that what at first looked like a gash also includes a scrape, as if Nick hit his face on something rougher than a fist. Andy carefully dabs at the scrape to clean it as best as he can. The cloth comes away discolored with blood and dirt. He folds the cloth and keeps dabbing with clean sections until he thinks that at least Nick doesn't have any pieces of the sidewalk left in his face.

"Do you have any bandages? Peroxide?" Andy asks.

"Medicine cabinet," Nick says.

It isn't until Andy's unscrewing the cap off the peroxide that he realizes his hands are shaking. And so with unsteady hands he pours some of the liquid onto a washcloth and carefully applies it to Nick's face. Nick winces, and Andy remembers the last time— the only time—he's ever done this for anyone, nearly a year ago in the newsroom. It feels much longer ago than that, as if it happened on the other side of a divide, because then he was helping a friend, and now he's helping—he's helping Nick, and he doesn't know what that means. He doesn't want to know.

"Sit still," Andy whispers.

"Sorry." Nick makes a sound that's almost a laugh. "I hate this."

"Nobody likes it, you dummy." But Andy doesn't think Nick's referring to the burn of the peroxide or even the fact of having gotten mugged.

These cuts seem—they seem bad, and Andy doesn't know if that's because they're dangerous, or because Andy is inclined to worry about everything, or because they're on Nick. But he thinks that maybe peroxide isn't enough, so he goes back to the medicine cabinet. When he returns, he begins to paint bright orange Mercurochrome onto the worst of the wounds.

Nick hisses, his fingers digging into his thighs.

"Who knew you were such a big baby," Andy murmurs, perversely mad at Nick for having let himself get hurt. But he takes one of Nick's hands and puts it on his own arm. He lets himself believe that he's siphoning off some of Nick's discomfort as Nick squeezes him.

The kitchen light casts an unforgiving light, Nick's cuts and bruises standing out stark and lurid, every hair in his five-o'clock shadow dark against his skin. Nick sits on the edge of the table, and in order to get close enough to be any use, Andy has to stand between his legs. He feels like he's never been so close to anyone.

Andy peels the paper off a couple of Band-Aids and does his best to cover the gash without the adhesive touching any broken skin.

"I think you might have needed stitches," Andy says when he's done.

"Yeah, well, that wasn't going to happen." Nick is still holding Andy's arm and Andy feels disinclined to mention this.

"You should take that shirt off so we can soak it."

When Nick takes his hand off Andy's arm, he leaves behind a smear of bright red blood. Andy grabs Nick's hand and turns it palm up. It's worse than his face had been. He checks the other hand, and it's better but still scratched up. It's only the palms, as if Nick landed on them when he fell, but not the knuckles. Andy wonders if this means Nick didn't fight back or if he didn't get a chance to.

"I'm sorry," Nick says.

"Why are you apologizing?" Andy asks, slightly hysterical.

"I must have hurt them when I fell."

Andy repeats the process of cleaning the scrapes and covering them as best as he can. "Well, I don't think you'll die of sepsis. At least not tonight," he says when he finishes.

"Thanks, Andy."

"Nothing to thank me for." The idea of not having been here—of Nick going to sleep with grit from the street still in his skin—makes Andy unaccountably furious. "This shirt is coming off now. No, don't you dare try to unbutton it with your hands in that state." He loosens Nick's tie and pulls it over his head, then undoes the top button, then the next, all the while trying not to think about the fact that he's undressing Nick. Which, he tells himself, is what he'd do for any friend in this situation. Hell, he'd probably do it for a stranger. But he doesn't think it would feel this way with anyone else. He doesn't think he'd be so conscious of their breath against his cheek as he bends to unfasten the buttons at their cuffs. He doesn't think that with anyone else he'd have to suppress the bizarre urge to kiss their temple when he finishes.

He balls up Nick's shirt and puts it to soak in the bathroom sink. Then, remembering the bloodstains on his own sleeve, he quickly strips off his shirt and puts it in there, too.

He braces his hands on the edges of the sink and looks at his reflection, surprised to see that he looks normal, almost calm. He feels as if he's been turned inside out, as if he just learned that a part of his heart is on the outside of his body, in the possession of somebody else entirely.

When he goes back out to the kitchen, Nick is still sitting on the edge of the table, staring at an empty spot on the wall. "Did you at least have dinner?" Andy asks.

Nick cracks a smile, but stops with a wince. "No. I'm not hungry anyway, and I don't think I could eat without messing my mouth up even more."

"Do you want to tell me what happened?"

"Not really."

It looks like Nick's mouth hurts when he talks, so Andy doesn't pursue the topic. Instead he gestures to the couch. "Television?" He checks his watch. "*The Tonight Show*'s on."

Nick sits on the couch while Andy looks for an ice tray in the freezer. There isn't one, which stands to reason since he doubts any part of this refrigerator gets below freezing. He takes out a cold bottle of beer and hands it to Nick. "Put this on your face. You're already going to have a black eye and a fat lip."

Again, Nick does as he's told, almost as if he's glad to have someone fuss over him and boss him around a little. Andy likes it himself when Nick looks after him, but the shoe has never really been on the other foot. He doesn't think he's ever looked after anyone in his life, probably because someone who needed looking after would go to anyone in the world before they went to Andy.

After turning on the television, Andy sits beside Nick. Usually he keeps to one side of the sofa, because it isn't terribly large and it seems only polite not to crowd its actual owner. But today he plants himself right next to Nick, maybe because he wants to reassure himself that Nick is all right, maybe for other reasons. Maybe he just isn't going to look too closely into any of his thoughts right now and instead watch some television.

Nick falls asleep almost right away, promptly tipping over onto Andy's shoulder. That can't be comfortable, so Andy tugs him lower, until Nick is using Andy's lap as a pillow.

Andy doesn't even try to pay attention to what's happening on the television. Instead he brushes Nick's hair off his forehead, and then—God, he hopes he isn't being a creep—combs his fingers through Nick's hair.

Nick's eyes blink open and Andy goes still. "No, keep doing that," Nick mumbles into the fabric of Andy's trousers. "Feels good."

And so Andy keeps doing it, careful to avoid any cuts or bruises, and lets his other hand rest on Nick's bare shoulder.

When Andy wakes up, there's nothing but static on the television screen and the sort of silence from the street below that means it's after four A.M. last call. Nick is still asleep, his head in Andy's lap, one hand hanging off the edge of the sofa and the other on Andy's leg.

He slides out from under Nick and gets up to turn the television off, then fills a glass with water and puts it on the end table within Nick's reach. He sets a bottle of aspirin beside it, then takes the blanket off Nick's bed and covers him.

He tells himself that the ache in his chest is what anyone would feel when a friend is injured. But Andy has dozens of friends and has never felt the urge to curl up beside them on the sofa. There's no need for him to stay near Nick. Nick's asleep, and he isn't so badly injured that he needs someone to hover over him all night.

Still, before stepping into his bedroom, he glances back for one last look.

CHAPTER SIX

When Andy wakes up on Saturday morning, Nick is standing in the kitchen, looking blearily into the refrigerator.

"Sit down," Andy says. "I can make coffee and toast."

Nick grunts and slopes off to the sofa. Andy tries not to wince when he sees Nick's face. One side is mottled with purple bruises mingling luridly with the lingering orange of the Mercurochrome. He's halfway to a black eye and his lip is puffy and red.

"You can tell me what happened now," Andy says as he measures out the coffee grounds. "Because what I'm imagining is probably worse than the truth."

"Guess it depends on what you're imagining."

Andy puts the coffee press on the stove top and turns on the gas. "You don't want to know what I'm imagining."

"Well, *now* I do."

Andy sighs. "I'm worried that you got hurt by someone who's trying to stop you from talking to a source. Because if they did that this time, what will they do next time?" He doesn't even suggest that Nick might be prudent and stop going after the story—that would only be an insult, and Andy would only get his stupid feelings hurt when Nick rightly tells him to mind his own business. "And I'm worried that if it wasn't that, then maybe you were hurt when you were doing the other thing I thought you might be doing last night." He waits for his meaning to register with Nick. Andy knows that sometimes men are attacked after approaching the wrong man, and sometimes people just attack anyone they think might be queer. Andy knows this, and the idea of it happening to Nick makes him want to kick the wall.

"It wasn't the second thing," Nick says.

"Okay." Andy shouldn't be relieved, because that makes him suspect it's the first thing: Nick was beaten up because of something to do with a story. But somehow, a journalist being hurt because he's on to a dangerous story seems less traumatic than someone being attacked for living his life.

"It wasn't a source, either. I mean, I met with a source. A woman in Spanish Harlem called me at the paper and said that her apartment was robbed a few years ago. The police confiscated a handgun as evidence and she never got it back. They told her it was procedure. She didn't want to disagree because she didn't want cops making trouble for her. After talking to her, I got on the subway, got off at Spring Street, and was mugged by a couple kids on the way here. I should have just given them my wallet, but I was tired and cranky and—anyway, I was an idiot."

Andy blinks. One of the first rules to surviving in the city is that you don't fight muggers. You don't run, you don't fight back. You give them your wallet and move on. The fact that Nick decided to resist a mugger—no, a *group* of muggers—is infuriating. Andy just wants Nick to be safe—or as safe as possible for someone whose job and personal life both involve some danger. And here Nick is taking *optional* risks?

"The next time you consider being that kind of idiot, can you imagine how I'd feel if you didn't come home? If I learned about your death in a police briefing?"

Nick looks stricken, like he's never considered the possibility of anyone being sad about his literal murder.

"Did they take anything?" Andy asks, mainly so he doesn't reach across the table, grab Nick by the shoulders, and shake him.

"Ten dollars and a roll of nickels."

Andy snorts. Nick always has at least one roll of coins so he never runs out when calling in a story from a pay phone.

"It happens," Nick says when Andy has been silent for too long.

It *happens*? Andy thinks he's about to part company with sanity for good. Nick being attacked is not something that *happens*. It's not like rainy weather or a pitcher with a bad elbow. He puts some bread in the toaster and doesn't turn around until he's pretty sure he looks somewhat composed, or at least not actively unhinged.

"Thanks for everything last night," Nick says when Andy brings him coffee and two slices of buttered toast.

"I already told you not to thank me. I'm glad I was here. You would just have made a mess of your face."

Nick takes a sip of coffee and winces when the cup touches his lip. "I think my face is a mess, regardless."

Andy's about to protest but has to concede the point. "Yeah, it's pretty bad. But I think it'll at least be less swollen by Monday."

Nick grimaces. "I hate to go into work looking like I got in a brawl. Half of them already assume that I get into bar fights in my spare time and the other half think I'm the janitor."

Andy presses his lips together. He can't deny it. The *Chronicle* isn't as snobbish as a lot of papers, but there aren't many Italian reporters, and none on the mastheads of any of the city's major papers.

"You know that if my father and Epstein and Jorgensen didn't think you belonged at the *Chronicle*, you wouldn't be there, right?" Not to mention the fact that everyone seems to be giving Nick surprisingly free rein with the dirty cop story. "Also, maybe I'm not supposed to know about your pay raise last month, but I do. And I know why you got it."

"Care to share?"

"So you don't get poached."

Nick cracks out a laugh. "Poached by who?"

"If the *Daily News* and the *Journal-American* haven't tried yet, they will."

"You're crazy."

"I was in the meeting when your raise was approved."

Nick scoffs. "The *Daily News* is even crazier if they think I want to write about actresses in bathing suits and the grisly details of mob crime." He takes a careful bite of toast. "You know the only reason I have the job I do is that the city desk was short-staffed and the old city editor was batty right before he retired."

"You came in '55, right after the *Brooklyn Eagle* folded, right?" He already knows Nick's history. Nick started working at the *Eagle* as a night copyboy when he was a teenager, then climbed the ranks—obituaries, then the dictation bank, then reporting. "There were plenty of reporters looking for work. Nobody was giving away jobs."

Nick rubs the back of his neck, somehow managing to look skeptical and pleased and extremely embarrassed all at once, which makes Andy want to keep going, keep telling him good things that he ought to already know.

The toaster pops up with two more slices. When Andy comes back to the couch, plate in hand, he finds Nick staring into his half-empty coffee cup.

"I'm safer than you think," Nick says.

"The left side of your face argues otherwise."

"I mean about—about men. I don't do anything risky."

"Okay," Andy says tentatively, because he doesn't know how it's possible for a man in Nick's position to do anything without risk, but he also doesn't know what he expects Nick to do about it.

"I know there are raids, but I steer clear of bars that have back rooms. And I wait for people to approach me. Also, I was joking about the subway men's rooms. I don't do anything in public anymore."

That *anymore* makes Andy slightly hysterical in about ten different ways, but he tries to look unbothered.

Nick insists on wearing sunglasses when they go out to breakfast, as if they do anything to conceal the state of the rest of his face. He also insists on stopping at the locksmith and getting his keys copied for Andy. Then, without much discussion, they go to a matinée and watch Tony Curtis and Jack Lemmon spend two hours cross-dressing before Jack Lemmon elopes with a man, which is just proof positive that the world has conspired to force Andy to think about queerness. Since when is there queerness in movies? Since never, that's when. He's feeling badly put upon by the time they stop at the grocery store to pick up ingredients for dinner.

"I don't know how you're going to cook anything with your hands all scraped up," Andy says.

"It's pasta and some sauce," Nick says, as if this answers the question.

Andy wants to remind Nick that he doesn't have to entertain Andy like a guest, that he can go and do whatever he ordinarily does on weekends, but it doesn't feel like Nick is going out of his way. It feels easy.

"I hope you like lasagna," Nick announces as they leave the A&P, each laden down with paper sacks filled with meat and vegetables.

"I'd probably like anything you cooked," Andy says.

"Says the man who orders a chicken salad sandwich every day for lunch."

"I like chicken salad," Andy says. "And it's the sort of sandwich that never gets all over your lap. It's the ideal lunch sandwich." *It's safe*, taunts a stupid little voice in Andy's head. Andy tells that voice to get lost.

At home, Nick begins chopping onions and garlic and threatening Andy with a wooden spoon when he gets underfoot.

"Come on, you can't expect me to lounge around all afternoon while you make dinner."

"You can go next door and ask Linda if she wants to come over for supper at about eight or so." Nick layers flat noodles in a pan the approximate size of a Major League infield. "Tell her to bring whoever she has lying around the place. And then tell Mrs. Martelli in 3A that I'll bring down a plate for her, so she shouldn't bother making herself any supper. After that, you can go to that bakery on Cornelia Street and get a loaf of bread. You can pick up a bottle of wine somewhere, too, because I just used up the last of this in the sauce." He holds up an empty bottle of Chianti.

"You're making up jobs to get me out of the house."

Nick grins into the pot of sauce. "My dad used to send me out to buy cigarettes and to place a bet with Gino."

"Gino?" This is maybe the third time Nick has ever mentioned his father, so Andy is curious.

"The numbers runner." Nick's smile is gone, replaced by something hard but a little wistful.

Andy knocks on Linda's door and reintroduces himself even

though they've run into one another half a dozen times in the past week. She's wearing overalls and is covered in paint and what looks like plaster dust. Her long dark hair is in a braid.

"Yeah, yeah, you're Nick's . . ." She waves her cigarette vaguely in the air. "Friend."

The implication is clear, but Andy doesn't know how to correct her without seeming like a jackass. She's the second person this week to assume that he's Nick's—whatever—and the idea makes his face heat with something he tells himself is plain embarrassment.

"And you were also Emily Warburton's friend," Linda adds. "Busy, busy."

Andy tries to fight back his blush and that works about as well as it ever does, which is to say not at all. "Nick's making lasagna and says you should come over for dinner. He says the invitation extends to any of your guests." That isn't exactly how Nick phrased it, but Andy isn't going to say *whoever you have lying around*.

"Any of my guests?" she repeats wryly. She opens the door a bit wider, and Andy gets a glimpse of a half-nude woman lying on what looks like a row of pickle barrels. It takes him a minute to see the easel and understand that he's looking at an artist's model. "Yeah, we'll be there. Thanks." Andy waves awkwardly at both Linda and the model, then goes downstairs and knocks on Mrs. Martelli's door.

Mrs. Martelli is, for all intents and purposes, identical to Nick's aunts who Andy met last week. She has gray hair, wears all black, and could be anywhere between sixty and a hundred years old. "Nick from upstairs says he'll bring you some lasagna for dinner." He speaks slowly, not sure if she understands English.

"Okay. Tell him thank you," she says, equally slowly, in completely unaccented English, then laughs and shuts the door in his face. Andy worries that it's his lot in life to be mocked by elderly Italian women.

He takes his time walking to Cornelia Street, which is only a few blocks away. It's still March, but either today or tomorrow is the first official day of spring, and for once the city seems to know it. The sky is clear, the air smells less like car exhaust than usual, and there are honest-to-God flowers in the window boxes of one of the buildings he passes. It feels like the city is poised for something beautiful to happen, even though you can count on the weather to be intermittently repulsive until May.

At the bakery, he buys two loaves of bread and then, when it occurs to him that Nick is essentially having a dinner party, he also chooses a dozen Italian pastries. At the wine store, he stares at the shelves for a quarter of an hour until the man behind the counter begins to clear his throat pointedly. Then he haphazardly chooses three bottles of Burgundy for three dollars each, which seems expensive enough to guarantee a decent wine but not so expensive as to be embarrassing if Nick ever finds out what they cost. On the way back, he passes a corner store that has bunches of daffodils out front, so he grabs a few of them, too. Candles? Surely Nick has candles, but he goes into the store and gets some anyway.

It's only as he's climbing the stairs that he realizes that he might have gone overboard. He can barely see over the flowers that stick out from the top of the bag as he attempts to unlock the door using his new key. He expects one of Nick's more exasperated looks at all the excess, but instead Nick glances over his shoulder and—well, he stares.

"Uh. Sorry," Andy says. "You probably don't want all this. But I did get bread and wine! You don't need to use the candles, but you may as well hang on to them in case there's ever a blackout, and I can throw the flowers away. It doesn't matter."

He's halfway to the trash can when Nick grabs his arm.

"No. Keep them."

"Okay," Andy says. He stares at the place where Nick touches him, his hand dark against the white cotton of Andy's sweater. Nick doesn't let go, and when Andy takes a breath, all he can smell are the daffodils' sweetness mixed with the aroma of whatever Nick's cooking. He has the same feeling that he did outside, of something lovely being about to happen. He tells himself the unexpectedly nice weather has gone to his head.

Then Nick lets go and turns back to the sink, where he scrubs a pot. A few minutes later, as Andy is attempting to arrange the daffodils in a couple of juice glasses—because of course Nick doesn't have any vases, what was Andy thinking—Nick comes over to the table. "Thanks. I mean—thank you."

"It's my pleasure."

The moment stretches too long, with Andy ineptly fiddling with daffodil stems and Nick watching him and something hanging in the air just out of sight, and if Andy keeps his eyes averted, maybe he won't have to see it.

They're well into the first bottle of wine when Linda knocks on the door.

"I brought Sylvia and her brother, Charlie," she says, indicating the model, who is now dressed, even if it's only in what appears to be a silk robe over a pair of jeans, and a young man who wears a black turtleneck sweater and round horn-rimmed glasses. They both have light brown skin with dark brown freckles; they're also both intensely gorgeous in a way that makes Andy hope he isn't staring.

"Catch up," says Nick, handing the bottle of wine to Linda.

Andy fetches two more juice glasses and an empty jam jar from the kitchen, because of course Nick doesn't have wineglasses, either.

"What happened to your face?" Linda asks Nick.

"Kids," Nick answers, kicking off a conversation about which of them's been mugged and in what neighborhoods and how much money they lost.

Andy hangs back at first, overwhelmed with a sort of social paralysis that hasn't afflicted him since he was in school. He isn't a born charmer, but he makes do. He knows how to make people like him. He might not have his father's charisma or his mother's force of personality, but he's good at turning the tables and making people talk about themselves, which is all they usually want.

But everyone else is charming and talkative and there isn't much for Andy to do but listen and be amused. The conversation darts from Linda's account of an art show she went to, to Sylvia's stories about modeling, and Charlie's relentless flirtation with Nick. Which is fine! And definitely doesn't make Andy feel strange at all.

"And then, just when I thought the plaster of paris was dry—"

"It turns out nobody's paid rent on that gallery on Tenth Street for months—"

"She said she was doing a series of landscapes, but there I am, naked as a baby—"

"Were you at Ed Wortman's party—he's the poet with all the screaming, you know—because I'm sure I recognize you from somewhere, darling—"

Andy pours himself another glass of wine, and when the bottle is empty, he gets the corkscrew and opens another. Not wanting to return to the living room just yet, he lights the candles and turns out the flickering overhead light. The timer dings, so he pulls the lasagna—which weighs about as much as a small child—out of the oven, then puts together a plate for Mrs. Martelli. He's about to take it down to her when he realizes that Nick is standing in the doorway.

"I'm going to bring this downstairs," Andy says when Nick makes no move to step aside. "I'll be right back."

"I can do that."

Andy shakes his head. "Go have fun."

Nick frowns. "All right."

"Do you think she'd want one of those pastries?" Andy takes the box from the refrigerator.

"You bought cannoli?"

Andy is close to mortification at how far he went overboard. "Yeah, I remembered you getting one that time we went past that Italian bakery on East Eleventh Street."

"Thank you." Nick isn't frowning anymore, but he looks dazed. Probably too much wine on top of the head injury. Andy ought to have put his foot down and stopped Nick from cooking.

Nick finally moves out of the way, but Andy feels his eyes on him as he leaves the apartment.

Andy's awkwardness is worn away fifty percent by red wine and mozzarella cheese and fifty percent by the brute force with which Linda drags him into the conversation. And once he calms down a bit, he notices that Charlie isn't only flirting with Nick, but with Linda, too. And possibly with Andy as well, but he can't quite process that, so he doesn't.

Nick only has three chairs, so they eat in the living room, Sylvia in the seldomly used armchair, Charlie and Linda cross-legged on the floor in front of the coffee table, and Nick and Andy on the sofa. At some point Nick stretches his arm across the back of the sofa, his fingers so close to the nape of Andy's neck that he can almost feel them, so close that Andy has a hard time thinking about anything else. When Nick gets up to bring the dishes to the sink, he claps Andy on the shoulder and, Jesus Christ, Andy needs to get a grip.

He tries to focus his attention on Sylvia, who reminds him of Emily in that she's both sharp and beautiful. "Emily would have had fun tonight," he says when Nick comes back.

Nick gives him an odd look, half sympathy, half something else. "You miss her."

"Yeah." Of course he misses her. He was ready to spend his life with her; it's only natural that he's feeling her absence and the loss of the life he thought they'd have together. But he isn't over here pining or anything.

Why isn't he, though? Is it strange that he doesn't feel worse? It's only been a week. He wonders if this is one of his deficiencies; maybe he just doesn't feel things the right way. But part of him always expected her to leave, and so he couldn't be too surprised when it actually happened. With the amount of wine currently in his system, Andy's able to admit that maybe he's always expecting people to leave. Maybe it's a little safer to assume everyone has a foot out the door, someplace more interesting to be.

"Oh, hello, darling," says Linda in a peculiar voice. Andy follows her gaze to where an orange cat is peering out of the kitchen doorway. "What's your name, sweetheart? Nick, I didn't know you had a cat."

"He doesn't," Andy says at the same time Nick says, "I don't."

But there is, undeniably, a cat in the apartment.

"It's a neighborhood cat." Nick sounds the tiniest bit defensive.

"We're on the fifth floor," Linda points out. "He didn't just wander in here."

"Nick leaves the window open for him," Andy says, remembering the kitchen window that has to be left cracked, allegedly for ventilation. Nick shoots him a betrayed look. "How have I been here a full week and not seen this fellow until now?"

"He doesn't live here. He isn't my cat. I just— Look, sometimes he gets up to the top of the fire escape and can't get back down, so I leave my window open and then carry him down to the street."

"You carry the cat down to the street," Andy says.

"Otherwise he screams his head off outside my window!"

"He lets you carry him down."

"*Lets* is a strong word. He doesn't actively try to kill me, let's say."

"What kind of cat can't get down a fire escape?" asks Charlie.

"I never said he was smart," Nick says, and the other four people in the room scold him.

Andy's had enough wine for the presence of a strange, likely flea-ridden cat not to matter much in the grand scheme of things, so he decides to ignore it. But he definitely wants front-row seats when Nick carries the poor thing downstairs. For now, he slides his mostly empty plate toward the cat, not that the animal looks like he's missed too many meals.

Somebody puts on a record, and Andy knows just enough to be able to identify it as blues. He waves away the joint that Sylvia passes him, because he's already boneless, so relaxed that he thinks he might never be able to get up again. He tips his head back, thinking to lean it against the back of the couch, but Nick's arm is there again.

For a moment, neither of them moves. And then Nick jerks his hand away so quickly, it nearly hurts, like he's pulling his palm away from a hot stove.

CHAPTER SEVEN

A ndy isn't expecting an epiphany at eight on a Monday morning when he's still mostly asleep, when his first cup of coffee is still hot in his hand. Honestly, Andy isn't expecting an epiphany *ever*.

Nick's in the bathroom, shaving with the door open, while Andy blearily wanders around the apartment, putting on one sock, then another, then topping off his coffee. Their conversation meanders from Khrushchev to the movies to whether there might be another spring blizzard like the city had last year.

The problem, really, is that Nick shaves without a shirt on. He stands there in his suit trousers but with no shirt, not even an undershirt, and tilts his jaw this way and that, and Andy can't help but *notice*.

He tries not to notice. Damn it, he's been trying not to notice, or at least not to notice himself noticing, for a while now.

Nick is . . . handsome. Everyone knows this. The fact that Andy is aware of it only means that his eyes work. But Andy doesn't think that the word for Nick's shoulders and arms, or—God help him and save him—the hair on his chest is *handsome*. Nobody talks about chest hair being handsome. Attractive, maybe? Compelling?

Andy is depending on the correct adjective to act as a key to unlock the confusion in his mind, to open a door that doesn't have "Congratulations, You're Queer" printed in huge letters on the other side.

But he doesn't have an adjective. What he has, unfortunately, is the beginnings of a hard-on and the certain knowledge that he wants to touch Nick.

Maybe on some other day he might have been able to convince himself that this was nothing new. After all, he's had these passing thoughts about other men and dismissed them in the same way he habitually dismisses any notion that will unduly complicate his life. But that cursed *Village Voice* article is still under his skin, even though he's crammed the newspaper itself under a stack of magazines that don't contain the word *homosexual* in thirty-six-point Bodoni Black.

It's one thing to know that he has this potential in him, a latent queerness that has no bearing on his life. It's another thing entirely to be attracted to a man—to Nick—who's standing right in front of him and who he knows is queer. Something theoretical has become something altogether too real, too concrete, and there's no wriggling away from the fact that this is very gay.

He's queer. The thoughts going through his head are inescapably queer, and so is he. Even if he never does anything about it, he's still queer. When he looks at Nick, he's consumed with a wanting so intense that it feels tangled up with the core of who he is. It's in there with newspapers and loneliness in the package deal that is Andy Fleming.

He tells himself that he can still ignore it. He can put this newfound knowledge to the side, stowing it tidily away. It's not like he's going to do anything about it, so it hardly matters, right?

"Andy." Nick waves a hand in front of his face. "Join us back on earth."

"Hmm?" He makes an effort to look at Nick's face, but can't help but notice that water droplets still cling to his chest.

Nick rolls his eyes, takes Andy by the shoulders, and steers him out of the doorway that Andy has, apparently, been blocking. Andy resists the urge to press his fingertips to the places where Nick's hands have been.

For the next few days, Andy is aware of having passed a point of no return, some kind of gay Rubicon. It's almost as if once he applied the word to himself, once he acknowledged it, he can't stop thinking about it. It's like his brain and some even less responsible parts have a decade of queer thoughts to get through in the span of a couple days.

If his brain wanted to give him a break for once, maybe it would allow the stream of semipornographic thoughts and images to feature Marlon Brando or the handsome man from accounts receivable, but instead it's Nick.

On the way back from lunch on Tuesday, Nick looks at Andy, sighs, and begins to rebutton Andy's coat so the buttons line up. Andy silently loses his mind. Nick isn't even touching him, just efficiently redoing the buttons on his overcoat as he's done a dozen times before. All those previous times Andy didn't think anything of it, except that it was kind of Nick to make sure Andy wasn't walking around looking like an unmade bed.

On Wednesday, they go out for drinks with a bunch of other reporters, and he and Nick wind up squashed together on one side of a booth. Andy can smell Nick's soap—the green bars of soap bought three at a time at the grocery store and which Andy now uses himself—and wants to press his face into Nick's neck and breathe it in. Like a *maniac*.

Thursday, Nick comes back from an interview looking rumpled and harried. When he finds the sandwich and cookie Andy left on his desk, he gets all flustered and thanks Andy like nobody's ever done him a favor, a rare blush high on his cheeks. Andy has to stop himself from buying ten more cookies.

On Friday morning, Andy is in the kitchen during that dismal period of time after getting out of bed but before the coffee is ready. When he stretches, Nick's gaze drops to Andy's middle, where the cold air of the kitchen hits Andy's exposed stomach, where the pajama shirt rides up and the too-big pajama pants slide down. That look could mean "Why doesn't Andy wear his own damn pajamas?" or it could mean something else. But even if Nick is looking at him . . . appreciatively, it doesn't necessarily mean anything. Andy isn't horrible-looking. He isn't in Nick's league, but who is? Nick can notice that Andy's objectively non-hideous without it being a big deal.

However. The idea that Nick might be looking back is outright catastrophic to Andy's peace of mind. It worms its way into his thoughts and infiltrates all his waking moments.

This is a problem. This is *Nick*, his colleague and his best friend. He needs to do something about this, and clearly his own mind is beyond help.

It occurs to him that maybe Nick is only looking at him because it's been too long since he's had any sex—it's been two weeks since Andy moved in, which isn't any kind of dry spell for Andy but might be for Nick.

Andy comes up with a strategy. He hasn't come up with a lot of strategies in his life, so it's a new feeling. He probably should have known better.

"Let's go out for drinks," Andy says after work.

Nick raises both eyebrows. "We're currently having drinks."

They're at O'Connell's, an Irish bar on Murray Street, along with a good portion of the *Chronicle* newsroom.

"I mean after we finish here. I was thinking," Andy says, his voice low, "that we could go to one of your places."

"What does that mean?" Nick's brow is furrowed, and Andy cannot believe he's going to have to spell this out.

Andy drops his voice to a whisper. "One of those places on Greenwich Avenue. Or Christopher Street, I guess?" he adds, as if geography is the real issue here.

Nick rears back so far in his seat that he almost knocks another reporter off the edge of the booth.

"Sorry, sorry, Andy startled me," Nick says, apologizing. *What the fuck?* he mouths to Andy.

"I don't want to stop you from . . . you know."

"Yes, I do know." Nick rolls his eyes. "And you aren't stopping me. Didn't we have this conversation last week?"

"No, last week you told me that you weren't going to go, um, make new friends and then come home and make omelets. Which still makes no sense, by the way."

"What are you suggesting?"

"That we go to one of those places, you meet someone and go home with them, and I'll go read a book in a coffee shop for a few hours."

"A few hours," Nick repeats, his mouth curved in a smile that makes Andy feel like he's melting. "Don't give me that much credit. Ten minutes in the john is more than enough."

"Fine, then," Andy says, trying and utterly failing not to think about the images that conjures up. "You'll do your thing, I'll finish my drink, and then we'll go home."

Nick stares at him. "You're serious."

"Yes, Nicholas, I'm serious."

"Why?"

"Because it's clear that you aren't going to go out without me."

"You're that dedicated to me getting my dick sucked."

Andy is going to *die*. "It's a mission of mercy. Somebody has to look after it."

It's dark, but Andy thinks Nick is blushing. "I'll think about it," he says, like it's this huge concession. "But you aren't coming with me. What if someone recognizes you?"

"What if someone recognizes *you*?"

"First of all," Nick whispers, "you're the one who was in the gossip columns not even two weeks ago."

"Do you think Walter Winchell is at a queer bar tonight?" Andy asks innocently.

"Not the point! Secondly, I'm actually—you know—so if I see someone there who knows me by name, it's fair, I guess."

"I'm sure these places are very well lit and have no shadowy, secluded corners whatsoever," Andy whispers back. "I'm sure every bar of the sort we're discussing is basically like stepping into Macy's window."

Nick sighs and passes his hand over his jaw. For a minute he doesn't meet Andy's eye. "You're going to harass me until I agree, aren't you."

"You're finally catching on," Andy says, beaming proudly at him.

"Jesus. Fine. Finish your drink and let's get out of here."

The bar is on West Tenth, right past the place where the streets in the Village completely forsake the grid pattern and leave Andy with no hope of knowing where he is. There's nothing out front to indicate that it's different from any other bar. Andy isn't quite sure what he was expecting, but he's seen bars with the infamous

"Raided Premises" police signs posted out front, a warning—or possibly enticement—that arrests for public morals offenses had taken place. This bar looks totally unremarkable.

On the inside, it's almost identical to the bar they just left: low lighting, polished wood bar top, hundreds of bottles behind the bar, balding and unfriendly bartender.

Only when Andy looks more closely can he make out subtle differences. At O'Connell's, there were a handful of women, mostly from the *Chronicle*. Here there are none. At O'Connell's, everyone wore a suit, but here there are a few young men in jeans and short-sleeved shirts.

Most of the men are minding their own business—nursing drinks, smoking, reading papers—just like at any bar. But when Andy pays attention, he notices the glances, the same sort of glances that he's becoming uncomfortably adept at identifying. There's a way men have of quickly looking at another man— assessing, appraising, covert—and then waiting for the look to be returned. Those looks are thick on the ground here.

"What do we do?" Andy asks.

Nick's been in a bad mood since leaving O'Connell's and Andy almost suggested that they drop the plan and go home. He remembers the way Nick has spoken of what he does with the men he picks up; there's often something grim and a little resigned in his tone, and maybe that's just because he doesn't want to talk about it with Andy, but at the moment Andy can't help but think Nick doesn't seem terribly enthusiastic.

Now Nick shoots Andy an unimpressed look. "Well, what you do is sit at the bar and read your book. What I do is best left undiscussed."

Andy's going to have a stroke and then that'll really ruin Nick's evening. He tries to get some control over himself.

Nick orders his usual Maker's Mark, neat. And Andy, unable to force his mouth to make intelligent words, just mumbles "same" to the grumpy bartender, earning a confused and skeptical glance from Nick, who knows Andy prefers a gin and tonic, heavy on the tonic.

"I need to know you aren't going to panic if some man approaches you," Nick says as they take seats at the bar, Andy's back to the door.

Andy will absolutely panic if some man approaches him, but not for the reasons Nick is worried about. "I'll behave myself," he assures Nick.

"What are you reading?" Nick asks. Andy doesn't know if it's his imagination that Nick is leaning a little closer to him than usual. He can feel the heat radiating off of Nick, and Nick's voice is quiet enough that it's just this side of a breath.

"What?"

"Okay. So, you see how you have a book with you? It has words in it. I think you've even read some of them. What's the book about?"

"This book?" Andy can't figure out why Nick is talking about books when he could be doing—his mind supplies images that it has no business thinking of.

"Right, so, what I'm doing right now is called making conversation. We've done this before, you may remember. Every day, even. Multiple times a day."

"Uh."

"I'm waiting to see someone I like the looks of," Nick murmurs.

"Oh," says Andy, feeling like a fool. Of course Nick isn't going to grab the first man he sees by the collar and drag him off to the restroom. He needs to wait for someone he finds attractive, and Andy wonders who that will be, what kind of men Nick is drawn to.

"And also I'm curious about the book because this is the fourth one I've seen you read by the same author," Nick adds.

So Andy tells him about the book, occasionally noticing Nick's gaze stray toward the door. Until, finally, he holds up a finger for Andy to pause and then flashes a look over Andy's shoulder. The look is—it isn't anything Andy's ever seen before. It's almost a smile, if smiles were made of molten metal and bad intentions.

Andy resists the urge to turn his head to see the recipient of this look. He doesn't have to wait long. A moment later, a man appears at Nick's side. He's older, maybe in his early thirties, with blond hair, slicked fashionably back. He has on a suit that looks, to Andy's eye, bespoke.

Andy recognizes this as his sign to start reading. He opens the book to his bookmark—or, where his bookmark was before he lost it and replaced it with a matchbook. Out of the corner of his eye, he sees Nick and the stranger move further down the bar. Nick takes out a cigarette and the stranger leans forward to light it.

The words on the page refuse to align themselves into any kind of sentence. All Andy can think about is the conversation happening just out of earshot. He turns his barstool a fraction to the left so he can at least see what's going on without craning his neck.

The stranger is leaning into Nick's space, one hand braced on the bar behind him. Nick does not seem to mind this encroachment in the least.

Andy wonders where they'll go—the blond man's apartment or Nick's. Surely Nick had been joking about taking care of things in the restroom. He hopes they go to the stranger's apartment.

Andy isn't much given to jealousy, truth be told. He was never bothered by other men looking at Emily, but that's because he was always sure that she'd ignore anyone who made a pass at her. He was wrong, it turns out, but he can't even find it in himself to be jealous of the man she left him for.

But right now he's being driven crazy by the idea that this stranger gets to light Nick's cigarette and lean in and whisper something that makes Nick laugh, soft and deep. He doesn't want this man to sit on their sofa, doesn't want him to drink out of any of the jam jars Nick uses as water glasses, doesn't want him to see the orange cat that comes through the window. This man shouldn't get any of that.

This can't be safe, can it? That stranger could be a cop. Granted, most cops probably can't afford suits as nice as the one this man is wearing, so that's some peace of mind, but still. He could be a murderer. Only last week Nick was attacked and Andy doesn't think he can stand the idea of seeing his friend getting hurt again.

The man puts his hand on the small of Nick's back and Andy wants to hiss at him. That strange smile is back on Nick's face, and Andy doesn't like that smile one bit, partly because it doesn't seem very happy, and partly because he thought he had seen all of Nick's smiles already.

Andy knows he isn't being especially rational. There are times when he couldn't possibly explain why he's doing a thing, times when a number of bad reasons somehow add up to a good enough reason. And that's what's happening here. The grim edges of Nick's smile, the fact that he's in a queer bar for the first time, fear for Nick's safety, the steady thrum of wanting that's been with him all week: all terrible reasons on their own, but put them together and you get something that looks almost like sense, if you don't look too carefully.

He slams his book closed and crosses the room.

"I need to leave," Andy tells Nick. He's surprised to hear that his voice sounds almost normal.

"You . . . what?" Nick says. He looks confused. Well, so is Andy.

"I need to leave," he repeats.

"Okay?"

"I need you to come with me."

Understanding dawns and a thundercloud passes over Nick's face. "Did something happen?" He turns to the stranger and makes an excuse, then walks with Andy toward the door before even waiting for a reply. "Did someone bother you?"

"No! God, no, nothing like that."

They're outside now. The temperature dropped while they were in the bar and now it feels like the dregs of winter.

"Care to tell me what the fuck just happened, then?" Nick asks. They aren't walking, just standing outside the bar, as if Nick thinks he might be going back inside.

"I didn't think it was safe." This isn't a lie, exactly. He's simply choosing not to mention the hot seep of jealousy that swept over him as he watched Nick and the other man.

Nick stares at him, and it occurs to Andy too late that Nick knows him too well to be taken in by a half truth. Nick knows he's prevaricating, but he doesn't need to know exactly what Andy's not saying.

Nick sets his jaw and looks away. Andy has seen Nick get angry before, but never at him. He doesn't like it one bit.

"It was your idea! This was your idea." Nick takes Andy's arm in a grip that isn't hard, but isn't messing around, either, and leads him away from any foot traffic, toward the doorway of a store that's closed for the night. "I didn't want to be here, but you wanted a field trip and I figured sure, why the fuck not. But you can't spend half an hour around f—"

"Don't say it!"

Nick stares at him.

"Don't say that word," Andy says, horrified that Nick has misunderstood him in this way.

"I don't understand you. I'm not even sure I want to understand you."

"If you think I have any trouble spending time with gay men, you haven't been paying the slightest bit of attention," Andy says. "I just don't want you to get hurt."

"Do you think I want to get hurt? Or arrested? Or publicly humiliated? Do you think I want any of that? Do you really think you get to decide what kinds of risks I take?" He throws his cigarette to the sidewalk and grinds it under his shoe. "I repeat, *this was your idea.*"

Andy swallows hard and scrambles to find a way to salvage the situation, and decides that the only way out is with absolute honesty. This is jumping in with both feet, reaching toward something he wants.

"I could do it."

"What?" Nick lights another cigarette, swears, and hands it to Andy before lighting another one for himself.

It's not too late to backtrack, but the truth is gnawing its way out. He *wants* to tell Nick. All week, since admitting it to himself, he's wanted to tell Nick, because not saying it feels like it's taking far more of an effort than it ought to. Why shouldn't he tell his queer friend that he's also queer? The more he thinks about it, the weirder it seems *not* to say anything.

And, yeah, he has an ulterior motive, which is that he's hoping that Nick will want to— He can't finish the sentence, not even in his head, but his thoughts supply a series of images: Nick's hands on him, Nick's mouth on his, Andy's fingers in Nick's hair. But that would be good for both of them, right? It could be—nice, maybe. It would be nicer than whatever goes on in restrooms. Safer, too.

"I could . . ." Christ. The fact that he still can't think of how to end that sentence can't be a good sign. "I could take care of you," he says, the words coming out in one crazy rush.

"What?" Nick's eyes are wide and his voice is hoarse.

"I could—if you wanted—"

"No," Nick says, looking horror-stricken. "Absolutely not. Have you lost your mind, Andy?"

Well, probably, but he doesn't think now is the time to say so. "It's an offer," he says, trying to get closer to honesty, nearer to the admission that he *wants* Nick. The words are right there, but he can't make himself say them.

"I can't deal with this—whatever this is—right now. I'm going for a walk." Nick turns on his heel.

"Wait."

Nick halts and looks over his shoulder.

"I want to. I mean. I . . . want to. In the way that anyone wants these things." And that probably would sound a hell of a lot better if he weren't such a prude, but at least it gets the point across.

Nick laughs, though, so maybe it hadn't. "You don't know what you want."

"Excuse me?"

"You're not thinking straight. You've had a rough couple of weeks. We'll forget this happened," he says with an attempt at a smile. "I'm going for a walk and you can let yourself into the apartment. When I get back, we'll pretend this never happened, okay?"

Andy knows he ought to be grateful to be let off the hook so easily, but it's so out of character for Nick, who's always digging and asking and looking for more. Nick is willing to sweep this whole situation under the rug and Andy hates it. It took so much effort for Andy to say something approaching the truth, to say out loud something he hadn't admitted even to himself until recently, and now Nick wants to pretend he never heard it?

Andy doesn't usually get angry. There aren't that many things worth alienating people over. But now his heart is racing. "That's insulting."

"It's *what*?"

"I told you what I told you, and you—" He stops himself as an alternate explanation for Nick's behavior belatedly occurs to him. Nick is letting him down gently. He doesn't want Andy to—he doesn't want Andy. And that's fine. It has to be fine. Andy's behaving like a child denied a toy, when Nick is a human being who's allowed not to want to do—whatever—with his friend. Jesus. He scrubs a hand across his face. "I'm sorry. I've ruined your evening. I'll head home and I'll see you later, all right?"

He turns and begins walking away before Nick can be the one who leaves.

"Wait!"

Andy turns at the sound of Nick's voice, a horrible swell of hope in his chest.

"That street up there is Seventh Avenue." Nick points in the opposite direction of where Andy was walking. "Turn left and you'll be at Sheridan Square. You can get home from there, right?"

"Yeah," Andy says. "Thanks." He drops his cigarette in a subway grate, because he never wants the things anyway. As he walks in the direction Nick pointed him, he tries to tell himself that he hasn't lost the only person in the world who really cares about him.

Part III

NICK

CHAPTER EIGHT

Nick isn't prepared for any of this. He's barely—*barely*—been managing to keep his own reactions to Andy under lock and key.

Hearing Andy suggest that he could, what—jerk Nick off as a favor? Jesus. That was enough to send all Nick's marbles scattering down Tenth Street.

He shudders at the idea of a pity jerk-off from Andy. Or, not even a pity jerk-off. A safety jerk-off. Nick laughs out loud. Two women in fur coats shoot him a baleful glance and quickly cross the street.

Nick tries to imagine how very much he would lose his mind if he let Andy touch him. He'd certainly lose his dignity. He'd probably say all kinds of soft and stupid things and it would be so embarrassing for both of them that they'd never be able to look one another in the eye again.

Hearing Andy suggest that he actually *wanted* Nick was even worse, but that wasn't Andy's fault. He wanted to do Nick a favor; Nick understands that much. Andy doesn't mean any harm, of course. He never does. Nick's done a decent job of hiding his feelings, he hopes, and so it isn't Andy's fault that he doesn't realize how cruel he's being.

Nick's usually perfectly content to take strangers to bed, men whose last names he doesn't know and doesn't want to know. Tonight, though, when he was talking to that man, all he could think about was Andy sitting a few yards away, drinking a drink he didn't want, reading a pulp detective story. The man Nick was talking to was good-looking and seemed nice enough, but Nick would rather have gone home with Andy and watched second-rate television. He should have just told Andy so and avoided the entire mess, but admitting that he'd rather watch the ten-o'clock news with Andy than have sex with virtually anybody was too close to admitting the truth.

Nick's past Fourteenth Street now, with nowhere to go, so he keeps walking.

It's about ten o'clock when Nick crosses East Sixtieth Street, and it's half past ten when he realizes where he's heading. And by then he's in such a state that knocking on Emily Warburton's door doesn't even seem like such a bad idea.

Jeanne answers.

"Nick?" she asks, obviously surprised. She's wearing a sparkly black dress and has probably just gotten home.

"I was in the neighborhood," he lies. "Is Emily in?"

"She is." Jeanne makes no move to get her sister, nor to ask Nick in. "You always seemed like a nice man, Nick, so if you're thinking of trying your luck with Emily—"

He almost laughs. "Jesus Christ, Jeanne, no."

"—then you'd better not. She's not in a good way."

"I'm definitely not going to put any moves on her or try to date her or take advantage of her or anything else. And she knows that I'm not—" Nick sighs. He supposes he ought to be glad Emily didn't gossip about him with her sister, but at that moment he almost announces that he's queer, right on the doorstep of the Warburton town house, just to make sure Jeanne doesn't hate him for the wrong reason. "She knows that I already have someone, all right?"

Jeanne raises an eyebrow. "If you say so."

"I promise." It's the truth, or close enough to it. Emily never came right out and said that she knew how Nick felt about Andy, but she never had to. "Look. I miss her. I miss both of you, actually. And I know I should have called ahead instead of showing up late at night like a creep, but here I am. If you want me to go away, I'll go."

"Come on in," Jeanne says, not sounding too enthusiastic about it. "Emily!"

"Did I hear the door?" Emily comes downstairs looking—well, looking better than she had two weeks ago, when she had mostly been composed of tears and ruined makeup. But now she looks different than he's ever seen her. Her hair is down around her shoulders, loose and straight, which isn't something you see on grown women every day, at least not outside the bongo-playing beatniks in Washington Square Park. She's wearing trousers and what looks like a men's shirt. "Nick?"

"Thought I'd stop by and say hi."

She raises a skeptical eyebrow but leads him up the stairs into the living room he remembers from the night of the dinner party. "Can I get you a drink?"

"Sure. Whatever you're drinking."

She hands him a glass of something clear and sits cross-legged on the sofa. He sits in an armchair. Jeanne, evidently convinced that her sister isn't about to get propositioned, has disappeared.

"What's the matter?" Emily asks. "And no, don't try to lie to me. It's past ten and this is well outside your usual stomping grounds."

"First tell me how you're doing."

"Nice try. Out with it. It looks like it's going to be juicy and I want to be entertained."

He shoots her a look, but she only shoots him one right back.

"Okay. You don't have any maids or—I don't know—butlers hanging around? Nothing I say will leave this room?"

"It's only you and me."

He believes her. For a minute he considers telling the story without using Andy's name, because he's in the habit of maintaining something like the secrecy of the confessional when it comes to anything even tangentially queer. He's always so goddamn careful that sometimes he feels like there isn't a person in the world he can speak freely to about anything that matters. But if Emily didn't even tell Jeanne about him, then she can keep a secret.

He lowers his voice as he tells her what happened that evening, starting from Andy's idea to go to the gay bar and ending with their quarrel on the street.

"He told you he was insulted?"

"Yeah." Nick doesn't know why that, of all things, is what catches Emily's attention.

"Listen, Nick. When I told him I cheated on him, he said that he'd be happy to go through with the wedding. He said that these things happen."

Nick takes a drink of what turns out to be a gin and tonic, in which the tonic is more theoretical than an actual ingredient. "Of course he did. Always the gentleman."

"No, that's not it. You're missing the point. You're right that Andy's a gentleman, but what's more important is that he doesn't quarrel. I think it must have to do with his parents going at it hammer and tongs."

"He never even gets angry."

"I think he does, but not at people. Anyway, if he's saying that he's insulted, that's the equivalent of anybody else stomping out of the room and slamming the door behind them, maybe throwing a glass or two at the wall."

"But why would he be insulted?"

She shrugs. "You know him as well as I do."

"You don't seem awfully surprised that your ex-fiancé propositioned me."

Emily raises an eyebrow. "If you're asking whether I ever suspected that he had secret homosexual leanings, the answer is no."

Before Nick can point out that Andy *doesn't* have secret homosexual leanings, that he just didn't want Nick to get arrested, Emily goes on. "But . . . honestly, that's not the kind of thing that would surprise me in anybody. And Andy has always adored you," she adds, as if that makes perfect sense.

It's definitely time to change the topic. "Now tell me how you're doing. How'd your family take the news?"

"Other than Jeanne? Awfully. Imagine, they all had their hopes up that I was finally going to do something right, and there I go and blow it all to pieces."

He and Emily are both intimately familiar with how familial disappointment can be both predictable in its consistency and infinite in its variety. He raises his glass to her.

"Are you going to tell Andy you came here?" she asks.

"Yeah," he says. "He's not holding a grudge, Em. I think he wishes he could still be your friend."

"He's a crazy person. He's supposed to hate me until his dying breath. So are you, actually."

"I can't really blame anyone for falling in love with the wrong person, can I?" He blames the gin for loosening his tongue, but saying the words is such a relief. "Have you heard from—" He realizes he doesn't know the name of the man Emily was involved with in London. He only knows the rough outline of events: Emily's mother had a heart attack. When Emily went to London to look after her, she fell for her mother's doctor. They started something that Emily thought was serious, but when Emily suggested that she might stay on in London, the doctor hadn't been interested. Nick hadn't asked for the details; in her shoes, he wouldn't want to pour his heart out, either.

"Gerald? No. I wasn't expecting to, though. It was a fling, evidently, and I'm the only one who didn't know the score." She drains her glass.

"I hate him."

"I don't." She sighs. "I wish I did. Jeanne would push him off a cliff, though, which is gratifying."

"Emily," he says, aware that he's whining a little and not caring, "Andy's future girlfriends are going to hate me. They're all going to be horrible compared to you, *and* they'll try to set me up with their single friends."

"I tried to set you up with my single friends all the time."

"Yeah, but your friends were the right gender."

She smiles. "There was that."

He finishes his drink and gets to his feet.

At the front door, he takes hold of her shoulder and kisses her temple. "Thanks."

"Nick, be careful with Andy."

"I'll look after him," he reassures her.

"That's not what I meant," she says.

Nick hails a cab, because no matter how he looks at the subway map he keeps in his head, he can't figure out how to get home without either changing trains twice or walking approximately a million blocks west from the Spring Street station where he was mugged last week. He's been drinking for six hours and is in no condition to think about crosstown buses.

When he looks up from the street, he can't see any lights on in his apartment. Andy has gone to sleep, then. It's past midnight, so that's good. They'll talk in the morning when they're sane and sober.

As he climbs the stairs, he hears the sound of a television coming from Mrs. Martelli's apartment and laughter and music coming from another. The baby on the third floor seems to have gotten past the stage where she had to holler for a few hours every night, so that has to be a relief for everyone concerned. Underneath one of the doors on the fourth floor, he can see the shadow of a dog lying down, waiting for its owner to come home.

Nick has a hard time with close friendships—if faced with the choice between lying to someone about who he is or keeping them at arm's length, he chooses the latter. He's no good at protracted dishonesty. But he likes being around people. He likes being sociable at work. He likes being friendly with his neighbors. He often wishes he could have more actual friends, but friendliness is a fine second best.

Andy's the closest friend he has, the closest he's ever had, and that fact means more to Nick than whatever happened tonight. He'll figure out a way to make things right between them. He hurt Andy's feelings—although he isn't quite sure how—and he needs to figure out a way to explain to Andy that his feelings were hurt, too. Or maybe he can skip that part. Andy matters a hell of a lot more to him than his own hurt feelings. He's going to do whatever it takes to put things back the way they were.

He turns the key in the lock as quietly as possible, then closes the door gently behind him. He takes off his shoes and is about to tiptoe into his bedroom when his breath catches.

Andy is asleep on the couch. He's fully dressed, the blanket from his bed draped half over him.

Nick could make his life easy and just go to bed. He probably isn't sober enough to have the conversation they need to have. But Andy either attempted to wait up for him or hoped that Nick's arrival would wake him, and Nick doesn't want to ignore that.

He sits carefully on the end of the couch near Andy's feet. Nick likes seeing Andy on his couch, likes seeing his dusty-blond hair spread over the faded green upholstery, likes the weight of his legs on Nick's lap when they land there while they watch television, likes the scent of his aftershave in Nick's home. He likes it more than he ought to, really. But that's no surprise.

Through the blanket, he puts a hand on Andy's leg and gently shakes him awake. "Andy." It takes a few more shakes before Andy's eyes open, and then he bolts upright. Nick has never seen Andy so alert so soon after waking. Usually it takes a full half hour of catatonia before Andy even attempts sentences.

"I'm home," Nick says unnecessarily. "You ought to go to sleep in your bed."

"I'm sorry," Andy says, rubbing his eyes. "I'm a jackass. I shouldn't have stopped you from being with that man."

"I don't give a shit about that," Nick says. And he really doesn't. That was annoying and kind of rude, but it's nothing compared to what came later. "Also, I'm sorry, too. I know you meant to be kind and I'm sorry that I overreacted."

As the words leave his mouth, Nick realizes that this is the first time in ages that he's apologized to anyone—not because he minds apologizing, but because in order to apologize, you have to be close enough to someone that you want their forgiveness.

"Thanks." Andy yawns.

"Let's go to sleep."

"Are we okay?"

"Yeah." Andy looks far too relieved. Did he really think that Nick would stay mad at him? "Hey, Andy? We're always going to be okay. At least on my end. Understand?" He reaches out an arm, meaning to clasp Andy's shoulder, but Andy ducks under it, and the next thing he knows he has an armful of sleep-warm Andy, his hair sticking up in tufts that tickle Nick's nose. Nick pats his back, takes a stupid minute to breathe in the scent of him.

"Thanks," Andy says again, his words muffled by Nick's coat.

"Shut up. You don't have anything to thank me for. Time for sleep," he says, and reluctantly lets go.

Nick is constitutionally incapable of sleeping past seven in the morning. He has some kind of godforsaken alarm clock in his brain that shakes him awake at about half past six every goddamn day, including weekends, including holidays, including days he's profoundly and regrettably hungover.

He levers himself out of bed, promptly stubs his toe on his dresser, and, swearing under his breath, gets some aspirin from the medicine cabinet. He swallows it down with a mouthful of water that makes his insides rebel.

Andy, of course, isn't awake yet. If Nick kept quiet, Andy could probably sleep all day. Even when Andy gets out of bed, he's still mostly asleep.

Nick dumps some coffee grounds in the top of the coffee press and then, thinking better of it, doubles the amount and puts it on the stove. Skeptically, he eyes the contents of his refrigerator. The idea of food makes his stomach turn, so he shuts the door.

He tries to remember exactly how much he had to drink last night, but it's a blur after leaving O'Connell's. Which makes sense, come to think, because there's no way he would have agreed to go to a gay bar with Andy if he'd been within a stone's throw of sobriety. He might have thought that the long walk to Emily's apartment would have burned off some of the alcohol, but evidently not. His head is filled with sawdust and nausea.

When the coffee is ready, he dumps some into a cup with a bit of milk and pours it directly down his throat, which—motherfucker. It's too hot. Too hot, by about ten thousand degrees. He drops his mug into the sink and it lands with a clatter. He fans his mouth, like an utter fool, as if that will even do anything.

"Shit fuck damn," he grumbles.

"Wow," says Andy from behind him.

"Drank boiling coffee," Nick explains, turning around. The sight of Andy, sleep-rumpled, wearing Nick's pajamas, his hair sticking up on one side, hits Nick like a sucker punch.

"I did that once," Andy says mildly. "Not a great experience."

Nick starts to laugh, because of course Andy's done that. "Only once?"

"The second time was hot cocoa."

"That's a different thing entirely."

"Exactly."

Andy grins and stretches. Nick's eyes are drawn to that sliver of pale skin exposed on his stomach. This happens every morning—Andy stretches and Nick gawks. He feels like a pervert, and even more so after last night's series of disasters.

"Are you hungry?" Andy asks, looking in the icebox.

"Andy, if you even talk about food, I'm calling the police."

"That bad?"

"Worse. I visited Emily and I think she gave me the equivalent of a fifth of gin, dressed up with just enough tonic that I didn't know how dire things were."

"Emily?" Andy's back is to him, so Nick can't read his expression.

"I needed someone to screw my head on straight." Nick decides not to mention that he walked all the way there. "Do you mind that I saw her? Or that I'm mentioning it?"

"Neither. I think it would be a lot weirder if you didn't mention it." He pours himself some coffee and leans against the counter, facing Nick. "So, what did she say?"

"That I owed you an apology."

Andy frowns. "Which you gave me last night. We don't need to have this conversation. Please. I embarrassed myself. It won't happen again."

"I hurt your feelings." He's hoping that Andy will give him a clue about where he went wrong so he doesn't make the same mistake twice, but Andy only flushes and looks away.

"That's unavoidable under the circumstances, and not something you need to apologize for."

Nick doesn't follow. Maybe there's still some gin in his system, or maybe his head is too full of rocks and garbage to do much in the way of thinking, but either way he doesn't understand exactly how he hurt Andy, much less how it was unavoidable. "It is, though. I don't want to insult you."

Andy gives him a confused look. "I mean, I know that, Nick. Anyway, I'm sorry. I meant what I said. I shouldn't have interfered."

Nick shakes his head. "I don't care about that."

"You don't need to say that."

Nick isn't just saying it. He can't even remember the man's name, or whether he even knew it in the first place. If he wants what that man had to offer, he can find it that very night, in one of any number of similar bars.

But that isn't what he wants, and that's the problem.

CHAPTER NINE

Nick ought to visit his mother this weekend, but he already knows that he won't. He just doesn't have any interest in surrounding himself with people who might hate him if they knew who he really was. He doesn't usually put it to himself that baldly, but Friday night still has him a bit shaky.

He loves his mother. He loves his nieces and nephew. Growing up, he was surrounded by family at every turn—aunts and grandparents, cousins and uncles and vague hangers-on. Being a part of that large, loud, fractious Russo family is as much a part of his identity as being a reporter or a baseball fan—or queer. But the knowledge that his belonging to that family is contingent on keeping a secret—on implicitly agreeing that a part of him needs to be hidden away—makes him feel fragile in a way he hates, and so he keeps his distance.

Before Andy came to live with him, Nick would sometimes stay on the subway for an extra stop in the morning, getting off at Fulton Street and walking to the fish market. He'd stick his hands in his pockets and watch the boats pass beneath the Brooklyn Bridge, solid and permanent, the time before its existence impossible to imagine, absurd as a concept.

Sometimes he imagines ships just out of sight, rounding the bend into the harbor. His father had been fifteen when he left Ragusa, he and his younger sister the last members of their family to survive both the war and the flu.

His mother's family had come earlier, aunts and uncles and cousins and what must have been half the population of a tiny fishing village on the Ionian Sea.

He can't quite imagine it, can't quite imagine having a village. He can imagine his father's journey more easily. He wonders if leaving everything behind is a Russo trait. As the crow flies, he's five miles from the place where he was born, ten miles from the house where his brother and mother live today. It feels like more.

Nick realized two things at about the same time: one, he didn't want to tend bar or work at the docks like most of the men in the neighborhood, and two, he wanted other boys in a way he wasn't supposed to. Those two things got tied up together in some ways that made sense and some ways that didn't. There was a general understanding in the neighborhood that anyone who didn't work with his hands was about one step removed from wearing lipstick and feather boas—one step removed from the queers by the naval yards, the fairies of the Village and Harlem. The people in the neighborhood had all but drawn him a map of where to find people like himself.

And so his after-school job as a night copyboy at the *Brooklyn Eagle* became a way out of the neighborhood and also a way he'd somehow be able to be queer. It worked, he supposes.

Nick never looked back.

Or at least he's trying not to.

"I have news," Andy says solemnly, coming up to Nick's desk. "And you can't get mad about it."

"Has telling someone that they can't get mad ever worked? Even once?"

"Okay." Andy looks like his heart is going a mile a minute. He's twisting his tie so aggressively that Nick wants to slap his hand away. "So, I have tickets to opening day at Yankee Stadium. They're playing the Red Sox. And you're coming."

"Oh no. Andy, *no*."

"Andy, yes," he says, nodding.

"You're going to wear a Red Sox cap and we're going to get murdered—literally murdered, Andy—on the way from the subway to the stadium."

"Ah!" Andy says triumphantly. "We can take a car."

"Oh, so we're Rockefellers now, are we?" Nick narrows his eyes. "Where are these seats? Why do I have the feeling that they aren't going to be up in the nosebleeds?"

"They're behind home plate."

Nick whistles. "Never tell me what they cost. Promise me that much."

"Think of how much I'm saving on rent!" Only the twitch in his lip gives the slightest clue that he's joking. Andy's apartment, the one with the bad plumbing, had been his mother's. He owns it outright and occasionally mentions that he ought to sell it.

"You've never paid rent in your life."

"You'll come with me to the game, right?" Andy asks.

Sometimes, for a smart person, Andy is incredibly dense. "Yes, I'm coming with you to the game," Nick says patiently. "You'll need someone to be your bodyguard."

For some reason, that makes Andy blush a little and shove his hands in his pockets and then make an excuse to go somewhere else. That's been happening a lot in the week since what Nick is coming to think of as the Proposition. As best as Nick can guess, Andy's embarrassed. He probably can't believe how narrowly he avoided having regrettable gay charity sex.

Approximately seven trillion times a day Nick remembers Andy's words: *I could take care of you.* And he remembers Andy's voice—low and shaky and a little terrified but *fond.* Nick doesn't doubt, hasn't once doubted, that Andy meant what he said. He'd have taken care of Nick. He'd have done his best. The trouble is Nick can picture it—Andy, fumbling a bit like he always does when faced with a new task, but catching on, maybe even a little eager—

Christ. This is perverse, fantasizing about his friend. It's a waste of energy, too, because Nick can't have this. He can't even have anything like it, not with anyone, so he shouldn't let himself think about it.

It's just, when Andy blushes, Nick can almost imagine—

The thing is that Andy has no poker face. His thoughts are right there on the surface for the world to see, and since his thoughts are usually perfectly respectable, it doesn't do him any harm.

Except—sometimes when Andy blushes, he bites his lip, he looks away and then back, he stares at Nick's mouth. It's almost enough to convince Nick that there was something behind Andy's offer, some tiny spark—

But he can't let his thoughts drift down that path. He can already sense the easy equilibrium of their friendship tipping out of balance, something steady and fundamental slipping away.

Andy's probably just reacting to having his heart broken. He's been living in the Village, queer people around every corner, and his imagination has gotten the better of him. He looks at Nick, sees someone reasonably attractive, and wonders if he's feeling something queer when really he's just lonely. That would explain the blushes, the furtive glances. He's embarrassed and curious, that's all. Maybe he's even worried that he's secretly queer.

That feels plausible to Nick. God knows he looked at plenty of women when he was trying to figure out whether he was attracted to them. He did more than look.

It doesn't usually work the other way, though, not in Nick's experience. Men don't mess around with other men in order to rule out queerness. Apart from some pretty limited exceptions— the army, the navy, fourteen-year-olds out of their minds with hormones—men who screw around with other men are doing it because they specifically want to screw around with men.

But it isn't like Nick's an expert here. Maybe people like Andy— people who went to fancy boarding schools and were raised by card-carrying Leninists—have a more experimental approach to figuring out what gets their dicks hard. Maybe they don't have as much invested in the gender of who they fuck or something. Good for them, Nick supposes, even though it feels like cheating, because it took Nick most of a goddamn decade to get there.

The coffee maker in the grubby little kitchen next to the newsroom makes some of the nastiest swill anyone could ask for, but when deadlines are creeping closer and nobody, not even the copyboys, has time to run downstairs to get coffee from the deli, it's better than nothing. Until, one afternoon, it breaks.

"Fucker's busted," says Eugene from the sports desk, grimly standing over the defunct percolator.

"Did you try the fourth floor?" Nick asks.

"Their machine broke two days ago. I think it's ritual suicide, and they're all going to go off, one by one, until someone starts buying decent beans to put in them."

"Isn't there a jar of instant around here somewhere?"

"Fifth floor stole it. Their machine broke, too."

There's nothing for it but to go to the fifth floor and steal back the jar of instant coffee. It's an emergency. Besides, the fifth floor is mostly empty, only half its offices nominally occupied by a motley crew of editorial writers, columnists, and other people who can seldom be bothered to show up. Nick thinks his chances are good that he won't meet anyone before absconding with the coffee.

He doesn't bother with the elevator, just runs down the single flight of stairs and is immediately reminded why he never goes to the fifth floor.

"Kid," calls a gruff voice from inside one of the offices. "Who the hell is chasing you?"

It's just Nick's luck that Mark Bailey, who only comes into the office twice a week, tops, has to be here today. "I'm looking for coffee," Nick says, hoping he sounds normal. "Newsroom coffee maker's broken."

Bailey raises an eyebrow and gestures toward the kitchen with a single finger.

Nick hurries, thinking that maybe he'll be able to snatch the coffee and disappear. But as soon as he opens the cabinet, he hears footsteps behind him.

"Just pour yourself a cup," Bailey says. "Mugs are on the left."

"I'm looking for the instant. Our coffee maker's broken."

Bailey opens another cabinet and pulls down a jar of Nescafé, then hands it to Nick. "Still, pour yourself a cup. You don't want that stuff."

Nick glances wistfully at what appears to be a brand-new coffee maker, evidently bought to replace the one that killed itself in protest of bad beans. He feels like taking Bailey's coffee—somehow he feels certain that this is Bailey's own coffee maker, brought from home—will be a bridge too far.

"Jesus, kid." Bailey pours a cup and thrusts it into Nick's hand.

Two years ago, Nick was at the Everard Baths in Chelsea, doing what everybody does there, which is to say having semi-anonymous sex with other men. The place is an institution. It's been there as long as anyone can remember, having bounced back from God knows how many raids. Rumor is the cops actually own the place. Nick was just leaving when he caught sight of Bailey on the sidewalk outside, talking with another man. Neither of them was stupid enough to acknowledge the other by name, but they had met one another's eye and there was no denying that it had happened.

Nick hasn't gone back to the baths since. He's spent years trying to avoid Bailey, rarely going to the fifth floor, steering clear of him in the cafeteria. Not because there's anything wrong with the man, mind you. He's one of the *Chronicle*'s book critics, and he seems perfectly nice, Nick supposes.

It's just that there aren't a lot of people who know about Nick, and he's gotten used to people looking at him and only seeing what he wants them to see. Mark Bailey knows the truth and it makes Nick feel exposed, here at the *Chronicle*, where it's more important than ever for Nick to keep his secrets.

"Cream's in the refrigerator," Bailey says, and Nick realizes he's been standing there too long. Before Nick can decide whether to take the cream or make a break for the elevator bank, Bailey speaks again. "I didn't tell anyone. I'm not going to tell anyone. You know that, right?"

"I didn't think you would," Nick says, which isn't entirely true. It's not that he thinks Bailey would spread malicious gossip. It's just—Bailey had been with someone. *With* someone. He had been on the arm of another man, something comfortable and settled about the way they were standing. They had been together. And would it be so strange for Bailey, later on, to whisper to his— his lover, his boyfriend—that the young man with dark hair had been Nick Russo from the newsroom? Nick thinks it would be stranger not to, which means there's one other person who knows about Nick.

"I'm not going to hit on you, either," says Bailey, rolling his eyes.

"Shh!" Nick automatically looks over his shoulder, out the kitchen door.

"The floor's empty except for Archie Ross, and he's half deaf."

It's true, and besides, Bailey is speaking quietly. None of that does anything to make Nick's heart settle down. He's self-aware enough to understand that he's being unreasonably paranoid—it's the same skin-crawling sensation he gets when speaking freely even inside his own apartment or an empty subway car. It's been years: Bailey clearly means him no harm and has managed to be discreet enough that Nick's queerness isn't the talk of the *Chronicle*.

But Bailey's presence sets Nick's teeth on edge and somehow it's worse because Bailey is trying to be decent. A week after that awful meeting at the baths, he cornered Nick in the cafeteria and gave him a business card for a lawyer with another phone number inked in at the bottom. "Memorize both of these numbers if you ever have trouble," Bailey had said. Nick had been annoyed at the presumption but also grateful, because, yes, the phone number of a queer-friendly lawyer was a good thing to have, goddammit.

"I've been reading that series you're writing," Bailey says now. "It's funny. You're wasted on the news."

"*Funny?*" Nick repeats, outraged. "*Wasted?*"

"Those were compliments."

"Like hell they were."

"You're a good prose stylist."

"I'm a *what?*" Nick knows what those words mean separately and even together but not when applied to himself.

"Compliment, kid. You're good at what you do."

"But not at reporting news?"

"Didn't say that. Just meant that you'd be better at writing something else. Did you read that book I sent you?"

"No," Nick says with feeling.

Bailey takes out a pack of cigarettes and offers one to Nick, who shakes his head. "You should read it. I think you'd like it."

"That's what you always say."

A couple times a year, Nick finds a tale of gay misery and woe on his desk, because apparently Bailey has taken it upon himself to be Nick's personal sad gay librarian.

"You have shitty taste in books. Would it kill you to read something that isn't totally dismal?"

"I'm paid for my taste in books," Bailey says easily. "And I don't mind dismal things. I'm trying to be your friend, aren't I?"

Nick leaves before the conversation can get any weirder.

When Andy comes back from the afternoon editorial meeting, his face is drawn, his jaw clenched. That's how he always looks when he's been in a meeting, and these days he's spending less and less time in the newsroom, and more and more time in meetings.

"What happened?" Nick asks.

"The usual." Andy passes his own desk and comes to sit on

the edge of Nick's. "Circulation's down and department stores don't want to pay enough to advertise girdles." It's a truism in the news business that the entire fourth estate is propped up by dry goods manufacturers advertising underwear. "The fact is that fewer and fewer people get news from the newspaper, and every news editor in the room thinks the solution is to print more news and everyone in the marketing department thinks the solution is to decrease the news hole and run more ads. Every meeting we go over the same ground."

Nick tips back in his seat to look Andy in the eye. "What does your father say?"

"He wants to keep doing things more or less the way we have been. Not because he's particularly committed to it, but because he thinks everyone else is wrong."

"What about Epstein?" Nick asks. The managing editor might know more about this business than anyone alive.

"He wants more features. Expand the women's section. Expand the sports section. More columns of the throwing-spaghetti-at-the-wall variety. More series like what you're writing."

"More what now?"

Andy rolls his eyes. "I keep telling you. One, people talk about it. Two, they keep buying papers to find out what happens next. God knows what we need is people to keep buying papers."

Andy seems almost . . . interested as he says this. Tired, yes. Frustrated, definitely. But this might be the first time Nick has heard him sound like he cares about running the paper and also like he knows what he's talking about. But just as suddenly, his expression reverts back to a sort of hopeless exhaustion. "I can't believe my father expects me to sort it out. You should see them all during the meetings. The editors, the head of marketing, all of them—they keep looking at me out of the corners of their eyes, like they don't know why I'm there and would prefer that I go away. I mean, I would prefer that I'd go away, too, so really I sympathize."

Nick makes a scoffing sound. "They're probably just embarrassed that their future boss is hearing them sound ignorant."

Andy looks at him like he's lost his mind.

"Andy. Seriously. Do you really think that you could do any worse than what the publishers of most newspapers are doing? Have you *seen* newspapers lately?"

"You haven't seen the circulation numbers," Andy grumbles. "I don't want it to be my fault when the paper goes out of business."

Nick knows there really isn't anything he can say that will persuade Andy that he'll be able to run the *Chronicle*. He isn't sure if he even wants to say anything, when it's so obvious that Andy would be happier doing anything else. Instead he settles for a different kind of truth. "You should give yourself some credit for once."

To punctuate the point, he gives Andy's knee a flick—just the sort of borderline-friendly, borderline-annoying gesture he's done probably a thousand times, but today he somehow miscalculates and his hand collides with Andy's, their fingers winding up tangled together.

Andy's gaze meets Nick's and his expression is somewhere between embarrassed and horrified—no, it's the expression of someone who's been caught out, guilty and shocked, and Nick knows it because that's exactly what his own face does when he looks at the wrong man.

What the *hell*.

CHAPTER TEN

During the seventh inning, Nick decides that he'll attend as many Red Sox games as Andy likes, God help him. Even at Yankee Stadium.

The Yankees score two runs in the first inning, and then nothing happens at all for the following six innings. Well, nothing happens except Andy sitting at the edge of his seat, biting his nails, gasping every time a bat connects with the ball, actually covering his eyes a couple of times, and Nick wishing he could store all these antics on film so he could make fun of Andy later. And also because Andy is adorable like this, but Nick's trying not to think about that.

Nick used to take his nephew to see the Dodgers a couple times a year. They sat in the bleachers and Sal earnestly filled in his scorecard in his horrible handwriting, managed to drop at least one hot dog per game, and had all the dignity of a puppy. It was about as much fun as a person ought to be allowed to have.

Watching a ball game with Andy is a little bit like that, even though it's different for all the obvious reasons, and also because Nick has nothing invested in the outcome of this game. He wants the Yankees to lose, just on principle, but he can't go so far as wanting the Red Sox to win. He's in a state of pure impartiality, which lets him enjoy the beer and the sunshine, the crack of the bat against the ball, and the company.

In the seventh inning, the Red Sox even the score with two runs and the amount of pure joy radiating off Andy could have powered the electrical grid of all five boroughs.

Andy shamelessly cheers for the Red Sox, ignoring the dirty looks and pointed boos from the people in the surrounding stands. Maybe the folks in pricey seats will behave better than the crowd in the bleachers and they'll manage not to get murdered this afternoon. Andy cheers like he's never heard of a jinx, like he doesn't know what kind of a sorry deal optimism buys you.

But then in the bottom of the eighth inning, the Yankees score again, and the Red Sox aren't able to get on the board in the ninth inning, so that's that.

"That's baseball," Andy says cheerfully. "It's going to be a good season." They're lingering in their seats, not wanting to get crushed by the opening-day crowd pouring out of the stadium.

When the volume of people leaving the stands slows to a trickle, they get to their feet and make their way out to the street and toward the subway station. Andy hasn't, despite his threats, hired a car, and so they have a friendly quarrel about what subway line to take home.

"Actually, you're right," Nick says.

"What?"

"We should take the IND, because any train we get on will bring us to West Fourth Street."

"Did I . . . did I just win an argument about the subway? With you?"

"Shut up, will you." At some point in the last few weeks, Andy has gone from barely being able to use the subway unsupervised to having a pretty good sense of how to get where he wants to go. Also, he hasn't lost his keys, not once, since moving in with Nick. Nick hardly knows what to make of it.

"Wow, what's next. Have you heard the good news about extra base power?"

"Oh boy, here we go," Nick grumbles, and settles in for a lecture about the superiority of some crackpot theory Andy has about batting averages or something.

Nick kind of loves it though. He loves that Andy cares about statistics, of all the awful things, and he loves that Andy wants to talk about it. Nick will never understand more than four consecutive words that Andy says when he's on this particular tear, but he can see the light in Andy's eyes, the way he waves his hands around when he's excited.

The platform is still crowded as they wait for a train. Standing near them is a teenage girl in a summer dress, her hair in a ponytail, and beside her is a boy who looks like he's been scrubbed and combed into an uncomfortable degree of presentability. A scorecard sticks out of the boy's back pocket. There's a shy six inches of space between them, but they're holding hands. They must have been to opening day as a date, and based on the hand holding and a couple of bashful glances, Nick has to guess that it's been a pretty good date.

He looks at Andy, who's flapping his hands a bit in his enthusiasm over—Jesus Christ, it's long division, isn't it. Nick smiles without meaning to. Andy catches his eye and smiles back, never interrupting his own monologue.

Nick absently raises his wrist to check his watch, and when he drops his hand, he catches Andy tracking the movement. Even when Nick sticks his hand in his pocket, Andy keeps looking. It's hot, and Nick's sleeves are rolled up, and Nick might think Andy was judging him for being scruffy except for how Andy's sleeves are rolled up, too, and also he knows perfectly well by now that Andy doesn't give a shit about that sort of thing. Without thinking, he steps a little closer to Andy, shuffling along the sticky cement of the platform.

When Andy glances up, he catches Nick's eye and immediately looks away, the tips of his ears going pink. And, sure, the subway station is hot, everyone's a bit flushed, but Andy's blushing. He's seen Andy blush every day for over a year now and he knows what it looks like. Andy's blushing because Nick caught him looking.

Standing there on the crowded platform, watching Andy's Adam's apple work as he swallows, Nick has to acknowledge what he's looking at.

His mind starts to reel, his view of the situation shifting a full ninety degrees. At first he thinks he's losing his balance because of the train arriving in the station, that's how unsteady he feels. He goes back over the past few weeks, seeing all their interactions through a new, possibly demented, lens.

In the morning, when Nick only has on his undershirt and shorts, Andy sometimes looks a little too long, particularly at his arms and his chest. Nick chalked that up to Andy having some kind of WASPy aversion to people walking around their own homes in their underwear. Or maybe he just thinks Nick is hairy. Or maybe he isn't thinking at all, because they both know Andy's brain doesn't do much of anything until ten A.M. Who knows.

But there have been other times, now that Nick thinks about it. Whenever Nick rolls up his sleeves or loosens his tie, Andy's gaze immediately goes to the exposed skin. Again, Nick has assumed Andy thinks even partially disrobing is scandalous.

What if Andy meant what he said outside that bar? Not because he was offering a favor, not because he was curious or confused, but because he wanted to.

There's a chance— Nick stops himself short.

He glances at the couple.

This outing isn't a date. In order for it to be a date, they both would have had to agree beforehand, right? Nick has never been on a date, unless you count the times Andy and Emily brought him along as a fourth. He never contemplated the possibility that he might go on a date. Dates exist in the same universe as Sputnik: he's aware they exist and are important to a lot of people, but he's never expected them to factor into his own life.

Nick hasn't ever considered a future beyond sex with anyone. He isn't a fool; he knows that men can settle down together. He just can't imagine that happening to him; he's reluctant to give his last name to anyone he goes to bed with, for fuck's sake, let alone be open enough to actually get close. The degree of healthy paranoia that colors most of his life is a real check on anything like romance.

Anyway, this isn't a date. He doesn't know why he's even thinking about dates. Except—of course he does; it's because dates are what people like Andy do when they want someone. Even if Andy wants to—Nick doesn't know how to finish that sentence, even in his head—then it isn't going to be anything like getting off in the subway men's room.

Nick wants that—that thing that exists between people who are together for more than a night. And he's never going to have it, not with his head screwed on the way it is, but he at least wants a chance to go to bed with someone he cares about. He doesn't dislike the perfunctory, transactional sex he usually has, but sleeping with Andy would be—*more*. It would be more in ways that would result in Nick's heart getting broken at the end of it, but he wants it anyway.

And he wants Andy. God, he wants Andy. He's been trying not to think about it, but there's really no avoiding it, not with Andy there every morning and every night. His heart's already a little broken, so why not break it all the way through.

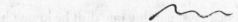

That night, when Nick is scrambling eggs for dinner and Andy is making a nuisance of himself by asking what every spice in the cupboard is for, Nick tries to figure out what to do. He's always done his best thinking when his hands are busy, and now is no exception. He chops some peppers, smashes a clove of garlic, and tries to think, rationally, logically, about what to do next.

But he can't. There aren't any logical thoughts to be found in the tangle of Nick's brain. It's all a soup of feeling. He's—fuck it—he's crazy about Andy, has been for a while. He's not even trying to pretend to himself that he isn't.

If Andy wants him in any way, Nick is going to take him up on whatever he's offering, and if what he's offering is nothing, Nick's going to be fine with that because he already is. All Nick has to do is figure out what Andy's offering.

He could, in theory, just ask, but that's a lunatic idea and he's having none of it. But what *can* he do? In the middle of supper, lean in and ask if Andy wants to revisit the topic of hand jobs? *Pass the salt, and have your attitudes toward jerking me off altered in the past few weeks?*

He tries to clear his head. He doesn't want to fuck this up, doesn't want to alienate Andy, but he's probably going to fuck it up anyway because he doesn't know what he's doing. But you know what, their friendship is solid enough to withstand a couple of fuckups. Andy propositioned him and they got over it, and they'll get over it if Nick screws this up somehow. He meant what he said when he told Andy that they were always going to be okay, and he thinks Andy feels the same.

"What's this?" Andy asks, holding up a little glass jar of cumin.

"It goes in polpette," Nick says, naming one dish he knows he has made Andy. "Meatballs."

"This?" Now it's a jar of red pepper flakes.

Nick takes the jar and sprinkles a modest quantity on the eggs. "You'll find out," he says, beaming angelically. "Set the table, pest." He carries the pan over to the table and puts it on a folded dish towel.

"Oh," Andy says a few minutes later, reaching for his glass of water, "so that's what the red pepper flakes do."

"Mm-hmm," Nick agrees, shoveling a forkful of eggs into his mouth. "You have maybe four flakes of pepper on your eggs, so don't moan about it. It's good for you."

"Likely story." But he keeps eating.

Steeling himself, Nick nudges Andy under the table with his foot. Andy looks up, curious. Nick fixes him with his best look, exactly what he'd use in a bar or even on the street in the right part of town.

Andy goes pink. Even his ears are pink.

Nick reaches out to push a loose strand of hair off Andy's forehead.

"What are you doing?" Andy asks.

"Uh," Nick says, because he isn't prepared with any kind of answer. He was hoping Andy would understand, would meet him halfway.

"Right." Andy sighs. "I don't think I can eat any more." He gets up.

Well, Nick supposes that settles it. Even if Andy's attracted to him, he doesn't want to do anything about it. Nick is mortified, but better to figure this out now than later. It'll be embarrassing for a few days and they'll get over it. That's the important thing, not the heavy lump of disappointment that's settled in his stomach.

Before he can figure out what to do next, what to say to return things to normal, Andy speaks again.

"So," Andy says as he rinses his dish in the sink. "I have news."

"Oh?"

He turns to face Nick, his hands gripping the edge of the sink behind him. "I'm going to Washington with Bob Diamond," he says, naming the *Chronicle*'s Washington correspondent. "Next weekend there's going to be a march for school integration. Dr. King is going to speak."

This, Nick guesses, is Andy's father's attempt to get Andy experience covering national news. It makes sense. It also means that Andy's time at the city desk is probably coming to an end.

But it's good news for Andy, and Nick tries to sound like he's happy about it.

"That's great," Nick says. "When are you going?"

"Tomorrow morning." Andy is resolutely looking at some spot just beyond Nick's ear.

"Tomorrow?" Nick frowns. "And the march is next weekend?"

"This way I can get the lay of the land beforehand."

Probably this means that Andy is going to spend the week shadowing Bob or meeting other reporters. Still, though. He's leaving tomorrow and hasn't thought to mention it until now? That isn't like Andy. He hasn't even packed.

"What time do you need to wake up?" Nick has a sense that all airplanes leave at ungodly hours.

Andy looks away. "I'm not sure. I'll have to talk to my father."

"He didn't let you know? Or—wait—you didn't plan on going until now." That's fine. Andy is allowed to make spur-of-the-moment decisions. He doesn't need to explain his every move to Nick. There's no reason for Nick to be taking this personally, but he's doing it anyway.

"It's a good opportunity," Andy says, which answers none of Nick's questions. "They're expecting tens of thousands of marchers."

"I hope—I hope you—I hope it's good," Nick says stupidly.

"Yeah."

"I'm sorry I put pepper in the eggs," Nick blurts out, apologizing for the one thing he can apologize for without making everything worse. Andy's Presbyterian; he can barely handle a shake of black pepper and Nick knows better. "Do you want me to make you something else? A fried egg, maybe?"

Andy's expression softens, and it's only then that Nick realizes Andy's been looking—not annoyed, but agitated. Anxious. "No," Andy says. "I really wasn't hungry. The eggs were fine."

"Okay." Nick isn't convinced. Andy does the dishes—that's his job, because Nick cooks—and Nick takes a shower. He turns the tap until the water is as hot as he can stand it, then shampoos the hell out of his hair.

When he gets out, Andy is on the couch watching television.

"What're you watching?" Nick asks as he sits on the couch beside Andy.

"*Alfred Hitchcock Presents* is about to come on," Andy answers without turning his head.

Something isn't right. Andy is sitting upright, instead of turning to stick his feet under Nick's thigh or putting his legs over the arm of the sofa or otherwise abusing both the furniture and his spine.

"I really am sorry about the eggs," Nick says.

Andy clenches his jaw. "I told you that I don't care about the eggs. Can we just watch the show?"

Nick wants to say that no, they cannot watch the show, not when things are weird and Andy seems mad at him. But he isn't going to get anywhere by pestering Andy.

"You hate this show," Nick points out after about thirty seconds. Andy likes sitcoms and shows about dogs, not this creepy shit.

Andy rubs his temple. "But you like it. Watch the fucking show, Nick!"

Nick's heart is racing. That's maybe the second time he's ever heard Andy swear. What he needs to do is act normal and just wait this out. He can do that.

This episode is about a reporter who's investigating a wax museum. "How come we never get sent to report on haunted museums?" Nick asks. "Just crime scenes and fires and building collapses. Never a haunting."

"First of all, we don't know that it's haunted."

"Come on, why would you have a show about a non-haunted wax museum?"

"Second, I'm pretty sure that if you find a haunted museum in the tristate area, Jorgensen will let you stay overnight and—oh." They both stop talking as a wax figure comes to life.

"Never mind. I love crime scenes and fires and building collapses."

"Me too. They're the best."

By the time they go to bed, things are maybe normal? Or almost normal? Nick can't tell. He's too anxious to do anything but call out a hasty good-night and shut his bedroom door.

Nick wakes to an empty apartment. It's quiet. Peaceful, even, without Andy dropping cans of shaving cream and begging for more coffee.

Nick hates it.

He checks the sink and it's totally empty, not even a coffee cup in there, which means Andy somehow managed to leave the apartment without coffee and without waking Nick up.

Nick hates that, too. If Andy mentioned needing to wake up early, Nick would have gotten up along with him, would have put on a pot of coffee.

But that's probably the sort of thing Nick shouldn't do. He needs to try to be a normal friend, not an overly clingy basket case who tries to put the moves on his best friend.

It was smart for Andy to leave. Nick made things weird, and Andy got some distance so that when he returns, they can forget about it. This is Andy being smart about people, as usual. Nick tells himself that he ought to be grateful that Andy knows how to handle this gracefully.

He hasn't lost anything. He isn't any worse off than he was yesterday morning, and he tells himself this very sternly as he gets dressed. If he's disappointed, that's on him, not on Andy. His feelings are his own problem, and he has plenty of practice keeping his feelings to himself.

CHAPTER ELEVEN

On Tuesday morning, after Monday has come and gone without a word from Andy, Nick gets himself to the *Chronicle* offices early and does something he hasn't ever done before: he takes the elevator to the seventh floor.

The seventh floor is sandwiched between the bustle of the newsroom and the commotion of the top-floor composing room. It's where the *Chronicle* brass have their offices. Technically the managing editor's office is here, too, but Lou Epstein spends most of his day on his feet in the newsroom.

When the elevator doors open and Nick steps out, he's assaulted by the quiet. It's not the quiet of emptiness, like downstairs in the morgue files or the semi-abandoned fifth floor, but rather the quiet of a deliberate hush, and that flies in the face of everything Nick has ever experienced at a newspaper. Nobody is shouting for a copyboy or shouting at their editor or shouting at all, which is just disturbing. The carpet is about twice as thick as any carpet has a right to be and isn't littered with a single cigarette butt or pencil shaving. No phones are ringing. The handful of secretaries, stationed at desks outside their bosses' offices, are even typing quietly. It's unnerving. Nick can't imagine Andy up here, can't imagine Andy anywhere so quiet and sterile and slow.

Off to the side he spots a woman who's been pointed out to him before as Mr. Fleming's secretary. She's about fifty and looks like she could moonlight as a nun: hair scraped back, plain dark clothes, general air of not being interested in your bullshit. Nick unconsciously straightens his tie.

His theory is that Mr. Fleming's secretary will know what hotel Andy is staying at in Washington. He approaches her desk, unable to shake the sense that he's about to get a demerit or learn that he's failing chemistry.

"Good morning," he says, and at least his voice doesn't crack. "Do you happen to know which hotel Andy—which is to say, Mr. Fleming the, ah, younger, is staying at?"

She blinks at him, and Nick hadn't known a blink could contain that much disappointment. The nuns at Nick's elementary school could have learned a thing or two.

"Send him in," comes a deep voice from within the office.

Nick freezes.

She blinks again, and this time the blink means that Nick better hurry if he knows what's good for him. Nick hurries.

Inside the office, the carpet is somehow even softer than in the reception area. At a desk the approximate size of a cathedral door sits a man he's only seen a handful of times. Mr. Fleming seldom leaves the seventh floor.

"Good morning, Mr. Fleming," Nick says, trying to sound normal. In the New York newspaper business, Andrew Fleming is nothing short of a legend. He dragged the *Chronicle* out of tabloid sensationalism into something respectable, something like an institution, a paper that gets mentioned in the same breath as the *Trib* and the *Times*, not the *Daily News*. When Nick was a copyboy at the *Brooklyn Eagle*, seasoned reporters read Fleming's HUAC testimony aloud to one another.

In real life, he's a gray-haired man of about sixty-five with a lantern jaw and broad shoulders. He looks nothing like his son, but Nick already knew that—Andy takes after his mother.

"Mr. Russo, is it? Shut the door, will you?"

"Yes, sir."

"Please, take a seat." Mr. Fleming gestures at a pair of leather upholstered chairs. "We haven't met. I told Andy he ought to bring you up to meet me. So now that he isn't here, I can satisfy my curiosity."

Nick sits in one of the leather chairs. It's aggressively uncomfortable. He's a hundred percent positive that the secretary picked it out. "I'm happy to answer any questions you have."

Mr. Fleming raises his eyebrows the merest fraction. "I don't have any questions. I only wanted to meet you." He picks up the phone. "Evelyn. Will you bring in two cups of coffee, please?" When he puts the phone down, he glances up at Nick. "Actually, I do have one question. Is Andy coping well after the debacle with Miss Warburton?"

Nick doesn't know how to answer that. If Andy wanted his father to know, he'd already have told him himself.

"Because," Mr. Fleming goes on, "when I ask, he tells me he's doing fine. He says that after the initial shock he was disappointed, but that he wishes her the best."

Since that's almost exactly Nick's understanding of the situation, he decides that maybe he won't be giving anything away by confirming it. "That's what it looks like to me, too, sir."

Mr. Fleming looks relieved. Nick knows that Andy thinks his father is completely indifferent to him except as the *Chronicle*'s future publisher, but Nick isn't so sure of that. Still, Nick's the last person to tell someone what to think of their family, so he'll probably be keeping this opinion to himself.

"I've enjoyed that series you're writing about the missing police evidence. Has Stanley spoken to you about doing another series?"

It takes Nick a moment to realize that Stanley is Jorgensen. "Yes," Nick says, and is spared explaining that he hasn't even pitched an idea yet, because the secretary enters. She sets a tray on the desk, then disappears, closing the door silently behind her.

Mr. Fleming takes off his glasses and begins to clean them with his handkerchief. "What did you need to know from Evelyn this morning?" Mr. Fleming asks. He puts down his glasses for long enough to bring his cup of coffee to his mouth, and Nick notices that his hands are shaking—except, no, that isn't quite right. He realizes that what he's seeing is a tremor of the sort his nonna had, only worse. Andy never mentioned his father drinking, and the man he sees before him doesn't look like he's in the late stages of drinking himself to death, so Nick doesn't know what to think.

"Did I hear you ask about Andy's hotel?" Mr. Fleming continues.

"He didn't tell me where he's staying."

"If you have a message, I can make sure it's passed on to him," Mr. Fleming says smoothly enough that it takes Nick a moment to realize it's a refusal.

"Don't worry about it." He starts to get to his feet. "I'll see him when he gets back."

"Mr. Russo. Drink your coffee." Mr. Fleming's voice is mild, and in it Nick can hear echoes of Andy. But there's an edge in the older man's voice. Something that speaks of decades of hard decisions and disappointment. "My son called me at five o'clock yesterday morning asking for the first flight to Washington. I doubt *he* even knew what hotel he'd be staying at."

Now Nick is alarmed. "Someone met him at the airport, didn't they? Andy's plenty smart, you know that, but if he's left to navigate a strange city on his own, I don't like to think of what kind of hotel he'd find himself in."

Mr. Fleming stares at him. "A driver picked him up at the airport, Mr. Russo."

"Good," Nick says, relieved. He isn't going to ask where this driver took Andy. Andy will either get in touch with him or he won't. And even if he doesn't, they can talk when Andy gets home. He just needs time or space, hence the last-minute trip to Washington. Nick understands that.

He gets to his feet. "Thanks for the coffee, Mr. Fleming. And it was nice talking to you."

"Likewise, Mr. Russo. I'm glad you stopped by."

Dimly, Nick notices that Mr. Fleming doesn't get to his feet when Nick leaves, which is odd because he seems like the sort of man to stick by his manners even when obliquely accusing someone of having caused his son to flee the city before dawn.

When Andy's around, he and Nick either go out to lunch or sit together in the *Chronicle* cafeteria, usually joined by whatever junior reporters are having lunch at the same time. But without Andy, Nick feels like it's his first day at a new school, despite the fact that he's been working here for four years and Andy's only been here for one of them. The day before, he had lunch by himself at the Automat, but today he bites the bullet and goes to the cafeteria.

He gets a chicken salad sandwich (which makes him miss Andy, because he is *ridiculous*) and finds an empty table, thinking he'll scarf down his food and go back to work. But no sooner has he sat than Mark Bailey comes over and pulls out a chair across from him.

"Thought you might want some company," he remarks.

"What's that supposed to mean?" Nick asks, too defensive.

"Just that you're wandering around like a lost dog without Fleming."

Nick almost hisses at him to be quiet, but he hasn't really said anything too pointed. The fact is that Nick *is* kind of moping around and Bailey isn't the first person to notice. Everyone in the newsroom is giving him a wide berth, and Nick would be embarrassed if his brain weren't busy with about half a dozen other emotions.

"Am not," Nick mutters weakly, then crams his mouth full of chicken salad so he doesn't have to say anything else.

"There you are," says a woman's voice. Lilian Corcoran bends to kiss Bailey on the cheek then hitches up her trousers and sits beside Nick.

It doesn't escape him that the only two queer people he knows at the *Chronicle* have suddenly decided to have lunch with him. "What is this, a club?" Nick asks.

"If it were, we'd hardly even have a quorum," says Lilian. "Only three of us? Please."

Nick lets the ramifications of this sink in. Lilian knows of others? He doesn't know whether he's curious or panicked at the idea that there might be a secret network of gay reporters who have all found out about him.

"I haven't seen you in a dog's age," Lilian goes on. "You've turned down two consecutive dinner invitations and I'm starting to think you're mad at me. Maureen's feelings are hurt."

"I have Andy staying with me."

"What, he doesn't eat?"

"I couldn't bring him to dinner at your place," Nick says. This is blindingly obvious to him: he couldn't bring Andy to the one-bedroom apartment Lilian shares with another woman.

Lilian regards him for long enough that Nick has to look away. "I see that it's an advanced case," she finally says, either to Bailey or to nobody in particular. Nick refuses to ask what she means. Bailey takes a bite of his apple.

"If someone can't have dinner with Lilian and Maureen, they probably aren't a very good friend for you," Bailey observes mildly, apparently paying more attention to his apple than he is to Nick.

Nick bristles. "It's not that. I don't share other people's secrets."

"Who asked you to? We could have had a perfectly sane conversation. I ask you to dinner, you say, *Well, actually, Lilian, I have your future boss staying with me, and either I stay the hell away or I bring him along.*"

When she puts it like that, it sounds so easy, but what was even easier was refusing to think about it. He's always known that Lilian probably guessed that he's queer, but she never actually said so, just like she's never come right out and said that she's queer, either. He hasn't wanted to have that conversation. Even asking whether it was all right to invite Andy would bring the topic of their shared queerness uncomfortably close to the surface.

He doesn't want to be queer at work, which sounds asinine, but there it is. Everything is so much safer if he draws a line between those parts of his life. He honestly isn't even sure he would have told Andy if he hadn't found out himself.

But here are Lilian and Bailey, comfortably eating lunch and apparently not bothered in the least. Thinking back over the past few minutes, he realizes that the two of them are friends. Bailey knows about Maureen. He remembers the relief it was to be able to talk freely to Emily and briefly imagines being able to do that on a larger scale. It's preposterous—absurd.

"You see that Robert Moses is trying to shut down the Shakespeare Festival?" Lilian asks Bailey.

"You've got to be kidding."

"Maureen's fit to be tied. He says it's no good for the lawn."

"Jesus Christ," Bailey grumbles. "That fucker."

Nick doesn't care even slightly about any Shakespeare festivals, but complaining about Robert Moses is practically his favorite hobby. For a moment he feels a swell of fellow feeling for Bailey. It's terrible.

He must look friendly or something, because Bailey turns toward him. "Did you read that book yet?" Bailey asks.

"Which book?" Lilian asks.

"*The Charioteer*," Bailey says.

"No," Nick says with feeling.

"Oh, Nick, you ought to," Lilian says.

"What, you've read it, too?"

"We bought a copy in England when we went on vacation a few years ago. It's a darling book."

"Darling?" Nick repeats, because if there's any word to describe the books he's gotten from Bailey, *darling* sure isn't it. For all the shit Nick gives Bailey, he understands why Bailey likes these books, and he understands that the endings have to be miserable in order for publishers to agree to put the books out. But Nick's tired of dead queers. Nick's tired of people like him having to suffer in order to provide the right kind of ending. He's done his time with shame and doesn't want any more of it. "So it's not going to make me want to stick my finger in an outlet?"

Bailey and Lilian exchange a look that Nick can't translate. "No," Lilian says.

Nick still isn't reading it, but he shrugs, hoping to let the subject drop. And it does. The two of them move on to some play that they've seen and that Nick can't bring himself to care about. They share the usual workplace chatter involving people Nick knows peripherally, and he wonders if these names also belong to the club. He doesn't ask, of course.

But he wonders. If there really are so many queer reporters, then it's that much less remarkable for any one of them to be queer. Safety in numbers, maybe. And there's something more than that—there's the sense of commonality, like when he realized that Jimmy from accounts receivable was from Nick's old neighborhood in Flatbush. It's something like kinship, a concept that he finds himself reaching for despite it never having done him any good. But he wishes he were the sort of person who could give it a try.

Nick hasn't really given the apartment a good cleaning since Andy moved in a month earlier, so with nothing better to do with himself after work, he dusts and mops and tidies. He borrows a vacuum from Mrs. Wojcik downstairs and shakes the carpets out the window.

Andy's detritus is everywhere—books left facedown all over the apartment, a mostly empty coffee cup on the bookshelf, ties draped across the furniture. He finds Andy's glasses—missing for over a week—on top of the *E* volume of the 1938 *Encyclopedia Britannica* that Nick bought secondhand. Nick has never known a grown man as careless with his belongings as Andy, but now these objects at least serve as solid proof that Andy lives here and will come back.

When he's done, the apartment smells like an unholy mixture of pine needles and lemon peel, so he throws the windows open. The idiot orange cat is sitting on the fire escape, so he scoops the animal up and brings him in. He doesn't feel like carrying him downstairs, so instead he opens a can of tuna fish and puts it on the floor, then watches the cat scream bloody murder at the can before realizing that it's food. Even the company of the world's least competent cat is better than no company at all.

Finally he sits on the couch and begins to go through the magazines that have accumulated. He quickly realizes that he can't throw any out, because Andy likes to tell himself he'll get around to reading them. But nobody has ever had enough time to read all the magazines Andy subscribes to. There's *Sports Illustrated*, *The New Yorker*, *Esquire*, *Time*, *Life*, and the *New Republic* and some others he picks up at the newsstand. Andy reads fast, but nobody reads *that* fast.

Tucked between two issues of *National Geographic* is a copy of the *Village Voice* dating from a few weeks back. That's got to be safe to throw out. But then he sees that Andy has dog-eared a page. Curious, he opens the paper and immediately flinches at the headline: "Revolt of the Homosexual." When he scans the article, words and phrases jump out at him: *platinum-haired freaks, perverse, pathological.* His gaze catches on the odd slur here and there. Seeing that language in print, instead of hurled at strangers in the street, muttered disapprovingly everywhere else, is a punch in the gut.

More from habit than anything else, he goes back to the top and forces himself to read the article through. This time it's a different set of phrases that stick with him: *We no longer have the energy to hide. You can't know the strain on a person in always pretending.* How many times has he thought something like that? He had a similar thought only yesterday, sitting with Mark Bailey and Lilian at lunch.

Every now and then he thinks that maybe it would be easier to tell the world, even though it would mean throwing away safety and saying goodbye to the life he's worked so hard for. He's always thought that this feeling is in the same category as standing at the top of a tall building and wondering what it would be like to jump off, a fleeting impulse of pure self-destruction that doesn't really amount to anything.

His breath catches when he gets to the queer person's response to being called *miserable* and *unworthy to live*: *We've finally rebelled against feeling this way because our human nature can no longer stand it.* If every queer person starts out feeling defective and ashamed, how many ever find a way to stop? He knows that for him, the trick was to get away from the people who would have thought he was repellent if they knew the truth—or at least the people who would say so to his face. There's no real getting away from it.

But he's never thought of his refusal to be ashamed as a rebellion and he's never framed the harm done to him as discrimination. It seems obvious now, seeing it laid out like this.

Why had Andy dog-eared this page? It has to be because of this article rather than the ads for spaghetti joints and bowling alleys that march up and down the side columns. Had Andy meant to show the article to Nick? Had he wanted to contact the writer on *Chronicle* business?

Or had Andy read this article and seen himself in the same way that Nick does? A month ago Nick would have laughed at the idea, but at this point he doesn't have much doubt that Andy is attracted to him, at least a little, at least in theory. Even if Nick's come-ons had made him flee to Washington, even if nothing ever happens between them.

He wonders, does Andy think of himself as queer? Did he read this article and think of those words as belonging to him, as describing him? If something happened between him and Nick, would he consider himself queer? Plenty of men wouldn't. Plenty of men sort of hated the men they got off with or wanted to get off with. He wouldn't have thought Andy was like that, but people get themselves all tangled up over less important things every day.

He thinks about lunch yesterday with Mark and Lilian and that odd sense of belonging he could almost—but not quite— reach for. He thinks of Sunday lunches at his brother's house, of weddings and Christmases where he holds himself carefully aside, not even thinking about the truth.

He sticks the newspaper back where he found it and shoves the entire stack of magazines onto a shelf. Then he wraps up the cord of the vacuum and returns it to Mrs. Wojcik.

As he climbs back up the stairs, he can hear his phone ringing. He takes the steps two at a time and scrambles to unlock the door before missing the call.

"Hello?" he nearly shouts.

"Nick?"

At the sound of Andy's voice, any and all of Nick's cool evaporates. "Thank God it's you. I was honestly beginning to worry."

"Sorry, I just—"

"You don't have to explain. How's your hotel?" Nick asks, half because he wants to steer the conversation somewhere normal before it has a chance to go wrong, and half because he wants to be able to picture where Andy is.

"I'm at the Mayflower. Let me tell you, I'll be bringing this up at the next budget meeting. The Holiday Inn would have been just fine, but instead I have about six acres of blue velvet all to myself."

"It's nice, though?" he asks, because that's safe. And boring.

"I guess so. I mean, it definitely is. But it's quiet. I hate waking up someplace so quiet."

"I know," Nick says, because he does. "It's too quiet here, too." That's the closest he can get to telling Andy that he misses him—both because of the operator who might be listening in and because he doesn't trust himself to say it calmly. *I miss you* seems like the key to a door that he doesn't know if he ought to open.

There's more silence, and it occurs to Nick that what Andy probably wants is chatter, something to fill up the silence of his empty hotel room.

"I've never stayed at a hotel," Nick says. "Never been much of anywhere."

"Where have you been?"

"Went to Hackensack once."

Andy laughs—strained and thin, but it's still a laugh. "Come on, you must have been somewhere."

"Jersey City, a couple of times, to visit a cousin. Long Island, for a christening."

Nick doesn't usually feel like his life is small or parochial, but compared to Andy's, it really is. Not only has he hardly been anywhere, he can't even think of anywhere he'd particularly want to go. He lives in New York, for Christ's sake. People come *here* when they want to see things. But now, Andy all the way in Washington and Nick in his tiny apartment, Nick has a sense of a widening, fracturing gap.

"What's your hotel room like?" Nick asks, wanting to picture Andy, to feel like he isn't so far away.

"It's blue."

"That's it? Blue?"

"No, really. You've never seen so much blue. Blue carpet. Blue bedspread. Blue curtains. Blue sofa and chairs. The *lampshades* are blue."

"Where are you sitting?"

"On the floor next to the bed."

"That can't be comfortable."

"The carpet's like marshmallows. I'm never getting up."

There's something about Andy's voice that's careful. Not anxious—Nick's well aware of how Andy sounds when he's worried—but deliberate. It's like he's holding back. There usually isn't much of a delay between an idea popping into Andy's head and it coming right out of his mouth, but tonight he's checking himself. This is probably how he is in meetings.

Nick hates it. He knows Andy's just trying extra hard to make things safe and normal between them, but he hates the sense that their interactions have to be filtered. He's gotten used to Andy holding himself open like a book for Nick to read. He's gotten used to Andy wanting Nick to read him.

"When were you going to tell me that you were going to Washington?" Nick asks, reaching for something real, something that will force an honest answer—not about the thing neither of them wants to talk about, but honest in general. "I mean, I get that you left earlier than maybe you meant to, but when were you going to tell me?"

Andy laughs, staticky and abrupt over the phone. "As late as possible."

"Why?"

"I've been at the paper a year. I've already spent too long at the city desk. When I get back, there's an office on the seventh floor waiting for me."

Hearing Andy say those words aloud feels like a door slamming shut and it takes all Nick's effort to sound unworried. "I figured."

"You did?"

"I mean, we knew you weren't staying at the city desk. It was only supposed to get your feet wet, right?"

"Yeah, I guess," Andy says glumly.

This conversation has gone wrong, somehow, and Nick desperately wishes he could see Andy's face. "When are you coming back?"

"Sunday morning."

"I'll see you then. Wait, no. Dammit. I told my mom I'd visit her this Sunday."

"Do you want company?"

"Really?" What Nick actually should be asking is whether it's a good idea for them to see one another for the first time after all this in front of twenty elderly Italian immigrants, but he doesn't want to be presumptuous.

"Give me her address."

Nick does, and also reads out his mother's phone number. "Do you remember how to get there?"

"Not even slightly."

Nick tries to come up with a route that will give Andy at least a fighting chance of not getting lost. "Go to the Prince Street station. You remember where that is? You go to the Chinese restaurant Linda likes and you keep walking for two more blocks. Get on the train that says *Fourth Avenue*." From across the line, he hears the scratching of Andy's pencil.

"Got it."

"We'd better hang up before you have to explain a five-dollar long-distance call."

"Probably."

"Andy?"

"Yeah, Nick?"

"I'm really glad you called."

"Me too."

Nick sits on the floor, holding the phone long after the line goes dead.

CHAPTER TWELVE

Nick tries to look calm, because if his brother realizes how well he's succeeding in pissing Nick off, it'll only encourage the bastard. They're sitting on the back steps, side by side, so at least they don't have to look at one another.

"It'll toughen him up," says Michael. "He needs it. It toughened you up, after all." He lets out a crack of laughter. "You were such a crybaby, even worse than Sal."

Nick lights a cigarette and doesn't bother offering one to his brother. Maybe getting beaten up after school did toughen Nick up; he doesn't know. He does know that at some point he just stopped talking about it. They had all been living in that shoebox of an apartment in Flatbush and nobody was getting any sleep because Sal had colic. Nick getting beat up was small potatoes.

His mother was waking up at dawn to scrub floors at the hospital and he didn't want to bother her. Johnny, his middle brother, was already off at the seminary. And Michael was around, but he was married with a baby of his own and working godawful hours trying to support his wife, child, mother, and brother. His idea of dealing with Nick's complaints about getting beat up was to smack him around a bit himself. So, yeah, Nick learned to keep his mouth shut.

"You learned how to defend yourself," Michael goes on.

Maybe that's true, too. Nick can hold his own against most people in a fight. But Nick gained thirty pounds and six inches his first year of high school. That was why nobody tried to pick fights with him anymore, not because he was good with his fists. The same thing might happen to Sal, but looking at him now—all skinny arms and legs—Nick wouldn't put much money on it happening anytime soon.

"You're a cop. You could go to their house."

"Christ, Nicky. Sal would never live it down."

Nick hates that this is probably true. "You could give him a choice of whether he'd rather have his father embarrass him or his classmates hurt him. You could act like you don't think those kids are doing him a favor by beating him up."

"He needs to learn how to act."

A chill goes down Nick's spine. "What does that mean?"

"You know what it means."

"Humor me."

Michael leans in and lowers his voice. "He acts like such a limp-wristed little fairy. He has to quit it. If this is a lesson he needs to learn the hard way, so be it." He actually shrugs. "You of all people know that I'm right."

Nick ignores these last words. He can't—not now, he just can't deal with that. But the rest of it is almost verbatim what Michael used to tell him back when Nick was the one getting beaten up, except back then he hadn't said *fairy*. Nice to know Michael at least has some standards where his son is concerned.

He hates to see Sal go through what Nick went through himself—other kids trying to hurt him, the adults in his life unwilling or unable to help, and the sense that it's all somehow his own fault.

"Nicky! Telephone!" his mother calls.

"Me?" he asks stupidly, already getting to his feet. There's only one person who would be calling him at his mother's house. He makes it into the kitchen in two strides, not giving a fuck what Michael thinks about it.

"Nick?" asks Andy. Wherever he is, it sounds like a wind tunnel.

"Where are you?"

"Well. About that."

Nick closes his eyes. "You didn't get on the train that said *Fourth Avenue*, did you?"

"Perhaps not," Andy says, and Nick can picture the crooked half smile on Andy's face, the same expression he always gets when Nick tries to be stern.

"Where are you? I'll come get you."

"I seem to be at Coney Island."

Nick snorts. He's pretty sure he knows what Andy did: he managed to get to the right station, even managed to find the correct platform, but then got on the first Brooklyn-bound train that pulled up.

"Are you at the Stillwell Avenue station?"

"Maybe?" A pause, during which Nick bets Andy is leaning halfway out of the phone booth in search of signage. "Yes, that's right. Stillwell Avenue."

"I'll find you. I'll be there in twenty minutes, maybe half an hour."

"Ma," he says when he hangs up the phone. "Can I borrow the car?" His mother has an ancient Ford station wagon that she uses almost exclusively to go to church and the grocery store in the winter, but last he heard it's still running.

"Michael's parked behind me and I don't want to move the car. Ask Michael if you can borrow his."

Nick sighs, not wanting to ask a favor of his brother. But if Andy needs him, then that's that, so he steps back outside. "Can I use your car for an hour?" He doesn't add a *please* or try to sound polite, because he's fully reverted to being the petulant little brother.

"What for?"

"I have to pick up Andy."

Michael looks at him for a long moment, but finally reaches into his pocket and tosses him the keys.

When Nick drives past the subway station, he doesn't see Andy. Since it's only April and Coney Island is still relatively empty, he's able to find street parking, so he parks the car and goes off on foot.

He looks up and down Surf Avenue and Stillwell but still doesn't see Andy. He ought to have given Andy an intersection where they could meet, but he was too busy thinking of how badly he wanted to see him and how badly he wanted to get out of that house.

If he were Andy, where would he go? He'd get off the train, re-alize his mistake, find a pay phone, and—he'd probably still be by the pay phone. Nick enters the station and, sure enough, there's Andy, sitting on a bench near the token booth.

Nick stands there for a minute, unobserved. Andy has on a shirt and tie, which likely means he hasn't changed since get-ting off the plane. He must have taken a cab home, dropped off his suitcase, and gone directly to the subway. On his lap is a magazine—*Sports Illustrated*, if Nick has to guess. He looks tired. He ought to be home eating soup or catching up on sleep, but instead he's here because—

Well. He could be here because he doesn't like to be alone or because he likes Nick's mother's cooking. But at least Andy isn't actively avoiding him. Nick still doesn't know if they're going to have a conversation about what happened last weekend or if they're going to sweep it under the rug. The first prospect is terrifying and the second is depressing.

At that moment, Andy turns and sees him. He looks the same as he ever does, and Nick doesn't know why it surprises him. It's only been a week.

"Oh, that's not creepy at all," Andy says, getting to his feet and grinning. And blushing, because of course. "How long were you there?"

"Thirty seconds, jerk."

"Likely story. You probably drew a picture of me to put in your scrapbook."

There it is, that smile that splits the difference between smug and bashful. Nick wants to kiss it off his face. Some of that must show in his expression because Andy looks away, that smile still in place.

"What if I did?" Nick asks, feeling ridiculously bold. But he thinks Andy's flirting with him, or at least trying to, and Nick wants to make sure he doesn't let the ball drop. His heart's in his throat.

Andy's smile doesn't falter, exactly, but it melts a little, going soft at the edges as his eyes go wide.

"Let's walk over to Shatzkin's. I'll buy you a knish," Nick offers.

It's sunny, one of those clear April days that make you forget it could rain for a solid week at any moment. The breeze that comes in off the sea is cool, but nothing a jacket can't contend with. And the boardwalk is almost empty, nobody but a few people out for a stroll, a beat cop, and some seagulls fighting over the contents of a spilled garbage can.

The beautiful thing about Shatzkin's is that they have exactly one type of knish on the menu, so Andy is spared the ordeal of making a choice and the man behind the counter is spared a coronary. They take the knishes outside and find a bench at a comfortable distance from the marauding seagulls.

"How was the rally? What was it like?" Nick asks.

"There were thirty thousand people there, or close to it. Did you know that one of the organizers is gay? And a communist, apparently."

Hearing Andy say *gay*—which Nick only hears from other gay men—makes him feel like the bench has turned into a seesaw. "He's probably neither of those things. Every civil rights leader gets called a communist. Every communist gets called a queer."

"Well, he was arrested for vagrancy, and it was the sort of vagrancy that involved another man."

The knish has turned to lead in Nick's stomach. "And people just . . . *know*? They talk about it? He still has a job?"

"Apparently." Andy shrugs. "It's an open secret."

"Jesus." Being a . . . *known homosexual*, or whatever the parlance is, seems bad enough. Being Black on top of that—and one who's involved in a movement that's already greeted with violence at every turn—is something Nick can't imagine.

"You okay?" Andy asks, nudging him with an elbow.

"Yeah, yeah."

The frame of a roller coaster looms in front of them, disconcertingly fragile, silent and still in the off-season, birds squawking from the rails.

"I missed you." Nick feels shy saying it, even though it isn't even close to the sappiest thing he's said to Andy, or Andy to him. But now *I missed you* carries an extra weight that's new and a little unwieldy.

"Yeah?" Andy says it as if he's surprised, the idiot.

"I like it better when you're around." He tosses a bit of knish to a seagull.

"Good thing I'm around, then."

They don't have to have this conversation. They could eat their food, sit on the bench, and trust that they're good enough friends that they don't need to clear the air about what went wrong last Sunday.

Nick's already worn out from talking with his brother and it would be so easy to decide that he's done with emotions for the day. Christ, he usually goes months at a time without having to say anything heartfelt and the idea of doing it twice in one day makes him want to go back to bed.

But even though Andy is sitting just inches away from Nick on the bench, even though his posture is loose, his legs stretched in front of him and his face turned up toward the sun, Nick thinks he can detect a strain between them. Maybe it's all in his head— maybe Nick feels guilty and is seeing things that aren't there. But he doesn't want it to happen again, and the fact of the matter is that he'd rather have an unpleasant conversation than risk hurting Andy.

"I need to clear the air about what happened before you left," Nick says, because he's practiced that sentence in his head for days now. Immediately Andy tenses, but Nick pushes through. "Because I made you run away and I don't want you to do that again." He takes a breath, because this is only the beginning. He has to figure out how to apologize for trying it on with Andy without either revealing too much of what he's feeling or—even worse—making it seem like he thought it was a good idea to hit on his best friend just for fun. But he also wants to do this in a way that leaves the door open in case Andy might be interested in . . . something. He rubs the back of his neck.

But Andy speaks first. "I felt like you were toying with me."

"Toying with you?" Nick repeats, baffled.

"Teasing me," Andy says, an edge of frustration in his voice. "Letting me think I could have something I couldn't."

"I— What?" He can't make Andy's words fit into his understanding of what went wrong between them.

"God, Nick, don't make me spell it out. You know how bad I am at talking about this sort of thing."

Nick has no idea what's going on, but Andy's pleading with him and it doesn't matter what he's asking for; Nick will give it to him. "Okay," he says placatingly. "Okay." He keeps spinning the set of facts in front of him, as if looking at them from a different angle might reveal something that makes sense, but right now all he can see is that Andy thought Nick was . . . leading him on? There's no way out of this without brutal, mortifying honesty.

"I was testing the waters," Nick says, squeezing his eyes closed.

Andy is silent for a moment. "What does that mean?"

"I thought you might be interested. In, um. Well."

"You thought I *might* be? Might?" Andy's voice raises to an almost shrill urgency. "I *told* you I was interested."

"Wait, what?" Nick opens his eyes and looks at Andy. Andy isn't looking at him, just staring straight ahead.

"That night outside the bar! I told you I *wanted*—" Andy breaks off and Nick can almost hear the unspoken *you*, unbelievable as it is.

"But when you said that, I—"

"You thought you knew better." Andy is pissed now, his food abandoned, his fists clenched in his lap. "You assumed I didn't know what I was talking about or that I was confused. You didn't believe me! And kept on not believing me for weeks, apparently! And *then*, right when I get used to the fact that you don't think of me that way, out of nowhere, you start making googly eyes at me! What was I supposed to think?"

Nick wants to protest that it would have been both delusional and dangerous for him to accept Andy's words at face value, that doing so would have meant taking the feelings that he keeps packed away in a safe corner of his heart and putting them out there for anyone to trample on. Nick tries hard not to think too much about that sad little parcel of emotion. The idea of anyone else seeing it, of Andy seeing it, makes him feel almost sick.

But here Andy is, laying himself bare, and Nick isn't sure he's ever seen anything so brave in his life. This is a man who plays it safe, a man who orders the same sandwich every day for lunch. And now he's taking a risk, and he's taking it for Nick.

"And so you thought I was teasing you?" Nick asks. "I wouldn't." Whatever direction the rest of this conversation takes, he needs Andy to know that first.

Andy looks at him, his expression softening a little around the anger. "I mean, once I got to Washington and had time to think, I knew you'd never hurt me on purpose. I just didn't understand what was going on. I couldn't actually believe . . ."

Andy looks away, his cheeks pink, and when he looks back at Nick, it's shy, almost embarrassed. His hand is resting on the bench now, six inches of green painted wood away from Nick's own. Nick desperately wants to reach over, but they're too exposed. His heart is beating so hard, he can barely hear the waves breaking on the shore, the cry of the seagulls, the distant hum of traffic.

"But, Nick, do you have any idea how rare it is that I actually know what I want? That I have any actual clarity?" Andy smooths out the fabric of his pants and Nick sees that his nails are bitten to the quick. "I go to law school because it seems like a good enough way to kill time, then I drop out of law school because it turns out I was wrong. I go to business school because I have to do something, and then I drop out because I'd rather eat my *foot* than spend another day doing *that*. I thought I wanted to get married, so I got engaged, but then when that ended, I wasn't even awfully sad, so maybe I didn't want that? I have no idea! I've been drifting, and—anyway, the one thing I do know is that I want to be with you." He takes a deep breath. "And you didn't believe me."

At some point during the last minute or so, Andy's anger has shifted into something else—determination, maybe. Nick knows what Andy looks like when he's indecisive, when he's filled with self-doubt, and this isn't it. There's a force underlying his words, a force Nick isn't used to seeing in his friend. The fact that this force is all for Nick isn't something he can begin to understand.

"I don't know how to do this," Nick says. "I've never—with a friend." The fact that he can't even get a verb into that sentence can't be a good sign.

"We don't have to! God!"

"I want to!" The words feel ripped out of him. "I want to. It's not a . . . new thing. Not for me." He doesn't know how to say that he's been crazy about Andy for the better part of a year; he doesn't even know if he wants to. He doesn't know whether he ought to explain that what he wants goes beyond sex and into places he doesn't even feel comfortable thinking about. Maybe that can all wait, though; maybe he can get through this bit by bit.

Andy goes still. "Yeah?" His voice cracks a little on that single syllable.

"Yes." Nick wishes there were a better word than *yes,* but even if there were, he isn't sure he'd have the guts to say it. "Fuck yes," he adds.

Nick musters up some courage and turns his head and finds that Andy's already looking at him, his face a little pink.

"Okay," Andy finally says, a bit like he's soothing a scared animal. "Okay."

Nick clenches his fist around the crumbled paper bag his knish came in. "Does it mean—do you want—shit. I don't— Why are we having this conversation in public, for fuck's sake?"

"What would you do if we weren't?"

Christ, what wouldn't he do. "I'd try to—" His gaze drops to Andy's lips, pink and a little parted.

"Would you try to do that thing with your eyeballs again?" Andy asks. "Because that's a dealbreaker."

Nick lets out a startled burst of laughter. "Oh fuck off. I hate you."

"No, you don't," Andy says in a singsong voice. "You really don't," he adds, sounding awfully smug. Nick makes himself look away.

In an effort to avoid Michael, they walk straight around the outside of the house to the backyard and play bocce with the old men. Conversation is minimal. They roll the ball, they drink some beer, and it's probably the best half hour Nick has ever spent at this house. Even dinner passes without much grief. He makes it through the usual questions about girlfriends and settling down, and manages not to look at Andy while he does so.

Andy gets abducted by the aunts again while Nick washes

dishes, and when Nick finally dries his hands on the dishrag, he finds Andy and his mother talking on the other side of the room. He can't overhear what they're saying and kind of wishes he could, because Andy's nodding along as Nick's mother delivers what seems to be a monologue. Next to Andy, his mother seems old. She *is* old, Nick knows, and he feels like an asshole for not visiting more often.

Andy must notice him watching, because he flicks a glance over Nick's mother's shoulder, a half smile and a raised eyebrow: *You okay?* Nick looks pointedly at the door: *Time to leave.*

When they're saying their goodbyes, his mother corners Nick in the kitchen. "You're getting skinny. Take some leftovers."

Nick isn't getting skinny. "I can cook, Mama."

"But do you?" She turns to Andy. "Does he?"

"Not as well as you," says Andy, diplomatically.

"You'll take the sauce."

"No, Mama. I don't need any sauce."

"You can boil pasta, can't you?" Again, she turns to Andy. "Can't he?"

"Yes," says Andy, with the look of a man who very much hopes he's giving the right answer.

"Then you'll take the sauce," she tells Nick, as if this settles things. "Otherwise it'll go to waste."

"Send it home with Mr. Esposito." Mr. Esposito is a widower and therefore regarded by the entire neighborhood as in danger of imminent starvation.

"He doesn't appreciate good things." She turns back to Andy. "I know! You take the sauce."

It isn't until they're on the subway, Andy holding a quart jar of Bolognese like it's a newborn baby, that Nick realizes that the sauce was his mother's ploy to figure out whether Andy is still living with Nick.

He tries to tell himself it's funny, that his mother is harmless. The fact of Andy living with him wouldn't even matter if Nick hadn't been so secretive about it in the first place, if he had just come out and told her at the beginning. But he had reacted with an instinctive if misguided sense of protectiveness over Andy, and now it's too late. He tells himself that it probably wouldn't even occur to her to mention his living arrangements to Michael. That even if she does, Michael won't jump to conclusions. That even if Michael does jump to conclusions, he won't tell their mother or use his pals on the force to make Nick's life hard.

And with Andy sitting beside him, cradling a stupid jar of sauce, occasionally flicking pleased, shy glances in his direction, he's almost prepared to believe good things, however far-fetched.

CHAPTER THIRTEEN

Nick goes straight to the icebox to make room for the jar of sauce. "Where does she even get jars this size?" he grumbles. "And how are we supposed to eat it all before it spoils?" He shoves aside a carton of eggs and leftover pizza and pushes the sauce to the back.

When he turns around, Andy is there, his hands in his pockets. He's loosened his tie and undone his top button. "So," he says.

"So," Nick agrees.

All day they've carefully preserved a few inches of space between them, but now Andy is close enough that Nick can see the pale tips of his eyelashes.

He doesn't know how to do this. All his experience is fast and furtive, either anonymous or near to it. He doesn't know how to translate that to this. He doesn't know how to exist in the space between mutually acknowledged interest and acting on that interest. They should already be kissing—fuck that, they should already be in bed—and instead Nick turns around and starts organizing the top shelf of his refrigerator, sliding a stick of butter to the right and a jar of mayonnaise to the left as if he's going to get an award for having all the condiments at right angles to one another.

He hears Andy huff a laugh behind him.

The fact is that he doesn't have any experience at all in whatever this is. He doesn't know how to make a move on his best friend. He doesn't even know if he *should* make a move. Is that even what Andy wants? Maybe he wants to go slower. Maybe he's nervous. Andy gets nervous, right? Nick is pretty nervous, too, now that he thinks about it.

"I have laundry to fold," he announces, and marches down the hall to his bedroom, where indeed he has a pile of laundry sitting on his bed. Yesterday he had gone to the laundromat instead of doing what he usually does, which is spend a stupid amount of money sending his laundry out. It turns out that no price is too steep if it means he doesn't have to fold his own clothes.

He stares at the mountain of laundry. Some of it's Andy's, since they've been piling their clothes in the same hamper since he moved in. "I have some of your clothes," Nick calls out, unnecessarily loud considering that Andy is leaning in the doorway, regarding him with an amused expression.

"So you do," Andy says. "Want me to come in and get them?"

That shouldn't be a difficult question, should it? But Nick doesn't know the answer. "Sure?" he manages.

They stand on opposite sides of the bed, sorting the wrinkled heap of clothes. Nick passes Andy a sock that definitely isn't Nick's. Andy passes Nick an undershirt. This is the opposite of seduction. If Nick quits the *Chronicle* and instead devotes his life to seeking out the least seductive activity, he'll never find anything worse than folding laundry.

Not that Andy is folding anything. He's just gathering everything under his arm in a ball.

"You aren't going to fold that?"

"Definitely wasn't planning on it."

"The ladies at the laundry place always fold it."

Andy raises an eyebrow. "The ladies at the laundry place aren't here to judge me."

"What are you going to do, shove it all in a drawer?"

"Got it in one."

"Barbarian."

"Set yourself free, Nicky. You don't need to fold your underpants."

Nick's face heats. Like a goddamn twelve-year-old, he's blushing because a boy mentioned his underpants. "I don't fold my underpants," he grumbles.

"No, the ladies at the laundry place do."

Andy crosses to Nick's side, dumping his crumpled ball of laundry onto the bed. Nick can't bring himself to look at him, but out of the corner of his eye he sees Andy lift a hand, and then he feels Andy touch his shoulder before skimming his palm down Nick's sleeve and taking Nick's hand.

"C'mere," he says, tugging Nick to face him. "You're so nervous."

"Am not."

"You could at least look at me."

Nick does. He flicks a glance at Andy and sees that his cheeks are a bit pink and that he's biting his lip. "I can't," Nick says. "I literally cannot look at you." He has the urge to close his eyes to hide from whatever is making his heart thud stupidly in his chest.

With his free hand, Andy touches Nick's face, gently nudging him so he has to turn his head. "I've been wanting to do this." His voice is little more than a whisper.

"Do what?" Nick asks, as if the answer isn't obvious.

Nick can't understand why he's so overwhelmed. He isn't new at this. Not by a long shot. He isn't even new to *Andy* touching him.

"You look like you expect me to pull out a switchblade at any moment," Andy says.

"Sorry."

"Are you sure you've done this before?" Andy teases.

"Not this." Nick swallows. "Nothing like this."

Andy frowns and looks at him carefully. A little too carefully. Nick is being too serious and he's ruining the mood. If there even is a mood, which Nick doubts.

"If I hug you, are you going to pass out?"

Nick brings a hand up to cover his eyes. "You're the worst."

"It's against all the rules for you to be the worried one, Nick. Come here." Andy steps closer and puts his arms around Nick's neck. Nick lets his hands settle on Andy's back, their chests flush together. He breathes in the unfamiliar scent of Andy's hair. He must have used different shampoo at the hotel. Nick wants to put him in the shower and scrub him down, and just the thought of *that* scenario is more than his mind can handle.

Or, well, more than his dick can handle, because it's hard and pressing into Andy's stomach.

"Sorry," Nick says.

"Shut up. Shut up shut up shut *up*." Andy turns his head, pressing his face into Nick's neck, and Nick can feel his breath, warm on his skin. "I want this. Do you?"

"Jesus Christ."

"That's not an answer."

"Yes."

"You always smell so good." As Andy speaks, his lips brush against Nick's throat, and Nick wants to groan. Andy's mouth is moving now, up and over, toward Nick's mouth.

When he finally slides his lips over Nick's, Nick involuntarily grips Andy's shirt.

"Hi, Nick," Andy says, and Nick can feel the smile against his mouth.

"Hi yourself," Nick mumbles, and he pulls Andy closer. He feels the wiry muscles of Andy's arms tighten around him at the same time Nick opens his mouth, just a little. Andy's hands go up to cradle Nick's face, cool against the flaming heat of Nick's cheeks.

They're pressed together now, chest to chest, no space between them, but Nick wants more, so he backs Andy up against the wall and presses him there.

"Oh shit," Andy gasps. He's hard now, too (*Thank God, thank God*, whispers the part of his brain that still needs reassurances), and Nick lets out a groan at the feel of him.

"Stop?"

"God no, don't stop." Andy twists them around so it's Nick's back against the wall, which is not a position he's ever spent much time in, but with Andy it's fine. Andy can shove him into however many walls he pleases.

"You want this," Nick says, his lips moving against Andy's. "You really do."

Andy pulls back, just enough to give Nick a severely unimpressed look. "I told you."

"I know, I know. You know what—" Here, Nick swears that he means to say *You know what you want*, but what comes out is "You know what gets your dick hard."

"Nick," Andy says, half laughing, but with this shuddering little rasp in his voice that makes Nick glad he has the wall to prop him up.

Andy moves one hand so it's braced on the wall beside Nick's head and the other goes to Nick's throat. He presses a kiss to the divot of Nick's collarbone. "You have no idea," Andy murmurs.

Nick isn't thinking clearly enough to understand what Andy's talking about, so he dips his head for another kiss. He bites Andy's lower lip and Andy makes a broken sound that goes like lightning through Nick's body. He wants all these clothes gone. Clothes are such bullshit, it turns out. He untucks Andy's shirt and pushes up his undershirt and gets a hand on his lower back, seeking out skin.

"Wait," Andy pants. "Hold up." But he doesn't move—he still has Nick pressed against the wall.

Nick drops his hands. "You okay?"

Andy leans back and looks at Nick, his cheeks flushed and his eyes a little wild. He looks slightly deranged, and all Nick can think is that at least he isn't the only one. "Time out."

Nick can do that. He can do a time-out. He doesn't know why they'd want to, but it doesn't matter. "Okay," he says. Tentatively, not sure if this is against whatever rules exist between them now, he puts a hand on Andy's hip. Andy drops his head to Nick's shoulder and sighs, his breath hot on Nick's neck.

"I think I'm probably very bad at sex," Andy blurts out, his words muffled against Nick's collar.

"How good do you think you need to be?" Nick asks, faintly stunned. "I was going to come in about two more minutes of that, so you can't be that bad."

Andy whines. "You know how I am with new things. Remember that first time we went bowling?"

"Gay sex doesn't have so much in common with bowling. You'd be surprised."

Andy swats Nick's head. Nick wants to tell him that he'll be careful and patient, wants to tell him that they'll figure this out together, that maybe that'll be half the fun. But he knows Andy, and knows Andy won't believe a single word of it. So he pokes Andy's shoulder. "Afraid you'll sprain your ankle?"

Andy coughs out a startled laugh. "Oh fuck off."

Nick takes Andy's hand, looks deep into his eyes, and says, "Afraid you'll slip on a banana peel?"

"Oh my God, please go to hell."

Andy is fighting back a smile, and even though Nick knows he hasn't exactly set Andy's mind at ease, he thinks he's done some good.

After that, the rest of the day should have been awkward, Nick is sure of it. Instead Andy makes coffee ("I know it's four o'clock, Nick, shut *up*") while listening to the tail end of a baseball game on the radio. Nick irons his shirts, cursing his decision not to have them sent out. It's so normal, it's almost anticlimactic.

But when Andy has to squeeze past Nick to get to the radio, he puts a hand on Nick's waist and lets it linger there. Nick nearly drops the iron. And then when Nick walks past where Andy sits on the couch, he bends down and kisses the top of Andy's head.

Andy doesn't even blush, the fucker.

"How are you so calm about this?" Nick asks. "I once saw you almost hyperventilate when the supermarket was out of your favorite brand of applesauce. But having a gay affair doesn't even ruffle your feathers?"

Andy snorts. "A gay affair. I mean, when you put it like that, it sounds alarming."

Before Nick can ask what on earth he'd call it instead, Andy goes on. "Besides, I'm not calm at all. It's just that you're clearly about to lose your marbles and there really can be only one crazy person at a time here."

Nick opens his mouth to deny it, but Andy is right. "Fair."

"What has you so agitated, anyway? I know you're, um, experienced."

Nick aggressively irons a wrinkle out of his shirt. "You're not some guy I picked up in the park and took home to fuck over the back of the couch."

Andy stares, his mouth slightly open, his eyes unfocused, as if he's picturing that. And excellent work, Nick. Great job coming up with a scenario that will put Andy right off the idea of sex.

"This couch?" Andy asks eventually. He looks accusingly at it, as if it's made a lot of mistakes in its life.

"Usually their couch, actually."

"Hmm." Andy swallows. "I'm not sure I'm game for that. At least not at the moment."

Nick can't look at him. He becomes fascinated by the cuff of his shirt, which he's ironed about fifty times in the last five minutes. "God. I wasn't going to suggest it. Give me some credit."

Andy goes back to listening to the game and Nick resumes ironing his shirt, thinking the conversation is done.

When the game is over, Andy flicks off the radio and wanders over to the bookcase. He does that all the time, taking a book out and examining the cover, flipping through a few pages and leaving it in some insane place, then reading a magazine or a detective story, so Nick only pays attention to him out of the corner of his eye.

But then he sees Andy's hand on a familiar blue book.

"This is the book Mark Bailey gave you," Andy says.

"It is," Nick says, hoping he sounds normal, then realizing that he never mentioned that it was Bailey who gave him the book. Nick probably should have realized Andy would figure out who it was, and now he feels guilty in addition to all the other useless things he's feeling.

Andy curls up in the corner of the couch and begins to read. Nick's palms are too damp with sweat to hold the iron, so he unplugs it. Burning the building down won't help anything.

Watching Andy with that book is like watching a kid play too close to traffic.

He doesn't want Andy to feel like what they're doing—like what they're on the verge of doing—is shameful or tragic. Which is probably ridiculous, because Andy is a grown man who knows real from make-believe, and Nick can't really go over there and snatch the book from his friend's hand.

That night, they sit down to watch *Alfred Hitchcock Presents*, each in their usual spot on the couch, a solid two feet between them.

But when Nick rests his arm along the back of the couch, Andy slides over a bit. Nick meets him in the middle, and then he has his arm around Andy, his palm cupping Andy's shoulder, his thumb close enough to Andy's collar that he can't stop thinking about it.

He's had his arm around other people, for fuck's sake. He's not a total stranger to affection and he doesn't know why every time he touches Andy today he feels raw, exposed.

By the time the show is over, Andy has his head on Nick's shoulder and Nick's hand is on Andy's waist, the soft cotton of Andy's shirt doing nothing to keep Nick's mind from the warmth of the skin beneath. Ordinarily, this is the point in the evening when they'd turn the television off, but there's no way he's leaving this couch unless the building is literally on fire. Andy is apparently of the same mind, because they both decide to act very interested in the detective show that airs next.

Nick slides his hand under Andy's shirt and hears Andy's breath hitch. He feels the smooth skin of Andy's waist, then spans his hand over his stomach. He keeps his movements slow, both to give Andy time to decide whether he likes it, and because he wants to enjoy the feeling of Andy pressed against him, warm and soft and a little uncertain. He doesn't move his hand lower than the waistband of Andy's pajama pants. Andy has one hand resting lightly on Nick's thigh, a little too high to be accidental, and occasionally strokes a fingertip over the inseam of Nick's trousers.

By the first commercial, Nick is hard, and Andy must be able to tell. It's taking a lot of effort not to move, not to search out some friction. When Andy sits up and pulls away, Nick almost whimpers, but then Andy swings a leg over Nick's lap and kisses him.

And oh *God*, the weight of him, the way his kisses are almost careful, the smell of his hair—Nick tries to sear these details into his memory, tries to map out every bone and muscle under the warm expanse of Andy's skin. He lets himself get lost in the heat of Andy's mouth, and somewhere at the back of his mind he realizes that Andy's taken over the kiss, that he's pressing Nick back against the couch cushions. Nick can feel the hard length of him against his stomach and groans. Andy gasps.

"This feel okay?" Nick asks.

"Yeah. Feels good."

"Me too. Why did you think you'd be bad at this?"

"I said I'd be bad at sex. This isn't sex."

"If you touched my dick, it would be in about three seconds."

Andy laughs, but then his expression sobers. "Is that what you want me to do?"

On the one hand, yes, definitely, Nick wants that very much. On the other, Andy looks . . . not exactly skittish, but not confident, either. He looks exactly the way he does when he realizes he's forgotten his keys or lost another handkerchief. Andy has always been shy, downright prudish, when it comes to talking about sex, so Nick doesn't think that his hesitancy has to do with Nick being a man, but rather with Andy being Andy.

"We can take it slow," Nick says. "We have time, right? I'm not going anywhere." He'll just beat off in the shower four times a day, no problem.

"Yeah," Andy says, and bends down for another kiss.

CHAPTER FOURTEEN

Nick is getting nothing done.

Nobody's at their best on Monday mornings, but Nick has never needed to be at his best to do what needs to get done. Maybe his focus has gone to the birds because he knows that outside it's a beautiful spring day. Or maybe it's because he only ate half his breakfast. Or maybe it's because Andy's lingering *looks* from across the table were why he hadn't bothered finishing his eggs in the first place.

They'd gone to sleep in their separate beds, a paper-thin wall between them. Then they'd woken up and gone through their usual morning routine in which Andy bumps into things and funnels coffee down his throat and Nick looks on and pretends not to be utterly, dementedly fond. Except—now he doesn't have to pretend. He will anyway, because he has *some* dignity, but now at least he can look his fill. When Andy came out of the shower with only a towel around his waist, Nick let himself notice the droplets of water that had collected at the center of his chest, the scattering of dark freckles over his shoulders. He could notice, and he could keep on noticing.

And now it's all he can think about. He's pretty sure he spends the half hour from ten to ten thirty sitting blankly at his desk and doing nothing but remembering how Andy bit Nick's lip the previous night. It's only the ringing of the phone that jolts him out of his reverie.

"Mr. Russo?" says the girl at the switchboard. "Phone call from a Mr. Hollenbeck."

Nick frowns, unable to remember which story involves anyone called Hollenbeck. "Thanks. You can put it through."

"Nick Russo here," he says after hearing the click.

"Dave Hollenbeck here from the *Journal-American*."

Nick sucks in a breath. Dave Hollenbeck is the *Journal*'s managing editor. "How can I help you, Mr. Hollenbeck?"

"I wonder if you'd meet me for lunch one day next week."

Nick doesn't ask why the managing editor of a rival newspaper wants to meet with him, because there's only one explanation, and it's that Andy hadn't been completely full of shit when he said that other papers were going to try to poach him.

He doesn't think that he wants to work for the *Journal-American*. What he wants is to keep working at the *Chronicle*, with his desk facing Andy's forever. But that's already impossible, with Andy upstairs and his old desk empty and uncluttered for the first time in a year, not so much as a gum wrapper in sight. Nick can hardly look at the thing.

He's never liked the idea of Andy being his boss. There's already a chasm between them, a pit filled with class and money and connections. Nick didn't like it even when they were ordinary friends; now that they're something else he really doesn't like it. He wouldn't want to be sleeping with someone much richer than he was; he really doesn't want to be sleeping with his boss.

Even entertaining the thought feels disloyal to Andy, but he doesn't think he's out of line in feeling the way he does. He's allowed to have his pride.

But there's something more, some small voice of reason that urges Nick toward self-preservation. There's going to be a time when Nick will want some distance from Andy. When this new thing between them comes to an end, he isn't going to want to run into Andy in the elevator. He sure as shit isn't going to want Andy's signature on his paycheck.

"We were thinking," says Hollenbeck, "that you might like a column. Maybe a bit more freedom to choose which stories you want to cover." And then he mentions a number that Nick at first thinks must be a mistake, a solid twenty percent higher than what he's making at the *Chronicle*.

Nick knows that the only reason other papers might want him is because they want to handicap the *Chronicle* by removing anything that might be a market advantage. Nick isn't *that* good.

There's no harm in hearing the man out, though. It's good to know what kind of opportunities are out there.

"Yes," Nick says. "I'd like that."

First thing Friday morning there's another fire in Gowanus. Jorgensen sends Nick to the crime scene. Ed Meyer has been covering this string of arsons, but he's stuck on Staten Island for some godforsaken reason and won't get to Brooklyn until noon, so Nick's on deck.

On his way out, he makes a detour to the seventh floor to let Andy know that he won't be around for lunch.

"I'll come along," says Andy, looking like Nick's bailed him out of jail. He springs out from behind his enormous new desk in his enormous new office.

Nick raises an eyebrow. Andy isn't even pretending not to hate his new job.

"Shut up," Andy mutters. "And put that eyebrow away."

It's raining when they get downstairs. The past few days were sunny and about as warm as April can get in New York, so this weather feels like a slap in the face, a lesson that nobody should get too comfortable.

Andy opens his umbrella and sighs. "I'm betting that if I suggest a cab, you're going to laugh in my face."

"No cabs in weather like this. Besides, the subway will get us there twice as fast." Nick turns up the collar of his coat and makes for the subway entrance.

The subway station is wet and muggy, with filthy-looking puddles littering the floor and drips coming from improbable places on the ceiling. It's the sort of day when nobody even looks at one another. It feels like everyone's mood is brittle, liable to snap at the slightest provocation.

When the train arrives, the car is half empty, so they keep a seat's worth of space between them. That empty eighteen inches of rattan is taunting Nick, as bad as the suddenly shitty weather or everyone's shitty mood or the shitty arsonist. Nick *hates* that empty seat. It feels unnatural to go from touching someone constantly every evening to acting like touching that person is the furthest thing from his mind.

Every night that week, they've fooled around—kissing, hands over the clothes, orgasms tacitly off the table. Nick has never done anything like it; he's never been with anyone without getting off being the mutual and immediate goal. But Andy seems to have done plenty of it. He has this way of slowing down once things get too heated: he pulls back a few inches, puts his hands someplace respectable, makes his kisses shallow and soft, so that by the time they separate Nick isn't even too frustrated.

After all that, they go to sleep in their separate beds. When they wake up, they go through their regular morning routine, except with approximately five thousand percent more touching: a hand on the other's back when passing in the bathroom, a kiss on the crown of the head when handing over a cup of coffee. Mostly chaste, sweet touches that Nick wants to hold in his hands and store someplace safe.

And then they leave the apartment and turn all that off like a switch. Which is fine. Everybody does that. Nobody gropes one another on the street. Except Nick feels too aware of Andy's presence a few feet away. It's all he can think about; he doesn't dare turn his head because he's afraid that everyone on the train will know exactly what he's thinking. He's more careful about preserving space between them and keeping his hands to himself than he'd even be with a stranger.

The address Jorgensen gave them is just over the river, close enough to the subway station that they don't even get soaked, at least not too badly. The fire's out by the time they get there. A fire engine is blocking the street, along with a handful of police cars. A river of dirty brown water flows down the street, carrying ash and debris and a nameless sludge. And the house—it's in one piece, at least. Probably it'll be condemned. If it's the same arsonist as the other fires, the stairwell will have been soaked in gasoline. Not much you can do with a building after that, other than tear it down.

Nick's been at this long enough that the faces of the people outside shouldn't startle him. Some of them have coats and hats. But—a girl in her pajamas. A boy holding a squirming dog. A pair of old women in housecoats and curlers.

Who the fuck burns a building down? Logically, Nick knows the answer: nine times out of ten, the arsonist is a landlord looking to get some insurance money. But the last few fires in this neighborhood don't fit that profile—the buildings were good investments and the landlords are pissed to be out a source of income. Sometimes kids torch an empty building—it's stupid and dangerous, but that's kids for you—but these buildings have all been inhabited and in busy neighborhoods. So: a firebug.

The residents don't want to talk to Nick, no surprise there. Nick would probably punch anyone in the face who tried to bother him if he were in their shoes. The firemen, smoke-smeared and waterlogged, keep their mouths shut. The fire captain and police will give a press briefing later on; that's standard.

Nick jots down what he sees, hanging around the smoldering mess with a clutch of other reporters. The rain picks up, and Andy adjusts his umbrella so that it covers about two-thirds of each of them, leaving just enough exposed that they'll both be a soggy mess by the time this is done.

He's been at this long enough that he recognizes a few of the reporters. That's Louise Ramirez from the *Daily News* in the rumpled trench coat—she was doing rewrites at the *Eagle* when he was a copyboy. And in the sharp hat, that's Len Brewer from the *Amsterdam News*. He doesn't recognize the man with the haircut like Andy's but would put money on his being somebody from the *Tribune*. Nick mimes tipping his nonexistent hat at Jim and when he catches Louise's eye, she mimes drinking. He nods—they're due for a catch-up.

Andy already has his notebook out and is jotting something

down. A year shouldn't be enough to make someone a compe
tent reporter, but Andy can hold his own. As publisher, he won't
alienate his reporters. For the first time, it occurs to Nick that he
might not be one of the people who work for Andy, that he might
be watching it all happen from a distance.

He drags his attention back to the crowd of bedraggled people
huddled under too few umbrellas on the sidewalk. Maybe he'll
offer to buy lunch for that pair of old women, slip them his business card if they feel like talking later on. He's glad he doesn't
usually report on fires; they're bad enough when they're in empty
warehouses. The smell of smoke and—yep, that's gasoline—is
thick in the air.

A uniformed officer emerges from a car, the door slamming
behind him with enough noise to draw everyone's attention. He
looks at the gathering throng of reporters with a little surprise and
a lot of disgust, his eyes scanning the crowd. Then he stops scanning and looks at Nick.

Nick has the feeling of time stopping, of the ground shifting
under his feet until he's in a different part of Brooklyn, skinnier
and reckless, afraid of all the wrong things.

He's always known it's a possibility, that he could run into a
cop who recognizes him. He's been banking on the hope that a
nice enough suit and a respectable haircut make him look different at twenty-six than he had at eighteen. He's been counting on
what he now realizes is enough optimism and faith to found a
religion.

"You're Mike's brother," the cop says, actually smiling, like he's
meeting an old friend. "Michael Russo? I used to work with him
at the Sixty-Eighth. Nicholas, right? You're with some newspaper
now. I heard about that."

He could deny it. He can almost taste the words: *Sorry, you must be thinking of someone else.* But half the reporters here know Nick by name, and the last thing he needs is a reporter wondering why he lied about his name to a cop. "That's right," he says. "We're here from the *Chronicle* about any new leads in the arson cases."

"Can't help you with that, pal," the cop says, holding his hands up and stepping backward. "Tell Mikey that Jimmy Walsh says hi." Nick can't tell whether there's a threat in there, because right now everything feels like a threat.

Andy doesn't say anything, which at least gives Nick some time to stop feeling like he's about to throw up. Nick doesn't dare turn to look at him, but he can still tell that Andy's watching him carefully.

"Want to talk about it?" Andy asks after a few minutes.

He isn't going to lie to Andy. But he doesn't think he can tell the truth, either, not now, at least. Not here. He's supposed to be working, and he's never let the bullshit inside his brain or the garbage in his past get in the way of doing his job.

He's used to coping with a certain amount of anxiety always simmering on the back burner—the old familiar fear of cops materializing out of nowhere, like they had that one time. He doesn't even mind it—that steady hum of fear is a reminder to stay quiet, to keep to himself. It keeps him safe.

Except that's a delusion. He was never going to be safe. Something like this was always going to happen, and it'll happen again. And eventually it will all come back to hurt him.

This is the usual fear, but instead of it being in his head, it feels like it's in his whole body, in his heart and fingers and toes. Like fear is the only thing holding him together, the only thing that stops him from breaking down into his component parts and dissolving in the rain.

"I gotta get out of here," Nick says, urgent and low. "Can you handle this?" He pushes his notebook into Andy's hand. He can't believe he's doing this, can't believe he's walking away from work, and he doesn't like to think about what he'd do if Andy weren't around to cover for him.

Andy nods, doesn't ask whether Nick has suddenly lost his mind. "You don't look great. Do you need me to—"

"No," he says with enough force that Andy doesn't finish the question.

"Where will you go?"

Nick has no idea. Just . . . not anywhere near the police. "I'll see you later."

And he walks away.

Andy finds him at O'Connell's, two hours and four bourbons later.

"I filed the story," Andy says. "Told everyone you were under the weather."

Nick kicks out a chair for him. "Thanks." Nobody will believe that, of course. For one, Nick has never taken a sick day. For another, those are two of the *Chronicle* copy editors over at the bar.

Andy holds up a hand for the bartender and gestures that he wants a round of whatever Nick's having. "You want to tell me about it?"

Of course Nick doesn't. But he'll do it anyway.

When their drinks come, Nick drains his in two gulps. "I don't want to tell you."

Andy doesn't say anything. He slowly sips his drink.

Nick lights a pair of cigarettes and hands one to Andy. A

minute passes, then another. "I don't want to tell you," Nick repeats, a pitiful effort for someone whose job is literally stringing words together. He's being infantile and irrational. Andy's probably annoyed with him. He dares a glance at Andy, and what he sees in Andy's face isn't irritation, of course it isn't. It's pure undiluted concern and that's a hundred times worse.

"Nick." Just that one word, just his name, spoken gently and without reproach, and Nick is ready to cry for the first time in years.

He lowers his voice and makes himself look Andy in the eye. "I was arrested."

Andy's eyes widen. "Okay." He doesn't ask why. Doesn't ask when. The number of questions Andy isn't asking could probably fill a book.

"Vagrancy," Nick says. "With another man at the Navy Yard. I was eighteen. That cop today was the arresting officer." He's dimly aware that he's managed to produce a succinct and comprehensive lead paragraph.

Andy is silent for a moment. His fingers twitch on the tabletop, as if he wants to reach over and take Nick's hand. Instead he takes a drag from his cigarette. "What happened after you were arrested?"

"I was booked but never charged. They let me go home with my brother." He still isn't sure exactly what Michael did that night. Presumably some buddy of his had been convinced to lose the paperwork or forget what he saw.

"Your brother pulled strings," Andy guesses.

"I know it's not right." Here Nick is, making a name for himself in chasing down dirty cops and the only reason he has a job in the first place is because his brother didn't follow the rules.

Worst of all, he's grateful for it. He's indebted to his brother and he always will be.

Andy's glass hits the table with a thunk. "What isn't right is being arrested for what you did."

Nick makes a dismissive noise.

"Come on," Andy says, as serious as Nick's ever heard him. "You know that, right?"

"I got special treatment. I don't even have an arrest record."

"Good."

"It's corrupt."

"*Good.*"

Nick snorts. "So you're a fan of police corruption now."

Andy narrows his eyes. "You do realize that I have a horse in this race." He gestures idly between them. "I do not give one shit how or why or under what circumstances you got let off, because I care about you." He lowers his voice so Nick has to lean in to hear. "And I don't give one shit how or why *any* queer gets let off, and that's for a slew of reasons, not least because I'm one of them."

Hearing Andy say that about himself makes Nick want to disagree for some stupid reason, wants to tell him that he never has to worry about getting arrested at the Navy Yard. But even as those thoughts take shape in his mind, he recognizes them as bullshit. Sure, Andy's going to get married and get a dog and a couple of kids in the bargain, but right now he's spending his evenings kissing Nick on the couch, and that's as much against the law as anything any queer gets arrested for.

"Is that cop today going to make trouble for you?" Andy asks.

Nick hesitates. "I don't think so. He plays cards with my brother every Saturday night."

"You need to get off that police corruption story."

"What?"

"You can't make enemies of people who have dirt on you. Come on, Nick."

Nick's stubs out his cigarette with unnecessary force. He's not going to argue with Andy about this—not now, at least. But he's not dropping that damn story. He's worked his ass off to get to where he is, and that story is the best thing that's happened to his career.

Andy seems to understand enough to change the topic. "I thought you said your family doesn't know. About you, I mean."

Nick shakes his head. "I told my brother I was trying to steal that guy's wallet." He feels a hot wash of shame, both at the idea that stealing from that man was better than blowing him, and also at the memory of the look on his brother's face when he got Nick out of that jail cell.

"He believed you?"

Nick still isn't sure. "If he doesn't, at least he pretends to."

Andy finishes his drink. "I told my father that I'm missing the afternoon meeting because I'm coming down with whatever you have, so let's get out of here." He gets to his feet before Nick can argue that this is insane; Andy's been working too hard to blow off a meeting for no reason at all. But Andy is already moving toward the door. "We're going home," he says, low and decisive. "And we're taking a cab."

CHAPTER FIFTEEN

A ndy is furious. It's coming off him in waves. In the cab, every time Nick glances over, all he sees is the firm set of Andy's jaw, the clench of his fists.

"I'm sorry," Nick mutters.

"Don't." Andy doesn't even look at him.

Nick isn't sure what exactly about his story has Andy all riled up, but supposes Andy can take his pick from any number of good reasons. Nobody likes when their friends keep secrets, especially secrets that might blow up in everybody's faces. If anyone finds out about Nick's arrest, they might start talking about Andy.

Nick should have told Andy about the arrest already, although he doesn't know when. Before asking Andy to stay indefinitely, at least. But he hates to talk about that night at the Navy Yard. It was the worst night of his life—a flashlight in his eyes, cuffs snapping around his wrists, his fly still unbuttoned. It had been humiliating and terrifying, and—worst of all—it's shaped the rest of his life.

It isn't so much that he's prudent to the point of paranoia when it comes to meeting men—he's hardly the only one always looking over his shoulder. The real difference between then and now is that he doesn't allow himself to get comfortable. Not anywhere, not with anyone. He's perpetually, constantly afraid.

Somehow, the fact that there are men like him who manage not to hide only makes it worse. He thinks of Ted, the museum curator. He's in the art world, though, and rules there are different. But then Nick thinks of that man Andy mentioned, the associate of Dr. King. He must have FBI agents following him around seven days a week. How in hell does he manage to even live a life? Is the real problem that Nick is a coward?

"We're here," Andy says. Nick looks out the rain-streaked window and sees that the cab has stopped in front of their apartment building. He reaches for his wallet, but Andy is already passing a five-dollar bill up to the cabbie, then waving away the change.

It's pouring now, just a godawful deluge of frigid rain. Nick nearly dried off in the bar, but now he's drenched again. With half-numb hands, he tries to take out his keys, but Andy already has the front door unlocked and is shepherding Nick inside.

All the way up four flights of stairs, Andy doesn't say a word. Nick can practically see the fury rising off him like steam from a subway grate. Well, at least Andy is going to be mad at Nick while they're together. He isn't leaving Nick alone and going off somewhere else to fume. That's probably a good sign?

Andy has the apartment door open now and Nick steps mutely through. He tries to toe his shoes off, but he's too cold and wet to manage it. He leans against the wall and starts in on his coat buttons, but they aren't budging, either.

"Let me." Andy's voice is as near to a snarl as Nick has ever heard it. He unbuttons Nick's coat, pulls it off his shoulders, and throws it onto the radiator before dropping to his knees and untying Nick's shoes.

"I'm sorry," Nick says.

"I don't know why you keep saying that. Lift your foot."

"Because I upset you. You're . . . mad."

Andy gets to his feet. "*You* didn't upset me." He takes Nick's face in his hands and kisses him. "I'm furious. I'm—fucking irate." Another kiss, then another that's more teeth than anything else. "When I think about what happened to you, I want to hurt someone. I want to burn down the courthouse and throw that cop into the river."

Oh. Only then does Nick understand what Andy is talking about. Andy is angry *for* Nick, not at him.

"I can't think of you in a jail cell. At eighteen! I couldn't even make toast at eighteen."

Nick doesn't know why Andy is loosening his tie and unbuttoning his shirt, but likes that Andy's hands are on him. "You still can't make toast."

Andy laughs, but it sounds a little damp. He shoves Nick's shirt off his shoulders. "I want you to be safe. I *need* you to be safe, Nick. I can't function in a world that won't let you be safe."

And that's too bad, because Nick has never heard of that world, but Andy looks so earnest and lovely and righteous that Nick has to kiss him.

"You still have on your coat," Nick says into the soft place under Andy's jaw.

"Just wanna touch you." Andy kisses Nick's exposed shoulder, then moves the neck of his undershirt aside to kiss his collarbone.

"Clothes," Nick says, plucking at Andy's wet coat.

"In a minute." He kisses Nick again, hungry and impatient, taking hold of Nick's loosened collar and pressing him into the door. Andy is apparently bad at listening today, so Nick begins tugging Andy's coat off, and—okay, that's probably a hundred-dollar coat sitting in a puddle on Nick's floor, and nobody cares.

All that matters is the grip of Andy's hands, the slide of his mouth over Nick's jaw, the press of his hips.

"Beautiful," Andy says, pulling back a little. "Could look at you all day." But he's a liar, because the first thing he does is shut his eyes and kiss Nick again. Nick isn't complaining, though. Nick isn't complaining at all. The warmth of wanting and being wanted start to push away some of the fear and sadness.

One of Andy's hands slides to Nick's belt and they both catch their breath, pulling back a little to stare at one another.

"Bed?" Nick asks. Leaning against the door is fine, but Andy on his sheets, in his bed, would be better. Andy is looking at him like words aren't getting into his brain anymore, and that's such an improvement over him looking furious that Nick has to kiss him some more. "Bed, come on. I want you in my bed."

They stumble down the hall, Nick pulling Andy's shirt over his head, Andy pushing Nick's undershirt up, Andy almost concussing himself on the doorjamb when he tries to take his pants off without getting rid of his shoes first.

Nick pushes Andy onto the bed because he probably can't hurt himself there, and starts working on his own pants. Andy props himself up on his elbows to watch. Nick hooks his thumbs into his shorts and pulls them down, too, hoping he hasn't badly misread the situation. Andy is staring. Nick strokes himself, just once.

"Bring that over here," Andy says, his eyes wide and his voice rough.

Nick does as he's told.

Maybe the past week of kissing on the sofa and in the hallway and against the icebox and just about everywhere else in this rat-trap has made Andy confident, because he reaches for Nick with a sure hand. Nick groans. This isn't going to last. "Get rid of your underwear," he pleads. And then: "Can I touch you?"

He wants to touch Andy anywhere he can reach, hungry for every point of contact. Andy seems to feel the same, his hands exploring, his breath catching whenever Nick likes something. And Nick likes everything. He's thought too much about this, imagined Andy in every possible way, and the reality of him flushed and naked in Nick's bed, the reality of his hands on Nick's body, completely undoes him.

They're both too desperate to have any finesse. It's been a week of buildup, a week of hard-ons left to subside, and now Nick has to shelve about a dozen big ideas and instead grab them both together in one hand and hope for the best.

Andy doesn't seem to mind. He looks like he's being dismantled, taken apart atom by atom, and Nick doesn't know how that can be when he's the one dissolving into nothing but want and need and too much fondness to even think about.

Nick rolls them so Andy is on top, then hooks a leg around Andy's hip to keep him close. This makes Andy's damp hair fall in his eyes, and into Nick's eyes, too.

He moves his hips so they rock together, and then after that there's nothing but gasped names and soft words, the two of them sheltered together in a warm safe place.

Afterward, Nick lies boneless and warm, Andy half on top of him and apparently insensate. His face is smashed into the pillow beside Nick's head, an arm and a leg flung heavily across Nick's body.

Nick reaches out and gropes around on his nightstand for a pack of cigarettes. Andy must hear the click of the lighter because he lifts his hand and makes a grabbing motion. Nick puts the cigarette into his hand and Andy shifts over, sitting up against the headboard.

Nick cranes his neck to look. Andy is still flushed, pink and rosy from what they did together. His hair is rumpled and his jawline and neck are red from rubbing against Nick's stubble. He looks gently debauched.

"You're staring," Andy says.

"Mm-hmm."

Andy rolls his eyes.

"Want me to stop?" Nick asks.

"Knock yourself out," Andy says, making a sort of *help yourself* gesture.

When they first met, Nick thought Andy was at best generically handsome, like models in the Sears catalog or ads for soap. He thought Andy's looks were bland, forgettable, boring WASPy straight-nosed pale-skinned dullness.

And then he started to notice the other things: the way Andy's ears stick out a little, the way his smile tilts to the side, how his expression never stays the same for more than five seconds and instead acts like a television screen, displaying everything that passes through his head.

None of that is in the least boring.

Now when he looks at Andy, he doesn't even see his component parts unless he makes himself pay attention. Instead it all coalesces into the shape of Nick's favorite person. Even when he looks at the parts he doesn't usually get to see—strong shoulders covered in the freckles of a dozen sunburns, the soft insides of his thighs, pink nipples and a dusting of dark blond chest hair— it's all still Andy.

"Jesus," says Andy, looking away. Another part of him that Nick doesn't usually get to see is taking renewed interest.

"You've been looking at me for weeks," Nick points out, stealing the cigarette from Andy's hand.

"You walk around half naked! It's impossible not to look."

"Is that so?" Nick crawls over Andy's lap and stubs out the cigarette in the ashtray. "You like what you saw?"

"Fishing for compliments is beneath you," Andy says, even as he smooths his hands down Nick's shoulders.

"I want to know what made you have your gay awakening." He waggles his eyebrows. "I want to know what about me is so powerfully attractive that it contributed to your degeneracy."

Andy suddenly looks serious. "I don't think I'm gay."

Nick gestures at Andy's hard-on. "Coulda fooled me, champ."

Andy smacks his hand. "I mean I'm not *only* gay. I definitely like women. And I like men, too."

Nick nods. "Okay, fair enough."

"I just mean that I wasn't living a lie or whatever. But if you really want to know what about you made me consider whether I like men, and we're going to pretend that the fact that you're my best friend has nothing to do with it, then it's this spot here." He touches the dip in Nick's clavicle.

"That?" He'd been ready to hear about his shoulders or his arms, or even his ass. Those are the things that get mentioned. He's not exactly unaware of his own charms.

"Every time you loosen your tie or unbutton your shirt, I can't look away. I love that spot." He reaches up and kisses it. "I couldn't be in the same room as that spot without eventually considering whether I might be at least a little queer. And then when I moved in here, I saw it every day, because you don't understand shirts, and now I'm committed to lewdness and homosexuality. And probably communism. We'll find out, I guess."

Nick likes the idea of Andy being seduced by his collarbone.

Plenty of people have looked at Nick and liked what they saw; he's pretty sure none of them thought twice about his clavicle. "You're already pretty committed to communism if you ask the *Daily News*. Or the FBI, for that matter."

"Shh," Andy says, as if there's anyone who might overhear, as if there's anyone who might see the two of them naked in bed together and focus on communism.

"What about you?" Andy asks. "What made you think about me like that?" He's a little breathless, and he's definitely looking for a compliment. Nick will give him compliments until his throat goes hoarse, if that's what he wants.

"It was these," Nick bends his head to kiss the triangle of freckles at the corner of Andy's mouth. "I love them."

"My birthmarks? Why?"

"They're like an arrow. Like a dare." He doesn't mention that he first noticed these freckles about six seconds after they were introduced and that it's been a steady descent into helpless infatuation ever since.

Andy pulls him down into a kiss but soon gentles it. "We should eat something. It's past six and you didn't have lunch, unless you count bourbon, which I do not."

"I can run out and get pizza," Nick offers.

"You really can't. I left a bruise under your jaw. You look obscene. I'll go."

"You can't, either. There's beard burn all over your face and neck."

Andy brings a hand up to his face and touches it with just his fingertips, as if he'll be able to feel the redness. "We still have some sauce."

Jesus. A week of pasta, meatballs, meatball sandwiches, and

more pasta and they're only half done with that jar. He lightly smacks Andy's hip. "Come on, you can help boil the water."

They fall back into bed as soon as the pasta bowls hit the sink, Nick kissing his way down Andy's chest, Andy responding with increasingly unhinged swearing and a fist in Nick's hair. They've taken the edge off, so now Nick makes it last, drawing helpless, sweet sounds from Andy. Nick loves doing this, loves that he can make Andy go from mild-mannered and lighthearted to *this*, frantic and grasping and desperate.

Later, he puts his head on Andy's thigh and catches his breath, but Andy begins trying to pull him up. "Get up here, come on, come on." And then his mouth, sweet and hot, trailing a line of kisses downward as he attempts to return the favor. The key that dangles from Andy's neck grazes Nick's chest, then his hip, then his thigh.

"Are you sure?" Nick asks. Andy glares at him and then— Jesus.

What follows is the sloppiest, funniest blow job of Nick's life. "Don't try to take it all in," Nick says, laughing as Andy coughs. "I swear, if I have to take you to the hospital— Holy mother of God, do that again. No, not *that*, you fool." He pushes at Andy's head.

Andy is laughing so hard his shoulders shake, but when he manages to collect himself, he looks up at Nick, earnest and open. "Just tell me what you like."

So Nick does, guiding him through it, step-by-step, and he's reminded of that first day in the morgue files, when he showed

Andy how to open the sticky drawer. He remembers Andy then, sweet and willing and grateful, and wonders what would have happened if he had known how inevitably his own heart would be on the line. If he had known that first day what it would be like, what that awkward stranger would come to mean to him, what would he have done? If he had known how things would play out, with his own unavoidable heartbreak, would he have kept Andy at arm's length? He doesn't think so. He doesn't think he *could* have. If heartbreak is the price, he'll pay it for this, for Andy in his life and home and bed.

Part IV
ANDY

CHAPTER SIXTEEN

It's entirely possible that Andy is going to die, right here in the seventh-floor conference room, and when they find his body, no one will be able to tell whether it was this cold that did him in or plain old boredom from staring at the columns of numbers on the report sitting in front of him.

The numbers have something to do with circulation and ad sales, and the first number is—as far as Andy can tell—a tiny bit higher this quarter than it was last quarter, but ad sales are still in the pits. And apparently paper has gotten more expensive and wages have gone up. He'd probably have a better idea about all of this if he could pay attention to what people at this meeting were saying, instead of trying to blow his nose in a way that doesn't draw attention to himself.

The man at the front of the room drones on. "It's imperative that advertising efforts target the sector of consumers that—"

Andy blows his nose and loses the rest of the sentence. He sticks the used tissue in his pocket with all the rest. That morning, Nick had taken one look at him and shoved a box of Kleenex in his direction. "One handkerchief isn't gonna cut it, pal," he had muttered. "You really ought to stay home."

Andy had rolled his eyes. Of course he couldn't stay home. People get colds all the time. Besides, there's really no point in being miserable and lonely at home when he can be miserable and not lonely at work.

He remembers being looked after by an efficient housekeeper when he got the chicken pox and his mother was overseas. He remembers getting tonsillitis while away at school and being looked after by a well-meaning nurse at the infirmary. He remembers using his best manners to ask for cups of juice and packets of crackers when all the while he had a vague sense that things might be tolerable if someone sat at the edge of his bed and stroked his hair. He didn't even know if anyone had ever done that for him, or if he had just seen it in a movie or read about it in a book.

And so now he's dying in a meeting about ad revenue or—no, now they're talking about the lease on the building, and doing something about the empty fifth floor. *Fill it with people writing interesting things*, Andy wants to say. *Don't sublet it to a reinsurance company, whatever that is.* But probably the grand strategy of having people write interesting things is one that has occurred to everyone in this room, which is just another reason why Andy has no business running a paper.

After the meeting, his frustration peaking, he waits until everyone has left except his father, then gets up and shuts the door. He opens his mouth to tell his father exactly how out of his depth he is, how ill-equipped and ignorant he is and always will be, and how what the *Chronicle* really needs is competent leadership, when his father sighs and leans back in his chair. Andy watches the expression of businesslike alertness slide from his face.

The man looks—he looks tired and unwell, there's no way around it. During the meeting he looked like his old self, and

Andy realizes that his father must be worn out from whatever effort that cost him.

"Do you need anything?" Andy asks.

He doesn't expect his father to say yes—his father has always had secretaries to fetch things for him and he certainly doesn't need Andy. "A glass of water," he says. "Please."

Andy pours water from the carafe that stands on a sideboard, then places the glass in front of his father. "You ought to rest," he says, even though it's none of his business.

His father cracks a weary smile. "I'll take a nap on the sofa in my office, as soon as I have the energy to get to my office."

Jesus. He hadn't expected his father to agree. His surprise must show on his face because his father goes on. "It's an unusually bad day."

It hits home, then, a truth that Andy hasn't wanted to face. His father can't keep running the *Chronicle*. He's not just shoving it at Andy on a whim. He's tired, he's unwell, he needs to rest, and he's at an age when anyone would be thinking of retiring. It's selfish for Andy to ask him to stay on.

Andy has never been good at asking for anything; it's always better to be the kind of person who doesn't ask, who doesn't cause too much trouble, who's *likable*. Part of him can't believe that he was about to ask his father for something as monumental as continuing to work at a job that's making him ill.

He waits until his father has finished his water and then helps him back to his office, seeing him settled on his sofa with a thick blanket pulled over his legs.

"Thank you," his father says. "It's good to have you here."

"I'm happy to help," Andy says, because it's true.

"I don't mean that. It's just good to see you."

Andy doesn't know what to say. There were years—decades—
when he only saw his father every couple of months for an awkward
lunch. He always assumed his father wasn't terribly interested in
him. He was born a few months after his parents' marriage and a
few months before his parents' divorce. You don't have to be especially good at math to see that Andy hadn't been part of the plan.

Andy has never been especially bothered by it. Most of his
friends were in constant conflict with their fathers, and not having one in the picture seemed to be a net gain. It hadn't ever occurred to Andy that his father might want more to do with him.

It's too late for that, isn't it? Andy's sure that he ought to think
so, that if his father really wants to open this door, then Andy
ought to shut it in his face, just on principle.

But he already knows that he won't do that. His father is the
only family he has, and while Andy isn't sure he ought to care
about that, the fact is that he does.

When Andy gets back to his desk, there's a manila interoffice mail
envelope sitting on it. Absently, he unwinds the cord and pulls
out the paper within.

How are you feeling? the sheet of yellow-lined paper reads. It
isn't signed, but it doesn't need to be.

On the same paper, Andy writes *fine*, crosses off his name on
the envelope and writes Nick's, then puts the note inside before
handing it to his secretary.

Maybe half an hour later the envelope returns, this time
brought by a copyboy who's carrying a brown paper bag.

"Mr. Russo said you're to eat this," says the copyboy, plopping
the bag onto Andy's desk.

"Let me guess," Andy says, opening the bag to reveal a white cardboard container of soup. He's too congested to smell what kind of soup. "He also told you to stick around until I've finished it." He gestures expansively at his barely furnished office. "Make yourself at home." He opens the envelope. This time there isn't anything written on the paper, but it's been folded up small. When he unfolds it, two chalky white aspirins spill out. It's just like Nick to assume that Andy doesn't have his own bottle of aspirin in his desk—he doesn't, of course, but Nick can't possibly know that.

He swallows the tablets and opens the container of soup—it's chicken noodle, boiling hot, and likely from the deli downstairs. Along with a plastic spoon, there's a little cellophane packet of oyster crackers, which he opens and crumbles into the soup. Even before his first mouthful, the heat and steam from the broth seem to work some kind of magic on his poor abused sinuses, and he momentarily feels like he can breathe a little.

As he eats, he writes a reply to Nick. *Thanks. Do you want me to stay at my old apartment tonight so you don't catch whatever this is?*

Later, when the empty soup container is in the trash and Andy's sinuses are stuffed up again, a reply comes.

Don't be stupid. I'd only worry that you were lying dead in a pool of your own snot. Besides, I'm already going to catch whatever you've got.

Nick's probably right. They spent the weekend in bed together, and even if they hadn't, they're forever taking bites of one another's food and stealing sips of one another's coffee.

Suddenly his office seems even emptier than usual. It's only three o'clock, not nearly time to leave, but Andy's not getting anything done. He's tried to make sense of the report, but the words on the paper in front of him have long since disintegrated into a blur. Maybe Nick won't mind Andy hanging around his desk for a bit. When he gets to his feet, the room wobbles in a way that rooms really shouldn't. He drags himself to the elevator and mumbles "six" to the elevator operator.

"Go home," says Nick, looking up from his typewriter when Andy approaches. "Don't sneeze on everyone in the newsroom. Meyer is going to throw you out the window if you even walk past his desk."

Andy looks over his shoulder and, sure enough, Meyer is giving him a look that dares Andy to come any closer. Andy holds up his hands in surrender.

"I don't need to go home," Andy says. His head is pounding and the floor is wobbly again, not that he's going to mention that to Nick. "It's just the sniffles."

Nick gets to his feet, takes hold of Andy's elbow, and steers him toward the elevator. "I'll be home by seven and your ass had better be on the couch."

"Fine," Andy grumbles. "I'm leaving."

Nick is by Andy's side, all but shoving him into a cab. When the cab pulls into traffic, Andy turns around and sees that Nick is still on the curb, watching, as if he thinks Andy might try to jump out of the moving taxi.

But Andy gets home in one piece, even if the stairs take three times as long as usual and have him wondering if it would really be so bad to curl up on a landing and sleep. Or die. Either one, really. When he gets upstairs, he drops onto the sofa and falls asleep almost immediately.

Andy wakes to a cool hand on his forehead and the blurry sight of Nick looking down at him with undisguised concern.

"I think you have a fever." Nick disappears for a minute and comes back with a couple of aspirin and a glass of water. "You're sicker than I thought."

Andy wants that worried look on Nick's face to go away. "It's nothing," he says, sitting up and doing his best to look normal. "I probably just got warm while I was sleeping."

Nick gives him a long, skeptical look but drops the subject. "I'm making soup for dinner. You want the television on while I cook?"

"No, I'll just watch you, like a creep." He attempts a leer, but ruins it with a sneeze. Nick rolls his eyes, then takes a handkerchief out of his pocket and throws it at Andy.

Andy sits up and rests his chin on the back of the sofa. He lets his eyes unfocus and his mind wander. He watches as Nick puts a grocery sack on the table and takes out an onion, some garlic, a dozen eggs, a couple of cans, a lemon, and some cheese. Then Nick washes his hands and rolls up his sleeves. Andy closes his eyes and is left with the rhythmic thwack of the knife against the butcher's block, the sizzle of onions hitting oil, Nick's off-key humming.

He must fall asleep, because when he opens his eyes, Nick is standing over him, brushing Andy's hair off his forehead. "Come and eat something."

Andy gets to his feet and stumbles over to the table, where a bowl of yellow soup and a piece of toast wait for him.

"Egg soup," Nick says, sitting down across from Andy. "It's good when you're sick."

Andy would eat a bowl of motor oil if Nick put it in front of him and it's completely insane that Nick doesn't seem to already know this.

He sits and takes a spoonful. "S'good," he says. "Lemony." He thinks he'd probably appreciate it better if his nose weren't so stuffed up, but the lemon and steam cut through some of the more nightmarish things happening in his sinuses.

"It's what my mother made when we were sick," Nick says.

"I miss my mom," Andy says. He's pretty sure he hadn't meant to say that, but he's tired and his head hurts. He's not even sure why he misses his mother now, of all times: God knows she never cooked soup or anything else in her entire life and was hardly the kind of person who could be described as nurturing. She would have *shot* anyone who called her nurturing, and that thought only makes him miss her more. But she was his mother and now she's gone, she's left him *again*, and Andy is all alone, and will always be alone, and—

After dinner, Andy lands on the couch and drifts off, waking to hear Nick's hushed voice.

"I don't have a thermometer, but he feels hot," Nick is saying, and then there's a pause. "Really hot. No, no cough." He must be on the phone. "Okay," he says a minute later. "Got it. Thanks, Bev."

The sofa shifts under Nick's weight. "Hey, I'm heading out to the drugstore to get you some medicine."

"Don't need medicine. I'm fine."

Nick snorts. "You have the flu, pal."

"Says who?"

"Says Beverly. She's a nurse."

Beverly is Michael's wife, Nick's sister-in-law. Andy doesn't know what to make of the fact that Nick went so far as to call his brother. "I don't get the flu," Andy says.

"That might be half the problem. She asked when was the last time you had the flu and I told her I didn't know."

"High school," Andy mumbles.

"Yeah, well, remember how bad the flu was last year?"

"Sorta." Andy does remember—they had called it the Asian flu and apparently it was almost as bad as the Spanish flu of 1918.

"Well, everybody else in the world got the flu last year, but you didn't, so you're getting it now."

Andy's too tired to argue that this can't possibly be how the flu actually works, so he shuts his eyes. When he opens them again, Nick is sitting on the coffee table with a paper bag in his hand. He's still wearing his coat. "These are the tablets Beverly said to get," he says, opening a red-and-white cardboard box.

"You didn't have to—"

"Oh, can it, will you." He unscrews the bottle and holds out his palm. Andy takes the two pills, swallowing them down with a cup of orange juice that Nick passes him. He hates that Nick went out to the drugstore at night, hates that he called his brother's house. Andy doesn't want to be any trouble.

"Let's get you to bed." Nick stands and pulls Andy into his arms, disgusting sinuses and all. Only then does Andy realize he's been crying. Jesus. He needs to pull himself together.

Nick leads Andy down the hall to his bedroom.

"You sure you don't want me to sleep in my own bed?" Andy asks. "I'll keep you up half the night wheezing. And I don't want you to get sick."

"I had the flu last year, right before you started at the *Chronicle*. Knocked me flat on my ass for a whole weekend. And anyway, I'm probably already swarming with whatever germs you've got."

This is true. Their faces were practically attached to one another all weekend. He might have said that aloud, because Nick snorts and says, "Very romantic."

Andy is still contemplating that word—*romantic*—and what it might mean, when he realizes Nick has somehow gotten him out of his clothes and into a pair of pajamas.

"Can you sleep with the light on?" Nick asks. "I might read while you're resting."

It's bizarre that Nick wants to be with him. From the neck up he's made entirely of phlegm and snot, each of which are objectively disgusting even on their own. But Nick strips down to his shorts and gets into bed next to Andy, sitting against the headboard.

Andy falls asleep to the feel of Nick's hand stroking his hair, and he can't remember if he asked Nick to do that or if Nick somehow knew.

He sleeps fitfully, waking to blow his nose using the box of Kleenex that Nick wedged between Andy's pillow and the headboard. Whenever he settles back down, Nick's arm lands heavy and sure around him. Nick murmurs things that may or may not be actual words, the sort of soothing sounds you make to wounded animals or crying babies.

"I'm right here," Nick mumbles at one point, when Andy wakes with his teeth chattering. Andy burrows into Nick's side, seeking his warmth. Nick has always been like a furnace.

Andy knows he really ought to go next door to his own room. Nick can't be getting any real sleep with Andy tossing and turning.

But Andy wants this—he wants Nick's warmth, he wants the feel of Nick's solid body pressed against him, he wants Nick's gentle words and the kiss he absently drops on the top of Andy's sweaty head. He's miserable and sick and inexplicably sad and he doesn't have enough strength to go away.

CHAPTER SEVENTEEN

The next day there isn't any question of Andy going to work.

"You ought to go to the doctor," Nick says as he brings Andy a cup of coffee in bed.

Andy doesn't have a doctor. He hasn't had more than a cold in ages. He's lucky that way. He supposes he could call his father's doctor, but he doesn't want to let on how sick he is—the last thing his father needs is one more thing to worry about.

"It's a cold," Andy says, managing to roll his eyes despite the throbbing in his head. "The doctor would only laugh at me."

"Do you need me to stay home? I could—"

"*No,*" Andy says with probably too much force, because Nick's eyes widen in surprise. "Don't be silly." If there's a big story and Nick isn't around, he'll regret it.

"Fine, but you'd better call me every couple of hours or I'm coming by to check on you. Or, worse, I'll send Mrs. Martelli to check on you. She'll come up here with prayer cards and the rosary and make you eat raw garlic."

Privately, Andy would rather have Mrs. Martelli and her garlic than he would an empty apartment, but he isn't going to admit this to Nick. When Nick leaves, Andy promptly falls back asleep.

He wakes up in the middle of the morning, achy and ragged. He wishes Nick were around to pet his hair. Around lunch, he runs out of orange juice, which is presently the only thing giving him a will to live. Before he can consider whether it's a good idea to go outside in his current state, he already has his shoes on. He's all the way down the stairs before he realizes he left his wallet on the kitchen table.

He sits down on the stoop and nearly cries. He just wants juice. He doesn't even have a dime to call Nick from the pay phone, not that he'd really interrupt Nick at work to ask for juice. Probably. It's just that juice is the only good thing in the world and now he doesn't have any.

Across the street is a uniformed police officer. Andy wonders if he'd lend Andy a quarter or two. It's not one of the regular beat cops, but a rosy-cheeked stranger who could play a kindly neighborhood policeman on a children's television show—he looks like he keeps lollipops in his pocket for kids and spends his days helping old ladies cross the street. But Nick would hit the ceiling if he found out Andy was asking for favors from cops, so Andy doesn't try his luck.

"Andy?"

Andy looks up and sees Linda carrying a paper sack. "Any chance you have orange juice in there?"

"Pigments, copper wiring, lug nuts, and plaster of paris," she answers. "No juice."

Andy doesn't cry, which is an accomplishment. "Can I borrow fifty cents? My wallet is upstairs and I don't have it in me to do those stairs twice today."

"Flu?"

It probably is, and for some reason Andy doesn't feel so bad about admitting it to Linda. "Yeah."

"Jeanne just got over it."

At the best of times, Andy can't quite wrap his mind around the fact that Linda, with her copper wiring and paint-splattered overalls, is part of Emily and Jeanne's world. The borders of that tasteful little bubble are more porous than he had once thought. But now, with a fairly significant headache, the fact that Linda Ackerman, Vassar class of '55, is standing in front of Nick's Barrow Street stoop seems almost mystically significant. If a girl who went to school with Jeanne and Emily Warburton could find her way to a pair of overalls and a paper sack filled with lug nuts, then maybe it isn't so strange that Andy is here, too. Maybe Andy can be in this world in a way that isn't temporary.

Linda shifts her sack to a hip and presses the back of her hand to Andy's forehead. "Not that bad," she says.

Andy wants to protest that actually he's dying, thank you very much, but his throat hurts quite a bit, so he doesn't.

She reaches a hand into the pocket of her overalls and gives him a dollar bill. "Get your juice, but when you come back, knock on my door so I know you're alive. Otherwise, I'm calling Nick."

Andy thanks her. At the corner store, he bypasses the frozen concentrate Nick usually buys and pays extra for a bottle of Tropicana. When he gets back to the apartment building, he stops at every landing and sits for a bit, drinking juice out of the bottle like a barbarian.

On the third floor, a door opens. Andy looks up and sees Mrs. Martelli peering out, a frying pan clutched menacingly in one fist.

"I heard someone out here," she says, lowering the pan. "Thought you were a vagrant."

"I'm a bit under the weather."

"It's the smoking," she says, narrowing her eyes.

Andy is too tired to argue. "Probably," he agrees.

"You smoke too much, then you turn out like me. I used to do these stairs four times a day with a baby in each arm and now look at me. I need to move in with my daughter on Long Island. Long Island!"

Andy refrains from pointing out that being able to climb any stairs at all at the age of approximately a hundred and fifty is pretty good. "You're moving?"

"I'm selling the building."

Andy hadn't even realized that Mrs. Martelli was the landlady. "Why not just move to the ground floor?"

"Too loud." She wrinkles her nose. "Also, I want the money. I'll send my grandchildren to college."

Andy wonders about the going rate for a five-story apartment building in this part of the Village, and also how many grand-children Mrs. Martelli plans to send to college. The other day he called a real estate agent about putting his mother's Upper East Side co-op on the market and learned it would go for what feels like an astronomical sum.

Mrs. Martelli snaps her fingers in front of his face. "Don't die on my stairs. I'll never get any money for this place if there are dead bodies. Do I need to walk you up myself?"

Andy assures her that no, she does not, and manages to haul himself up the remaining stairs in a single go. He barely remem-bers to knock on Linda's door before collapsing onto Nick's sofa, the glass bottle of juice still clutched in his hand.

One floor down, there's a dog who loses her mind when her owner comes home, running in circles and letting out little yelps of delight as soon as she hears the key turn in the lock. Lying on the sofa, Andy can hear the owner try unsuccessfully to quiet the dog.

This, minus the running in circles, is how Andy feels when Nick comes home. Because, in addition to being happy to see Nick, which he always is, Nick brings the certainty of hair-stroking and cuddling. Andy can't believe how utterly weak he is for hair-stroking and cuddling.

"Shh," Nick says into Andy's hair, even though Andy hasn't said anything. Nick still has on his coat and shoes, just dropped his bag by the door and immediately went to Andy on the sofa. "You feeling any better?"

"Yeah."

"Really?" Nick leans back to regard him skeptically, which is fair since Andy would probably have said he felt better even if he were on fire.

"I don't think I have a fever anymore."

Nick puts a hand to Andy's forehead and must be satisfied by whatever he finds there, because he doesn't press the point. They have more soup for dinner. Andy is coming to realize that Nick believes that soup is basically a prescription drug designed to cure all illnesses and also, probably, bad moods. He doesn't protest.

Later, when they get into bed, Nick pulls Andy against his chest. Andy drifts off, then wakes when he feels a familiar hardness against his back.

"Had no idea that wheezing did it for you," Andy manages. "Or is it the snot?"

"Fuck off," Nick says gently. "It's a Pavlovian response or whatever you call it. It's never had a chance to be this near to anyone unless there's a very specific agenda. Ignore it."

Andy thinks about that as he drifts in the space between asleep and awake. Does Nick do this with the men he sleeps with? Does he hold them in bed or pet their hair? Is Andy the only person Nick's been with like this? The idea makes him feel greedy, smug with satisfaction. It's pathetic, but he wants to know that he's special, that what they're doing is new for Nick in some way. He definitely shouldn't mention this to Nick.

"Do you not cuddle the men you fuck over the back of the sofa?" Andy asks, because he's hopeless.

"Jesus, Andy." Nick's laugh is soft and warm on the back of Andy's neck. "No. Definitely not."

"Not even afterward?" He feels his cheeks heat and he blames the flu for all of this.

"Not like this," Nick says, and it doesn't even sound like an admission, just a fact freely offered up for Andy's satisfaction. Surely Nick knows what Andy was getting at with his questions, but he let Andy have it anyway, held out his own morsel of vulnerability in exchange for Andy's.

By the second full day of being stuck at home, feverish and achy, with no company but soap operas, Andy's well enough to be bored beyond belief. When he turns off the television and switches on the radio, he's rewarded with the dubious pleasure of listening to a Yankees day game. He lies on the sofa eating burnt toast and cursing the Yankees bullpen. His brain is melting inside his congested head. He drifts off sometime in the seventh inning.

When he wakes, the phone is ringing and the light coming in from the window is already faded with dusk.

Before this week, the only time he's been in the apartment alone is when Nick is out running an errand—and even then, Andy usually goes along. He's never needed to answer Nick's phone and he isn't sure if he should. But he supposes it's technically his phone, too, even if few people know it—just the other day he gave Nick forty dollars for his half of the rent for May and a few dollars for the phone and electricity. And besides, it might be Nick calling to check on him.

That last thought settles it. Andy levers himself off the sofa, switches off the radio, and answers the phone. "Hello?"

The line is silent for a beat too long. "Is that—" A pause. "Andy?"

Andy puts out a hand to lean against the wall. "Emily?"

"I was calling Nick. Just to—never mind. I'm sorry. I'll call back when he doesn't have company."

"Wait! Don't hang up. Nick hasn't gotten home yet."

The line goes silent again. "Then why are you there?"

"I've been staying here ever since—since March," he says, as if alluding to the breakup might be rude.

Emily doesn't say anything for a moment. "He didn't tell me. I mean, not that we talk a lot. Or at all, really," she adds hastily.

"Emily. It's fine. It's good. You're friends. I've told him the same thing."

She's quiet again. "Thanks."

It annoys him a little that she's thanking him for allowing her to be friends with Nick, who was her friend before either of them met Andy. "Stop," he says, and hopes she understands.

"You sound awful."

"It's just a cold."

"Jeanne just got over the flu. I wanted to burn all her things in a giant bonfire like in *The Velveteen Rabbit*."

Andy laughs, which hurts both his throat and his head, but it's worth it. "Excuse me, we don't talk about that book."

She goes silent again. "How have you been, Andy? Other than being sick."

"I've been really well," he says immediately. "Everything is good. What about you?"

"Better. Jeanne keeps reminding me that I'm twenty-five and rich and beautiful and it's my job to have as much fun as I can manage, so I've been giving that a go."

Emily has always liked going out. It occurs to Andy for the first time that maybe, just maybe, they wouldn't have suited one another as well as they once thought. Andy could stay home seven nights a week and count himself a lucky man. Eventually either Emily would have gotten bored or Andy would have gotten exhausted. It's a strange realization.

"You should come over for dinner," Andy says, making himself say the words before he can think better of it. "You and Jeanne both. Nick's a good cook. And did you know your friend Linda moved in next door? We could invite her, too."

"Wouldn't that be awkward?"

His instinct is to deny it, but— "Who cares? A lot of things are awkward, right?"

"True," she says dubiously.

"Look, if you want to say no, that's fine. No hard feelings. But why don't we see if we can be friends? If we can't, we can't. No harm done." He takes a deep breath. "And I think Nick would like it."

"You want to make Nick happy," she says, and it isn't a question, so he doesn't try to answer. "Okay. Tell me when and I'll be there."

"I invited Emily for dinner," Andy says when he hears the door open. "I told her you were a good cook."

"Dinner tonight?" Nick comes over to the sofa and looks bemusedly down at Andy.

"A week from Saturday." He half expects Nick to make a joke, to say that Andy must be feverish if he's inviting his former fiancée to dinner with his current—whatever he and Nick are to one another.

But Nick just nods. "Okay."

"She called and I answered the phone. We talked for a bit. It was nice."

He examines Nick's face for jealousy, but there isn't anything there except maybe a trace of worry. Andy doesn't know if Nick isn't jealous because he knows Andy isn't hung up on Emily or because he doesn't particularly care.

In general, he doesn't know what Nick is thinking when it comes to . . . whatever it is they're doing. He knows Nick cares about him, obviously, but he's known that for as long as he's known Nick. He knows Nick wants him, and he also knows that the . . . affectionate aspect of this thing is sort of unprecedented for Nick. But he doesn't know what it means when you put all that together; he doesn't even know whether it *does* mean anything.

Maybe if he knew what Nick was thinking, he'd have a clue as to what he's thinking himself, because he's pretty much at sea. All he knows is that he sees Nick and his heart acts like it's magnetized, pulling at his chest like that's what it's meant to do.

If he were sleeping with a woman, he'd know it was serious— headed for the altar, or at least in that direction. Or would he? People do fool around without it going anywhere, even if Andy isn't usually one of those people. Andy likes certainty; he likes knowing where things stand. For as long as he can remember, he's wanted to get married and have a family. It doesn't take any great feats of introspection for him to understand that he's craving something he didn't have enough of as a kid, but that doesn't bother him because there's nothing wrong with wanting a wife and kids and a nice house somewhere green. These are all very normal things to want.

Whenever he's dated a woman, it's been with that end in mind. He's looking to settle down in a very predictable and defined way. It's something every girl he's dated understood as the goal as well, which made things incredibly easy, he now realizes. If he had to start every date with an explanation of his goals and dreams, with the hope that his goals matched those of the person sitting opposite him at the refined but slightly boring sort of French restaurant he always chose for first dates, he'd never date anyone.

When he looks at Nick, merrily puttering away in his kitchen, he has no idea whether Nick views what they're doing as fooling around or as a prelude to something else. Because he can feel it, that possibility of *something else*—there might not be a wedding or a house in Connecticut, there might not be children and a Labrador and the settled vision of life he's always longed for, but Andy knows in his heart that he could hold on tight to Nick and keep doing what they're doing and have that be *it*.

He's pretty sure this ought to frighten him more than it does.

CHAPTER EIGHTEEN

Maybe something in that accounting report actually stuck in Andy's head, or maybe being away from the office gave him some perspective, because when Andy goes back to work, all he can think about is that empty space on the fifth floor.

Somebody could do something with that; somebody really ought to. And for the first time since starting to work at the *Chronicle*, Andy thinks: maybe.

When he thinks of his name going on the *Chronicle*'s masthead after his father retires, he feels faintly sick. He feels the way he did after his mother's funeral, when he had to clean out the refrigerator, dumping pickles and mayonnaise and turkey into the trash can, and then going out for a sandwich, because the idea of actually eating the contents of his dead mother's refrigerator seemed impossible. That night he cried because he didn't have any jars of mayonnaise left that his mother had touched. It was not a good month.

And maybe part of his reluctance to think about any kind of future at the *Chronicle* is because it depends on his father leaving. Lately he's been all too conscious that he has one remaining parent and is pathetically invested in keeping him.

His father has spent the last year trying to teach him the business and Andy would still be just as ignorant after another year or two or ten. Give him maybe another decade of experience and he'd probably make a decent features editor; he could probably take over the sports section in even less time. But he'll never be his father.

Except—there's business, meaning ad revenue and what to do if the delivery truck drivers go on strike again, and then there's the business meaning *news*.

Andy's pretty sure he knows the latter. He isn't confident about a lot of things, but he's sure of that. News was the only way he ever had of reaching either of his parents. It's his first language.

That night, while Nick's cooking, Andy pours an extra glass of wine and knocks on his neighbor's door.

"What paper do you read?" he asks Linda, handing her one of the glasses.

"Is that a trick question?" Linda beckons him in and gestures for him to sit on an overturned milk crate.

"Nope. Call it market research."

"Honestly, Andy, if there's big news, I'll see it on television or my mother will call me. I pick up the *Journal-American* every now and then."

"Why?"

Linda shrugs. "I like their funny pages. But listen, Andy, what good is a newspaper ever going to do me? If a bomb is coming, I'd rather not know. And so much of the rest of it makes me miserable. There isn't much I can do right now about schoolkids in Alabama or pogroms in Russia. I want to know what's happening, but not every single day."

She addresses the words to her wineglass, a bit of an edge to her voice, as if she thinks Andy is judging her. And she's kind of right: the idea of not wanting to know the news is vaguely shocking to

Andy. He has to remind himself that not everyone was raised the way he was.

Linda is an outlier. Just look at her: today's work must have involved paint—at least, he hopes it did, because her dungarees are covered in crimson splotches and the only other explanation probably makes him an accessory after the fact to murder. Her hair is tied into a long braid that looks like it fell in the paint pot a few times, she has not a speck of makeup on her face, and he's pretty sure that's a men's shirt she's wearing. Nobody should care what papers she reads or doesn't read because, as she said herself, she doesn't read the newspaper.

He changes the topic and finishes his wine while listening to Linda talk about some gallery opening she went to. As she talks, he scans the apartment. It's the mirror image of Nick's but missing the wall that creates the second bedroom, and consequently is a bit brighter. There are makeshift shelves cobbled together from planks of wood and cinderblock, and crammed on the shelves are jars of paintbrushes, a basket of apples, a variety of objects that he can't identify, a slew of paperbacks, and stacks of magazines.

Which—there has to be something to that, right? She doesn't read newspapers but has a stack of magazines. There's *Life*, *The New Yorker*, the *Atlantic*, and something arty he can't make out the title of.

He crosses over to the shelf and picks up a magazine at random. It's out-of-date by several months and it's good to know Linda's just as bad as he is about getting rid of back issues. He flips through it, already knowing what he'll see: short fiction, theater reviews, long-form reporting, a couple of essays that probably could have been published at any point in the past three years. The publication seems to be financed entirely by ads for whiskey, cruises, and expensive shoes.

He thinks about that *Village Voice* article and wonders if something like it could appear in any of these magazines. Definitely not. Perhaps an essay on the ethics of police entrapment? Probably not even that. Maybe, though. Maybe *something*.

He makes a note to ask his father if they have numbers on whether magazine ad sales have tanked as badly as newspaper ad sales. There's probably not anything he can do with that information—after all, he's not running a magazine.

But when he goes back next door, Nick looks at him and raises an eyebrow. "You seem pleased with yourself."

"Just a little bit," he says, and presses a kiss to Nick's jaw.

"I swear to God, Andrew Fleming, if you use the word *canoodling* one more time, my dick will never get hard again."

"I was *just* pointing out that I'm not sneezing every five seconds anymore, so I think we can do *that* again." It's Friday night, and they've been reading in bed, sitting up against the headboard, their shoulders pressed together.

"*That*, huh?" Nick's tone is faintly mocking, and Andy knows he deserves it, but before he can complain, Nick is swinging a leg over his lap and Andy is already tilting his face up for a kiss.

He'd never have guessed that this would be the easy part, that sex, of all things, and with a *man*, no less, would feel easy and natural. But everything with Nick always feels right. From the beginning, all the things that usually are jagged and dangerous have been smoothed down, like rocks after centuries on a riverbed, like something he can hold safely in his hand. It's never hard to ask Nick for help or to let him see the frightened and awkward parts that Andy usually keeps hidden away.

Maybe that's why it feels so good and safe and right for Nick's hands to be on him. There has to be a reason. Two months ago he hadn't even let himself imagine touching a man, and Andy is, to grossly understate the case, not what you'd call easily adaptable. He isn't sure why he isn't having a crisis about this. Maybe he's just full up on crises and doesn't have time for another.

He rubs his cheek over the stubble on Nick's jaw, then presses his lips to the spot where his neck meets his shoulder, because that always makes Nick groan. "Lie down," he whispers. "Let me."

Nick lies down and tugs at the hem of Andy's pajama top. Andy takes the hint and pulls it over his head. As usual, Nick is already mostly naked. The undershirt, it turns out, had been a concession to modesty, because ever since they first got one another in bed, he's been walking around utterly shirtless. Andy is not complaining.

Andy bends down to kiss Nick and Nick's hands slide down his back, sure and firm. Andy starts to shuffle down the bed and pull Nick's shorts off, but Nick holds him in place.

"I was going to—" Andy hasn't gotten to the point where he can say *blow you* with any sense of composure. "I was going to use my mouth," he says, rolling his eyes at his own prudishness.

"Not yet," Nick mumbles, and pulls him down so their bodies are pressed together. "Wanna touch you for a bit. Missed being able to do this without getting sneezed on."

Apparently what Nick has in mind is lazy kissing combined with some groping and the sort of murmured praise that makes Andy feel like he might dissolve into a puddle. It turns out that *sweetheart*, when said by Nick, low and rumbly, sends all thoughts fleeing from Andy's brain. Which is fine, because Andy doesn't need thoughts at the moment. Or his brain, for that matter.

Andy's paid attention to the things Nick likes, so now he rubs a thumb rough over Nick's nipple and follows it with his mouth.

Nick bites off a curse and Andy feels himself respond, Nick's urgency feeding his own.

When Andy lightly bites Nick's lower lip, he feels Nick's hands slide down low, past the waistband of his pajama pants, cupping his ass.

And that's—Andy doesn't know what to think about that, even less so when Nick lets the grope turn downright filthy, his fingertips dipping low. Letting them linger.

Nick will stop if Andy asks him to, or even if Andy just doesn't give him the go-ahead. And so instead, Andy pushes back into his touch, just a little, just enough to make Nick suck in a breath.

He feels exposed, and not only physically. Every time he discovers something new about Nick that he likes, something he can't get enough of, he feels like yet another brick comes down from a wall that he hadn't known he was hiding behind. And this, Nick's hands on his body, the stubble of Nick's jaw rasping against his lips, their hardness pressed together—this isn't even the worst of the exposure. The worst is when Nick says *Andy, sweetheart*, and Andy says nothing at all because the only words his mouth could possibly form are *I love you* and he can't say that.

That's the thing about walls. They don't tend to appear for no good reason; they're either closing something off or holding something up, and you can't just wish them away.

"Feels so good," Nick groans when their bodies rock together. "Why is this so good?" He says it like it's an actual question, like he doesn't know the answer, when to Andy it's the most obvious thing in the world. He doesn't know how anything between them could be anything but good.

But he can't say any of that, so he asks Nick for more.

Later, when they're lying side by side, Andy stares at the ceiling and steels himself. "Do you want—well. I know we haven't. But we could." He clears his throat. "It's just—you mentioned that you did. And so. We could." He's pretty sure there isn't a single coherent thought in that mess, but maybe Nick can sift through it and find some sense.

Nick rolls over and searches his face. "You're talking about . . . fucking."

Andy nods in relief that he isn't going to have to draw a diagram or act out some kind of pantomime.

"So," Nick says slowly. "I've only ever done it the one way. And it's not the way I think you'd be interested in." He pushes Andy's hair off his forehead. "I've never been fucked. I'm not against the idea; it's just never come up. I'd give it a go, though."

Andy does not know how Nick manages to say that sort of thing and not die on the spot. "You would?"

"Yeah." He shrugs and gives Andy that lopsided smile that makes his insides feel like they're melting. "People seem to like it."

He means that men like it when he fucks them, and the thought makes Andy feel like he might explode right then and there. "Let's table that issue." Andy is so grateful that Nick doesn't laugh at him—not at his inability to get the words out or his reticence or his need to change the topic.

"Okay." Nick drops an arm over Andy and presses close.

The truth is that other than detective stories, Andy doesn't read much fiction, never really has. He isn't sure why anyone would want to, when news exists. But he's been reading that book, the queer one Nick got from Mark Bailey, just a few pages at a time, waiting for something to happen.

And the thing is, it's queer. It's queer from the jump, and

unapolegically so. Andy expected something vague and gauzy, at most a couple longing glances.

"The guy in this book gets mistaken for a rent boy twice," Andy calls out from the sofa. Nick's in the kitchen, frying something for dinner.

"How do you even know what a rent boy is?" Nick calls back.

Andy doesn't roll his eyes, but only because Nick wouldn't be able to see him do it. "He gets mistaken for a rent boy and doesn't seem to mind. Everyone in this book knows he's gay. Which stands to reason, because all he does is ogle the boring pretty one and stay out too late with the dashing one."

"They're all going to wind up miserable at the end." Nick appears over the back of the sofa, still holding a cast-iron frying pan and looking like he wants to grab the book from Andy's hand.

"No, they won't. I read the final chapter."

"You did what?" Nick sounds scandalized.

"I'm not wasting my time on things that make me sad." He learned that lesson with *Old Yeller*, thank you very much.

"Andy, you publish a newspaper. It's the saddest thing anyone could want to read."

Andy makes a dismissive noise. "Anyway, the book ends up with one couple happily together. Not ecstatically happy, mind you, but England's being blitzed, so that's a factor."

Nick is quiet for a moment. "I suppose that's why nobody would publish it here." He disappears back into the kitchen and Andy resumes reading. He can't believe this book is going to make him read *Phaedrus*. It's possible that at some point he knew something about Plato, but it's vanished along with calculus and the order of the planets. "Do you have a copy of *Phaedrus*?" he calls out.

"Do I have a what?"

"Plato's *Phaedrus*."

"Oh yeah. Sure, it's right over by the— No, I fucking don't have any Plato in my apartment, for fuck's sake, Andrew."

This time Andy does roll his eyes. God forbid anyone point out that Nick has literally hundreds of books in his apartment.

"Are you really enjoying it?" Nick asks later when they're sitting down to eat.

"Yeah," Andy says, surprised. "It's sweet."

"Sweet."

"And very, very gay." He puts his fork down. "There's gay sex."

Nick's eyes widen. "Mark Bailey is reviewing this for the *Chronicle*."

"I mean, it isn't explicit. But it happens anyway."

"What happens afterward?"

"Huh?"

"After the sex?"

Andy thinks back. "Cuddling, I guess? They're asleep on the sofa together. And then one character asks the other to move in with him." He doesn't say that everything leading up to the sex is, for lack of a better word, romantic. When she was packing for an airplane trip, Andy's mother used to bring these novels in which handsome doctors fell in love with their nurses ("It's escapism, and the only thing that keeps me from worrying about plane crashes," she used to say before shoving three battered fifty-cent paperbacks into her bag). This book is as romantic as any of those (which Andy knows, because he used to skim them, hungry for any point of commonality with his mother).

"They don't regret it?" Nick asks, voice oddly aggressive given that they're talking about a pretty sappy novel.

Andy realizes that Nick doesn't believe him—he thinks Andy's misread the book. He absolutely does not believe that the little blue paperback sitting on their coffee table contains a story that is both queer and non-tragic.

"No, not at all," Andy says, but then reconsiders. "No, I'm wrong. They don't regret the sex, but they're all constantly disparaging themselves for not liking women. That's getting on my nerves, to be honest."

"That's how it is for some people," Nick says, and that's when Andy realizes that they're having two separate conversations. Nick isn't talking about the book at all—or, not only about the book.

"Oh?"

"Yeah." Nick pushes away from the table and brings his plate to the sink.

"Nick."

"I mean, I hate to be the one to break it to you, but people like me are supposed to be ashamed of ourselves."

Andy swallows. "People like us."

"Right, right. But—how on earth are you not?"

"Ashamed? Are you?"

"*No.* But it took time."

Andy realizes that Nick's waiting for Andy to change his mind, waiting for a crisis Andy isn't going to have, and he doesn't know how to go about reassuring him. "Nick, I don't know. The fact is that I don't have anything to lose, do I? I've lost the person who meant the most to me and the person I have left doesn't seem to mind that I'm queer."

"Your dad?" Nick asks.

"Oh my God." Andy isn't sure whether he wants to laugh or cry. "I'm talking about you."

"Oh." Nick looks far more surprised than he should.

"But my dad doesn't mind, either. He assumed we were sleeping together back in March. So he's not going to disinherit me or anything. I'm rich—"

"Finally, you admit it." Nick gives him a look that manages to be skeptical and soft and a little bit annoyed all at once, and then shifts abruptly into alarm. "Wait, did you say your dad knows we're sleeping together?"

"I didn't tell him. He just assumed when I moved in with you."

"And you didn't deny it?"

Andy doesn't know how to explain that for all his father was never much of a parent, Andy doesn't doubt for a minute that he can keep a secret. Andy might not think much of him as a father, but he respects him as a man. "I trust him."

"You hardly know him!"

It's true, but it stings. "He's notorious for not naming names. He didn't even name my *mother* to HUAC and they hated one another." Andy thinks that possibly Nick won't receive this as the proof of good character that it is, but a bit of tension leeches from Nick's posture.

"I don't like it." Nick's voice is awfully small.

Andy's kicking himself for not watching his mouth. "Think of it like this. You aren't going to get fired for being gay."

"He already knew? About me, I mean?"

"Must have."

"I was so fucking careful."

"I'm sorry. I should have denied it for you."

Nick lets out a strangled-sounding laugh. "No, I wouldn't like that, either. There's no winning with this." He starts piling dishes into the sink.

"Leave that." Andy gently shoves Nick away from the sink. "I'll wash up."

"If you use soap on that pan, I—"

"You'll hunt me down, I know, I know. Go put on the television. I've never known anyone so fussy about pans."

"You've never known anyone else who has pans," Nick says, and he's right. He doesn't leave the kitchen, like he expects Andy to say something else, or like he's trying to say something himself. But whatever it is passes, and a moment later Andy hears the sound of the television coming to life.

Andy's having a hard time sleeping—it's a few degrees too warm in the apartment and Nick always runs hot—so he wriggles out from under Nick's arm and slips off to the living room.

He's debating whether turning on a lamp will wake Nick when he hears an odd pounding noise coming from the kitchen and nearly jumps out of his skin. He takes a deep breath. He doesn't believe in ghosts, and burglars probably don't spend much time in the cabinets, which is where the sound seems to be coming from. Mice, maybe? A lot of mice?

He pulls the chain on the kitchen light and sees that the door to the cabinet under the sink, where they keep the garbage can, is thwacking against its frame.

He's frozen in place, not because he's frightened but because this is inexplicable, when he sees an orange paw emerge from the cabinet door. Andy throws the door open, revealing a cat sitting inside the garbage can, the remains of table scraps all over its face.

"You're filthy," Andy says, as if an animal sitting in a trash can could be anything else.

The cat produces a little yowl that Andy chooses to interpret as agreement. Then it wiggles, and Andy realizes that the poor idiot doesn't know how to get out. "Jump," Andy suggests. "Or climb. You got through the window. You can't be totally helpless."

In response, the cat makes a beeping sound, as if arguing that no, he can definitely be that helpless.

"I really don't want to pick you up." Andy doesn't want fleas. He doesn't want to get scratched or covered in garbage, either. But he can't leave a cat sitting in a trash can. He gets a bath towel and, hoping for the best, flings it over the cat and picks him up. God, this cat is about twice as heavy as he was expecting. Which, he supposes, stands to reason if the animal makes a habit of eating inside trash cans full of table scraps. At that point Andy realizes he has no exit strategy. What's he supposed to do with this cat? He drops the whole bundle, towel and all, into the sink.

The cat mewls plaintively.

"Yeah, you and me both," he agrees.

Experimentally, he wets a corner of the towel with warm water and uses it to clean the worst of the mess from the animal's face. He doesn't think cats are supposed to like water, but this cat doesn't seem to know what cats are and aren't supposed to do, because he goes along with the whole procedure, even after Andy adds some soap to the towel. Andy wonders if the cat would put up with a flea bath.

"What the fuck?" says a groggy voice. Nick is rubbing his eyes.

Andy shrugs. The situation is, unfortunately, pretty self-explanatory.

"You do this every night?" Nick asks, and it's unclear whether the question is being addressed to Andy or to the cat.

"He was stuck in the garbage can," Andy says. "Or maybe he wasn't stuck. Maybe he just likes garbage cans."

Nick is looking at him like he's crazy, but honestly Nick is the one who rolled out the red carpet for this poor unfortunate creature. Andy knows for a fact that nobody else in the building, or possibly the world, leaves their windows open so feral cats can wander in.

"I don't know how he isn't dead yet," Nick says.

"Have you thought about keeping him inside?"

"He's a wild animal."

"He's the opposite of that." The cat tries to swat at a floating soap bubble, missing by a mile.

"If you want to keep him, I'm not going to stop you."

"Really?"

Nick shrugs.

Andy wonders if they'd have the same conversation if this hadn't happened in the middle of the night. Nick is barely awake. There's a red line on his face from where it was pressed against a crease in his pillow, and his eyes aren't quite focused.

Andy's never had a pet. As a kid, it would have made no sense, what with his mother never being around. After that, he was away at school. Since then, he guesses he could have gotten a cat, but he doesn't trust himself to look after another living creature. Although, looking at the animal in the sink, he couldn't do much worse than this cat has been managing on his own.

But it doesn't seem right to start bringing animals into what's really Nick's apartment. He's said Andy can stay, but open-ended isn't the same as permanent. At least Andy doesn't think so. He feels like there ought to at least be some kind of conversation about it, but he can't imagine what that conversation would even sound like.

"I probably ought to bring him downstairs," Andy says, and proceeds to do exactly that.

CHAPTER NINETEEN

On the day Emily and Jeanne are coming for dinner, Nick wakes Andy at seven in the morning.

"It's Saturday!" Andy protests, grabbing a pillow and holding it over his head to block out the sun. "This is obscene."

"If we have guests and not enough food, I won't be responsible for my actions. We need to do the shopping."

Some barely awake part of Andy's mind registers that Nick could buy groceries on his own and let Andy sleep in like a normal person, but Nick knows how much Andy hates waking up alone. This is Nick's idea of a compromise.

"Okay, okay." Andy lets himself be tugged out of bed. Obviously Nick has lost his mind, because walking to the Christopher Street A&P, getting groceries, and walking back takes no more than an hour. They've been doing it every week for two months now. But Andy will humor him.

Nick throws a shirt at him and sticks a cup of coffee in his face.

It isn't until he stumbles down the steps and out onto the sidewalk, into a shockingly warm and sunny spring morning, that the penny drops: Nick is nervous.

"You know," Andy says slowly, "you could make lasagna like you did when Linda and her friends came over."

Nick glares at him as if he suggested putting bowls of cereal out for supper. "*That* is the problem. I made lasagna when Linda came over the last time. And anyway, lasagna is . . ." He makes a dismissive gesture. "I've never had a dinner party."

Andy doesn't point out that Linda has scrounged food from Nick a dozen times. Apparently the addition of Emily and Jeanne means something. He considers telling Nick that he's seen Emily eat caviar with tiny mother-of-pearl spoons and he's seen Emily eat Chex mix out of her palm, and, with the expansive taste of people who have been raised with everything, she doesn't seem to really prefer one over the other. But Nick will not be making Chex mix for Emily and Jeanne Warburton and probably would be offended by the idea, so Andy keeps his mouth shut and follows Nick down the street.

"What's the deal with that cop who's always across the street now?" Andy asks. It's the friendly-looking cop straight out of central casting again.

"They probably think junk's being sold out of that jazz club," Nick grumbles.

"Before eight o'clock on a Saturday morning?"

"Neighborhood's always crawling with cops. You'd think they'd have better things to do."

First, they go to the A&P, where Nick buys noodles, canned tomatoes, and a lot of weird-looking vegetables that Andy refrains from commenting about.

"They're eggplants, Andy," Nick says, so maybe Andy's face is doing some commenting of its own. "Trust me."

"I do," says Andy, maybe a little too earnestly. "Everything you make is delicious."

Then they go to the bakery on Cornelia Street, where Nick gets two loaves of bread, glowers away Andy's offer to pay, then hands the grocery bag to Andy to carry. A few doors down is a cheese store that Andy has passed a dozen times but is too intimidated by to consider going in.

"Where else are we going?" Andy asks when Nick emerges with two paper-wrapped parcels of mysterious cheese that he dumps into Andy's shopping bag.

"Just the butcher." The butcher Nick likes is a block away on Jones Street, a hole-in-the-wall that's long since passed old-fashioned and ascended into a sort of battered permanence. The floor is covered in sawdust and meat hangs in the window. There's no need for Andy to go in—he could wait on the sidewalk as he had at the cheese shop and say hello to all the dogs that come past. Except. Well.

Nick greets the butcher in Italian. He's told Andy that he only speaks kitchen Italian, but this is a flat-out lie because right now the butcher is clearly trying to sell him what looks like beef and Nick is saying no, no, he wants something else. The butcher asks a question, Nick answers, and, honestly, somebody speaking a language that literal millions of other people speak shouldn't affect Andy in quite this way. In fact, there's the butcher speaking Italian right now, and Andy in no way wants to push that man against the counter and do lewd things to him. It's just a language! Jesus.

As he watches, Nick leans a hand against the counter and laughs at whatever the butcher says, again refusing the offered cut of meat. When most people laugh, they become more attractive. But with Nick, who's already about as good-looking a person as Andy has ever seen, laughing transforms his face into something accessible—he exposes a crooked tooth and a pair of fillings, his eyes scrunch up so you can no longer see their warm brown depths, and a road map of creases appears around his eyes and mouth.

And if Andy hadn't already known he loves Nick—if Andy had managed to tuck that truth away where he keeps everything else he doesn't want to deal with—he would have known it then, watching Nick laugh with the butcher on a sunny May morning.

After humoring Andy by letting him chop the eggplant, Nick sends him out on an errand.

"Wine," Nick says. "Three bottles of red, plus another for the chicken."

Andy makes a mental note to buy at least five bottles. Or maybe a full case of wine? Is that the sort of extravagance that might bother Nick? It isn't as if they aren't eventually going to drink twelve bottles of wine, right? And buying a case brings the cost down, so maybe it's the opposite of an extravagance?

"And . . ." Nick's voice trails off as he stirs a pan of onions. "Remember when you brought me—when you got those flowers?"

Nick is facing away, so Andy can't be sure, but he thinks Nick might be blushing. He repeats Nick's words to himself. *When you brought me flowers.* He remembers Nick's expression when Andy walked through the door with all those daffodils; it had lodged in Andy's memory because it didn't quite make sense. At the time, he hadn't been able to tell whether Nick was embarrassed or pleased or something else.

If Nick wants flowers, then Andy will fill the apartment with every bouquet and posy and arrangement he can get his hands on. He'll raid a florist. He'll break into a funeral home—which, all right, maybe not that.

Except, no. He imagines Emily and Jeanne and Linda walking into an apartment filled with flowers. They wouldn't know what to think—or they would, which might be worse. All right. He needs to buy flowers. Just some. A normal, non-alarming quantity of flowers. Not all the flowers in the world. He can do that.

He's still standing at the door, his wallet in his hand, and Nick is staring at him.

"Haha," Andy says. "I'm going now. Bye!" And he flees.

At the wine store, he makes life simple by buying a case of the same wine he bought the last time, because he knows Nick likes it. Then he pays extra to have it delivered within the hour, because carrying a crate of wine anywhere, let alone up four flights of stairs, is something he will happily pay somebody else to do.

When he bought the daffodils, he had just seen them outside the corner store. They weren't anything fancy. Today, in front of that same store, there are only scraggly bundles of carnations and he isn't having any of that. There's a flower shop near Washington Square Park, though, so when he returns to the apartment an hour later it's with an armful of sweet peas.

"You're back," Nick says, stirring something at the stove. "Too bad there's no wine left in Manhattan because it's all at our house. I tipped the kid fifty cents." With the wooden spoon, he gestures at a crate on the floor next to him, then turns around and sees Andy. And the flowers, presumably.

After looking at every flower in the shop, much to the consternation of the florist, Andy settled on sweet peas because one, they're pretty; two, they smell good; and three, they don't look expensive, at least to Andy's notions of what expensive flowers look like. He chose a jumble of pinks and whites and purples, no greenery, no baby's breath or other bullshit filler, on the theory that it would look less stuffy. And if he puts them in the quart jar that used to hold Nick's mother's spaghetti sauce, they might look like they belong.

"I got these for you." Andy makes himself tag on those last two words so Nick will know this wasn't an errand; it's a gesture. It's someone bringing flowers to the person he loves. Simple as that.

Nick doesn't say anything, but he calmly sets the wooden spoon on the rim of the pot, crosses the room in a few strides, and kisses Andy hard. He crushes Andy against the door and Andy has to move his arm to the side to avoid ruining the flowers.

Andy figures there has to be some official etiquette regarding how to greet an ex-fiancée, but if so, he's never heard of it.

"Do I hug her?" he asks as he haphazardly putters around the apartment. "Shake hands? Kiss both cheeks?"

"How do you usually greet Jeanne?" Nick has finished cooking and is now showering with the door open.

"I kiss her cheek," Andy calls out.

The taps turn off. "Then do that." Nick steps out of the shower and wraps a towel around his waist. "Should I shave?"

Andy is surprised enough by the question that he drags his attention away from Nick's damp chest. Nick always shaves. Sometimes he even shaves twice a day. But apparently he's noticed how obsessed Andy is with Nick's stubble. He might have noticed this because Andy has said so, out loud, maybe a dozen times, usually while running his lips over Nick's jaw.

Andy grins. "You know what my answer's going to be."

"Pervert."

Andy kisses Nick's jawline as he passes by on the way to the bedroom. "Your pervert."

"What do I wear?" Nick stands in front of his closet.

"No tie. Gray pants. Sleeves rolled up."

Nick shoots Andy a skeptical look over his shoulder. "Sleeves rolled up? That's part of the dress code?"

"Yeah. It would be bad manners for you to hide those away," he says, gesturing at Nick's forearms. "Sorry you didn't know that."

"Lucky I have you around." Nick drops the towel, which is unfair since Andy has to get into the shower immediately if he wants to have time.

"Such a tease," he laments, and strips off his own clothes.

Nick has no restraint, no scruples, no *ethics,* because he kisses Andy and kisses him again and follows him into the bathroom and into the goddamn shower and it's nothing short of a miracle that they're both decent when the buzzer sounds.

"Should I go downstairs?" Andy asks.

"I could throw them the keys?"

Andy is of the opinion that throwing keys out a fifth-story window is a surefire trip to the emergency room and possibly the police station, but they've already had this conversation, and Nick insists that the throwing of the keys is entirely normal apartment-building behavior.

"We could both go down?" Andy counters.

Nick nods. He goes to the window, leans out far enough that Andy yelps, and shouts that he's on his way.

On the last landing, Nick grabs Andy's shoulder. "Even if you're awkward, she won't be. Emily Warburton is the antidote to awkwardness."

This is an excellent point. "Thanks."

At the front door, the question of air kisses versus hugs is rendered moot because Jeanne immediately hugs Andy. He briefly wonders if the sisters settled it between them beforehand, because it's the perfect solution: after Jeanne and Andy hug, of course Emily and Nick have to, and then it's natural for Emily and Andy to hug as well.

It's all significantly less bizarre than it might have been, embracing the woman he once thought would be his wife, the mother of his children, his partner through thick and thin. It shouldn't be this easy. It feels like greeting an old friend.

Upstairs, they knock on Linda's door, and she must have made a real effort because she's noticeably less paint-splattered than usual, with only trace quantities of plaster dust in her hair. Emily and Jeanne enter the apartment armed with anecdotes to smooth over any awkwardness—Emily talks about her new job at *Vogue*—she's still writing about sofas, but very expensive ones now—and Jeanne talks about a cat that had kittens in the broom closet at the museum. All Andy has to do is pour drinks and make the appropriate conversational noises.

Emily has on slim black trousers, a white sweater, and flat shoes, and it takes Andy a moment to realize that he's never seen any of these clothes before. He also hasn't seen her hair that way—sort of half up but loose around her shoulders. When they hugged earlier, he noticed that she changed her perfume.

It's strange, how he can look at her and see that she's beautiful, see all the things that used to make his heart race and his hands ache to touch her, but not feel anything about it other than a diffuse and not unpleasant sort of nostalgia.

Nick puts on a record—the kind of jazz where the individual notes refuse to organize themselves into a melody—and Andy keeps everyone's wineglasses filled.

One afternoon this week they went to Andy's old apartment and packed up a couple things to bring to Nick's—Andy's summer clothes and tennis gear, a dozen wineglasses ("a dozen people could not fit in this apartment, Andrew"), four chairs, and a stack of dishes. When they sit at the table, Emily looks at the dishes and does a double take, probably not expecting bone china to make an appearance in Nick's apartment. She glances at Andy and raises an intrigued eyebrow. Andy smiles as if he has no idea what she's getting at. So what if he brought his grandmother's wedding china with him to Nick's, carried in the back seat of a cab like a sack of groceries? It doesn't have to mean anything, and it isn't as if Nick knows. Besides, the wineglasses are from Woolworth.

The dish Nick made is chicken stewed in tomato sauce with mushrooms and fried eggplant, and he serves it along with a bowl of spaghetti. "Chicken cacciatore," he says, plonking the dish onto the table as if daring anyone to argue with him.

"Nick," Emily says after a few bites. "I had no idea you could cook."

"That's because you don't know anyone at all who can cook," Andy points out.

"I can cook," Linda interjects. "I mean, I don't, but I *can*." Linda's family is relatively normal, compared to the Warburtons.

"Don't tell me you helped," Emily says, looking at Andy.

"Oh, no," Andy says seriously. "I'm not allowed."

"I let you chop the eggplant!" Nick protests.

"When he's doing serious cooking, he sends me on errands to keep me out of his way," Andy says.

"Well, you're a menace," Nick says, utterly failing to keep the warmth from his voice, and Andy doesn't dare so much as *look* at him.

After dinner, they sit around in the living room and Andy opens the windows to let out some of the heat. The sounds from the street below—the occasional honking car horn or person hollering—drift up and mingle with the music from the record player and the hum of conversation. They're well into the third bottle of wine, not counting whatever Nick put into the stew, and everyone is pleasantly loose.

Emily moves toward the open window and gestures for Andy to come over.

"I want some fresh air," she says. "Let's sit on the fire escape."

Nick coaxed Andy out there a few days earlier on one of the first genuinely warm evenings of the season, insisting it was safe, telling him stories about sleeping out on the fire escape during the hottest part of summer when he was a kid. They sat side by side, watching the people in the building across the street and down the block doing the same thing, cigarettes lighting up the night like fireflies.

Andy climbs out first and automatically offers Emily his hand. Her hand feels small and strong in his own, at once strange and intensely familiar. As she lowers herself to sit, he crouches down and feels around in the potted basil plant and finds a pack of cigarettes with a lighter tucked inside. He holds it out to Emily, then leans in and lights it before lighting his own. Nick has lit almost all his cigarettes for nearly two months. It's a meaningless statistic—Andy hardly smokes in the first place—but it pleases him anyway.

"You look good," she says.

"So do you. You look happy." He realizes as he says the words that he hasn't seen her happy since before she went to London.

He's glad she looks happier now, and his gladness is the relief of a friend; if her former unhappiness had anything to do with him, that's over and done with. The engagement feels ancient, almost irrelevant, a funny thing that happened to them on the way to friendship.

"I think I am," she says.

"I'm glad." He leans back, the stone of the wall cold and rough through the fabric of his shirt. "Do you want to tell me why we're out here?"

She breathes out a puff of smoke. "Maybe later. First we have the customary death threats."

Andy coughs out a lungful of smoke. "What have I done to deserve the honor?"

"You know how when someone begins dating your sister, you have to say something about how if you hurt her, you'll break their knees?"

"You've been spending too much time at the movies."

"Well, I doubt Nick has anyone to threaten you. Or, rather, I doubt anyone knows that they ought to. Which is where I come in," she says cheerfully. "If you hurt Nick, I'll break your knees."

Andy has no idea what to say. He knows that Nick told Emily about that night outside the bar, but how does she know that anything actually happened between them after that? Did Nick tell her? Or is this another instance of Emily's irritating ability to see these things? Is the woman some kind of dowsing rod for homosexuals? Secondly, acknowledging out loud that he and Nick are . . . whatever they are, is terrifying. He remembers when Nick had joked about worrying that vice police might appear out of thin air. Now he realizes that it hadn't entirely been a joke. He swallows. "How did you know?"

"Oh, *Andy.*"

"That obvious, huh?"

"Maybe not to people who don't know both of you."

Andy puts his head in his hands and moans.

"The point, darling," Emily goes on, "is that you had better not hurt Nick, because I know how he feels about you."

Andy goes still. "He said something?"

"No, no. Andy, keep *up*. I've seen how he looks at you."

"Tonight?" Andy supposes they've been making eyes at one another all evening.

"From the beginning."

"Of the evening?"

She laughs in his face. "From when you met him. He's adored you from the jump." She pauses. "No, *adore* isn't the word. I adore ice cream. You adore handmade suits and baseball. Nick *loves* you. He's in love with you."

Andy's throat feels thick and he knows he's blushing. He turns his face away, watching a teenager ride his bike in lazy circles in the lamplight. "Don't be silly," he finally says, because this is typical Emily hyperbole. Nick has always *liked* him, obviously, and Emily is reading too much into it. There's no way Nick had been—attracted to? sweet on?—Andy for all that time. The implications are more than Andy can grapple with.

Emily stretches her legs out so her feet dangle over the edge of the fire escape, one flat black shoe hanging precariously from her toes. "I've had four glasses of wine and I'm feeling very honest, so I'm going to tell you this, even though it's probably a bad idea."

"Now you have me intrigued."

"When I was with Gerald, I know that's how I looked at him. I could feel it on my face. Gooey devotion." She brought her cigarette to her mouth. "I had seen it on Nick's face a thousand times, so when I felt my own face doing it, I knew."

It takes Andy a minute to remember that Gerald is the cardiologist. "How *is* Gerald?"

"Don't change the subject. I don't know what you're doing here with your china and your dinner parties. If you let him think that you're—I don't know, setting up house with him, then make sure you mean it."

"I mean it," Andy says.

Emily is quiet for a moment. "I'm not the one you need to tell," she finally says.

When they come back inside, Jeanne is sitting on the floor, Linda's head in her lap, Nick's record collection scattered around her. Linda is smoking a neatly rolled joint. When Andy sits down beside them, she offers it to him.

"Don't give it to Andy," says Emily from the sofa. "He won't know what it is or what to do with it, the poor lamb."

"I know what it is," protests Andy, and honestly he might be a little insulted. "That," he intones, using his best Walter Winchell voice, "is a jazz cigarette."

Linda, evidently under the influence of the cigarette in question, starts giggling.

"I'm afraid this means you're all beatniks," Andy continues. He's at the stage of tipsiness where it's time to either slow down or fully commit to a lost evening. "You smoke your funny cigarettes and play the bongos and attend jamborees."

"Anyone who brings out a bongo will have me to answer to," Nick says darkly, leaning in the kitchen doorway. He hadn't been in the room when Andy came in from the fire escape and now Andy feels himself smile up at him, helpless and fond.

"I have bongos," Linda says. "And I've been to jamborees."

"Nick should write a profile on you and sell it to *Life* magazine and become famous," Jeanne says.

"I've read that profile," Nick says, still leaning distractingly. "At least three of them. Nobody needs another. If I wrote a profile of you, it wouldn't be because you're a beatnik."

Andy wants to know what Nick would write about, but Linda speaks first.

"Nick, how do you have a hundred records and not a single one you can dance to?" Linda complains.

Nick kneels down beside them and shuffles through the records. His sleeves are rolled up to his elbows and his top button is undone. Andy knows he's staring and isn't sure he can stop. "Here," Nick says, handing a record to Linda. "And this one, too."

"Now you have to dance with me," Jeanne says, her words the tiniest bit slurred. "It's the law."

"Well, in that case." Nick holds a hand out and helps her to her feet, then waits as Linda fiddles with the turntable.

Nick is, unfortunately, an excellent dancer, and Andy has no idea how he's supposed to take his eyes off him as he spins Jeanne deftly around the room. "Fly Me to the Moon" plays, and Nick guides Jeanne over Andy's and Linda's legs and around the coffee table.

"We should probably move the sofa against the wall," suggests Emily. She's lying on the sofa, a cigarette in one hand, displaying no signs of wanting to get off the sofa, let alone move it.

Andy, who was raised to believe it's a mortal sin to sit out a dance if a woman needs a partner, gets to his feet and holds out his hand to Linda.

"What am I, chopped liver?" calls Emily.

"You jilted me," answers Andy. "I'm only dancing with people who haven't jilted me." He blows her a kiss and she sticks her tongue out at him. He catches Nick's eye over Linda's shoulder, and he's looking fondly between Andy and Emily, and something gives way in Andy's heart, some final defense he hadn't known he still had.

When Andy graduated high school, his parents made a rare exception to their policy of never seeing one another, never mentioning one another, and encouraging Andy to participate in the delusion that the other parent didn't exist. They both attended his graduation and even went so far as to jointly take him out to lunch afterward. They both clearly hated every minute of it and it was a miracle the meal hadn't ended with the table being overturned, but for that hour Andy had gotten to have both of his parents, the only family he had ever had, in one place. He had been almost overwhelmed with it, hardly able to believe that this was normal for most people, that this was how most people experienced family.

The idea that he could have that, or something like that, opens up inside him and takes root.

The room is warm despite the open windows and there's a sink full of dishes Andy will have to deal with later. The record is playing too loudly and it's only a matter of time before Mrs. Wojcik from downstairs has something to say about it. But meanwhile, Andy gets to be in a room with his favorite people, dancing with someone who might be a worse dancer than he is, and he's happy.

He and Linda careen into the sofa.

"I have to lead," Linda says. "Sorry, went to an all-girls school and I was too tall to follow. And right now I'm too stoned to learn new things."

Andy puts aside his worries about twisted ankles and adjusts so his left hand is on Linda's shoulder and braces himself for the worst.

"Guess we're going to die," he says when she starts moving.

"Man up, Andrew." She twirls him around with surprising competence and Andy promptly trips over his own foot and smacks his face into her arm. He starts laughing, because it's ridiculous, because it's silly, because this might be the first time dancing has ever been fun.

"Do it again," he says.

This time he manages to duck under her arm when he's supposed to. Or, rather, he manages to let himself be pulled along where she wants him. It's exhilarating, and, sure, some of that is the wine talking, but the rest of it's just Andy having fun while doing something badly. The song changes to something faster and unfamiliar, and he's doing more stumbling than actual dancing, but somehow it doesn't stop being fun.

"I'm cutting in, you oafs," says Jeanne, tapping Andy on the shoulder. Andy isn't sure when Jeanne stopped dancing with Nick, but now Nick is dancing with Emily, and someone has opened a fourth bottle of wine. Andy turns away from Linda to dance with Jeanne, but apparently he's gotten it wrong because Linda and Jeanne are waltzing right into the kitchen.

He collapses onto the sofa and watches. It's only natural for him to watch Nick now, right? What else is he supposed to do? And Nick is looking back at him with a small secret smile that doesn't belong in public, but maybe this isn't public. This is their home, and maybe they're safe. Realistically, everyone in this room already knows about them—if Emily knows, then Jeanne probably does, too. And Linda lives next door and has seen them often enough to draw her own conclusions. Linda is also dancing cheek to cheek with another woman, and girls' school or no, that's mighty interesting.

So he lets himself enjoy the sight of Nick moving, the way he leans close to whisper something to Emily while never taking his eyes off Andy, the way he can almost imagine Nick's big hands on him instead.

When the record ends, Jeanne looks at her watch and shrieks. "It's past midnight."

"Pumpkins," Emily says somberly.

"Little talking mice," Linda agrees.

Andy levers himself to his feet and participates in the hunt for purses and cardigans and cigarette cases.

"I'll walk them downstairs and put them in a cab," says Nick, leaning close to Andy's ear. "You look beat."

Andy kisses and hugs both sisters good night. There's a general round of futile late-night attempts to plan another gathering and then they're gone, leaving Linda and Andy alone in the kitchen.

"I won't say a word," says Linda as she watches Andy fill the sink with water and dump in some dish soap. She sounds deadly sober.

Andy doesn't pretend not to understand. "I trust you."

"I trust you, too," Linda says.

Families might usually be bonded by blood, but maybe sometimes they're bonded by shared secrets, by a delicate mixture of caution and faith, by the conviction that hiding together is better in every way than hiding alone.

CHAPTER TWENTY

A ndy is piling dishes in the sink when he hears the door open and close, then the slide of the bolt in the lock. There's the familiar sound of Nick kicking off his shoes, and then a minute later he hears the window sliding closed and the curtain being drawn. Music starts playing—not the record they had played earlier, but something else.

"Come here," Nick says, hooking his chin over Andy's shoulder. "Leave the dishes."

Andy dries his hands on his pants and turns in Nick's arms.

"Earlier," Nick says, "I wanted to dance with you."

Andy had wanted that, too. "You weren't missing out on much."

"Bullshit." He takes one of Andy's hands and puts his other hand on Andy's shoulder. Andy lets himself fall into position, his free hand landing at the small of Nick's back. When Andy steps into the dance, he feels Nick go along with him.

"You're letting me lead."

Nick's voice comes low in Andy's ear. "A concussion is not what I have planned for the rest of the night."

Andy shivers, as if he hasn't already been thinking along the same lines. Nick's chest is hard against his own, his hand firm on

Andy's shoulder, his frame broader and bulkier than Andy's, and it's so different from dancing with a woman that Andy can't avoid thinking about it. When kissing Nick, even when in bed with Nick, Andy seldom thinks about how what they're doing is different from his past experiences, probably because he just hadn't had that much experience before Nick.

But he's danced with many, many women. School formals, debutante balls, college parties, friends' weddings, nightclubs. Andy seldom sits out a dance. And so the feel of Nick's body against his, the stubble scraping against his cheek, the lack of a skirt brushing against his trousers, the fact that they're almost the same height—the differences stack up until he feels like he's doing something shocking and brave and new.

"Have you ever danced with a man before?" Andy asks.

"A couple of times." A few bars of the song pass. "But nothing special."

The implication is that this *is* special, which Andy knows, or should have known. Nick's made it clear that in the past his encounters were mostly quick and efficient, but now Andy wants to hear it again. "Have you ever done . . . this before?" He trusts that Nick will understand that he doesn't mean dancing.

Nick shakes his head. "Never."

Andy shifts his hands and it takes Nick a moment to catch on. "You want me to lead?"

"Yeah," Andy admits, not quite understanding why it's an admission in the first place. He wants to be danced with the way he's seen Nick dance with other people. He wants Nick in all the ways that he can have him. He kisses the slope of Nick's neck, feels the answering shiver.

Nick maneuvers them into the living room and, with one hand, switches records, hardly missing a beat. Andy knows this song—

"You Send Me." The hand at the small of Andy's back pulls him closer, holds him in place, and the dance shifts into something else. Against his neck he feels Nick's breath, hot and humid.

Andy has to keep repeating the bare facts of the situation to himself, checking and rechecking his math like a baffled child. This is a love song—at the very least a romantic song—and Nick deliberately chose it. He adds this to the other facts: Nick's pleasure at receiving flowers, Emily's words on the fire escape. The rest of it—Nick's perpetual kindness to him, the way Nick looks after him—could all be explained by friendship, couldn't it? The sex itself doesn't enter into the calculation: people have sex all the time without this other, softer feeling.

Andy swallows. "I like this," he whispers, because he can't say any of the other honest things.

Nick lets out a soft exhale, a sound like he's giving up, giving in. He lets go of Andy's hand and holds his hips instead, and Andy wraps his arms around Nick's neck. The hard press of Nick's body against his mimics the weight of being pressed into the mattress, and Andy decides that they've gone long enough without kissing. He kisses Nick's throat, his jaw, his chin, and when he finally connects with Nick's lips, they both gasp.

Andy feels himself being steered backward until he hits the wall, Nick still kissing him, still pressing against him, the record still playing. Andy sucks gently on Nick's bottom lip and Nick's grip tightens. He wants to get closer—he needs more, he needs everything, and he doesn't trust his mind to come up with the words. He hooks his leg around Nick's hips, and Nick groans, grabbing Andy's ass and lifting him, until both his legs are wrapped around Nick's waist. Then Andy's frantically popping open the buttons of Nick's shirt, searching for skin, for the warmth of him, for more and more and more.

"Bed," Andy gasps, and Nick actually starts to *carry him down the hall*, which is about enough to give Andy a small, if pleasant, stroke. "Down," he manages. Nick lets him go with palpable reluctance, his arms tight even as Andy's feet hit the floor, and it's a miracle Andy doesn't sink to his knees right then and there. But he wants whatever's about to happen next to happen in their bed.

They get there, they even manage to get their clothes off, and then Andy is on his back, his head on the pillow, one knee bent. Nick comes over like he's a puppet and Andy's just pulled his string. "I want you," Andy says, drawing Nick close, between his legs. "Will you?" He's relying on Nick to get the message, to not make Andy say it.

Andy's not sure he's ever seen Nick look so frantic. "You." His voice is hoarse. "I thought—"

"I want you to," Andy repeats, more firmly now, but he's pretty sure he looks as wild as Nick does. "I've been thinking about it." A deep breath, and he puts his arms around Nick's neck. "Is that something you want?"

"Is it—Jesus, Andy— *yeah*." The only light is coming from the lamp still on in the living room, but it's enough for Andy to see that Nick's eyes are dark and steady, and he hopes that Nick can see how much Andy wants this, how serious he is.

"Good." He rocks his hips up, feeling Nick's hardness with his own. Nick swears and the sound ricochets through Andy's nerves.

Andy actually has thought this through. He figures that if Nick does it to him first, then the worst-case scenario is that Andy will know what to do if he does it to Nick. But he thinks he'll like it. Conceptually, at least. A jealous streak he never knew he had will only be satisfied if he has Nick in every way Nick's been with other men. But more than that, when he thinks about it—Nick in him, having him, enjoying him—it makes his mouth go dry, makes his skin feel a size too small. He wants this.

One of Nick's hands is cradling Andy's head as they kiss, the other fumbling in the bedside drawer for what Andy realizes is a jar of Vaseline. He puts two and two together and feels a flush spread across his whole body as desire and curiosity and annoying embarrassment mingle together into one powerful, heady thing. And then—Nick is kissing his way down Andy's chest, and his mouth, his *mouth*, Andy will never get enough of it.

He tries not to think about exactly what's happening and instead focus on the sensations, but he can't stop thinking about Nick's hands, his fingers, how things can be lovely and strange and good and too intense all at once, and how there's probably a metaphor in there, but he's too worked up to think straight. So he pushes up on his elbows to watch what Nick's doing.

Nick catches him watching. "Jesus," he mutters. "Killing me, Andy."

And then Nick is braced over him, whispering things, talking him through it, slowly, slowly breaching him, tense with the effort of holding back. That's, maybe, when it starts to feel good, when Andy realizes how much work Nick is putting into being gentle. And that's what's always done it for Andy, isn't it, the fact that Nick is just so good to him. He tries to tell him so, but all that comes out is "so good," which is also true.

And then things really start to get good when Nick stops being so gentle. After that, it's Andy's mouth on Nick's shoulder, his hand on Nick's back, the steady thrum of desire coiling inside him. "Sweetheart," Nick rasps.

Afterward, Nick's arms are around him, his face in Andy's hair, and only then does Andy realize that Nick is unusually silent. When he turns his head, he sees a muscle tensing in Nick's jaw.

"Are you all right?" Andy asks.

"Jesus Christ, yes."

"I don't mean your dick, Nicholas. I mean your brain."

Nick snorts at this. "I'm good." And he kisses Andy long enough that he forgets he had anything to worry about.

Andy wakes to an empty bed and a quiet apartment. He doesn't hear the shower running or the percolator bubbling. He doesn't hear off-key humming or the sizzle of eggs in a pan.

When he gets out of the shower, there's still no sign of Nick. He probably went out to get the paper and some bagels, like he does most Sunday mornings. But usually he waits until Andy's awake. Usually he asks if Andy wants to come, because he knows that Andy's a giant baby about being alone, but he's too kind to mention it and instead lets Andy tag along on all his errands like a well-behaved dog.

Andy is reminding himself that nobody gets mugged or beaten at ten A.M. on a Sunday when he hears the door open. And, sure enough, Nick comes in with a bag of bagels, a couple of Sunday papers, and a stricken expression.

"I thought you'd still be asleep."

"I just woke up," Andy says, which is an obvious lie because he's standing there in a towel, dripping wet.

"I thought about waking you, but you looked . . ." He breaks off, his face doing something complicated.

"No, it's good. I needed the sleep."

Nick stares for a minute, clutching the bagels and papers to his chest like a life preserver. "I'll." He clears his throat. "Coffee." He disappears into the kitchen.

Nick is weird sometimes. That's all. Today he's just weirder than usual. Andy gets dressed and when he goes back to the kitchen, there's coffee and a bagel waiting for him next to the *Times* Sunday supplement and a freshly sharpened pencil.

He's on his second cup of coffee, halfway through his bagel, reading an article about yet another atrocity Robert Moses wants to commit in Lower Manhattan, when he realizes Nick hasn't said a word the whole time. He isn't even looking at the newspaper open in front of him.

"Okay, out with it," Andy says, folding up his paper and tossing it aside. "What's eating you?"

Nick makes a noise, a single syllable of confusion. "Nothing?"

"Oh my God, stop. Don't lie to me. Do you need me to get out of here for a few hours? I could visit my dad."

"Why would you think that?" Nick looks like he's been slapped.

"Because—you're not acting like you want me here!" Andy knows he isn't being fair. Nick's unusually silent for one meal and Andy's jumping to conclusions. He's not being fair at all.

The truth is that after last night, Andy feels like his body has been rearranged in some subtle way and that now it belongs to Nick; it's a stupid thought but he's having it anyway. He's worried that what they did somehow ruined things, and that this is why Nick can't look at him normally, as if everything they were to one another hinged on a secret No Sodomy clause that neither of them knew about. He's just filled with dumb ideas this morning, but they're the only ideas he has, so he's keeping them.

"I always want you here!" Nick's on his feet now. He steps around the table and kneels in front of Andy. "That's the problem."

"Care to explain that?"

"Not really."

Andy sighs. Operating on the idea that if a man's kneeling at your feet, he probably isn't cross with you, Andy touches Nick's cheek. Nick presses into the touch. "Try anyway."

"I should have tried to get you and Emily back together."

Andy is too stunned to come up with anything more incisive than "What?"

"That would have been best for everyone, right? You loved one another and you could have made it work again. Then you wouldn't have to worry about being found out."

He strokes a thumb over Nick's perfect cheekbone. "I'm not worried about that."

"Christ, Andy. You should be."

"We're careful."

"Come on, Andy. There are going to be rumors. The two of us living together? Neither of us dating women? What happens when those rumors start?"

Andy doesn't have an answer. "I've been trying not to think about it," he admits. When he does think about it, he reassures himself that people have brazened out all kinds of rumors. His parents both have. Plenty of people still think his mother was a Soviet spy, for crying out loud, and that never stopped her.

For a minute he lets himself imagine the worst—if he and Nick are exposed, if rumors start to fly. Andy has connections, a little money, an entire fucking newspaper. He can leverage that into some kind of future. Nick has none of that. He's still starting out and has no resources to fall back on. Brazening it out isn't an option. "I want you to be safe. Do you want me to start taking girls out to dinner?"

"No," Nick says darkly. "I just thought—what was Emily

saying to you out on the fire escape? Was she— Is she—" Nick doesn't seem to be able to get the words out. "Does she want to try again? With you."

Andy can't help the laugh that forces itself up from his chest. "Um, no. She told me that if I hurt you, she'd break my kneecaps."

Nick looks appalled. "Why would she say that?"

Andy can't very well tell him that it's because she believes Nick has been in love with Andy for a year. And he certainly can't say that he's starting to think she's right. "Honestly, I think she just enjoys threatening violence." He tips Nick's chin up. "I don't want to get back together with Emily, you jackass," he says gently. "Tell me you know that." Nick looks away and grunts noncommittally. Andy rolls his eyes. "I'm with you. Aren't I?"

He means for it to sound rhetorical, but the question comes out too earnest, a little desperate, every bit of doubt in his mind finding its way into those few syllables. It's one of his worst qualities, this need for reassurance, this fear that he's not wanted. But they are together, aren't they? Nick could just confirm it, couldn't he?

Nick doesn't do that. "I keep thinking that whoever you date next—whoever you marry—won't like me half as much as Emily does. I would have still—if you and she had gotten married, I'd still have gotten to be around you."

It takes Andy a minute to realize what Nick is saying and when he does, he slides onto the floor beside him. He's not the only one in this room who needs reassurance, apparently. "This is all my fault," he says, wrapping his arms around Nick's neck. "I thought you understood. But I forgot that you're a goddamn *idiot*." He kisses the corner of Nick's stupid mouth. "I love you. I love you and I'm *in* love with you. I don't know how to make this clearer. I'm not biding my time here. I'm *here*."

"But you shouldn't be," Nick mumbles into Andy's hair, but then pushes him down onto the kitchen floor, kissing him and kissing him.

"Are you going to be this brainless after every time you fuck me?" Andy asks, a little breathless. "I just need to know so I can plan in advance."

Nick doesn't answer because he's too busy shoving Andy's shirt up and unbuckling his belt, and the linoleum is hard against Andy's back but he doesn't care, he doesn't care at all.

CHAPTER TWENTY-ONE

On Monday morning, Andy gets off the elevator with Nick in a sad attempt to put off going to his too-quiet office upstairs.

He misses the newsroom, not only the things he likes—the noise, the constant sense of things being discovered and history being written—but the things he actively hates—the cigarette butts and pencil stubs that litter the floor, the overhead light that flickers, that one copyboy who seems to function as the office bookie. Being here now, he feels homesick.

When he gets to Nick's desk, he really ought to say goodbye and go upstairs, but he hangs around. There's an envelope on Nick's desk—it's not an interoffice envelope, but it hasn't gone through the post office, either. There's no stamp, no address, just Nick's name written in blocky capitals. Nick rips the flap open and peers inside, then dumps the contents onto his desk. It's a pile of photographs.

Nick seems frozen in place, so Andy fans the photographs out, spreading them across the desk. They're all photographs of Nick. There he is lighting a cigarette outside the *Chronicle* building, and there he is leaving O'Connell's. There's a picture that's obviously shot through the window of a luncheonette of Nick sharing a table with a blond woman Andy recognizes as Nick's source at the Property Clerk's Office.

There's a picture of Nick and Andy carrying groceries two days ago. One of Andy letting himself into Nick's building carrying an armful of sweet peas. Another of Nick and Andy sitting on the fire escape just last night.

"Shit," Andy says.

"There's nothing incriminating," Nick says—whispers, really. "We weren't doing anything wrong."

"It's a threat."

"A threat to do what, expose that I buy groceries? I'll stop meeting with that secretary, though."

It's true that there isn't anything explicit in those photographs. Looking at them, Andy can't tell if he's standing too close to Nick, if that expression on his face is too fond, if there's anything inherently queer about goddamn sweet peas.

"It's a threat," Andy repeats. "They're letting you know that the minute you do anything, you'll be exposed." The minute Nick goes to a gay bar, the minute he talks to the wrong man in public, it's over for him. Nick effectively has no privacy now and neither does anyone he's with. They're careful in public; of course they are. And since they've been together, Nick hasn't gone to gay bars or anyplace like that. Otherwise, these pictures could very well be in front of a judge, not on Nick's desk.

It's a threat, and not just to Nick. Andy's in more than ten of these photos. He can't believe Nick doesn't see it—Nick, who only yesterday was worried about rumors.

"Who's 'they'?" asks Nick.

"You can't be serious. The police. We already knew they were angry about that evidence story. There's been a cop outside our building for weeks, ever since—shit."

"Ever since what?"

"Ever since we ran into that cop at the fire in Gowanus." Andy remembers the way the cop's eyes had narrowed when he realized that the Nick Russo who was writing the stories about the missing police evidence was the same Nick Russo he had once arrested. Andy hadn't put it together at the time, and Nick had probably been too shaken up to realize, but now it seems all too clear.

Something happens to Nick's face, and Andy knows he's watching the last shreds of denial get whisked away. He wants to take Nick in his arms, but they're in the middle of the newsroom. Instead the best he can do is squeeze Nick's shoulder and tell him to talk to Jorgensen.

One of the photographs catches his eye. It's the one where they're each carrying two sacks of groceries. Andy's caught mid-laugh, his face turned to Nick. It's a good picture, and that might make Andy angriest of all, because under any other circumstances he'd want to keep it. But he can't keep it, because it's sordid. It's a weapon. He and Nick laughing and buying groceries is now an ugly, dangerous thing.

"Are you going to drop that story?" Andy asks mildly that night while they're clearing the table after dinner.

"What? Hell no."

Andy forces himself to sound calm. "Why not?"

"Those photographs are just more proof that they have something to cover up. They wouldn't have bothered otherwise."

"Did you tell Jorgensen?" Andy asks, already fearing the answer.

"If I showed those pictures to anyone, it would be as good as admitting that I'm queer, and that you are, too. Jorgensen's smart enough that he'd figure it out right away."

He's right. The fact of the photographs is an announcement that whoever took them knows Nick has something to hide. Even if Jorgensen doesn't have any problems with a queer reporter working for him, the news would get around. There's nowhere in the world gossip travels faster than at a newspaper.

"You're right," Andy concedes. "Okay. You can find a pretense to drop the story, then."

"I already said no."

Andy's known for over a year that Nick is stubborn, but this is ridiculous. "Listen, Nick. They're not going to be able to hurt you with those photographs, right? You haven't been doing anything incriminating in public lately. So they're going to try something else. How do you know those kids who mugged you weren't put up to it by the same people who took those photographs? And even if they weren't, the next people who hurt you will be."

"You're overreacting."

"Nick. I can't stand the idea of you getting hurt. I can't."

"This is my job," Nick says, something grim and closed off in the way he says it.

For as long as Andy's known Nick, he's understood that Nick keeps people at arm's length, and for good reason. This is how Nick stays safe—or thinks he does. But sometimes there's a fatalistic edge to his isolation, as if he thinks that he's doomed to be alone. Or, in this case, that he's doomed to go do stupid, dangerous things.

Nick squeezes his hand but doesn't say anything and Andy doesn't pursue the topic because the thing is, it never works. He probably asked his mother a dozen times not to take a dangerous assignment, and she never listened, because she went where the story was. That was her priority, not her son's worry.

He isn't sure why he expected any different from Nick.

After finding the photographs on Monday morning, the rest of the week is quiet. It isn't even strained, because Andy won't let it be, and Nick meets him halfway. Andy's heart is working double time, but he thinks he's doing a good job of hiding it.

On Friday, Andy lingers after the usual morning meeting. He watches as the editors file out of the room, the last one shutting the door behind him.

He's been meaning to ask his father about expanding the Sunday supplement. Right now it's a Frankenstein's monster of syndicated columns, recipes, television listings, and a seemingly random assortment of features. Andy wants to know what it would cost to turn it into a proper magazine—a magazine with the *Chronicle*'s editorial perspective and the cachet to be financed by something other than ads for department store underwear sales. What he's not comfortable saying—what he's not even sure he's comfortable thinking—is that the *Chronicle*'s editorial perspective is something he can change. If—God help them all—he's this paper's publisher, then that's very much in his job description.

And he's not sure he can separate his own perspective from the paper's. He's not sure he should. Right now Andy's perspective is shaped by too many things to count: the values he had passed on to him by his parents, the things he saw in Washington, the fact that Nick's been shutting the curtains before so much as cooking dinner in case someone across the street has a telephoto lens.

For now, though, he's only asking about budgets.

But his father speaks first. "Have you decided whether to put your mother's apartment on the market?"

Andy had offhandedly mentioned this plan last week, but the idea of actually getting rid of all his mother's things is daunting both physically and emotionally. And he's a little hesitant to sell the apartment without Nick having said— Well, Andy isn't sure what he's expecting Nick to say. He isn't expecting an engraved invitation to spend the rest of their lives together, but he needs to know that Nick actually wants him to stay.

That isn't quite accurate—it's pretty obvious that Nick does want him there, but deciding to settle down with someone can't possibly be as simple as Andy not moving out. He feels like there ought to be a conversation, some kind of confirmation that what they're doing actually is settling down. He's had this thought so many times that the phrase *settling down* has ceased to carry any meaning.

"Not yet," Andy says.

"I wondered if you needed help finding a new place to live."

"I don't," Andy says, feeling churlish for not offering any more information than that. His father is trying.

His father takes off his glasses and polishes them. "There's always room at my apartment."

"Thank you," Andy says, "but I'm happy where I am."

His father puts his glasses back on, regards Andy, then apparently thinks better of it and resumes polishing his glasses. "During the war I knew men who . . ." He sighs, polishing his glasses some more. "I know that 'enlightened minds' would have us think of it as an affliction, and before that it was just garden-variety sexual perversion, but . . ." He trails off again, and Andy thinks he'll never recover from hearing his father say the word *sexual.* "But I never thought so," he says now, looking Andy squarely in the eye.

The fact that Andy can follow his father's thoughts through sentence fragments and lacunae—and that his father knows he can—reveals any secrets Andy might have wanted to keep. Andy can hardly believe he isn't blushing, and is pretty sure that's only because he's gone pale. "I see," he manages.

"During all that . . . unpleasantness with the senator, homosexuals had a bad time of it as well." The senator, of course, was McCarthy. "Still do. I've never figured out how homosexuals are supposed to be especially vulnerable to communism. It does make one wonder what they all thought went on at IWW meetings."

Andy laughs, just one startled involuntary cough of a laugh. His father joking is rare enough. His father joking about communist orgies is something else altogether.

"My point is that there are other homosexuals in this business, of course. Even at the *Chronicle*. Some are discreet. Some are lucky. And it doesn't matter to me, except insofar as I'll do my best to protect them from the vagaries of law and public opinion."

It takes a moment for Andy to understand that his father is offering acceptance—not a silent sort of acceptance or a tacit agreement that neither of them would mention Andy's love life, but something overt and undeniable. Maybe it shouldn't be a surprise—his father has made a career out of disagreeing with conventional wisdom. And more than that, his father, for all his failings as a parent, is a good man and a broad-minded one. But it's a surprise anyway, and Andy doesn't know how to respond.

He remembers that Nick was distressed when Andy mentioned that his father had more or less guessed that they were together. Andy could probably still deny that anything's going on, and his father might even believe him. But that would cheapen what his father is offering, put distance between him and his father, and relegate Nick to a dirty little secret. And more than that, it means something to Andy—something he can hardly put into words— that his father is speaking up when he could have remained silent.

"What did my mother think?" Andy blurts out.

If his father is dismayed to hear his ex-wife mentioned, he doesn't show it. "Your mother was always ready to champion any-one whose rights were trampled upon," his father says carefully, coming close enough to paying a compliment to Andy's mother that Andy's a bit taken aback. "You know that."

It's pitiful, probably, to crave his mother's posthumous ap-proval, but he does, and he's grateful his father managed to give it to him.

"Thank you," he says. Nick would probably pay any price to hear his mother say half of what Andy's father has told him.

He realizes that his father is trying very, very hard to be a parent—or maybe a mentor, or maybe just a decent person. He thinks of all the ways his father has tried to reach out to him in the past few months: the repeated offers of a place to stay, the fact that he didn't even blink at the idea that his son might be queer, and—maybe most of all—his conviction that Andy can, in fact, successfully run the paper. His father is trying.

In the spirit of honesty and disclosure or whatever is happen-ing right now, Andy almost tells his father everything—that he doesn't know what to do, that he's fallen in love with a man who won't keep himself safe. That he's afraid he's going to make him-self miserable and ruin the *Chronicle*.

But before he can formulate a sentence, his father puts his glasses down.

"Oh! That reminds me. I heard from David Hollenbeck—managing editor of the *Journal-American*—that we're going to be losing Mr. Russo. Give him my congratulations, will you?"

Andy only stares. He must have heard that wrong. "I— What?"

His father is silent for a moment, looking as if he'd like to crawl into a hole and polish his glasses in peace for an eternity. "Perhaps Dave and I got our wires crossed."

"Dad."

"I wouldn't have said anything if I thought you didn't know."

"*Dad.*"

"They offered Mr. Russo a column and a salary that we wouldn't have been able to match."

Andy is reeling. He's in free fall. "Thanks for telling me."

"I didn't mean to tell you," his father laments.

"But thanks anyway," Andy says, already at the door.

"Talk to him!" his father calls, and Andy hardly even notices that this is the first advice his father's ever given him.

It's cowardly, but he asks his father's secretary to phone down to the newsroom and ask Nick to meet him in the morgue.

He's already leaning against a tall filing cabinet when Nick walks in.

"What's the matter?" Nick asks.

Andy leads Nick to a corner in the back of the room. "Why in hell didn't you let me know you were leaving the *Chronicle*?" he hisses. "My father just told me!"

Nick looks hurt, which is mighty rich. "I'm not sure what your father heard, but I'm not leaving the *Chronicle*. I decided to turn down the offer."

Andy waves this away. His heart is racing and facts feel highly unimportant. "I can't believe you'd even think about leaving without telling me!" He's panicking. He knows he is, feels the fear swirling around in his head and his gut, displacing anything like logic or goodwill. This is twice in one week that he's made his dumb brain into Nick's problem and he knows it isn't right, but fear and anxiety are driving the car.

"I'm *not* thinking about it. They made the offer, I'm turning it down, the end."

That was future tense—Nick hasn't turned down the offer yet. "When? When did they offer you a column?"

"They called two weeks ago."

"Two weeks!" That was two weeks where Nick could have turned down the offer but didn't, could have told Andy but didn't.

"And I had lunch with Dave last week."

"Lunch!"

"I told you, I'm turning it down."

Mother of God, Andy's eyes are burning. He's going to cry in the goddamn morgue. "I don't know what I'd do without you here. I can't—I don't want to. *Nick*."

Nick's hand twitches, like he wants to reach out and take Andy in his arms, but they both know he can't. Secluded corner or no, that's too much of a risk. Instead he takes Andy's hand. "I'm not going anywhere."

"When my father leaves. I—I won't have anyone. I don't. I can't." This is all panic. This is one hundred percent desperate, ugly, anxious clinginess and he should stop, but he can't.

"Listen to me." Nick's voice is low. "Sweetheart, listen."

But Andy doesn't want to listen. "I don't want you to leave me."

"Baby, I'm not leaving you. I told you, I didn't accept the offer."

In some inaccessible part of his brain, Andy knows that Nick is being very patient. Andy ignores this part of his brain with all his being. "Well, you should have."

Nick drops his hand and takes a step back. "Andy, what the fuck."

"My father said it was a good offer. A column and much more money. You'd have free rein to write about what you want." He doesn't add that maybe a column would make Nick take stories that didn't put the cops' hackles up. Maybe a column would keep Nick safe, even if Nick wouldn't do that much for Andy.

"I'm going to need you to make up your mind here about what you want me to do because my head's spinning."

"You have to do what's best for you. I want what's best for you. But I don't want you to leave me."

Nick throws up his hands. "This is nuts."

Andy can't disagree with him there, but he also can't come up with any way to make this conversation less nuts.

"Besides," Nick goes on, "you already spend most of your time in meetings. It's already not like it was a year ago."

Andy cannot believe he isn't crying. He's almost impressed with himself. But he doesn't know how to explain that this isn't about him wanting to keep things the same; it's about him not wanting to be left. He knows it's unreasonable, but that doesn't make it any better.

"And we both know," Nick goes on, picking up speed, annoyance building in his tone, annoyance that Andy knows he richly deserves, "that when you're the publisher, you aren't going to be able to live in a rattrap apartment with one of your reporters. You just aren't."

Andy's aware that Nick's argument has holes, but he's too worked up to find them. He has just enough sense to know that he needs to quit before he makes Nick angrier, because then Nick really will leave. He wants to tell Nick that he loves him, but his entire experience with that phrase is that it does nothing to stop anyone from leaving.

When Andy doesn't say anything, Nick goes on, more gently now. "You must have thought of this already, right?"

Andy hasn't, though. He hasn't thought about it in the same way that for months he didn't think about the dip of Nick's collarbone, the restless urge to touch him, what all of that meant. He pushed that thought safely to the side, out of view, where it couldn't bother anybody.

And now he's furious that Nick made him look at it.

Andy can't take it anymore. "There's nothing I can say to that, is there? I'm going to go home. I'll see you tonight."

"Andy—"

"No, I can't do this anymore." He gestures at his face, hoping that Nick sees how dangerously close to tears he is.

"I'll put you in a cab."

Like hell he will. "I'm a grown man. I can take the subway."

Nick looks stung and Andy doesn't even care.

CHAPTER TWENTY-TWO

Andy's anger dissipates by the time he takes his first breath of stale subway air. All that remains is his shame and the too-familiar dread of being left. He's tempted to go back through the turnstile, climb the stairs, and return to the *Chronicle*. He could apologize to Nick, do his best to patch up the mess he's made.

But he has enough sense to know that this would only add to the day's dramatics. He needs to make sense of what that argument was about. They had been quarreling about too many separate items, tangled together in ways Andy will only be able to pick through if he's calm. Nick's career is ultimately Nick's decision, and Andy knows that he needs to either back off or be supportive. Likewise, Andy's dread about running the *Chronicle* is really not something he needs to drag Nick into. That all seems straightforward now that he's sitting in a half-empty subway car taking him away from Nick, away from work.

More worrying is Nick's belief that what they're doing is only temporary. This isn't the first time that Nick has said something like that. He's right that rumors are inevitable, and Andy already knows that he can't ask Nick to endure that. He's pretty sure Nick thinks Andy will walk away before they even get to that point.

Andy wants to somehow persuade Nick—and maybe himself—that there isn't an inevitable end to this. But he has a sinking sense that he'll lose that fight, that no matter how long they stay together there will always be a piece of Nick waiting for the end, and that breaks Andy's heart.

When Andy gets home, someone is sitting on the stoop. Andy takes one look at the olive skin and mop of dark curls and wonders how Nick managed to get here first. He quickens his step.

But this is a kid—skinny, hunched over, and, Andy notices with a sigh, bleeding into his handkerchief. Could be one of the neighborhood toughs, but toughs probably don't wear shirts and ties.

He's about to offer to buy this kid a Coke and give him a subway token when he recognizes him.

"Sal?"

Nick's nephew looks up abruptly, his fists clenched, as if he's ready to throw a punch. From the looks of his face, it wouldn't be the first fight he's had that day. One of his eyes is swollen and there's a cut on his chin.

"I'm friends with your uncle Nick. We met at your house. My name's Andy." Sal looks at him blankly. "Your grandmother sent me home with a bucket of tomato sauce," Andy adds, as if this will be the decisive information the kid needs.

"What are you doing here?" Sal asks.

"I think that's my line."

Sal scowls. "I'm here to see my uncle."

Andy looks at his watch. "It's not even noon. He'll still be at work."

"I can wait."

Andy glances across the street to where that cop had been stationed for the past two weeks. He isn't there, so that's one less thing to worry about.

"Sure, if you want to dehydrate and get sunstroke. Your uncle will love that. I can let you into his apartment and we can call him."

Sal narrows his eyes. "Why do you have a key to his apartment?"

Andy can't remember if Nick's said anything to his family about Andy still living with him. "I keep a spare in case he locks himself out."

"Why are you in Uncle Nick's neighborhood?"

He goes with the first definitively heterosexual excuse that presents itself to him. "My girlfriend lives next door." Linda, with any luck, will find this funny and play along. "So do you want me to let you in and find you a couple of Band-Aids and a glass of water or do you want to sit out here and bleed all over yourself?"

Sal gets up and grudgingly follows Andy inside, as if he's doing Andy a huge favor. He starts grumbling at about the third floor and doesn't let up.

When Andy pulls out the key he still keeps on a string inside his shirt, he knows he's probably giving the lie to his story about just happening to have a key in case Nick locks himself out. He hopes Sal is too immersed in his own angst to pay much attention to what Andy's doing. Andy's pretty sure fourteen is the least gracious age for human males. On the other hand, he's equally sure that Nick was exactly like his nephew at this age, and finds that he's reluctantly charmed by the kid's sullenness.

He fills two glasses at the tap and brings one to the sofa, where

Sal is somehow managing to slouch miserably. "Will you let me take a look at your face?"

Sal shrugs and Andy peers at him. In addition to the swollen eye and the cut under his chin, there's also a gash across one eyebrow and a couple of old cuts still healing, along with bruises in various stages of fading. "I think some soap and water should do the trick," he suggests. "How'd this happen?"

Sal rolls his eyes. "I walked into someone's fist."

"How many someones?"

"Just one this time."

He wants to ask whether the person who hurt Sal was his father or someone else, but can't figure out how to ask, so he wets a cloth and begins gently dabbing at the worst of the cuts.

"Why'd he do it?" Andy knows as soon as he's spoken that it's the wrong question. There's no good answer, and it sounds like he's asking the kid what he did to deserve a beating.

Sal snatches the cloth from Andy's hand and begins wiping his face himself. "Oh, the usual. I'm a f—" He breaks off. "The usual things. Don't tell Uncle Nick."

Andy can fill in the blank perfectly well. "Nick can keep a secret."

Sal scowls. "I *mean* don't tell him that anyone *calls* me that. I'm not—Jesus. People just say those things when they don't like you. What are you, new?"

Obviously, Andy knows all this. He's heard that word and all the rest of them. But this is the first time since he could reasonably apply them to himself that he's thought about them as generic insults. He tries not to look like he's reeling.

"Do your parents know where you are?"

"I ran away, genius. No, they don't know."

Andy is in over his head. "I'm going to call Nick." He goes over to the phone and dials the *Chronicle* switchboard and a minute later learns that Nick isn't in the office anymore. He isn't surprised—Nick had planned to go to City Hall.

"Right," Andy said. "We need to call your parents."

Sal gets to his feet and heads for the door.

"Hear me out," Andy says. "I'm afraid that your father is going to send some of his cop buddies over here and get your uncle in trouble for, I don't know, kidnapping you or something."

"And telling my dad exactly where I am will prevent that *how?*" He sounds ticked off, but his eyes are suspiciously shiny. Andy has the sense that one wrong word will send him either into tears or back out onto the street.

Andy has no answer for Sal, though. All he knows is that under no circumstances should any cop enter this apartment. The sheets alone would get them arrested. Andy's things are scattered all over Nick's bedroom. Jesus. Okay. He has to think.

"We're going to go next door and say hi to my girlfriend and then all three of us are going out to get pizza." He figures Linda ought to at least get a slice or two out of this. "Why don't you wash your face and take a couple of aspirin while I see if she's home."

He knocks on Linda's door, sending up a silent prayer to any nearby deities that she's home. She answers the door in her usual state: hair piled on top of her head, overalls paint-spattered. "You're a sight for sore eyes," he gushes. "Which is great because you're my girlfriend now."

"Oh boy. This'll be good."

Inside, he explains. "But what I need now," he concludes, "is for you to have Sal over for ten minutes while I clear Nick's apartment of, uh, incriminating evidence."

Linda blinks, apparently unfazed. "Send him over."

Sal grudgingly goes to Linda's for a tour of her studio and Andy tidies up the apartment as he's never tidied anything in his life. He changes the sheets. He stuffs his razor, toothbrush, and most of his clothes into a suitcase and crams it under Nick's bed. He makes up the bed in the spare room and only then does he realize what he should have noticed from the start.

That room at the end of the hall has to be the entire reason Nick chose this apartment instead of a more affordable one-bedroom, or an even more practical room in a boardinghouse. He hadn't meant to use it as a study or whatever it is people do with spare rooms. When Andy moved in, it was already made up as a guest room, its little bed with its cheerful yellow sheets unslept in, its closet empty, the bookcase bare except for a collection of comic books.

The room has always been meant for Sal.

Of course. Of course Nick keeps a bed for the nephew who's being raised by a man Nick doesn't trust. He's kept the room ready and waiting in case his nephew needs a refuge. It's just like Nick, and it's equally like Nick never to mention this to Andy. God forbid he mention his family, not that Andy can blame him, because he can hardly think about Nick's brother without wanting to kick the wall.

But the fact that there's a room for Sal means that there can't be room for Andy. Sal will be Nick's priority, and rightly so. Andy needs to leave. He doesn't know what this means, other than that this isn't Andy's home and it never could have been. Even so, Nick is—Andy's thoughts stutter over how to complete that sentence. Nick is *his*, and Andy will make sure he's safe.

He leaves a note for Nick on the kitchen table, then takes another sheet of paper and writes a note asking Linda to get the suitcase from under Nick's bed and store it in her apartment. This second note he folds up small. Next door, he kisses Linda's hand (she rolls her eyes) and presses the note into her palm. "We'll meet you at the pizzeria in ten minutes, darling."

This is probably how spies feel. Andy is glad he isn't a spy. His heart is pounding and all he can hope is that he's done a good enough job keeping Nick safe.

When they get back from the pizzeria, having put away an entire pie and a half between them and carrying home the remaining slices for Nick, the apartment is still empty. It's only two o'clock. Andy calls the *Chronicle*, but Nick still isn't there.

"You don't have to babysit me." Sal isn't any less sullen after lunch.

"Well, I'm not getting arrested for contributing to the corruption of a minor by leaving you unattended," Andy says.

"I don't think that's a real offense."

"Do you think that'll stop your father's friends from arresting me for it?" Andy asks, slightly frantic.

Sal shrugs, conceding the point. This does not make Andy feel any better. Every time he hears the building door open below, he's convinced it's the police. He is not cut out for this.

Distantly, he hears the building door open again. Andy glances warily at Sal. Since arriving, Sal's started to look progressively wearier, a gray semicircle appearing under his unbruised eye, a brittleness to his surly teenage bravado. Andy wishes he knew what to say or do.

There are footsteps on the stairs, close by, as if they're heading here. Andy holds his breath, and then hears the key in the lock.

About a dozen emotions flicker across Nick's face in quick succession as he opens the door. "I'm glad you came," he tells Sal.

And apparently those are the magic words, because Sal's lower lip quivers and the next moment he's in Nick's arms doing a version of Definitely Not Crying that Andy knows all too well.

Andy probably shouldn't be here, but he can't just leave without explaining to Nick where he's going, or in fact confirming that he *is* going, because that aspect of the problem may not even have occurred to Nick yet.

"Did you have anything to eat?" Nick asks.

"Andy and his girlfriend took me out for pizza," Sal says.

Nick gives Andy a look.

"I found Sal on the stoop when I was stopping by to say hello to Linda," Andy says, hoping he sounds smoother than he feels. "And now I probably ought to be going."

"Sal, do me a favor and scram for two minutes. Your room's at the end of the hall."

They wait until Sal has shut the bedroom door.

"I had to come up with a story on the spot," Andy whispers. "I changed the sheets and got rid of all my stuff. Look, I'd better go. I'm sorry for everything before. I was out of line."

Nick gives him a funny look. "I understand. You know I do, right? And what do you mean you have to go?"

"I can't *stay*," Andy says, gesturing down the hall.

"Oh. Right." Andy can see the moment reality catches up with Nick and something hard and determined flickers over his face. "Thanks for looking after Sal and, uh, ridding the apartment of sexual deviance. Hey, did that cop across the street see Sal?"

"No, he wasn't there when I got home."

"He's not down there now, either. Huh. Anyway, where will you go?"

"Oh, you know." He waves a hand vaguely uptown, not wanting to admit that he's going to stay in his dad's spare room and probably cry about Nick and his mom and a dozen other things.

He even manages a smile before he leaves because it won't do Nick any good to know that he's falling apart.

CHAPTER TWENTY-THREE

When Andy lets himself in to his father's apartment, it's empty. He drops his suitcase, turns on the lights, helps himself to a gin and tonic, and settles on the sofa with a copy of last month's *National Geographic*. But he can hear the clock ticking, the drip of a faucet in the bathroom, and the apartment is so quiet and empty that each sound seems to echo.

He thinks about calling Nick, but the next conversation they have ought to be face-to-face. Andy will make things right when he sees Nick; he thinks he might already have gotten most of the way there. Nick wasn't upset when he got home. They'll figure out how to talk about things sensibly and probably manage another baker's dozen equally inane fights before they get anywhere. That all makes Andy sick to his stomach, but it isn't what he'd call a crisis.

The crisis is that Nick doesn't think they can stay together. And if staying together means living together, Andy might have to concede the point. Being roommates isn't an excuse that will stand up to much scrutiny—not indefinitely, at least. But they could be together without sharing a roof. Andy would miss the shared bed, the morning coffee, the hours of watching Nick cook. But it's better than nothing.

Andy's notion of happiness has always hinged on sharing a home with someone, and he might not get to have that. The past few weeks with Nick have been the first time he really felt like he had a home—not an empty apartment, not a dormitory. A home. He's been fixating on the notion of settling down, of having someone to come home to, but that's only possible in a world where you're allowed space to settle. Maybe Nick's known this all along.

But maybe what Andy needs is to learn to be alone. Maybe he needs to get used to the idea that he isn't going to have the sort of life he can share with anyone. Maybe what he needs is to make peace with a life of waking up alone and learn for that to be enough.

At the sound of a key in the lock, Andy turns to see his father leaning heavily on his cane. He looks awful.

"Andy," he says, sounding surprised but not displeased to see his son. "Everything all right?"

Andy's already on his feet. "Where's the chair?"

"Coat closet." Andy has the wheelchair out and next to his dad in seconds. His father collapses into it with a sigh. "I'm going to need to start having bridge games here," he says.

For lack of any better ideas, Andy pours his father a scotch. "What brings you here?"

There's no point in lying. No point in being anything other than perfectly honest. "Nick's fourteen-year-old cousin is paying him a visit, so I needed to find somewhere else to stay."

"You're always welcome here. Did you, ah, talk to Mr. Russo?"

Mortified, Andy remembers that he had fled from his father's office in an obvious state that morning. "Yes, and I was an enormous baby about it. It's fine now," Andy says.

"He should have told you himself about that job offer," his father says, and Andy remembers Emily on the fire escape threatening to break Andy's knees. His father wants to be in his corner, Andy realizes, touched. "He's a very good reporter, though," his father adds, as if that covers a multitude of sins.

"He really is," Andy agrees.

Once they're settled in the living room, Andy waits for his father to finish his drink and then refills it. He figures this is as good a time as any to bring up what he wanted to talk about after the meeting that morning.

"Has anyone suggested investing in the Sunday supplement?" Andy asks. "Turning it into an actual magazine?"

"It came up a few years ago," his father says carefully. "At the time we decided it was too costly. We'd have to bring on new staff, of course, but also invest in new printing presses."

That's not a refusal, though. Andy seizes on it. "Can I draw up a potential budget? Just to get your opinion," he adds. "Something has to be done to increase circulation, even if it's only Sunday circulation, and people who don't care about newspapers still read magazines. If we're willing to invest, we could attract talent— essays, features, long-form pieces."

"You don't need to persuade me. In less than four months I'll be retired and you can do what you please."

Andy feels like he's going to scream. What he really doesn't need is a reminder that his father is effectively abandoning him— *again*, some very unhelpful voice in Andy's head whispers. "No," Andy says.

"I'm sorry?"

Andy takes a breath and starts over. "I know you aren't up to running the paper. I respect that. I want you to look after your health. And I want to run the *Chronicle*."

This part is mostly true.

The fact is that he doesn't particularly want to be a newspaper publisher. He knows it's his legacy, and a good legacy at that. He and his father are each all the other has by way of family, however distant their relationship, and the *Chronicle* is their point of connection. Andy wants to at least try to maintain that.

But a newspaper is more than a legacy or a job or a family business—it's a mouthpiece, a microphone, a way into the hearts and minds of hundreds of thousands of people. And Andy isn't going to give that up lightly. There are probably dozens of people more deserving and better qualified than Andy to wield the power that publishing a newspaper would give them, but the fact is that Andy's the one who does have this power, and he's going to use it.

He spent his childhood watching his parents use their positions to influence the world—he's not sure either of them would put it so baldly, but that's what they did. His father's still doing it, with every column inch he devotes to civil rights, with every story that treats progressive politics as something other than crypto-communism.

Andy can carry on doing that. He keeps thinking about that *Village Voice* article and he doesn't know if it's just wishful thinking, but if people like him are going to get the law on their side, then having a newspaper sure isn't a bad thing.

"I want to run the *Chronicle*," he repeats. "But I don't want to do it by myself, Dad. I've spent too long doing things by myself." He doesn't mean for it to be a rebuke, but he also doesn't mind if his father takes it that way. The fact is that he's never asked his father for anything. But he's asking for this, and he needs his father to hear it.

"What I was thinking," Andy goes on, "is that I take over as publisher in September, just as you planned. But you stay available as an adviser."

"An adviser," his father repeats.

"Someone with a lifetime's worth of wisdom and experience who I can consult as I need to. You wouldn't have to go into the office if you didn't want."

His father is silent for too long, staring at Andy, his drink forgotten in his hand. "You're asking whether you can telephone me to ask for advice?"

"Well, yes."

"Andy. Son. I— Of course you can."

It's really only then that Andy realizes what he's asking for. He's asking for his father to be a father. And it feels like the biggest favor he's ever asked of anyone. He nearly apologizes, nearly explains that he doesn't make a habit of asking for things, that he hates being a bother. But he thinks his father just figured that out.

His father is still looking at him, shocked and a little ashamed. Andy has to say *something*.

"I think it'll be fun," Andy says, bringing his glass to his mouth. "I have all kinds of ideas."

"I always thought it was," his father agrees, and raises his glass.

After his father goes to bed, Andy checks his watch. Somehow, despite having been awake for what feels like forty-eight hours, it's not even ten o'clock.

He kneels in front of the television, searching for something to watch. A detective show, a police show, another detective show. No thanks. What Andy really wants to watch is the sort of sitcom that revolves around impish kids who get into minor scrapes, their well-dressed parents, and the adorable family dog. Obviously, he knows nobody's life is that perfect; obviously, he knows the reason he likes those shows so much is because they're a glimpse into a kind of stable family life he's never known, but neither of those facts stop him from wanting to watch them.

It occurs to him, though, that hardly anybody he knows grew up that way, either. Nick certainly didn't. Emily and Jeanne went to boarding school. Linda's parents got divorced when she was a kid. Andy had always figured he'd have that kind of life when he grew up, but now that he knows queer people aren't allowed it, he doesn't want it. He feels cheated, like he's gotten to the last page of a book and it turns out the whole story was a dream. The dog dies in the last chapter. You never find out who stole the diamond necklace.

The fact that this thing that's been a source of such comfort to him probably never existed in any meaningful way makes him feel rattled. Everyone he knows is trying to assemble some kind of life from the spare parts they have lying around, just like Andy.

And, fuck it, that's what Andy's going to do. He doesn't care if the world wants to give him space to make a life. He's going to push and shove until he and Nick have the space they need and then he's going to build the kind of life they want. If he wants someone to come home to, and if Nick wants to be that person, then Andy's going to make sure they have it.

Part V

NICK

CHAPTER TWENTY-FOUR

It's only after Nick gets off the phone with his brother that he notices how thoroughly Andy has scrubbed the apartment of all traces of himself. Sure, his fancy dishes are still stacked in the cupboard and his chairs are still arranged around the table. But the bits of detritus that follow Andy around—gum wrappers and envelopes and books open facedown on every surface, including the stove—are gone. His razor and hairbrush are gone. His coffee mug has been cleaned and put away. The pajamas that Nick now thinks of as Andy's are folded neatly at the foot of the bed.

Nick has never hated his apartment so much.

"Okay, slugger," he says to his nephew, who's sitting on the couch, halfheartedly watching *American Bandstand*. Nick has confiscated all the cigarettes and Sal is pretty unimpressed. "Your dad isn't as pissed off as you might have thought."

"Glad to get rid of me," Sal mutters, which Nick suspects isn't far from the truth. "Is he gonna let me stay with you tonight?"

"For the weekend." Nick isn't sure if that's good enough. He still doesn't know exactly what precipitated Sal running away that morning, only that he got on the subway to come here instead of getting on the bus to school. Nick retreats to the kitchen, not returning until he has a glass of bourbon that's a little too full, and sits down on the couch next to his nephew. "Is he hitting you?"

"Jesus, no. I keep telling you that he isn't. My mom would murder him with her own hands."

"Yeah, but I have to ask."

"He doesn't hit me," Sal went on. "He never has. He doesn't hit the girls or Mom, either." His voice is awfully gentle, like he's reassuring Nick, when really it ought to be the other way around.

Shit. Sal had been maybe three years old when Nick hit his growth spurt and nobody—at home or at school—wanted to smack him around anymore. Nick hates to think of Sal—fat-cheeked baby Sal—remembering that.

"I'm glad, kid. I just needed to make sure, you know? I'm not trying to turn you against your father." Nick's glad Michael has his act together. "But who messed your face up?"

"Assholes at the bus stop."

"And so you came here after?"

Sal scowls. "The other day, Dad said that if those kids went after me again, he was showing up at their houses in a patrol car. So I couldn't go to school after that, obviously."

Nick almost laughs, because as far as he can tell this is Michael being something like a decent parent. Something in that ballpark, at least. Go fucking figure. "I guess cops are good for something," he says, and Sal snorts.

Sometimes, when Nick is feeling charitable, he remembers that Michael came home from war to four people who depended on him. He had been twenty-two and had spent his entire adult life in the Pacific Theater. The fact that he came home and took some of his anger out on his kid brother was—it wasn't okay, it might not even be forgivable, but Nick could hope that maybe the person Michael had been in 1945 wasn't around anymore.

When he's feeling less charitable, Nick is pretty sure that now his brother just smacks people around at work. Cops have all kinds of ways to vent their anger.

"Sometimes he calls me names," Sal says, "but nothing like what he called you."

A familiar swirl of panic begins to take root in Nick's gut, the feeling of having been caught, of having been seen for what he is. He can't fill his lungs with air.

Nick is twenty-six. There's no reason in the world why he should be so fucking rattled by memories of being smacked around and called names over ten years ago. Since the night of his arrest, Nick's been telling himself that he shouldn't hold a grudge anymore. The slate is clean between them. Michael's an asshole, sure; but then, Michael saved Nick's future and never so much as mentioned it to Nick or anyone else. That was decent, right?

Except he does sort of mention it. Every time Nick sees his brother, there are sly comments and insinuations. As far as Nick knows, Michael's never told anyone else about Nick's arrest, but those comments make it so the arrest is hanging over Nick's head anyway.

And it's not as if what Michael did for him actually erased the smacking around. So now Nick can't speak, because all he's thinking about is his brother hitting him a dozen years ago and his brother—maybe—tacitly threatening to tell their mother, maybe even threatening to do worse. He thinks again of that envelope of photos, and how easy it would be for someone on the force to unravel Nick's life.

"Uncle Nick?"

"People shouldn't call you names," Nick says uselessly.

Sal snorts and looks at him like he's crazy. "It doesn't *mean* anything. Knowing that my dad called you those things sort of takes the sting out when kids at school say all that stuff to me. Because you're—" He makes a sweeping gesture at Nick.

Nick stares into his half-empty glass. "Kid, the reason it's wrong to call people names is because it's a shitty thing to do, not because it's inaccurate."

"Yeah, but—"

"I mean, do you think I'm not any of those things?" Nick wants to go back in time and talk to himself when he was Sal's age, when he was realizing that all the schoolyard taunts actually applied to him. He wants to see that kid and—and what? What can he possibly tell that kid?

Sal stares at him.

"All those insults do is convince everyone that being, I don't know, sensitive or queer or skinny are the worst things a man can be. And what fucking good does that do anybody? It doesn't matter whether the person being insulted actually is any of those things, but I can tell you that it feels a hell of a lot worse when it's true."

Nick's mouth is dry and his collar feels too tight. He feels exposed. In danger. As if having said that much to his own nephew could come back to haunt him. Sal could tell anyone. Word could get around.

But for the first time, anger outweighs the fear. It's not that the fear is less, only that the anger is more, tipping the scales decisively. All he wants to do is be himself, do his job, and love his boyfriend, and instead he's ready to black out from nerves in his own goddamn apartment.

When Sal turns his attention back to the television, Nick sits next to him, trying to act like the music on this show isn't making him suffer. He keeps thinking of how miserable his fourteen-year-old self would be if he had known that this was his future—afraid in his own home, afraid of his own family, which was pretty much exactly how he'd felt at fourteen.

Sticking out from between the couch cushions, he sees a corner of white linen. It's one of Andy's handkerchiefs. He wonders how many others are in there. Is that where they all go? If Nick took the cushions off, would he find two hundred linen handkerchiefs? Suddenly, he knows exactly what he'd tell his fourteen-year-old self: *You'll be loved by the best person you know.* And that's— Christ, it's not enough, but it's enough to start with.

He goes to the bathroom and splashes some water on his face. When he comes out, he finds Sal standing in front of the refrigerator, the television still playing in the background, the worst music in the world sounding tinnily through the apartment.

"Help yourself to whatever you find in there," Nick says. "I made pork chops last night and there should be a couple left. It's the dish covered in foil."

Sal gets the dish out and puts it on the table. He already has half a slice of pizza in his hand.

"Want me to warm it up?" Nick asks.

"Too hungry," he says through a mouthful of pizza crust.

Nick rolls his eyes and hands the kid a fork and knife as a concession to standards.

"Hey, Uncle Nick," Sal says a minute later. "You never bring girls home." His full attention is on his plate. He's cutting that pork chop as if it's the most fascinating thing in the room, maybe even the world. His cheeks are dark red.

Nick could still walk back what he said earlier. He could tell the lie he's told dozens of times before. He doesn't have time for a steady girlfriend; he's keeping his options open.

Lying would be the safest thing to do. But he thinks he can trust Sal. Even if Sal told his parents, Michael already knows.

Nick swallows hard and admits to himself what he's known all along—Michael has to know. There's no way Michael ever bought Nick's excuse about trying to pick that poor guy's pocket.

Still, lying would also be the easiest option, and not only for Nick. If Nick tells Sal the truth, won't that only make things awkward for Sal?

But if he can't tell one of the only people in his family he actually cares about, then what is a family even good for? He doesn't have an answer now, any more than he did when he was fourteen.

Besides, this is Sal asking for confirmation. From the blotchy red of his face, he knows exactly what Nick was getting at earlier and now he wants to hear it.

"I'll never bring a girl home," Nick says. "I don't like girls that way. Never have."

For a second, poor Sal looks like he wishes he hadn't asked. He shoves more food into his mouth, probably to buy himself time.

"It's okay," Nick says, taking pity on the kid. "You don't have to say anything." There really isn't anything to say, is there? Nick can't imagine that there is. This is the first time he's told anyone so directly, so he wouldn't know.

When Sal swallows, he looks more composed. "I won't tell anyone."

"Thanks, Sal, but I know I can trust you." Then something occurs to Nick. "Do you still want to stay?"

Sal stares at him. "Uh. Yes?" He shoves some more food into his face. "What are you making for dinner?" he asks, his mouth still full.

Nick snorts and takes inventory of what he has in the refrigerator.

Nick needs to talk to Andy, to apologize for this all happening so abruptly and to thank him for taking care of Sal and making the apartment look . . . safe. He hates how they left things that morning and he hates that they haven't had a chance to talk it through, but he doesn't really care about any of that now. He needs to see Andy, even if it's only for two minutes.

When Sal falls asleep, Nick knocks on Linda's door. "Can I talk to Andy for a minute?"

Linda frowns. "He's not here. He left hours ago."

"I thought he said he was staying with you." Nick distinctly remembers Andy gesturing at the wall they share with Linda when Nick asked where he was going.

"He told me he was staying with his father."

Nick pinches the bridge of his nose. The wall he shares with Linda is in the vague direction of uptown—at least if you're Andy and don't know where anything is. He feels suddenly bereft: the idea of Andy next door is so much easier to take than the idea of him sixty-odd blocks uptown.

It's past ten, too late to call Andy's father's apartment. He'll need to wait until tomorrow. But when he goes back to his own apartment, Andy's absence hangs in the air. It feels so implausible that Andy was ever there, that Nick got to have the past few weeks. He never thought he would, so Andy's absence makes sense in a grim sort of way. Now Nick feels foolish, like he tricked himself, believing a fairy tale that was never his to begin with.

Andy's reaction to the *Journal-American* offer was, Nick knows, a bit on the irrational side. The fact that Andy took Nick possibly leaving the *Chronicle* so personally is another reason Nick doesn't love working for his boyfriend. But when Andy said that he didn't want to be left, he felt every inch of that. And after the kind of life Andy has led, being passed like a hot potato between parents and schools and God knows who else, it's no wonder. But Nick hadn't been prepared for it this morning. If he had a little time, he might have been able to come up with something reassuring to say, but Andy left before that.

And then Andy went home to find himself effectively kicked out.

Yeah, there's no way he's particularly happy with Nick right now. But it would be a lot better if he could be mad at Nick in person rather than sixty fucking blocks away. Nick hates the idea of Andy that far away.

Nick goes to bed, but he can't sleep.

At two in the morning, Nick takes Andy's folded-up pajamas from the foot of the bed and moves them up so they're on the empty pillow next to his own. At two fifteen, he decides he's being a sap and gets up to put the pajamas in the closet, where he won't be tempted to make a scene with them. When he opens the closet door, the faint streetlight shows far too much hanging from the rail. Reaching out, he touches the linen of one of Andy's stupid summer suits. Andy's clothes are all still there. Nick's heart does something awful and he holds the pajamas to his chest like a child clutching his teddy bear.

It means Andy's coming back.

Or it just means Andy has approximately three dozen shirts and can't fit them all into a suitcase.

He wishes Andy were here. Then they could talk it out, figure out what they're going to do, come to some kind of understanding.

Some very unhelpful voice in Nick's head points out that it doesn't matter if they come to an understanding, that whatever they have between them wasn't going to last anyway, that it's just as well for it to end with a quarrel as it is for it to end when they both get too terrified of being exposed to even look at one another or when Andy decides he needs to move on.

Except—for two months he's counted on knowing that each day would begin with bringing Andy coffee and end with Andy either in his bed or in the next room; he's taken for granted the presence of Andy on his couch, underfoot in his kitchen—on *their* couch, in *their* kitchen. He's happy. Andy's happy. Throwing that away for any reason at all feels . . . twisted. Backward.

Andy might not even want it. Andy might decide that Nick isn't worth the trouble, and Nick wouldn't blame him. But even as that thought crosses his mind, he imagines Andy rolling his eyes.

By eight o'clock in the morning, Sal has eaten every last crumb of food in Nick's kitchen and he's still hungry. Nick has a healthy appetite himself, but it turns out he has nothing on a fourteen-year-old boy.

"We'll go get bagels," Nick offers. After that they'll have to do something about clothes for the kid, because he isn't going to fit into anything of Nick's and he can't keep walking around in his wrinkled school uniform.

The weather is decent, so they walk to the good bagel place on MacDougal. They each order a bagel with cream cheese, and then Nick orders another half dozen plain bagels. He figures Sal will have put away three by the time they get home.

As he's placing the order, Nick remembers all the other times he's bought bagels during the past two months, usually with Andy at his side, bleary-eyed and begging for coffee. It's become a Sunday morning ritual, and even though it isn't Sunday, Nick feels its absence.

"You know what?" Nick says when they step outside into sunlight that suddenly seems blinding after the dim bagel shop. "I

nearly forgot. I have to go see Andy about something. Come on."
He begins to walk toward the Bleecker Street subway station.

"You see him every day at work," Sal points out.

"It's urgent."

"You could call him. There's a pay phone across the street."

"Pipe down and eat another bagel."

The holy mother and all the saints must be smiling down on them because a Lexington Avenue Local rolls into the station just as Nick and Sal reach the platform. And by another miracle, Nick remembers Andy's father's address from the New Year's Eve party. It can't be more than five minutes before Nick and a bewildered but bagel-drunk Sal emerge onto Sixty-Eighth Street. They stop at a Chock full o'Nuts and get a pair of coffees in little paper cups, one with about a pound of sugar and the other the way normal people like it. Sal gets a doughnut.

"Nick Russo here to see Mr. Fleming," Nick tells the doorman when they arrive at the building, wishing he were wearing something less scruffy than a pair of Levi's and the first shirt he managed to lay his hands on, which is somehow already rumpled, and the sleeves of which are rolled up. He looks like the janitor and Sal looks like an urchin he rescued from a street fight. Jesus Christ. They're going to wind up in jail.

The doorman picks up a telephone receiver. "Mr. Fleming says to go on up. Seventeenth floor," he says a moment later, looking as if he wishes Nick and Sal would hurry up and get on the elevator and stop cluttering up his lobby. Nick grabs Sal by the sleeve and tows him along. The elevator operator manages not to look scandalized. He probably has better things to do than judge however many hundred people he sees in his elevator every day.

"Jeez," Sal says. "This elevator is nicer than most churches."

Sal's not wrong. The elevator is fitted in shiny brass and polished wood. Nick remembers when he first visited Andy's old apartment to fix his sink and spent the rest of the day vaguely disoriented to realize that he was now friends with someone who not only was rich, but lived like a rich person, with gleaming dark doors and soft carpets and hallways that didn't smell like the neighbors' cooking. He had felt like he was seeing Andy in his natural habitat for the first time. Now when he thinks of where Andy belongs, he sees bare feet on the old green sofa, and he doesn't know whether he's deluding himself.

Nick knocks on the apartment door, knowing that Andy will be expecting him after the doorman called up, but acutely nervous despite, or maybe because of, that. When the door opens, though, it's Mr. Fleming. He's leaning on a cane.

"Sir," says Nick, trying not to look dismayed.

"This is a surprise," Mr. Fleming says, not sounding remotely surprised. "Come in."

"I came to see Andy. For work. He's here, isn't he? I think he's here?" This last bit comes out like a prayer. "And this is my nephew, Salvatore. Sal, this is Mr. Fleming, he's the publisher of the *Chronicle*."

Sal was raised right despite Michael being a dirtbag, so he swallows his doughnut, puts on his best manners, and says that he's pleased to meet Mr. Fleming.

"Andy's still asleep," Mr. Fleming says.

Nick reflexively looks at his watch. It's a few minutes past nine. He almost tells Mr. Fleming that if left up to his own devices, Andy would sleep until noon, but then decides this is probably too familiar. Then Nick remembers that Mr. Fleming *knows* and it's only the thought of seeing Andy that keeps him from fleeing the premises.

"Dad? I thought I heard—"

Nick looks up and sees Andy rubbing his eyes and wearing an unfamiliar pair of plaid pajamas, his hair disorganized in the way it always is in the morning. He stares at Nick like he's the eighth Wonder of the World.

"I'm here about the City Hall situation," Nick says, hoping it will get that dopey grin off Andy's face, even if Nick wants to remember that expression forever. He wants it printed on playing cards and commemorative plates.

"Right," Andy says. "The City Hall situation."

"Smooth," Sal mutters.

"I brought coffee," Nick says, holding up the cup that's ninety-nine percent sugar. "And a bagel. From the good bagel place." He's brought Andy coffee so many mornings. He hopes Andy will see that he's trying to preserve their morning ritual even if they didn't sleep in the same apartment.

The goofy look is back, so Nick guesses that he was successful.

"Why don't you sit down," says Mr. Fleming. "I have a phone call to make. Good to see you, Mr. Russo. You'll have to come for dinner sometime soon." He makes his way out of the room, one hand on his cane and the other braced on the furniture he passes.

They sit around a surprisingly normal-looking kitchen table. There isn't much Nick can say with Sal there, but he thinks that maybe he said all that he needed to by showing up like a lunatic at nine o'clock on a Saturday morning.

They manage a three-way conversation about baseball, and it isn't until Nick is finished with his coffee that he realizes Sal and Andy have been doing most of the talking. Andy's going on a tear about goddamn slugging percentages and Sal is listening with the zeal of the newly converted.

When Sal excuses himself to go to the bathroom, Nick talks as fast as he can. "Sal's going home tomorrow night. Do you want to come back? It's okay if you don't. We can still—if you want. I mean, the ball's in your court."

"Yes," Andy says simply. "Yes to everything. I'm sorry about yesterday morning. I was out of line."

"You had me worried," Nick said. "You were so worked up. I didn't know what to do."

"I— What? Why aren't you mad at me?"

"I was, for maybe thirty seconds. I mean, I don't ever want you to be upset, but you wear your heart on your sleeve. It's sweet." Nick can't believe he said that out loud and meant it. "But even if I were still mad, you'd still be you. And I'd still be—" The most unhelpful part of his brain wants to finish that sentence with *crazy about you*, but Nick can't say it. Not in Andy's father's kitchen, maybe not anywhere. And, also, that's not the point. "We'd still be friends. You'd still be my best friend."

Across the table, he can see the tension leak out of Andy like a deflating balloon, so he guesses he got that right.

"We're *friends*," Andy says. And it doesn't feel like an understatement or a euphemism; it feels like the bedrock of the truth, the inescapable fact of who they are.

"If I leave the *Chronicle*, it doesn't mean I'm leaving you."

"I know that, I swear. But in that moment, I didn't."

In that moment he had been like a kid who lost his mom at the zoo. Total panic. Nick had wanted to hold him, but they hadn't been in private. And they still aren't in private, not private enough for Nick, at least, but now he can squeeze Andy's hand, so he does.

"I'm not leaving you," Nick repeats. "Maybe the *Chronicle*, but not you. Never you."

"Want me to go to the bathroom again so you can keep talking?" Sal asks from the doorway just as Nick and Andy let go of one another's hands.

"Jesus Christ, kid," Nick grumbles. Andy laughs.

"You know," Andy says, "the Yankees are playing the Senators this afternoon. We could see if we can get tickets."

"We all hate the Yankees here," Nick clarifies, seeing the mildly horrified look on Sal's face.

"I wonder if some clothes of mine will fit you," Andy says to Sal. "Even if they don't, they'll be more comfortable than a school uniform, I think."

Sal winds up wearing thirty-dollar trousers from Brooks Brothers to sit on the bleachers at Yankee Stadium. Between them, Andy and Sal lose three pencils while attempting to fill out their scorecards. Andy gets a sunburn across the bridge of his nose, Sal eats four stadium hot dogs, the Yankees lose miserably in a shutout, and it winds up being one of the best days of Nick's life.

"Want me to come with you when you bring Sal back home tomorrow night?" Andy quietly offers on the subway back to Manhattan. Sal is across the car, half asleep from the sun and the gluttony.

Nick does. Of course he does. Andy's presence is always an improvement. "No," he says. "I need to have some words with my brother."

Andy bumps his shoulder against Nick's. Nick, holding his breath, lets his knuckles rub against Andy's, a silent promise.

He has no idea how they're going to manage to make it work, but they have to find a way because Nick has never, in his whole life of wanting things that were just out of reach, wanted anything so bad.

CHAPTER TWENTY-FIVE

When Nick and Sal get off the subway in Bay Ridge, Nick's stomach drops the way it always does. He never especially wants to talk to Michael, but today he wants to even less.

"You sure you did all your homework?"

Sal sighs with the put-upon weariness of a teenager. "Yeah, same as the last seven times you asked."

It's late Sunday afternoon and the neighborhood is quiet. From the top of the hill, Nick can almost catch a glimpse of the water and Staten Island beyond. A whole stretch of Seventh Avenue has been condemned to build the bridge that will span the Narrows, and God knows how many people will have to leave the neighborhood. This part of Brooklyn has never been Nick's home, but it is home for a lot of people—for generations of families. He thinks he'll pitch a piece to Jorgensen tomorrow, maybe interview some of the Norwegians who have lived here since their sailor ancestors settled in Brooklyn.

Or maybe he'll pitch it to a magazine. Maybe *The New Yorker*? They've printed stranger things in the past year, God knows. He'll talk to Andy about it later.

Sal knocks on the door, which is opened almost immediately by

Beverly, who must have been waiting at the door for Sal to arrive. She thanks Nick as if he's rescued her firstborn child from a volcano rather than just fed him about six pounds of carbohydrates over the course of the weekend and taken him to a ball game.

"Ma's on the phone," Bev tells Nick. "Want me to get her?"

"Don't bother. But is Michael around?"

Bev raises her eyebrows. "Yeah, come on in. He's in the backyard."

Nick goes through the kitchen, where he finds his mother on the phone. "You're not going to find escarole at the A&P," she's saying. "Use spinach." He kisses her cheek but gestures for her not to bother putting the phone down, then grabs the bottle opener and a pair of beers from the icebox and goes out the back door.

Michael is on his hands and knees, pulling weeds from a garden bed. When he sees Nick, he sits back on his haunches and wipes sweat from his brow with the back of his hand, streaking dirt across his face.

"I forgot how much teenage boys can eat," Nick says. He opens one of the bottles and holds it out to Michael, who takes it. "I watched him put away three pork chops and a loaf of bread without so much as breathing."

"I swear he eats twenty dollars' worth of food a week," Michael says. "I'm gonna need a second job."

Nick sits on the step. "Thanks for letting Sal stay with me. It was fun to have him around. He's welcome anytime, you know." It's funny, but now that he knows Michael is a halfway decent—or at least not actively violent, let's not get carried away—parent, Nick can almost stop caring about him. He doesn't want to be having this conversation, but he can do it for Sal's sake.

"He's a pain in the ass, is what he is. But I guess all teenagers are."

Nick forces himself to drain a good part of his bottle before speaking. "Well, if you and Bev ever need a break, I have a spare room."

Michael makes a noncommittal sound and shrugs. Nick thinks about what Michael hasn't said: he hasn't said that his son can't visit his queer uncle. Nick is grateful for this bare minimum, but then feels something deep within him revolt at the gratitude.

"There's something I wanted to talk to you about." Nick remembers the words he rehearsed all afternoon. "I want to thank you for what you did at the police station that time."

Michael becomes very interested in a weed. "I wasn't gonna let Ma find out you'd been— Jesus, Nick, what's the point of being a cop if you can't do that much?"

Nick decides not to answer that, and instead finishes his beer. "But do you think you can not mention it anymore?"

"When have I ever mentioned it?"

"I'm talking about the insinuations."

Michael sighs. "You always were too sensitive." Nick can't tell whether this means he'll agree to Nick's request or not. Nick supposes he'll find out. If Michael doesn't knock it off, Nick will stop coming around or he'll time his visits for when Michael's on duty. Maybe he can convince his mother to come into the city. But at least he's tried.

"While you're at it," Michael goes on, still not looking at Nick, "you can thank me for clearing up that mess with Jimmy Walsh."

Nick goes still at the name of the cop who arrested him, the cop he had seen at the Gowanus fire. "What mess?"

"His partner was one of the cops involved in that story you keep writing about. He and Jimmy followed you around, took a bunch of pictures. I thought they sent them to you?"

"Yeah," Nick says, his mouth dry. "They did."

"They'll stop now. Christ, what a fucking mess. I'm going to have to find another poker game. I don't have the negatives, though, so you're on your own there."

"There wasn't—" Nick starts, meaning to say that there wasn't anything incriminating, that it was just a couple of pictures of him living his life.

"I don't want to hear about it!" Michael protests, holding up his hands. "And before you ask, I don't have enough favors to fix this kind of thing another time. Can you try not to piss off cops who are connected, Nicky? Jesus. Or at least try not to do things that make it easy to blackmail you? One or the other? It ain't healthy to do both."

Nick isn't sure there's any kind of blow to the pride worse than when your least favorite person is right about something. Andy had said the same thing a few days earlier, but Nick had been too frightened and angry to think straight.

And he never wants to have to thank his brother for getting him out of trouble ever again.

"Thanks," Nick says. "I mean it."

"I don't know why you have to make your life so hard, though. Find a girl, for Chrissake."

Nick manages not to roll his eyes. Yeah, being queer isn't exactly easy. Hiding is hard. Knowing what his family thinks of him is hard. But then there's Andy—loving him, and letting Andy love him back, are the easiest things he's ever done.

He goes back into the kitchen, where his mother is still on the phone. "Let it simmer twenty minutes, maybe?" Nick wonders who his mother is on the phone with. It can't be one of his aunts or cousins, because then she'd be speaking at least half in Italian, and his mother would never say *white beans* when she could say *cannellini*. Probably some non-Italian from church.

"You know, this is why mothers want their sons to marry nice girls. Someone to look after them and make them good food. Men need someone to do that." She goes silent for a minute, listening to the person on the other end of the line—now Nick's money is on the new bride of an Italian man from church. "So you'll make him some nice supper."

Nick leans in and kisses his mother's cheek before heading out into the street.

Instead of taking the train all the way home, Nick gets off while he's still in Brooklyn. There's still plenty of light left, so he walks from the Court Street station toward the Navy Yard.

He knows that there isn't much happening there these days, even though at least one ship is being built. When he was a kid, the whole neighborhood was teeming with sailors, shipbuilders, and dockworkers. That had slowed down by the time Nick was old enough to become interested in the Navy Yard for reasons other than its ships. The waterfront from there to the Brooklyn Bridge was always good ground for cruising. There had been more than one queer bar, not to mention alleys, bathrooms, and all the usual places.

It had been maybe a fifteen-minute walk from the old *Brooklyn Eagle* building. Between the paper and that neighborhood, Nick discovered the first corner of the world where he belonged.

But as Nick walks along streets that had once been familiar, he realizes he can't get to the Navy Yard. The street he used to take is gone, torn up to build a highway. He'd known the BQE was going to cut through this part of Brooklyn, but he hadn't realized it would take this whole street off the map. He scans the area, looking for a way through, but he isn't enough of a fool to start prowling around empty construction sites right before dusk.

In the back of his mind, he meant to look at the place where he'd been arrested. He thought that maybe seeing it would defang the memory a little, that maybe he'd see it was just an alley or something. But now he can't even get to the memory. It's like that whole messy time is closed off, bricked up, and he doesn't know whether to be grateful or sad. That time is gone, that version of himself is gone, and there's nowhere to go but forward.

He walks back to the subway stop and gets on the train to Manhattan.

At the top of the stairs, there's a light under his door and the smell of garlic wafting out into the hall. Nick's heart starts to pound, but he tells himself not to get his hopes up: it's probably Linda heating up takeout next door, and the light he's seeing is just a bulb he forgot to check earlier that day.

But when he turns the key in the lock, he's holding his breath, and when he sees Andy at the stove, he feels something ease up inside of him, even if Andy anywhere within three feet of a gas burner is a pretty terrifying sight.

Nick goes over to the stove and puts his arms around Andy, hooking his chin over Andy's shoulder. "Hey," Nick says.

"I'd turn around and kiss you, but I don't want to mess this up." Andy's stirring what looks like—

"Is that minestrone soup?"

"That's what it's supposed to be. Only time will tell what it actually is."

"It smells good." Nick presses his face into Andy's neck. "You smell good, too."

"I thought you might need soup," Andy says.

In all the weeks Andy's been living here, rarely has Nick come home to find Andy already there. Andy has a thing about being alone, and Nick usually tries to avoid making it an issue. But today Andy let himself in and cooked.

Nick tightens his arms around Andy. "I do. Thank you."

"Are you going to let go of me so I can finish cooking?"

"No." Anyway, the soup's done, as far as Nick can see. He kisses beneath Andy's ear, right where a strand of hair curls when he's due for a trip to the barber. "I'm so glad you're here," he says. He doesn't know if he's ever said as much out loud, which probably makes him a jerk, but he hopes that this isn't news to Andy. He can feel Andy smiling, can feel the thump his heart just gave.

"Me too."

Eventually Nick pries himself off and they eat soup and crackers at the table. "This tastes like how my mother makes it," Nick says, trying not to sound too surprised. Andy still can't scramble eggs without nearly ruining a pan, and what's more, he's always leery of trying something new and then failing.

"It should," says Andy, not looking at Nick. "I used your mom's recipe."

"My mom has a recipe?" He can't imagine his mother using a recipe. And then the rest of his brain catches up. "How? How did you get it?"

"I called her. I hope that's okay." Andy stirs his spoon in the last inch of soup, where he's left all his rejected bits of carrot.

"This afternoon? You called her today?"

"Yes. Is that— Did I cross a line?"

"No. I— Thank you." So that was Andy on the phone with his mom this afternoon. That was Andy she was walking through the process of making soup. That was Andy she was telling that men need someone to look after them—and, apparently to that end, she taught him how to make Nick's favorite soup. And now Nick has a lump in his throat and he can't talk.

"You okay?" Andy looks concerned.

Nick shakes his head. He forces himself to take a drink of water and look at the ceiling for a minute. "The last few days have been . . . not good," he says when he returns his gaze to Andy's face. "I missed you." It's only been two days and it's fully ridiculous that Nick's even admitting any of this. He blames Andy. He's a terrible influence.

"Me too."

They have to talk; there are too many things unsaid hovering between them. But that conversation will keep for a while and so will the dirty dishes. He stands up and holds his hand out to Andy, then pulls him to his feet.

CHAPTER TWENTY-SIX

Over the next few days, Nick occasionally finds himself thinking that things are back to normal—or whatever passed for normal before that fight on Friday—but then he'll catch Andy's eye and realize he's wrong. The fundamentals are the same—dinner and coffee and sex and the easy sort of conversation that they've always had. But every step of the way it feels . . . deliberate, maybe. Like when he's bringing Andy coffee he's accomplishing something with capital letters, like a truth that used to be inside him is now set in print, notarized, undeniable.

It feels like the beginning of something, or maybe the end of something else, and Nick might know what if he thought about it, but instead he doesn't. He feels his heart trip in his chest when Andy comes to his desk in the evening when it's time to leave; he feels his face heat when Andy rolls toward him in bed, a proprietary hand on Nick's hip.

Sometimes when Andy looks at him, it's like the radio has tuned in to the right station, the static dropping away and everything going momentarily clear. The plausible deniability that Nick has been holding on to with both arms isn't there anymore and he has no choice but to see the truth of things—Andy's here, he isn't going anywhere, he doesn't want to go anywhere, they could keep doing this, or something more than this, indefinitely.

It's terrifying. People will likely connect the dots and realize why they're living together. If Andy stays forever—Christ, this should not make him so goddamn giddy—that likelihood changes to a certainty. He tells himself that there's a difference between being exposed by dirty cops and people who know the two of them guessing the truth, but they both feel like the same kind of danger. He knows they aren't, but there's something about the inevitability of exposure that feels like cold handcuffs snapping around his wrists.

Honestly, he's used to it. Fear of exposure has been a constant in his life; he doesn't know how to stop being afraid any more than he knows how to stop his heart from beating. Sometimes he feels like the fear is crowding out everything else, though. He wants the good things in his life to take up the space they deserve, but he doesn't know how to go about doing that, or even if it's possible.

"It's a dog and pony show," Nick grumbles when he gets his assignment.

"And we cover those, too," says Jorgensen.

Today's the annual Operation Alert drill, a nationwide exercise in collectively engaging with the fiction that hiding under desks and avoiding elevators will do anything to help you survive a nuclear attack. That, and it's a not-so-subtle reminder of the dangers of communists or Russians or not voting for Eisenhower—take your pick. Tomorrow, most papers will run the government's accounting of how much death and destruction the fictional attack would have caused: millions dead, cities destroyed.

"It's pro-nuclear propaganda," argues Nick.

Jorgensen throws up his hands. "You're covering the protests!"

That's not much better. Last year the protests consisted of a dozen or so tired picketers from the Catholic Workers and a couple of vagrants who didn't want to leave their benches and take cover. They were all arrested, most sentenced to thirty days. It had been monumentally depressing.

Still, Nick does what he's told. The weather's irritatingly sunny and Nick peels off his jacket on the way to City Hall Park. Lilian's been assigned as the photographer, so he's got that going for him, at least. She gauges Nick's mood and doesn't bother with small talk, wordlessly accepting Nick's offer of a cigarette instead.

The drill hasn't started yet, so the protesters are marching with homemade signs, they're nearly outnumbered by the cops who are hanging around, ready to arrest them as soon as the sirens sound.

Nick checks his watch. They have twenty minutes to get their quotes and photographs, and then Lilian can get some shots of the creepily empty streets.

He isn't sure if it's his imagination or if there are more protesters compared to last year. The nicely dressed middle-aged people are the Catholic Worker crowd—he's pretty sure that lady in the black dress is actually Dorothy Day herself—but there are also a few young men with beards and overgrown hair and young women in trousers or with their hair down. It's the Washington Square Park bongo demographic and they're so young that Nick is torn between feeling jaded and optimistic.

There's also a woman with a stroller and two kids. The one in the stroller is still a baby and the older one is maybe four, with pigtails and scuffed saddle shoes and an expression of pure belligerence. He nudges Lilian and they head in that direction. When they get closer, he sees that the woman is younger than Nick by

several years, but with purple smudges under her eyes that suggest
that the baby who's currently fast asleep in the stroller might be
nocturnal.

He gets her name—Christina Mendoza—and asks her why
she doesn't have a sign.

"We came to feed the ducks," Mrs. Mendoza says, all indig-
nance and a Brooklyn accent even thicker than his own. "How
am I supposed to know there's all this malarkey going on? And
if a bomb were to go off in five minutes, I'd still rather feed the
goddamn ducks first."

Nick wants to know where this woman thinks she's going to
find ducks anywhere in Lower Manhattan but decides this might
be of secondary importance. "The purpose of the drill," he says,
gritting his teeth at repeating the government line, but spurred on
by some instinct that he needs to keep her talking, keep her mad,
"is to foster a sense of readiness among the citizens—"

"Readiness for what?" she asks, shaking her head as if in pity at
Nick's idiocy. "I hug my kids every night. I kiss their dad before
he leaves for work in the morning. I'd say I'm about as ready for
nuclear war as the next person. And I'm just too tired to get back
on the subway, so if they want to arrest me, they can try."

Nick writes all that down and they get a couple pictures of her
and the kids, then move on to the people who actually intended
to be at the protest. They get a couple good quotes about how the
only way to survive a nuclear war is by not having one in the first
place, and then the sirens sound. Lilian gets a picture of cops arresting a bunch of sweet Catholic grandmas. They don't arrest the
mother, probably at a loss for what to do with the kids, instead
escorting them all into City Hall, two cops awkwardly hauling
the stroller up the stairs.

As they walk back to the *Chronicle* building, through streets emptier and quieter than they are even in the middle of the night, it's the mother's words that repeat in Nick's mind. She hadn't said anything especially new, but the way she said it still hits him like a punch in the gut. Maybe she can't do anything about the disaster that other people want to bring about, but she can hug her kids, she can kiss her husband, she can live her life. No, it's more than that—she was willing to get arrested just to make a point.

It worms its way into Nick's mind as he types his story and files it. His lead is that line about feeding the ducks before a nuclear holocaust and Jorgensen can fight him on it later if he wants to.

If anyone asked him whether he's afraid of nuclear war, his knee-jerk response would be yes. Of course he is—everybody knows that any attack on America would hit New York. But if he starts thinking about it—his mother hurt, Sal frightened at school—he won't be able to do anything else. He can't contemplate nuclear death and also go grocery shopping and leave milk on the fire escape for the idiot cat and make sure Andy has clean handkerchiefs.

And maybe it's like that with everything else. Maybe the trick is to put fear in its place so it doesn't take over. He can relegate the vice cops and petty rumors to the same corner of his mind where he puts atom bombs and other lurking evils.

What he can do is— God, he keeps thinking of that woman. He can feed the goddamn ducks and he can kiss his boyfriend. He can believe that the future they have is worth more than his fear, and he can do what it takes to make that future as safe and happy as possible.

Nick gets up from his desk and goes to find Andy.

"I'm dropping the police evidence story," Nick tells him. Andy's in the process of taking over a shitty old conference room next to the newsroom and making it his new office because he says the seventh floor is too quiet to get anything done, too far from everything that matters. Lou Epstein has been watching this with covert approval; the managing editor is going to be in Andy's corner even if Andy turns the place upside down.

Andy drops his half of the desk they're moving. "You sure?"

"Yeah. You were right."

"You sure you aren't doing this for me?"

Of course Nick's doing it for Andy. If Nick gets exposed, Andy gets exposed, and Nick isn't letting that happen. And he keeps thinking about what it would mean if he got hurt—what it would mean to Andy. When he thinks about that, he figures he ought to keep himself safe. At some point he had gotten used to the idea that, when it came to his job, he could take whatever risks he liked, because ultimately he was on his own. But Andy's had enough people putting him last and Nick isn't going to be one of them.

"Don't like to think about you waking up alone," Nick mutters.

Andy stares at him.

"If you don't already know that, I'm really making a mess of things," Nick says. "Look, if I have to choose between work and you, between a story and you, between anything and you, I'm picking you."

"I don't—"

"Yeah, yeah. I know. You're not asking me for anything. I'm just telling you the way it is. It's no sacrifice. Just a fact." And it is a fact, settled and steady, something he's known for a while. Andy's first.

"I want to write about neighborhoods," Nick tells Andy. He's pitched a series to Jorgensen, who sent him to Epstein, who gave him the go-ahead. "A series. Robert Moses might be an asshole, but I don't think he'll send goons to follow us around."

He knows that Andy will hear what Nick isn't saying. He's moving away from covering news. Not all at once, but that's the direction he's heading. When he thinks about what he likes about his job, what he's best at, it isn't reporting hard news, but telling stories, and he's kind of pissed that Mark Bailey was the one to put the idea into his head.

"Can't wait to read it," Andy says, his mouth tipping up in a smile.

It takes Nick two hours to catch the cat. That little fucker wanders into Nick's apartment every few days, but the one time Nick actually wants him he's nowhere to be found. He isn't outside the fish store or the coffee shop or even in the dumpster behind the deli. Nick finds about fourteen other cats and a lot of animals he doesn't want to think about, but not the one he wants.

"Have you seen that orange cat?" he asks a group of kids playing stickball in the lot next to St. Veronica's.

"The stupid one?" asks a girl in braids.

"The one who gets stuck on fire escapes?" asks another.

"The one who sleeps in dumpsters?" asks a third.

"Yeah, yeah," Nick says. "That one."

The kids all point in different directions. Useless.

Nick eventually finds him curled up next to the laundry, enjoying the hot steam seeping out from the cellar door despite the fact that it's got to be seventy-five degrees today. He gives a half-hearted hiss when Nick picks him up.

"Swear to God, if you give me fleas," Nick mutters. The cat

manages to look bewildered and offended the entire trip back to the apartment and up the stairs, as if he hasn't been in this stairwell dozens of times.

Andy's having dinner with his father and an advertiser, so Nick still has time to get this thing presentable. He drops the cat into the sink and immediately fills it with warm water, keeping a hand on the back of the cat's neck just in case. He's never given a cat a bath before and doesn't think this is going to be a good experience for either of them.

On his way home that afternoon he went to Woolworth and bought a litter box and some cat food, then got a flea dip at the drugstore. He already has the flea dip waiting in the kitchen, next to a bottle of his own shampoo and a big fluffy towel.

"The goal here," Nick says, carefully soaping the animal's back with shampoo, "is not to get this in your eyes."

The cat lifts a paw and very deliberately scratches him.

"Ow," he says. And then he hisses when soap hits the broken skin. "Jesus, does that make us even?"

The water is filthy, so Nick drains the sink and starts the process over again. The cat seems patient, if infuriated, but lets Nick have his way. "It's just that we both know Andy's going to let you all over the furniture, and I won't have the heart to stop him, so we at least need to get the street filth and some of the fleas off you. You have no idea how lucky you have it. You're going to be as round as a beach ball in no time."

The water is a less alarming color this time, so Nick drains the sink, towels off the cat, and starts dabbing on the flea stuff. "Look, nobody's going to tell you this smells good," he says, "but it needs to be done."

"I know I've had too much to drink," comes a voice from behind him, "but it really looks like you're giving a cat a bubble bath."

Nick nearly jumps out of his skin. He turns and sees Andy leaning against the front door, his tie loose and his hair mussed, his jacket thrown over his shoulder. He must have come in while Nick was running the faucet.

"Hi," Nick says, trying to play it cool. "How was dinner?" But he must be distracted because he takes his hand off the cat long enough for the animal to make a flying leap, soaking Nick in the process.

"Oh, hello, little friend," Andy says, crouching down and offering the cat a hand. "Did you wander in here again?"

It's on the tip of Nick's tongue to say yes, that the cat came of his own free will and Nick didn't spend his whole evening chasing him down. But the entire point of the cat is for Andy to *understand*. "I, uh, helped."

Andy raises his eyebrows. "You helped."

"With a little kidnapping. But he went along with it." He sighs and rubs the back of his neck. "You wanted to keep the cat. The other week." Nick still doesn't know exactly why Andy had refused to keep the cat, whether it was because he didn't know if he was staying permanently with Nick or because he didn't want to be a bother. Both seem typically Andy-ish. "You live here now."

Andy's still crouched on the floor, still holding a hand out to the cat, but he looks up at Nick. "Is the cat supposed to be an incentive? Because I really don't need one."

God, Nick was getting this all wrong. "No, no. This is your home, so you should have a pet. Or do whatever it is people do in their homes. Rearrange the books, get a new shower curtain, I don't know. We don't have to keep the cat."

"I want the cat." Andy gets to his feet and for whatever reason this sends the cat skittering into the living room. "I think he's on top of the bookshelves."

Nick's pretty sure he hasn't gotten his point across at all. He takes Andy's hand, and he doesn't know whether it's to stop Andy from leaving the room or because he needs the contact. "I want this with you. I want everything with you. And I need you to know that. I don't know how we'll make it work, but I want it anyway."

"I love you," Andy says. Something hot and awful, lovely and mortifying curdles in Nick's blood, just as it had the other time Andy said that. Nick opens his mouth, but Andy's palm is there, preventing him from speaking. "I love you," Andy repeats, "and I want to be with you, and that's all there is to it. The rest is details. The rest is . . . administrative."

Andy has Nick's face in his hands now and is looking at him with more intent than Nick knows what to do with. Some other version of Nick in some other universe might have been able to bring the conversation back to someplace less terrifying. Some other version of Nick might still have some scraps of self-preservation Scotch-taped around his heart. But this version of Nick has been worn down by Andy for weeks, for months, for as long as they've known one another.

He shuts his eyes and rests his forehead against Andy's. "You're it for me." He doesn't know how to make this clearer, but he wants all his cards on the table. He doesn't want Andy to have the smallest particle of doubt. There's enough to worry about in the world; he doesn't want one of Andy's worries to be about how Nick feels. "Do you understand what I'm getting at?"

"You love me," Andy says.

Nick opens his eyes and scowls. "Of course I love you."

"I know, I've been trying to tell you so for weeks."

"It's more than that, it's—fuck. I want a life with you. I want this to be—I want more than we can have."

Andy is looking at him so carefully, too carefully.

"But I want it anyway," Nick admits.

Nick has never thought of himself as sentimental, but that's only because he's a damn fool. That first time Andy brought him bodega daffodils and Nick felt like Cinderella at the goddamn ball ought to have been clue enough.

He doesn't know why having admitted that he loves Andy ought to matter; they've both known it for a while, haven't they? It shouldn't feel like a confession. Nick can't look away from the truth, and the truth is that he feels for Andy every goofy thing anyone's ever felt about anyone else.

And it's just more proof that his brain has gone rotten that when kissing in the kitchen turns into stumbling toward the bedroom, Nick finds that he wants to take it slow this time; he wants to make it nice and sweet. But they wind up pulling all their clothing off in a desperate hurry like always, and Nick, in a dizzying rush of clarity, supposes they'll have all the time in the world for nice and sweet and slow. Tomorrow, next month, next year—Jesus. He gets on the bed and tugs Andy over him. He presses his mouth against the soft skin of Andy's neck and murmurs, "I want you to do it to me this time." He can't believe he's primly avoiding rude words, the way Andy does.

Andy opens his eyes. "You want me to fuck you?"

The word ripples through Nick's body, his hips hitching toward Andy's of their own volition. "Only if you want."

"Yeah—God—of course I do." Andy's looking down at him, eyes dark and intent, the color in his face high and hectic. "You'll talk me through it," he says, not a question, just a soft statement of fact. "You sure about this?"

"I want every first with you," Nick says, because he can't shut up. It's like all that honesty earlier has loosened his tongue and now he's going to say every stupid thing that never needed to be said out loud. He's dead sober, but he feels like he's been drinking. Or like he's been cursed by a witch to babble.

But the look Andy's giving him is . . . hungry, almost, like he wants to hear Nick embarrass himself some more. "Yeah?" He reaches for Nick and strokes him, as if he's ready to reward Nick for talking.

And fuck if Nick can't give Andy anything he wants. "Everything feels like a first with you anyway. Every fucking minute, and that's just because—because it's you." He's saying this all wrong, and there's a petulant note in his voice that doesn't belong there, and it's all Andy's fault. "Fuck, this is the stupidest I've ever been."

"Don't sell yourself short," Andy says, and Nick pinches him.

And maybe all they have to do to make things nice and sweet and slow is to put Andy in charge, because Nick finds himself taken apart with patience and gentle hands and a crazy-making lack of urgency. Andy is always, always so eager to please, and Nick can't help but bask in it. Sometimes Nick will whisper something along the lines of "you're so good" and Andy looks like he'll die on the spot. Andy's always been sweet, so it's no surprise that he's sweet in bed. And they've always had fun together, so it's no surprise that sex is fun—and sometimes silly—in a way that Nick couldn't have guessed he'd find appealing. And—fine—they love one another, so it's no surprise that this comes through in bed, too.

What is a surprise is this urge that Nick sometimes has to just turn his body over to Andy and let him do whatever he wants. And now, with Andy kneeling between his legs, that's how he feels.

Nick has never particularly wanted to do this, but he wants to watch Andy do it to him, he wants to feel Andy do it to him. If there's a contradiction there, then that's just going to have to be okay. Sex with Andy is full of contradictions, anyway: a little clumsy but always easy; a little rough but always tender. When he's buried deep inside Andy, he feels exposed, but also as safe as he's ever felt.

And it turns out that when Andy's inside him, he feels the exact same way. "This okay?" Andy asks about fifty times, asking again even as his rhythm falters and his breathing goes ragged. One of his hands has found its way to Nick's, clasping it against the mattress. Nick can't stop watching his face, can't stop watching the emotions play out over it—pleasure and concern and love. Nick pulls him closer and kisses the triangle of birthmarks at the corner of his mouth.

"Don't leave," Nick says later, when Andy is half on top of him, boneless and sweaty.

"Not going anywhere," Andy mumbles into Nick's shoulder. "Can't make me."

"I mean, forever." He's not sure he made that crystal clear before, and besides, he's on a roll with saying embarrassing things.

Andy lifts his head a little bit to look at Nick.

He smiles, as if he's slowly realizing that Nick is in the palm of his hand, and Nick never could have imagined that this would be a good feeling. "There's nowhere else I want to be," Andy says.

CHAPTER TWENTY-SEVEN

It's sheer bad luck that Nick happens to run into Mrs. Martelli on the stairs. "Let me get those," he says, taking a string bag from her hand and giving her his arm.

"God willing I'll only have to do this a few more times," she says when they reach her door, making the sign of the cross.

"You moving to the ground-floor apartment?" If you ask Nick, that's what she should have done years ago.

"I'm moving to Long Island," Mrs. Martelli says. "I'd have thought your nice young man would have told you."

"Andy? What does he have to do with it?" Nick asks, pretending he didn't hear the part about Andy being his young man.

"He's made an offer on the building," she says, as if talking about the drains or the water heater or something, not Andy buying a *building*.

Andy isn't home yet—he has some top-secret dinner with the editors—so Nick has plenty of time to turn this new information over in his mind. Andy knows that Nick isn't keen on the idea of Andy being his boss—why on earth would he think being Nick's landlord would be any different? And that doesn't even touch on how ridiculous it is that Andy has the kind of money where he can just *buy a building*. What's Andy going to do with a building, anyway? Is he going to fix people's broken windows and leaky sinks?

Nick pours himself a glass of bourbon and settles irritably on the couch. Toward the bottom of the glass it occurs to him that it isn't like Andy to do something that he knows would bother Nick without at least giving him a heads-up.

That's the thought that finally settles him down. It *isn't* like Andy. So either Mrs. Martelli has her facts wrong or Andy has his reasons. If it turns out that Andy's lost his mind and impulsively bought a building, Nick knows perfectly well that Andy would sell it if Nick asked.

And Andy's always been rich enough to buy a building—the fact that he actually *did* doesn't make his wealth any more annoying than it already was; it's just proof that, until now, Andy's been making sure that his money keeps a low profile. Nick can't actually expect Andy to keep his money hidden away in a savings account or a shoebox or wherever rich people keep their money the whole time they're together—and at that thought, the implications of their time together stretching out indefinitely, his stomach gives a little lurch that's halfway between nausea and happiness.

Nick's on his second drink by the time Andy gets home. He flops onto the couch beside Nick, planting a kiss on his cheek, then takes his shoes off, launching them in the direction of the door.

"Hi," Andy says.

"You smell like wine."

Andy takes a sip of Nick's bourbon, as if in response. "Weird thing happened today. Or not weird, just—odd. I guess that's the same thing. Rather, well, I don't know how you're going to take this." He bites his lip and starts playing with the end of his tie.

Nick decides to put him out of his misery. "Let me guess. You bought the building." At Andy's astonished look, he says, "I ran into Mrs. Martelli." He tucks his toes under Andy's thigh.

"I didn't buy it yet. I only put in an offer."

"You should have mentioned it to me first."

"I know. It's been killing me all night. I did it all backward. I was hoping to wait until I sold my mother's apartment, but Mrs. Martelli wants to act fast. Then I wasn't sure the bank would give me a mortgage, which is mortifying to think about. But it all came through this afternoon, so I put in an offer right away."

"You have a mortgage?" Nick asks. Michael has a mortgage. It seems like such a normal thing, such a mundane way to buy a house. And maybe that's when the penny drops—Andy bought a house. He wasn't just throwing his money around for fun. He bought a house—a home, their home.

"I'm not going to pay cash for real estate," Andy says, whatever the fuck that means. "And it won't be a huge mortgage."

"You're not raising anybody's rent, right?" Nick says dubiously.

Andy looks mildly insulted. "Of course not. And the numbers work out so that a superintendent—this building really needs a super, Nick—can have Mrs. Martelli's old apartment."

"Why, though? Why buy the building?"

Andy steals Nick's glass and takes another drink. "I need somewhere to go when Sal visits."

He's right, of course. Sal will visit again, hopefully under less urgent circumstances than last time, but Nick isn't going to share a bedroom with Andy while his nephew is around—he's not going to put the burden of that kind of secret on a kid, and he isn't going to give his brother ammunition against Andy. "You could stay in the guest room," Nick suggests.

"And put Sal on the sofa? No," Andy says firmly. "You want him to feel like he has a home with you if he wants it, right?"

"So, what—you're going to take another unit in the building and leave it empty except when Sal visits?" That seems extravagant.

"Actually I was thinking about knocking out the wall between this apartment and Linda's. That'll give us another bedroom and space to spare."

For a minute Nick doesn't know what to think. "You're kicking Linda out?"

"No, no. She mentioned looking for someplace with a service elevator and better light when her lease is up this fall. Apparently carrying bags of cement up four flights of stairs isn't her idea of fun."

"What'll we do with all that room when Sal isn't here?"

"You'll probably need an office if you want to write for magazines. You can't really use a typewriter on the kitchen table unless you want me spilling things all over it." He says this casually, as if he hadn't been devastated two weeks earlier about the possibility of Nick leaving the *Chronicle*. "But only if you want. We can leave things how they are and figure out another way."

Nick grasps at this like a lifeline. "Really?"

Andy looks surprised. "Of course. I can withdraw the offer. Do you want me to?"

Does he? Nick isn't sure. It's not that he's bothered by anything Andy suggested; it's just—this is a lot. "I can't believe you bought the whole building," he says, nudging Andy with his foot. "Who are you, the Monopoly man?"

Andy goes slightly pink. "I'm using my mother's life insurance money as the down payment. Do you want me to withdraw the offer, Nick?"

Nick's probably always going to be uncomfortable about Andy's money, but right now it's buying them a kind of security they wouldn't be able to have otherwise. Other people might be able to go get that for the price of a five-dollar marriage license at the city clerk's office, but Andy has to buy a building in order to get them a future where people won't look too closely at them. When Nick looks at it that way, it feels like Andy's just making things fair, and that if Nick's annoyed, he ought to be annoyed that not everyone in their position is so lucky.

Nick thinks of the Andy of a year ago and can't imagine that kid buying an apartment building, taking on the responsibility of dozens of tenants, in order to have a safe place—a safe home. But Andy's always wanted a home, and he wants Nick, and maybe the problem was that Andy just never really wanted anything before. Looking at him now, seeing something almost flinty in the warm depths of his eyes, Nick wouldn't want to be someone who stood between Andy Fleming and what he wanted.

"No," Nick says. "I don't."

"I don't even know where to start," Andy says. He's hovering in the doorway to his mother's apartment.

"We don't need to do this today," Nick says.

"I want to get it over with."

They've been through this a couple of times: Andy is determined to sell his mother's apartment and that means he needs to sort through his mother's belongings. Or, rather, he needs to put aside the things he wants to keep and have the rest sold at an estate sale.

Nick's been here a few times already, but now he's paying attention. The reporter's notebook on the desk by the window is filled with handwriting that isn't Andy's. A copy of the *Herald Tribune* wedged behind the typewriter is two years out of date. He imagines Andy living here alone and it breaks his heart.

"I don't know what I'm going to do with all these books," Andy says. Along one wall are shelves with books shoved in at any and all angles.

"If you want them, we'll get another bookcase. Hell, we can take that one." Nick pulls a familiar-looking volume off the shelf. It's a crisscross New York phone directory, an older volume of the same thing all reporters keep at their desks. He pages through it idly and two receipts, a lace-edged handkerchief, and a dollar bill fall out.

"Christ. You came by it honestly, I guess."

"What's that?" Andy asks.

"Was your mother as scattered as you are?"

"No, of course not," Andy says, offended.

Nick gestures at the collection of items that fell from the book, then at the haphazard arrangement of books on the shelves, the typewriter almost obscured by a stack of paper, the Pulitzer being used as a paperweight.

"I'm not so sure about that," Nick says. After living with Andy for three months now, he'd recognize it anywhere, this habit of absentmindedly leaving things in odd places, and he'd bet that Margaret Kelly was like her son in other ways, too. If he read her old stories, he wonders whether he'd hear Andy's voice in them.

As they poke around the apartment, they find four pairs of

women's reading glasses. "She was always losing hers," Andy says. "So she kept extra pairs lying about."

Nick gives him a pointed look.

In the end, they pack up three boxes of books, all the notebooks, a couple photographs, the Pulitzer, an ancient-looking bed quilt, and the typewriter. Then they break open one of the bottles of wine they find in the kitchen. Andy's eyes are red, and Nick can't tell whether it's just from all the dust they've dislodged.

"It's been nearly two years," Andy says. "I shouldn't feel like I'm coming right from the funeral." They're sitting on the floor of Andy's mother's bedroom.

Nick doesn't know what to say to that, so he bumps his shoulder into Andy's. "You're doing fine."

"I want to say that you'd have liked one another, but I don't even know if that's true."

"I grew up reading everything your mom wrote. Are you kidding me? It would be like meeting Captain America or Roy Campanella. I'd have made sure she liked me."

He hears a sniffle and doesn't turn his head, just squeezes Andy's thigh and pours some more wine into his glass. Andy needs to get nice and soused, then watch a sad movie where a horse dies or something so he has an excuse for a good cry.

Nick takes out a handkerchief and passes it to Andy, then makes a mental note to order another dozen.

Nick doesn't know what finally makes him pick up that book. Probably it's because Andy's been pointedly leaving it where Nick will see it—on top of the percolator, the edge of the bathroom sink—but also because Andy's apparently on a campaign to befriend every queer staffer at the *Chronicle*. The third time he waves Mark Bailey over to have lunch with them, Nick concedes that he's probably almost nearly friends with Mark, not that he'll admit it out loud or anything. So maybe he should just read the damn book.

One Saturday morning in the middle of June, while Andy is still asleep, Nick sits on the sofa, taking care not to dislodge the cat, who's sprawled in a patch of sun. He opens *The Charioteer* to the first page.

The book is—well, Andy had said it was a bit sappy, which is true, but it's not bad. It's not the sort of book he'd pick up on his own, and privately he thinks this group of queers in this fake city in England are all too dramatic for their own good, but they're in the middle of a war and getting bombed all day—who wouldn't be a little overwrought? That might be what turns the tide and makes Nick enjoy the book, at least a little. These men are finding time and energy to flirt and have queer parties and get jealous and fall in love despite bombs and injuries and death. That feels like the truest thing he's ever read.

"Did you finally read it or can we keep mocking you?" Lilian asks one evening. Apparently now Andy's Queer Club gets drinks after work even though Andy's still in a meeting.

"I read it, I read it," Nick says. "I didn't hate it."

"And?"

"I could have done with another chapter," Nick admits. He's already lent it to Emily so they can decide which actors they'd cast as the various characters. He bets she'll manage to get Paul Newman in there. She always does.

Conversation turns to how one of Lilian's cats had kittens, and she passes around snapshots of Maureen covered in fluffballs. Nick takes out his wallet and shows Lilian and Mark a picture of the idiot cat hiding on the top shelf of the cupboard. Andy had gotten some wallet-sized prints made because he thinks he's funny, but Nick's the sap who put one in his wallet next to a school picture of Sal.

Everyone duly praises the cat's stupidity and Nick feels very pleased with himself.

He doesn't know when it happened, but he doesn't feel panicky anymore when he thinks about how Mark and Lilian know about him. Now he doesn't feel exposed so much as oddly and unexpectedly warm, like he downed a cup of hot cocoa or put on a pair of mittens. It's sort of how he felt as a little kid, when everywhere he looked there was an aunt or a cousin.

Maybe this is what it's like, having friends, real friends, friends who know him. It's—well, it's a bit much, sometimes, and he's blaming Andy for all of it.

Later that week, Nick's source at the Property Clerk's Office calls and tells him that the police department has changed their procedure for how they log evidence and how many cops have the combination to the evidence safe. It's all but an admission that cops have been stealing evidence, and it's a small—but likely ineffective—attempt to stop the practice. It's not a victory, nothing that big, but it's proof that Nick's writing did something other than keep people entertained on their morning commute.

As soon as the ink is dry on the deed and Andy (and Chemical Corn Bank) officially own the building, something loosens in Nick, some old tension evaporating almost immediately. It's alarming, because he isn't expecting it—he had been a little ambivalent about Andy buying the building, but now that it's done, Nick feels like he has about a dozen fewer things to worry about.

He tells himself that he's only pleased because it means Andy really is here to stay, and maybe that's part of it. But honestly Nick had already known Andy would stay and he doesn't need a building as proof. It's something simpler and more material than that: the guarantee of a roof over his head.

It's the ability to lean on someone. It's something Nick hasn't had—maybe hasn't let himself have—since he was a child.

It's space. It's room to breathe.

The idea of not having to worry about steady work lets Nick imagine a world where life doesn't revolve around the predictable arrival of his paycheck. Andy already knows that Nick's getting ready to pitch a couple of ideas to some magazines. A year ago Nick would have rejected the idea out of hand—he was a city reporter, and that was that. That had been the safest and best place for him. But now he thinks he can carve out another, better place for himself.

"I mean, you're right," Andy says later when Nick, abashed, explains all this to him. It's late enough that half the lights are out in the newsroom, but Andy and the *Chronicle*'s treasurer have been burning the midnight oil, trying to find money for the kind of equipment they need to put out a glossy magazine on Sundays. "It goes both ways, you know. If the paper folds, figuring out the next step is less of an emergency since you'll probably have work."

Andy says this so simply and with such total faith in the idea that Nick is on board with the entangling of their lives and their futures, Nick is momentarily speechless.

"Did I get that wrong?" Andy asks, his face going blotchy with rising color.

"No," Nick says quickly. "It's just—it's good, you know?" A wild understatement, if ever there was one, but Andy seems to get the point. "It just, uh, made me sort of happy to hear you say that, I guess?" He feels deranged saying that sort of thing out loud, but it makes Andy so transparently thrilled that Nick has decided to get over himself.

Andy is sitting in Nick's chair and Nick is leaning against his desk. They probably ought to move this conversation into Andy's new office, but Andy looks too tired to move, and the truth is that anyone in the newsroom who was going to jump to conclusions about the two of them has already done it or will do it soon enough.

"The *Saturday Evening Post* wants to pay me twelve hundred dollars for that article," Nick says.

"Shit," Andy says, because he knows that's about what Nick makes in two months at the *Chronicle*. "Congratulations." He sounds like he means it. "When should I expect your resignation?"

"You shouldn't. Not yet. I'm not sure yet if those offers will keep coming in." This means Nick will be busy for a while, pitching articles and writing them while also doing his job at the *Chronicle*. But Andy's busy, too, and it feels like they're building something.

"I was talking to Mark," Andy says. "He used to give out a lawyer's phone number to queer men if they were arrested."

Nick thinks of the business card with the inked-in phone number that Mark had given him years ago.

"In any event," Andy goes on, "I was thinking of giving the paper's number out like that—along with the number of a lawyer, of course. I want to spread the word that we'll publish stories about gay men who have been entrapped by plainclothes cops."

Nick takes a moment before responding. He knows Andy's running this by him because it'll add grist to the rumor mill. But Nick is almost positive the *Post* has run stories like what Andy's suggesting, and nobody's going around saying that Dorothy Schiff is queer, as far as Nick knows. The *Chronicle* has always championed underdogs and been suspicious of cops; this is consistent with the paper's unstated mission, and there's a good chance readers will think the police are behaving unfairly. Nick doubts it will change anything, but he already knows that he's a bit of a fatalist. Andy is not only an optimist, but—Nick is realizing—the kind of optimist who will cheerfully bulldoze anything that stands between him and the things he wants. "I'm surprised the *Chronicle* hasn't been doing this all along," Nick finally says.

"We did," Andy says, looking a little proud of himself. "A couple of times, at least. In the thirties."

Nick caught that *we*, and wonders if Andy did, too.

This seems like a drinking sort of occasion, so Andy gets the bottle of bourbon out of the bottom drawer of Nick's desk and pours a couple inches into a pair of clean-looking coffee mugs.

Nick takes his cup, holding it up in a silent toast, and neither of them need to mention what they're drinking to. It's too many things to fit into a toast anyway—it's making peace with the future and also with the past; it's looking forward but also holding tight to the present. Nick knows that when Andy thinks too hard about the *Chronicle*, he still feels a little sick to his stomach, and Nick's own demons make sure to say hi a dozen times a day. But they have one another, an unmapped future, and the bone-deep certainty that they can figure it out together.

EPILOGUE

Andy

It's Linda's idea to have the party on the roof. Andy feels betrayed.

"I don't think we're supposed to go up there," Andy says.

Nick and Linda stare at him. "You own the roof," Nick says.

"The door is locked," Andy attempts, and they both shake their heads at him.

It turns out that one of the keys on the huge, jangling key ring that Mrs. Martelli handed Andy on her way to Long Island fits the lock to the roof stairs. The stairs are unlit (Andy makes a mental note to have the new super see to that) and narrow, but when they push open the rusty old door, the roof itself isn't the fetid death trap that Andy was imagining. It's dirty, in the way that everything outdoors in New York has a respectable patina of grime, but there aren't any obvious signs of animal infestation and the roof itself is penned in by a wall that would take some effort to topple over. Not that Andy's going anywhere near the edge.

"I'll tackle you to the ground personally if you get within two yards of that wall," Nick promises.

The night is clear, and even from the safe center of the roof, the view is kind of breathtaking. There are dozens of buildings just like this one, interspersed with the occasional church or school. The Jefferson Market Courthouse is visible in the distance alongside the hulking women's prison. To the north, he can see the skyscrapers of Midtown; to the south, he can see the buildings near Wall Street. He can't see the *Chronicle* building, but he knows where it is, nonetheless.

From this vantage, the skyline isn't composed of concrete towers, but rather of laundry lines and rooftop water cisterns; of people smoking on stoops and children shouting unintelligibly at one another. It's a neighborhood, and it's his neighborhood. It is, he thinks, the first home he's ever had.

Nick comes over and squeezes his arm. "I'm thinking that if I don't let go, you won't fall off."

"Fine by me," Andy says. After all, almost everyone they've invited knows the lay of the land between him and Nick, and those that don't are welcome to connect the dots.

The party is, nominally, just an end-of-summer party, something to entertain friends who are stuck in the city over Labor Day weekend, but really it's because Andy's about to take over as publisher, Nick is about to give notice, and a contractor is about to knock down that wall in their apartment when Linda moves out in a few weeks.

The night of the party, Nick pays one of the kids from downstairs a dollar to stand by the front door and send anyone who's there for the party up to the roof. The bathtub is already filled with ice that Nick hauled up the stairs that afternoon and bottles of beer and white wine that they've carried up in stages over the past few days. Nick finds an extension cord long enough so that if they put the record player on a table near the edge of the roof, they can dangle the cord into the bedroom window, where Nick plugs it in.

The cat is sitting on Nick's pillow, regarding these proceedings with intense skepticism. When Nick sees this, he doesn't even bother to shoo the cat away, and Andy pretends not to notice.

When the first guests arrive, Andy is carefully lighting some candles that Mrs. Martelli left behind, squat little candles in jars that have the images of saints painted on the glass. He's suddenly, unaccountably nervous, as if he's never been to a party before, as if all the people coming didn't deliberately choose to be there. Nick plants himself by Andy's side, shoving a bottle of beer into his hand.

The first guest is only Emily, thank God. "Jeanne's running late," she announces, kissing Linda on both cheeks. "Something to do with work."

Lilian's next, and she's brought Maureen. A couple other people from the *Chronicle* arrive. When Mark Bailey shows up, Nick actually leaves Andy's side to go say hello. Andy's kind of shocked and proud. It's like seeing a kid go off to school for the first time.

Andy happens to turn toward the roof door when a stranger passes through it—lanky and bespectacled, wearing a suit and tie, every item of which is badly wrinkled. He's scanning the crowd, obviously looking for someone, when a voice says, "Oh my God. *Gerald*."

And that was Emily, which means Gerald is—

Nick's a few feet away, talking to Mark, when Andy catches his eye. Nick mouths a questioning *Heart doctor?* and Andy almost loses it, almost laughs as he watches Emily get caught up in the arms of this strange, disheveled man.

"You could have called!" Emily says, but her rebuke has no sting since she's murmuring it into the man's collar.

"I tried," says the man, says Gerald, "but your damned telephone rings and rings. Doesn't anyone at your house ever pick up?"

Andy probably shouldn't be eavesdropping, but is it really eavesdropping if this entire conversation is being held two yards away from him on his own roof? Frankly, he doesn't care. He's keeping an eye on this fellow. If he does anything to upset Emily, he can just fall right off the edge of the roof, what a terrible accident. From Nick's dark expression, Andy isn't the only one with this idea. Jeanne, who's only now emerging from the doorway, and evidently is the reason this man knew to look for Emily here, will have a lot of explaining to do.

Andy tosses back the rest of his drink and goes to introduce himself to his uninvited guest. "Andrew Fleming," he says, sticking his hand out.

"Gerald Williams, and I wouldn't have crashed your party if it weren't urgent. I got on the first airplane after the call from Columbia-Presbyterian, you see," he says, as if this explains everything. His glasses are not only smudged and crooked, but one of the arms is broken. He's looking at Emily as if he's been bitten by a snake and she has the antidote.

"Columbia-Presbyterian?" Emily says. "The hospital?"

"Yes, well. I figured, you see." He stops, looking suddenly at a loss. "People in New York have hearts, too, don't they?"

And Emily must really love him if she's susceptible to a line like that. She kisses Gerald, laughing a little as she does it.

"I will murder you if you hurt her," Andy says cheerfully, remembering that this is what Emily considers the behavior of a decent friend in this situation.

"Oh, Jeanne's already taken care of that," says Gerald, altogether too easily for a man who's been threatened with murder twice in one evening.

Andy isn't surprised when they leave shortly thereafter, slipping away down the stairs.

The other night, they were late in the newsroom, waiting for a jury verdict to come in, and Andy could feel the presses rumbling beneath his feet, thought he could almost feel the heartbeats of all the people in the building, all of it ready to depend on him, and it didn't feel horrifying anymore. The paper isn't a burden or a debt he has to pay, but an opportunity he has.

He's already run two stories about police entrapping men at queer bars and he can run a hundred more. He can keep running them until people care, until something changes. A few months ago he told himself that his choices—that any queer person's choices—were either to hide or brazen it out, and that's still true. But there's another possibility: pushing back against the injustices that force people to make impossible choices.

Maybe that's not the best way to run a newspaper, but as far as he can tell, nobody knows how to run a paper going into this new decade. They're all making it up as they go along and hoping for the best. Andy can try new things—he can make the Sunday magazine glossy and slick; he can fill up the pages with feature-length stories; he can pack in the foreign correspondents.

Andy had always hoped there was a right way to do things, or at least a right destination, and it turns out there isn't, at least not for him. He has to make that up as he goes along, too.

Later, as the sun begins to set over New Jersey in the distance, and the third or so drink hits Andy's bloodstream, he leans against a structure that Nick says used to be some kind of pigeon coop. He's surrounded by the chatter of people who like him, people who know him, and beneath that, music coming from Nick's record player.

He shuts his eyes for a minute, and when he opens them again,

Nick is beside him. He hadn't noticed Nick's approach, but he isn't surprised; of course Nick is there. It strikes him all at once— the collision of past and future he's been experiencing over the past months. This place—this building, this apartment, their home—will be the place where they lived when they were young. One day they'll be somewhere else, and the things that are new and exciting now will be old and familiar then; they'll learn to take for granted easy kisses and morning coffee. He can feel the wispy end of a filament that could stretch out to infinity, the end of a rope that reaches to an anchor at the bottom of the sea. For now he reaches for Nick's hand.

Author's Note

There's a pervasive belief that in the 1950s queerness was never discussed in public or private unless to disparage it, but this was not the case. In March of 1959, an article by Seymour Krim appeared in the *Village Voice*; the headline was "Revolt of the Homosexual." The text from that article as it appears in this story was quoted verbatim. *The Charioteer* was released in America in the spring of 1959. *Some Like it Hot*, the same-sex romantic pairing and cross-dressing of which violated the Hays Code and which was released without approval from the Motion Picture Association, became an enormous success. The idea for this book came from imagining what kind of impact these texts and their depiction of queerness might have had on a deeply closeted and justifiably worried young man. It might be a stretch to say that any of these texts normalize queerness, but they refuse to sideline it or hide it away.

While most historical events in this book are rendered with an attempt at accuracy, a few I took the liberty of altering. Money disappeared from the New York Police Department evidence safe in 1958, but all the details surrounding it are of my own invention. There was an Operation Alert nuclear drill in the spring of

1959, but it took place a month earlier than it does in this book. Dorothy Day and her Catholic Workers did show up at the protest and were, as usual, arrested. At the 1959 protest, a woman with children was present and was interviewed in the *New York Times*; the woman who appears in this story is entirely of my own invention, as is everything that character says. The *Chronicle* is fictional but it occupies the old *Sun* building in Lower Manhattan.

Martin Luther King Jr. did hold a march in the spring of 1959 in support of school integration; there were over twenty-five thousand people in attendance. The gay associate of Dr. King mentioned in this book was, of course, Bayard Rustin, who went on to organize the 1963 March on Washington and whose contributions to the civil rights movement and other progressive movements throughout the century are too vast to detail in this note. He never kept his sexuality a secret from his friends and colleagues; it's not too much of a leap to imagine that senior staff at a progressive newspaper might know about it as well.

Some resources that were invaluable in the research and planning of this book include Hugh Ryan's *When Brooklyn Was Queer*, George Chauncey's *Gay New York*, Arthur Gelb's *City Room*, and Richard Kluger's *The Paper*.

Acknowledgments

I'm always grateful for the support and encouragement of my agent, Deidre Knight, but perhaps never more so than when I told her that, oops, I wrote a whole book set in the fifties and could she make sure it found a home! I'm so grateful that Elle Keck and Tessa Woodward at Avon believed in the potential for this kind of story in this kind of setting. My wonderful and talented editor, Sylvan Creekmore, came aboard when an early draft of this book was already a fait accompli and proceeded to adopt it like it was her own stray orphan baby animal; her incisive comments helped shape it into something so much more. I am so very grateful for the support and expertise of everyone at Avon who helped make this book a reality and get it into readers' hands.

My family has had to hear more about newspapers and pre-Stonewall gay rights than they ever wanted to know, and to them I can only apologize. My parents fielded dozens of questions about life in New York City in the 1950s, in particular life among Italian Americans in the outer boroughs. Many thanks to the people of the Discord, for their moral support, answers to inane questions, and pet pictures. As ever, Marikka took an early look at this book and performed the invaluable service of confirming that it was not, in fact, terrible.

About the Author

CAT SEBASTIAN writes queer historical romances. Before writing, Cat was a lawyer and a teacher and did a variety of other jobs she liked much less than she enjoys writing happy endings for queer people. She was born in New Jersey and lived in New York and Arizona before settling down in a swampy part of the South. When she isn't writing, she's probably reading, having one-sided conversations with her dog, or doing the crossword puzzle. Cat is the author of many series, including the Turners, Seducing the Sedgwicks, the Regency Impostors, and the London Highwaymen.

EXPLORE MORE BY
CAT SEBASTIAN

THE LONDON HIGHWAYMEN SERIES

The Queer Principles of Kit Webb, Book 1

"The Queer Principles of Kit Webb kept me up all night! I simply couldn't put it down."

—Tessa Dare,
New York Times bestselling author

Critically acclaimed author Cat Sebastian pens a stunning historical romance about a reluctantly reformed highwayman and the aristocrat who threatens to steal his heart.

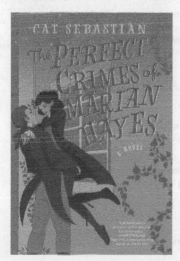

The Perfect Crimes of Marian Hayes, Book 2

"Cat Sebastian is an author at the absolute top of her game."

—Erin Sterling,
New York Times bestselling author of
The Ex Hex

Cat Sebastian returns to Georgian London with a dazzling tale of a reluctant criminal and the thief who cannot help but love her.

Celebrate the summer with more books selected by Bridgerton's

JULIA QUINN!

UNLADYLIKE LESSONS IN LOVE

"Sizzling romance with a splash of intrigue."
—Julia Quinn

The first in a dazzling romantic mystery series, a half-English, half-Indian society hostess must grapple with her past, prove a man's innocence, and face off against a handsome yet infuriating man who seems determined to hate her—or does he?

WE COULD BE SO GOOD

"A spectacularly talented writer!"
—Julia Quinn

Casey McQuiston meets *The Seven Husbands of Evelyn Hugo* in this mid-century rom-dram about a scrappy reporter and a newspaper mogul's son, perfect for *Newsies* shippers.

HOW TO TAME A WILD ROGUE

"I am in awe of her talent."
—Julia Quinn

In this next installment of *USA Today* bestselling author Julie Anne Long's charming Palace of Rogues series, an infamous privateer sees his limits put to the test when he finds himself holed up with a prickly female companion at the Grand Palace while waiting out a raging tempest.

DUKE SEEKS BRIDE

"Simply delightful!"
—Julia Quinn

Christy Carlyle takes readers to the breathtaking coast of Ireland where a pretty, young countess's secretary agrees to impersonate her mistress to help a duke appease his fortune-hunting family … until he falls for her instead.

Discover great authors, exclusive offers, and more at hc.com